The Baby Arrangement

Baby, I'm Yours

Baby, Be Mine

SAMANTHA CHASE

sourcebooks casablanca

Cover design by Dawn Adams/Sourcebooks, Inc.
Cover image © Getty Images/Maxsaf/(istock)

Published by Sourcebooks Casablanca, an imprint of Sourcebooks, Inc.
P.O. Box 4410, Naperville, Illinois 60567-4410
(630) 961-3900
Fax: (630) 961-2168
www.sourcebooks.com

The Baby Arrangement was originally self-published individually in ebook format in 2014.

Baby, I'm Yours was originally self-published individually in ebook format in 2014.

Baby, Be Mine was originally self-published individually in ebook format in 2014.

Printed and bound in Canada.
MBP 10 9 8 7 6 5 4 3 2 1

The BABY ARRANGEMENT

Prologue

"WHAT ARE YOUR PLANS FOR VALENTINE'S DAY?"

"*Ugh.* I'm not ready to think about it yet. I've still got…what? Five, maybe six weeks?"

Kayleigh Mitchell stood and looked up at the obscene number of red and pink hearts dangling from the ceiling of the SuperTarget and sighed. Valentine's Day was not her thing. She looked over to where her friend and coworker Carol was flipping through racks of red lingerie. Once again, there would be no one for Kayleigh to look forward to surprising with racy lingerie, and the next day she'd have to sit through hearing all about everyone else's superromantic dates.

"Well, you better get yourself ready because the big V day will be here before you know it."

Kill me now.

Resignation weighed her down as she walked over to catch up with Carol. "So I'm sure Joe really appreciates this kind of stuff, huh?" She sounded uncomfortable and ridiculous even to her own ears.

"Are you kidding me?" Carol said with a laugh. "We have been married for five years and we dated for three years before that, but all I have to do is flash a little red lace, and it's like we're teenagers again. It's become kind of like a game for us; each year I try to find something sexier and more daring. I'm not big on leaving my comfort zone, but once a year I can handle."

"Wearing sexy lingerie is leaving your comfort zone?"

Carol looked at her with pity. "When was the last time you purchased anything slinky?" The answer was too depressing to admit out loud. "'S what I thought," Carol said before turning back to the rack and looking at her options. "Wearing sexy things isn't out of my comfort zone; it's the sexy things the lingerie leads to that pushes my boundaries." She held up a red silk nightie. "See this? The first few years we were together, I'd wear something like this. It hits mid-thigh, it covers everything, and the spaghetti straps make it feel more like a slip than pajamas, but for the most part, it's tame."

Tame? She watched in fascination as Carol led her around the lingerie department and described each item she held up—the garments grew smaller and smaller, and after a while, Kayleigh had to wonder why a person would even bother wearing one.

"I'm pretty much down to needing just a thong this year," Carol said finally. "I'm not quite as fit as I used to be, and I'm a little self-conscious about wearing just that, but hey, I know Joe will be thrilled."

Kayleigh thought of her flannel boxers and T-shirts. Would any man be thrilled by that sight? Somehow she doubted it. Still, since no one was going to be seeing her in them anytime soon, it didn't really matter. She knew who she'd like to have see her in them, but somehow she was sure that particular man would be less than enthused by her unsophisticated sleeping apparel.

"If you want, I can fix you up with one of Joe's friends for Valentine's Day. You know, we can double-date and go out for dinner or something. What do you say?"

I'm pathetic. "Thanks, but…I'm good. Valentine's Day doesn't seem like the best night for a blind date."

Carol shook her head and made a tsk-ing sound. "When are you going to admit you're fighting a losing battle?"

"What are you talking about?"

"You never go out, you don't date, and you spend most of your Friday nights babysitting your nieces and nephews. It's time for you to leave *your* comfort zone, Kayleigh. A knight in shining armor isn't going to come searching for you, and if he does, he's not going to be looking at your siblings' houses. It's time you stopped letting your family take advantage of you and thought about yourself."

It wasn't a new concept. Kayleigh knew she needed to get out more and babysit less, but she didn't want to hang out at clubs or bars. She knew the man she wanted. She just needed him to notice she was alive.

Chapter 1

There was a whirlwind of activity going past the customer service department. Kayleigh had looked up several times from her tiny cubicle at the raised voices and the fast-paced movement of people running by.

"I wonder what's going on," she quietly whispered to Carol, who was sitting in the adjoining cube.

"I bet Brian's done something wrong again," she replied with a snicker.

Kayleigh shrugged her shoulders, figuring Carol was right. The Sloan brothers' nationally recognized textile distributor, Sloan Design, catered to clientele that included some of the most exclusive hotels, resorts, and spas in North America and, soon, abroad. Their grandparents had started the company some thirty years earlier and had retired just five years ago, leaving their grandchildren in charge. Since then, the company had more than quadrupled in size.

Derek, the older brother, was the company president and the brains of the whole operation. He had come to work for the company while still in high school and Gerald Sloan had groomed him to take the helm one day. Brian, five years younger, held the title of vice president but had no real interest in the company. Everyone who worked for the Sloans knew Brian was a playboy who enjoyed the perks of the family's wealth and success but did nothing to contribute to it. Derek had to bail his little brother out of one predicament after another.

The sound of a baby wailing brought Kayleigh's head back up. She looked over at Carol. "Was that what I think it was?"

"If you thought it was a baby, then you'd be correct."

Kayleigh looked around the department to see if anyone else seemed as distracted by the goings-on as she was, but most of her coworkers appeared unfazed. The sounds coming from the executive end of the hall were most definitely of an infant crying. Loudly. After several moments, the others seemed to catch up with Kayleigh's initial reaction and looked at one another with raised eyebrows, nearly getting whiplash when Derek's normally reserved and in-control assistant Eileen came running by them—and away from her office.

Several moments passed before she ran back to her boss's executive suite and slammed the door.

"Well, that was odd," Carol commented while punching numbers into her computer, clearly still uninterested in what was going on.

Kayleigh said nothing but inwardly felt great distress. The infant's cries grew louder and more heartbreaking. "Why is that poor baby still crying?"

"Who knows?" her friend replied casually, still not looking up from her work.

After looking at her clock and seeing that the cries, along with raised voices, had been coming from Derek Sloan's office for nearly thirty minutes, Kayleigh could no longer remain in her seat. She strode purposefully down the wide, carpeted hallway toward the one office she had never been invited into.

She knocked and waited for a reply. The raised voices made it impossible for her to be heard. Gently turning the knob and opening the door a mere slit, she was assaulted by the argument going on inside.

"I am *not* a babysitter, Derek! If that's what you need, then you better find one fast because that is not in my job description. And so help me, if you don't do something about this situation right now, I'll quit!"

Kayleigh admired Eileen's ability to stand up to her boss, but under the current circumstances, while an innocent baby was so obviously in distress, she didn't think it was right that the woman would stand there and yell.

"What is it you'd like me to do, Eileen?" Derek asked. His booming voice caused Kayleigh to jump and retreat slightly from the partially opened door. At thirty-five, he was the handsomest man Kayleigh had ever seen. His six-foot-two frame towered over most people in the office and he was built like a linebacker. His impeccable appearance and commanding presence made him an entity unto himself.

Most Sloan employees rarely saw the man in person because he was either holed up in his office or traveling on company business—a problem that plagued Kayleigh daily. After being with the company for a short time, she had found herself coming into the office earlier than necessary just so she could catch a glimpse of Derek's raven-black hair and smell his distinctive cologne.

Breaking out of her fantasies, she opened the door farther and stepped tentatively inside. The boss and his assistant were still arguing and the baby continued to cry. Kayleigh spotted a wicker basket on the floor and noticed a tiny red fist flailing around.

"I suggest you remove this child from the building and go find your brother," Eileen snapped, clearly at the end of her rope. "It's probably *his* responsibility anyway."

Kayleigh nearly gasped at the woman's harsh words. Who knew that a woman who looked like a saintly grandmother could have such a hard heart? Kayleigh was about to comment, but the sight of the tiny child screaming and squirming in what could only be described as a lunch basket grabbed her attention once again.

No longer caring what anyone thought at this point, Kayleigh entered the room and swiftly went to the child and picked her up. Her motions went undetected until the child instantly quieted.

"I have no idea where…" Derek stopped speaking midsentence when he noticed how loud his voice was and how quiet the room had become. He looked across the room with confusion and noticed a pretty, self-assured young woman holding the baby who had been dropped off in the lobby of his building earlier that morning.

Eileen started to speak again, but he held up a hand abruptly to silence her. Derek had a feeling the woman in question was probably an employee of his, but he couldn't be sure if he'd ever seen her before. She was humming softly, and the child had calmed down considerably. The woman's voice was like that of an angel, and for the briefest of moments, she looked like one. The light streaming in from his wide window hit her just right and gave her a kind of celestial glow.

Derek walked over to her. She looked up at him with the bluest eyes he had ever seen. They were so wide, so round, and showed such emotion, Derek felt like he wanted to dive right in and see into her very soul. His stomach clenched and he suddenly felt an overwhelming urge to take care of the lovely woman standing before him.

Long, chestnut hair pulled back in a tortoiseshell clip framed her heart-shaped face and she smiled shyly at him with a full, sensual mouth. He wondered what that mouth would feel like on his bare skin.

"I'm sorry, Mr. Sloan," Kayleigh said in a soft voice, careful to keep her tone soothing for the infant in her arms. "I just couldn't bear to hear the baby cry anymore."

Derek stood transfixed. That this woman was bold enough to come into his office without being asked or invited *should* have irritated him, but he was bothered more by the implication that he wasn't handling this situation well.

"I think she may be hungry," Kayleigh said softly as the child attempted to latch herself to Kayleigh's breast. She looked up to see Derek staring at the same spot the baby so desperately wanted to be.

He certainly couldn't blame the child.

"Look, Miss…um," he prompted.

"Mitchell. Kayleigh Mitchell. I work in customer service," she supplied, feeling a little dejected that indeed he had no idea who she was. It was no more than she should have expected and yet it still stung.

Derek ran his hand through his hair in frustration. "Miss Mitchell, what I am about to say is to be held in the strictest confidence, okay?" Kayleigh nodded. "This baby was left here this morning with nothing more than a note telling us her name and age and that she's my responsibility now."

Eileen chose that moment to chime in. "Well, it didn't say *you* specifically. I still think this has Brian written all over it."

Derek glared at his assistant. "That may very well be the case, Eileen," he growled with irritation, "but I can't reach him at the moment. He's apparently gone off on an African safari trip and will be incommunicado for at least two weeks! For the time being, this child is *my* responsibility!"

At the sound of his angry voice, the baby began to cry again. Kayleigh snuggled the child against her, turning her back on Derek and Eileen as she began to rock and sing softly to the baby. Looking over her shoulder, she quietly asked the child's name.

"Emery," Eileen answered stiffly. "Her name is Emery, and she is two weeks old. Now you know as much as we do."

Kayleigh did not like this woman's tone for a minute and couldn't understand why Eileen had an attitude toward her. *She* at least had the good sense to try to comfort the child while these two had argued and ignored her!

Poor little thing. She looked down at one very tiny, very angry, red face. "What kind of woman leaves her newborn?" Kayleigh regretted asking the question as soon as it left her lips. Two irritated sets of eyes turned to her.

"I…I'm sorry," Kayleigh stammered.

Derek sighed with frustration and sat down behind his desk. "Don't be. You haven't said anything we haven't been saying all morning."

"Did the mother leave any supplies for her?"

"I have no idea," Eileen snapped, glancing over at Derek.

Rolling her eyes, Kayleigh walked over to the basket and found one small bottle, along with some diapers and a change of clothes. Taking the cover off the top of the bottle, she offered the nipple to Emery. The child eagerly latched on and suckled with gusto. Sighing with relief, Kayleigh went to sit on the black leather sofa against one wall of Derek's spacious office.

"If I'm no longer needed, Derek," Eileen stated, "I'm going to lunch." Without waiting for a response, the woman left the room, the door slamming behind her, leaving Kayleigh and Derek alone.

Kayleigh kept her focus on baby Emery, but she could feel Derek's eyes on her. When she carefully pulled the bottle out of the baby's mouth so she could burp her, she looked up at him.

"Do you have any children, Katie?" he asked in a weary tone.

"It's Kayleigh, sir," she carefully pronounced, "and no, I don't have any children."

"You're good with them." He nodded toward Emery. "You knew exactly what to do."

"Well, I've been babysitting since I was twelve years old, and I am the youngest of four children. All of my siblings have kids of their own now, and I babysit for all of them as well."

"I see." The silence returned and stayed until Emery gave a hearty little belch and Kayleigh leaned back to feed her the remainder of her bottle.

"She's so tiny," she said with wonder as she examined the little fingers and then stroked the baby's cheek. "How could anyone not want you?" she cooed to the baby.

Derek's head ached as he watched Kayleigh. She was exactly what he needed right now. He had to have someone to help him with this child and there was no time to go through an agency. If she worked for his company, then she had already been vetted. It made perfect sense!

"Would you consider helping me out with Emery?" Derek asked suddenly.

Kayleigh's eyes shot up at his words. Derek Sloan wanted her—no, he *needed* her. Her, little Kayleigh Mitchell from customer service! It was like a dream come true! "You mean for today?" she asked casually, not wanting to seem too anxious. "Sure, I'll just let them know out in customer service I'll be in here today."

"That's not what I meant. Not fully," he said awkwardly. How was he supposed to ask this woman to help him for an indefinite period of time? She had a life of her own, maybe even a husband to go home to.

Damn, but that thought bothered him.

"I need someone to care for Emery full-time until I can get all of this settled. She may be my child. I don't know. I can't think who her mother could be—well, that's my personal problem and besides, as Eileen pointed out earlier, she could very well belong to my brother. He's gone for at least two weeks, and in the meantime, she needs to be cared for."

"You could call an agency—"

"No," he said firmly. "I don't have time for that, Kayleigh. You saw what it was like in here earlier. I have no clue what I'm doing where a baby is concerned, and finding someone reputable could take some time. I'll pay you double what you're making out in customer service, and I can guarantee your position will be waiting for you when you return."

It was quite an offer. One she couldn't take lightly. Kayleigh was a smart career woman, even if her job right now wasn't giving her any real challenge or motivation. She had graduated from college at the top of her class in interior design, but jobs in the field were hard to come by, and starting out on her own required financial backing she didn't have.

Five years ago, she had come to Sloan Design with the idea that she would work there temporarily until she found a "real" job. Now she was ashamed to admit that once she had seen Derek Sloan, she had all but stopped looking for work elsewhere. No one in her department had a clue she harbored a crush on their company president and that was the way Kayleigh preferred it. They'd tell her she was crazy to be wasting her time and talent at a dead-end job just because she liked to look at a man who didn't even know she existed.

Until now.

"Kayleigh?"

"Oh, sorry. My mind wandered for a minute." She took the empty bottle from Emery's still pursed mouth, draped a cloth over her shoulder, and positioned the baby so she could burp her again.

Standing up, Kayleigh began to pace around the office nervously. "Oh, I don't know, Mr. Sloan. I've never been a nanny before."

"You've been taking care of children for most of your life; you said so yourself just a few minutes ago."

He had her there. "I suppose I could do it," she said. "I mean, I can get to your house before you leave for work and we can work out a schedule so I have Emery settled in before I leave at night. Then—"

Derek cut her off. "No, I need a live-in nanny. Babies don't have regular schedules. That much I *do* know. I need someone to be there around the clock to take care of her. Besides, I don't keep banker's hours. I never know when I'll get out of here most nights. It would be easier for you to move in and take care of Emery."

"You want me to move in with you?" Kayleigh croaked out the words, forcing a lump down in her throat. Could this day get any better?

"Yes." His gaze met hers.

In her wildest fantasies, she never could have imagined this—living with Derek Sloan, caring for sweet baby Emery. It was insane!

Emery let out another unladylike belch, and Kayleigh chuckled. "I just don't know…"

Derek couldn't afford to have her refuse. He had to act quickly to ensure Kayleigh moved in with him today. "Please, Kayleigh. You obviously know what you're doing and Emery seems to like you. Please." He reached out and grabbed one of her hands and gave it a gentle squeeze. She looked up at him, her large eyes filled with pure wonder. "Will you help me, Kayleigh? It will only be for two weeks, maybe three tops. I promise." At her hesitation, he added, "I'll triple your pay."

Kayleigh looked at him and studied his pleading expression. She longed to promise him she'd stay as long as he wanted her, but in the end, she held on to her composure.

Taking a deep breath, she replied, "Okay."

Derek sagged with relief. "Oh, thank God," he

murmured. Giving Kayleigh a pleased grin, he stepped back, looking as if a great weight had been lifted off his shoulders. As he turned to walk back over to his desk, Kayleigh stopped him.

"Babies need a lot of things, Mr. Sloan. Do you have anything at home for her?"

"Like I said, she showed up here this morning, and before that, I had no idea she even existed." He sat back behind his desk and grabbed a legal pad and a pen. "I suppose we should make a list of what she'll need and then hit the stores to get it all."

"May I make a suggestion?" Kayleigh began cautiously.

"Absolutely."

"I don't mean to sound like a nervous Nellie or anything, but...if the mother was cold enough to desert her own infant, it makes me wonder what kind of care Emery has gotten so far."

"I'm not sure I'm following you."

"I think you should have her checked out by a pediatrician to make sure she's healthy."

Derek braced his elbows on his desk and rested his face in his hands. After a moment, he dragged them back down his face. "That's a good point. I never would have thought of that. How do I find a pediatrician?"

Kayleigh gave him a smile that filled him with hope for the first time that day. "You happen to be in luck. My oldest brother is a pediatrician and has a practice not far from here."

Without waiting for a reply, Kayleigh placed the now-sleeping Emery back in her ridiculous basket before reaching across Derek's desk and picking up the phone. She had no time to catch the stunned expression on his face at her actions. Dialing her brother's office, she perched herself on the corner of the desk and waited for his receptionist to answer.

"Dr. Mitchell's office, how may I help you?"

"Hey, Lindsey! It's Kayleigh. Is Jared available? It's an emergency." She was put on hold and her brother picked up in less than a minute.

"Kayleigh? Is everything all right? What's the matter?" Her brother's voice held a controlled-yet-panicked tone.

Kayleigh gave him the *Reader's Digest* version of events, and he agreed to see them just as soon as they could get there. "Thank you so much, Jared. We'll see you soon." She hung up the phone and related the news to Derek. "Now we only have one problem."

Derek arched an eyebrow at her. "Just one?" He chuckled, and though the sound washed over her like pure silk, Kayleigh could tell he was still nervous.

"We are going to need a real car seat to take Emery in, not this crazy basket. It's not legal for a child to ride in the car without an approved car seat. I could drive over to the Walmart and pick one up while she's sleeping if you'd like."

"*No!*" Derek frantically reached for the phone and punched in some numbers. "Eileen?" he barked into the phone. "Yes, I know you're at lunch, but I need for you to run a quick errand for me... No, it won't take long... Yes, I'll make the time up to you!" He went on to tell his assistant what was needed and asked her to please hurry back. After hanging up, he looked up at Kayleigh.

"Eileen will pick one up and bring it back with her." He seemed pleased with himself for solving their problem.

"It really wasn't necessary to bother Eileen. I could have gone myself."

His eyes widened at her words, panic clearly setting in. It was a side of Derek Sloan Kayleigh found endearing. "What if Emery had woken up while you were gone?" he asked.

"Mr. Sloan," she began diplomatically, "you're going to have to learn to take care of her on your own at some point. She could be yours, you said, or your niece, and if you're her father or uncle, you'll have to learn to handle her without being afraid."

When Derek remained silent, Kayleigh feared she had gone too far. After all, not only was he her boss, but he was also a very intimidating man no one dared disagree with. Now, in a short amount of time, Kayleigh had managed to question his ability to handle just about every aspect of his life. Filled with dread, she stood stiff as a poker and waited for him to do or say something. It would really be stupid of her to finally get this opportunity to get close to Derek and lose it because of her own big mouth.

Derek leaned back in his chair and raked a hand through his hair, which was now in total disarray and sexy as hell. While staring at him, Kayleigh noticed the color of his eyes for the first time. They were golden brown, like honey. How had she never noticed before?

Because before today, he's never even looked at you!

Kayleigh could tell her words had indeed made him uncomfortable. Unable to stand the silence any longer, she blurted out, "How about we work on that list?" She motioned toward the legal pad and then reached for it herself. A list maker by nature, she felt she would be less likely to forget something Emery would need if she was the one to write it down.

Fifteen minutes and two full pages of items later, Kayleigh finally thought they had covered everything.

"Are you sure? I don't think we've covered her first car yet," Derek teased, and Kayleigh laughed. He liked the sound of her laughter. Her whole face lit up and he was finding it remarkably easy to let his guard down with this woman. He was usually always on alert with the women in his life. They all seemed to want something from him and few, if any, had understood his company meant the world to him. It would always come first and Derek had no time for emotional entanglements at this point in his life.

But now he was faced with the reality that Emery could be his daughter. If he hadn't been able to find time for more than a casual affair with a woman, how was he supposed to handle being a father? His heart began to race and he felt his face form a frown.

Kayleigh reached out and touched Derek's hand. "Are you okay?" The concern on her face was genuine, Derek realized, and it touched him that she was worried about him.

"I guess the reality of all of this is just starting to hit me," he admitted honestly.

With a small smile filled with understanding, she said, "I'm sure it's all very overwhelming."

"You have no idea." Their eyes met and held, and Kayleigh thought, for just an instant, he was going to come around the desk and kiss her. Just thinking about it made her go warm all over.

Just as she was enjoying the butterflies tumbling

in her belly, the door crashed open and Eileen walked through carrying a large box that contained the infant carrier they'd requested. Breaking the eye contact, Derek rose and took it from her, thanking Eileen for taking the time to help him yet again. Kayleigh, in turn, took the box from him and immediately began to unpack it and set it up while Derek paid his assistant for the purchase.

Within minutes, Derek was amazed to find Emery changed into a fresh diaper and clothes and safely secured in her new seat. Several sets of curious eyes watched their progress as they walked down the hallway for their trip to the pediatrician, but one sideways glance from the boss had most people returning to their work. Kayleigh stopped at her desk to grab her purse before continuing down the hall to the elevator. Hanging back several steps, Derek took a moment to appreciate Kayleigh's figure. Wearing a simple navy skirt that came to just above the knee, a toast-colored twinset, and navy pumps, she made a very elegant picture. The soft sway of her hips and the confidence in her stride made his mouth go dry. She seemed oblivious to the stir she was causing both within the office and within him.

How the hell long has she worked here, and why have I never noticed her? Was he so obsessed with this company that he no longer even noticed an attractive woman unless she was blatantly throwing herself at him? At once coming to the realization that he was staring, he made a quick left turn into the customer service area and went directly to the department supervisor's desk to inform her of his arrangement with Kayleigh.

Chapter 2

DEREK MET UP WITH KAYLEIGH IN THE PARKING LOT. Pulling his sunglasses out of his jacket pocket, he watched her standing in the middle of the lot with a look of confusion on her face. Quite the turnaround from the confident woman of a few minutes ago.

"What's the matter?"

"Well," she began while still looking around the lot, "I was wondering whose car we should take."

"Mine," he replied as if it were the obvious choice.

"Well, I guess we could, but…" Kayleigh looked over at the sleek and sporty Porsche and frowned, fortifying herself to say what was sure to offend him. "It's a little small for the three of us."

The flash of annoyance was brief but noticeable. Then Derek shook his head at his own lack of foresight again. "Where's your car?"

"It's the silver Pathfinder on the end," she said as she started walking in that direction.

Once Emery's seat was fastened securely, a task Kayleigh handled with ease, they were on their way. Silently. It was a short drive and yet it felt like an eternity. Kayleigh wanted to be sensitive to Derek's needs, and if he needed some quiet time to think about the direction his life was taking, then she was willing to sit as quiet as a mouse. Although after several stolen glances at him, she began to frantically think of something witty to say to fill him with confidence.

Her mind was a blank.

True to his word, Dr. Jared Mitchell had a room waiting for them when they arrived and saw them right away. The two men eyed one another as if sizing each other up. *Men!* Kayleigh thought irritably. Jared was a protective big brother, and she knew immediately that even though Derek was merely her boss, her brother would still view him as some sort of enemy out to threaten his sister's virtue.

"Tell me about your daughter, Mr. Sloan," Jared began.

Derek paled at the question and snapped his head in Kayleigh's direction. Luckily she was quick on the uptake. "As I mentioned to you over the phone," she began, "Emery was left at the Sloan office this morning with little more than a note for identification. It's unclear whether she is Derek's daughter or his brother, Brian's."

It was the first time Kayleigh had called Derek by his first name and he smiled. *Focus, dammit!*

After weighing and measuring her, Jared handed Emery back to Kayleigh for dressing. "Any ideas who the mother could be?" Jared asked as delicately as he could.

Derek didn't keep a mental timeline of his relationships and had to rack his brain for a moment. It wasn't as if he had a harem at his beck and call. He'd sometimes go for months at a time without being with a woman. Brian used to dangle his female companions in front of his brother in hopes of luring him out of the office. But ever the professional, Derek put the company first. A little fact Brian seemed to be oblivious to—with no one running the company properly, no more cash flow. Why couldn't Brian be more damn responsible? Why was all the weight on *his* shoulders while Brian went out and acted the playboy? Derek thought to himself miserably.

But the fact remained, he *had* been intimate with several women in the past year; he just needed to remember their names. God, what a piece of crap he was that he couldn't even remember the women he'd slept with! And not because there were so many of them, but merely because they had been nothing more than a needed distraction. Correction, a *temporary*, needed distraction. He never made a commitment that went beyond the evening. It just wasn't his style. There was no time in his life for a relationship. Sloan Design was growing and about to go international. Why? Because Derek Sloan had made the commitment to take it global, and by God, he was going to succeed!

He could remember pattern numbers for every design his company had created in the last five years; surely he could remember a couple of names! Before he could reply, Jared added, "It might be a good idea for you to do some research, so we could have an accurate medical history for Emery."

Derek cursed the fact that he hadn't jumped on the idea earlier. Grabbing the cell phone out of his pocket, he punched in some numbers and turned his back on the Mitchell siblings.

Jared watched him through narrowed eyes for a moment before turning his gaze to Kayleigh.

"So," she began hesitantly, "is she all right? Has she been well cared for?"

Jared scribbled some notes onto his chart. "As far as I can tell, she's the picture of health. My guess would be she's a full-term baby. You mentioned you gave her a bottle earlier. Any idea what kind of formula was in it?"

Kayleigh shook her head. "I have no idea. It was just in a bottle." Glancing at Emery and smiling, she quietly asked Jared, "Are you sure she's okay? She seems so tiny."

He laughed. "Not everyone gives birth to ten-pound babies like our family does, Kay. Don't worry. She's responsive and her coloring is good." He paused before adding, "Besides, she's not your concern. I mean, I think it's great you got him to bring Emery in for a checkup and all, but honestly, her well-being is Derek's responsibility."

"Well, get me some answers, dammit!" Both Jared and Kayleigh's heads snapped at Derek's loud voice, and Emery started to cry. Turning around to face their looks of astonishment, Derek mumbled a quick "I'll call you later" into the phone and put it away. "Sorry."

Picking the baby up to comfort her, Kayleigh walked around the room while Derek conferred with her brother about Emery's health. By the time they walked out of the office several minutes later, their arms were filled with formula samples, spare diapers, and pamphlets on everything anyone could ever need to know about the health and care of a newborn. Derek's eyes had glazed over and he was very subdued as they climbed back into Kayleigh's car. In all of her wayward fantasies about spending time alone with Derek, *this* bizarre little scenario had never come to mind. What exactly was she supposed to do here? Was it her place to offer him comfort? Words of encouragement? And if so, what could she possibly say? Or would she be expected just to act as an employee and pretend not to notice his mood and focus fully on her charge? Oh, why didn't this damn day come with a handbook?

When several minutes had passed and she hadn't started the car, Derek turned and tapped her on the shoulder. "I guess it's off to shop now, right?" There was no joy or even the slightest inflection to his voice—it was very flat and monotone.

Kayleigh had never been known to be overly cautious with her words and she wasn't about to start now. "Are you all right, Mr. Sloan? I mean, that was all great news in there. Emery is healthy. You should be relieved."

"Oh, you're right, Kayleigh," he began sarcastically. "I should be just over the friggin' moon I've had a baby I know nothing about dumped on me this morning. I can't be sure if she's even mine! And hey, never mind the fact that my irresponsible brother could be behind this and he's conveniently out of the country—yet again leaving me to clean up a mess! But thank God the baby's healthy because otherwise this could be a real problem."

In an instant, she saw red. Not just red with annoyance, but full-blown *I'm gonna let you have it, mister* red. Facing him, she poked a finger at his chest. "Now you listen to me. I am well aware you did not ask to be put in this position, but neither did Emery! Now, I was more than willing to help you and Emery out, but I will *not* sit back and listen to any more of your bitching because you've been inconvenienced. If anyone's being inconvenienced here, mister, it's me!

"All I did was come to work this morning like I always do, and for the last couple of hours I've had to put up with your foul mood, your assistant's nasty attitude, a heartbroken baby, and a lecture from my brother! And besides, I haven't even had lunch yet, thanks to you." She took a deep breath and squirmed in her seat when she saw the surprise in his whiskey eyes.

By this point, Kayleigh was trembling and she didn't care. She took a deep breath. "And to tell you the truth, Mr. Sloan, I don't think I can help you. I think this has been a complete mistake. It would be best if you called an agency because I am just not up to this kind of situation and—" Derek's mouth crushed against hers and thoroughly brought an end to her tirade.

At first Kayleigh was too stunned to respond. Then her brain got on board and she found herself participating in what could only be described as one heck of a hot kiss. Her mouth opened under his, and in an instant his tongue swept inside. Kayleigh heard herself sigh and that small sound had her breaking the contact.

Derek had no idea what had caused him to act so recklessly and kiss her. Watching her bristle across from him and seeing the force of life, energy, and passion behind her words had been his undoing.

Kayleigh was the first to speak. Clearing her throat, she began in a subdued voice, "As I said, Mr. Sloan, I don't think this is a good idea." There was no way she could look him in the face, so she merely stared at her hands, meekly folded in her lap.

Leaning his head back against the leather seat, Derek let out a loud breath. "I'm sorry," he said slowly. "I know I am not handling this day very well. I'm not used to having to take other people's needs and feelings into consideration." God, he truly was a jerk. "The thing is, Kayleigh, I really do need you."

He reached over and gently took one of her hands in his.

Kayleigh finally turned to look at him. Her blue eyes were filled with confusion.

"I have no idea what I'm supposed to do with a baby, and you came to my rescue and Emery's. We both need you. There's no time to go through an agency—I wouldn't trust someone I didn't know to come and live in my home."

"You don't know me either, Mr. Sloan," Kayleigh added sadly.

"I think after the kiss we just shared, it would be best for you to call me Derek," he said silkily, and watched as Kayleigh's face reddened with remembrance. "I may not know you very well, Kayleigh, but you work for me. Your supervisor gave me a quick rundown on your history with the company, so now I have references to the type of person you are." When she made to interrupt, he went on. "I have witnessed, firsthand, how carefully you've cared for Emery, how you've put her needs first. *That's* the kind of person I want taking care of her. Someone who's honest, trustworthy, and loving—all qualities you've shown in just these last few hours."

Well, Kayleigh thought breathlessly, *that was one hell of a compliment*. How could she possibly walk away now? If that was what he'd noticed in just a short amount of time, how much more would he learn about her while she was living under his roof? Besides the fact that she was quickly getting attached to the baby, there was the added perk of being able to get closer to Derek as well. *What on earth is wrong with you, Kayleigh*

Marie? The baby's welfare should be your top priority, not cozying up to the boss!

"Okay, Derek," she said cautiously and smiled at the obvious relief on his face. "I'll stay for Emery's sake—but only until your brother gets back and you figure out exactly what's going on."

"Thank you, Kayleigh." Derek smiled. Genuinely smiled. She was going to stay and help him. He had been afraid she would walk away—particularly after their out-of-the-blue kiss. Derek could only hope he would be able to control himself while she was living with him.

After a quick stop at a convenience store for a bottle of water, Kayleigh headed back into Raleigh to the only baby superstore she knew of. If they were going to need as much as they thought, it would be best to get it all done in one place.

"Are you sure she really needs this much?" Derek asked wearily as they headed down the third aisle. "She's really small to require this much stuff."

With a chuckle, Kayleigh continued her quest through the store with an overanxious salesclerk hot on her heels, checking inventory on the larger items they needed. By the time they were standing at the checkout, Derek's vision had blurred and he felt as if he'd run a marathon. After some haggling and then outright arguing, Derek had convinced the store manager to have several employees in the delivery truck follow him home with all their purchases.

Two hours and what seemed like thousands of dollars later, they were finally headed to Derek's town house.

Kayleigh had let him drive her SUV, figuring it would be easier than trying to concentrate on following his directions while making sure the enormous truck holding all of Emery's necessities was still following them.

When they turned into the exclusive neighborhood where he lived, Kayleigh could barely contain her gasp. Shocked at her reaction, she quickly cleared her throat and prayed Derek didn't think she was one of the Clampetts! His town house was the end unit facing the golf course and had a lovely lake view in the back. It was positively breathtaking.

The delivery truck pulled in directly behind them, and while Kayleigh retrieved Emery from the vehicle, Derek opened the front door and shut off the alarm. "Remind me to give you the code so you can come and go as you please," he said easily as he tossed his keys onto a small table in the entryway.

Kayleigh stepped inside and came to an abrupt halt. His home was impressive. True, she lived in a small one-bedroom apartment that would almost fit in his entryway, but that was beside the point. Once she got beyond the initial shock of the beautifully polished hardwood floors and the wonderful use of earth-toned colors, she was overwhelmed with the view of the lake—which she could clearly see through the two-story-high windows in the living room. No, there would be no hardship in living here. The hardship would be when she would have to go home.

Behind her, the sounds of the moving men and Derek's voice hit her. With the baby asleep in her arms, she watched as the men set up the furniture and stored the furnishings that had been in the spare bedroom. It was amazing how some extra money could motivate these men to move so quickly.

A glance at her wristwatch showed it was going on two thirty. Lunch was obviously not going to happen, and she was sure Derek was champing at the bit to get back to the office.

As if on cue, he came strolling down the stairs, talking on his cell phone to Eileen. The movers came down shortly afterward and soon began bringing in all the smaller packages containing the necessities for the baby—clothes, diapers, bottles, formula, blankets, the works. That was Kayleigh's department, so she followed the men up the winding staircase to the second floor, where she got her first glimpse of where she would be staying.

The major furnishings in the nursery were all in place, and Kayleigh smiled when she noticed the rocking chair she had admired in the store earlier that day. Her heart did a funny little beat at the thought of Derek buying it for her. He was turning out to be a little less of an ogre than she had originally thought, and that made her smile.

After running up and down the stairs, situating the kitchen and nursery until all the secondary items were in place, she thanked the movers and watched them leave, still in awe at all that had been accomplished in such a short amount of time. Emery was asleep in her new bassinet and Kayleigh took advantage of the time to collapse in the mahogany rocker. With her eyes closed, she didn't notice Derek's approach into the room. It was the smell of pizza that brought her back around.

"Is that pizza I smell?" she asked with a smile, her eyes still closed.

"Well, someone pointed out to me earlier that she had missed lunch." He really was even more attractive when he relaxed and smiled, Kayleigh thought as she opened her eyes. She had never seen him so disheveled—his tie was long gone, as was his jacket, and the sleeves of the expensive silk shirt he wore were pushed up to expose a nice expanse of tanned forearms. "I don't want to be accused of creating poor working conditions for the woman who saved my life today."

Kayleigh rose from the chair and followed Derek down to the kitchen. The breakfast bar was covered with black granite countertops, and that was where she found the source of the wonderful aroma permeating the air. Without asking permission, she opened the box, grabbed a slice, and began to eat. Midway through her second bite, she noticed Derek hadn't joined in.

With a discreet lick of her lips, she asked, "Aren't you hungry?"

Derek was watching the movement of her tongue and for a brief moment couldn't respond. She made quite a vision. Her hair had started to come out of its tortoise-shell clip, her makeup had faded slightly, and yet she still was possibly the most alluring woman he had ever seen. When he noticed her eyes had gone wide with question, he remembered she had asked him something.

"I was just waiting to make sure I wasn't going to get my hand bitten off," he said lightly, delighted when Kayleigh threw her head back and laughed. When her laughter subsided, he noticed her cheeks had reddened slightly.

"I guess having been the youngest of four kids, I'm just used to diving right in in case the others beat me to it and there is nothing left." When Derek continued to just look at her, she added, "Believe me, it's happened." Then she continued to devour her long-awaited lunch.

He reached for a slice of pizza and gave her a reassuring smile. "While you're here, I'll remember to make sure there's plenty of food to go around." He gave in to the urge to smile and relaxed his shoulders. Maybe everything was going to be okay. Maybe he would survive this monstrous change that had been thrown at him. And maybe, just maybe, he would actually enjoy it.

Chapter 3

THEIR FIRST TWO DAYS WERE FILLED WITH MAJOR adjustments and apologies. With all that had been put into action to get Emery settled, both Kayleigh and Derek had neglected the fact that *Kayleigh* would need to get settled in as well. After Derek had gone back to his office late that first afternoon and the baby had woken up from her nap, Kayleigh loaded her into the car again and headed over to her own apartment to pack up the things she would need for her extended stay as a nanny.

The first night was rough. Emery had no real schedule, and Kayleigh realized sleep was going to be a thing of the past until the baby settled in. Babysitting for her nieces and nephews had in no way prepared her for the full-on demand of spending 24-7 with an infant. Derek had made himself scarce, and Kayleigh was hardly aware of his comings and goings. With her new surroundings thrown into the mix, Kayleigh was more than a little frazzled and was thankful there were no real eyewitnesses.

After reading every pamphlet her brother had given her several times—front to back—Kayleigh was just beginning to feel at ease with Emery. By the end of the third day, they were bonding, and a schedule of sorts had been established. Everything was going to be all right. She and Emery were going to make this work.

Until that night.

It was a little after midnight when Emery's restlessness came through the monitor Kayleigh kept beside her bed. Looking at the bedside clock and grimacing, she rose. It would be better not to let the infant get into a state of panic before going to get her.

"Hey, sweet girl," Kayleigh whispered as she walked into the nursery. Reaching into the bassinet, she carried the baby to her changing table to put on a fresh diaper and then carried her down to the kitchen to make a warm bottle. Kayleigh cooed and sang lullabies to her during the entire process. With Emery securely snuggled on her shoulder, Kayleigh tested the formula, turned—and very nearly let out a scream. Derek stood less than a foot away, with only the light above a restaurant-quality stove for illumination.

"Derek," she whispered, "you scared me half to death!" Emery startled on her shoulder, but a brief pat on the back settled her.

"I'm sorry," he said with a slight chuckle. "I thought you heard me moving around. Is everything all right? Why is Emery awake?" When the man said he didn't have a clue about babies, he wasn't kidding.

"She gets up at this time every night for a bottle. Don't you hear her?"

"The last two nights I haven't gotten home until after two." He didn't make any attempt to elaborate on his whereabouts—not that he needed to—but Kayleigh couldn't help but wonder where he was until such an hour.

"Oh." Without another word, she turned to head back up the stairs to the safety of the nursery. Being so close to Derek in the dark was making her heart hammer, and she didn't want him to know just how nervous his closeness made her.

"Nice jammies," came the deep voice from behind her. It had never occurred to Kayleigh to throw a robe on—her flannel boxer shorts with a ribbed tank top had seemed rather boring. But now under his gaze, she felt positively indecent. She gasped and hurried toward the stairs. "Kayleigh." It was her name, nothing more, spoken in a tone that beckoned her to turn around and face him—half-naked and all.

"Yes?" she replied softly, staying safely in the shadows at the foot of the staircase.

"You don't have to run back upstairs. Please. Come sit in the living room with me. I was going to grab something to eat and watch some TV, but it would be nice to have someone to talk to." It was a simple request—one she knew she wouldn't deny, even without a robe.

Walking into the dimly lit kitchen, she shifted the baby in her arms. Derek started opening cabinets in search of a midnight snack. "I, um, I saved you a dish," Kayleigh stammered, hoping she didn't sound like a complete idiot.

Derek turned and stared at her as if she had two heads. "What? Why?"

Oh, great, she thought to herself, *I am a complete idiot.* "I just thought maybe you didn't get a chance to eat dinner with the hours you keep. I have no idea what your schedule is, but…"—she hesitated for a moment—"but I was cooking for myself and made more than I could possibly eat, so I covered it and left it for you." There. That sounded reasonable, right?

Opening the refrigerator door, Derek stood stupefied. There was not one covered dish but three—one for each night she'd been here. He took a moment to let that sink in. The last person to care about his well-being had been his grandmother—and he hadn't lived with her in well over twelve years. He'd been taking care of himself just fine, thank you very much, but the thought of Kayleigh cooking a little something extra for him made him smile. He didn't realize just how alone he had been until that moment.

When he made no attempt to move, Kayleigh padded quietly into the living room. The reflection of the moon on the lake made for a breathtaking view. She sat in an overstuffed suede chair, curled her feet under her, and settled Emery in for her bottle. She didn't try to strike up a conversation with Derek; she was too enthralled with the setting—the infant in her arms, the moonlight, the view, and Derek Sloan's house. In her wildest dreams, she never would have thought this possible, yet here she was.

The beeping of the microwave snapped her out of her reverie. Soon Derek was sitting on the sofa facing her. The sofa and her chair sat on either side of an enormous stone fireplace. Kayleigh wondered how it would be to have a fire roaring while she and Derek made love in front of it. *Stop it!*

"So," Derek began after tasting a forkful of Kayleigh's shrimp Alfredo, "are you and Emery getting into a routine?"

"Yes." Her voice was barely above a whisper, and she had no idea why she was feeling so shy in front of him all of a sudden. After all, she'd worked for him for years, and on the day the baby arrived, they'd shared a lot with each other.

"Do you have everything you need? Did we forget anything?"

"We're fine, thank you."

Derek dropped his fork, resting his elbows on his knees as he looked at her. Kayleigh knew he was irritated; it was written all over his face. That and pure exhaustion. "If you didn't want to sit with me, you just should have said so," he said with a weary sigh.

She wasn't sure how to respond to that. It wasn't that she didn't want to spend time with him, but this was her third night of interrupted sleep. How could she possibly explain that he was overwhelming to her?

"Kayleigh?"

"I don't mind sitting here with you. It just feels so…" She hesitated.

"So?" he prompted.

"It just feels a little…intimate." There, she'd said it. He raised an eyebrow at her choice of words and now she felt the need to explain. "I mean, you're my boss. I barely know you, and yet I'm sitting here in a dimly lit room in your home, feeding your child, while I'm barely dressed." Well, maybe she could have left last part out.

Derek's eyes grazed over her. She did look delectable, with her long hair mussed from sleeping, the snug tank top revealing the fullness of her breasts, and the moonlight shining on the silkiness of her legs. With Emery curled in her lap, she looked like a Madonna. He swallowed hard and tried to think of something to say to put her mind at ease, but by the startled look on her face, he knew she could read his mind.

Kayleigh was the first to look away, focusing her attention on the baby in her arms. Emery was nearly finished eating and soon would need to go back to sleep. Most nights Kayleigh enjoyed sitting in the dark, cuddling her, but tonight she was just hoping to survive Derek's thorough perusal of her.

Was there a graceful way to jump up with the baby and run from the room, or would she end up looking like some frightened little girl? Good Lord, the last thing she wanted to do was to look like even more of a fool in front of him.

Derek resumed eating and, after another forkful of food, asked, "So how is Emery during the day? What kind of schedule is she on?" Kayleigh breathed a sigh of relief at the direction of the conversation. If he had asked her anything personal, she was unsure how she would have responded.

"She's a very good baby. She gets up around eight and by eleven is back down for a short nap. After lunch we've started going out for walks since the weather has been so lovely. She really seems to enjoy that. I think she's settled into a schedule of eating every four hours."

"That doesn't give you much rest at night, does it?" he queried.

Kayleigh laughed a little, and the action brought Derek's eyes first to her smile—which he was coming to adore—and then to her breasts, which were shaking under the thin, ribbed material. "I was kind of aware of the sleep deprivation aspect of the job. I figured I could handle it on a temporary basis." Lifting Emery to her shoulder, she began patting her back and talking softly to her. "She's really a wonderful baby. You're very fortunate to have her."

Derek's eyes shot to hers in a state of near alarm. For the last several days, it had been almost possible to forget the situation he was in. Kayleigh had been nearly invisible, as had Emery. His home still looked like his home on the downstairs level—upstairs was another story altogether. He had a private investigator trying to find out who the child's mother was, but so far he'd had no luck locating a birth certificate in the immediate area. Of all the irresponsible times for Brian to leave the country!

"Have you had any luck contacting your brother?"

Derek polished off the last of his food before answering. "Unfortunately, no. I do think it would be wise to set up a paternity test, so maybe some things will be resolved by the time Brian does get back." He leaned back in the chair and sighed. "Who knew one little person could change a life so much?"

Kayleigh wanted to remind him that thanks to her, his life really hadn't changed so much. He had taken no real interest in Emery since Kayleigh had moved in, and if it weren't for this chance meeting in the kitchen, he still wouldn't know what was going on. But it was late and not the time for hashing those things out. Eventually the situation would have to be dealt with, and she would move on with her life and so would he. Snuggling Emery close, she only hoped it would be an easy transition for all of them.

"I think she's ready to go back to sleep," Kayleigh whispered, her voice bringing Derek out of his own thoughts.

"Thank you for sitting with me," he said quietly, careful not to startle the sleeping child. "And thank you for dinner. I wasn't looking forward to eating microwave popcorn." He smiled and Kayleigh thought her heart would melt. It was devastating. Seeing Derek in that environment was going to make it so much harder to see him around the office when everything was all over. "Good night, Kayleigh." He stood as she did, and for a brief moment, she thought he was going to walk over to her. Instead, he placed his hands in his pockets and stood rooted to the spot.

"Good night, Derek." Turning, she headed up the stairs, thankful for the darkness swallowing her form and hiding the nervous trembling of a body too aware of the man in the living room.

The rest of the week flew by. Derek had to go out of town for several days on business and left Kayleigh at ease around his home. She and Emery were bonding and had developed a routine where they went out frequently. It was a suggestion both her brother and his wife, Sarah, had presented her with—get the child used to being on the go, and soon enough, you should be able to take her anywhere without a fuss. Amazingly enough, it had worked.

They went food shopping together and had an outing to the mall just for the fun of it. Derek had given her a credit card for groceries and necessities for Emery, and she tried not to abuse the privilege. Once again, she had been assaulted by the number of decorations up proclaiming it was almost Valentine's Day. *Isn't there another way of doing it without being so...obnoxious?* Red balloons and hearts and flowers were everywhere, and all it managed to do was make Kayleigh hate the holiday even more.

It had been so long since Kayleigh had had so much free time that she was unsure of what to do with herself. There were lunches out with friends, and even a night with Kayleigh's family, when Emery was the star attraction even among all the grandchildren.

Kayleigh was sitting on the couch in her parents' den, watching her charge sleep on a blanket on the floor, when she found herself wondering about the little girl's future. She knew Derek's parents had died many years ago and both he and Brian had been essentially raised by their grandparents. What kind of family would that be for Emery? It broke her heart to think the child might never know the closeness the Mitchells had. If Derek were her father, would he put her in boarding school so parenthood wouldn't disrupt his career? Would Brian hire some hot nanny to care for her—and for him at night? *Ugh*. The thought of it all sickened her.

Her mother noticed the frown on her face and inquired into its source. "I just hate the fact that Emery may never know what it's like to be part of a loving family."

"That's a pretty big assumption to make, don't you think?" Kathleen Mitchell asked. She was the older version of Kayleigh—short, dark auburn hair streaked with silver and more laugh lines on her face, but still a vision. No one would have guessed she was over fifty.

"You haven't met the Sloan brothers."

"What about their grandparents? What do they think of this whole situation?"

Kayleigh had wondered about that very thing, and assumed Derek didn't want to burden them until they knew for sure who Emery belonged to. She shared her theory with her mother.

"What if the mother comes back and has a large family?"

Kayleigh chewed her bottom lip. That thought had never occurred to her, and now it angered her. After deserting the child, she felt the birth mother had given up any rights to the precious baby. And if the woman happened to be a former lover of Derek's and they married and…and… *Oh!* Just the thought of Derek with another woman raising Emery made her want to cry.

"I guess we'll just have to wait and see," Kayleigh said softly, and quickly asked about her nieces' and nephews' interests to take the focus off herself.

Derek arrived home late Sunday night and found himself anxious about being there. A glance at his watch showed it was barely after midnight. Would they be awake? Would Kayleigh remember he was due home and have food waiting for him?

Jeez, get a grip, man. She's the nanny, not your wife, for crying out loud. The thought stopped him cold. He never imagined himself coming home to a wife and kids—it just didn't fit into his plans—but somehow, in the last week, the thought had become less scary and more appealing. After all, if Emery was his and her mother never came back, he'd need someone to care for her. Wouldn't it be better if that caretaker was his wife rather than the hired help?

Shaking his head at the wayward thoughts, he slipped the key into the lock and went inside. While resetting the alarm, he heard Kayleigh's voice coming from the living room. Quietly dropping his bags by the door, he walked toward her and stood in the shadows.

She was sitting on the couch this time, curled into the far corner. Emery was suckling loudly on her bottle and Kayleigh was singing a lullaby to her. He actually felt an ache in his chest he'd never felt before. When he stepped forward slowly, Kayleigh noticed him and smiled, never once breaking the song she was singing or alerting the baby that anyone else was there.

Kayleigh's heartbeat accelerated wildly. He actually looked relieved to be home, and though he was slightly rumpled from his travels—a far cry from the model of perfection he presented at the office—he still looked good enough to eat.

Loosening his tie, Derek advanced into the room. "Hi," he said softly, walking behind the sofa to get a better look at Emery. "How's she doing?"

Looking up at him and willing the tremor out of her voice, she replied, "Fine. She's going for a little longer between bottles, so our nights are getting better."

"That's good," he said, his eyes still on the baby. It seemed like an eternity before he moved away and headed for the kitchen.

Before he could even ask, Kayleigh called out, "There's a plate for you in the refrigerator." Derek smiled. So she had remembered he was coming home. The thought pleased him immensely.

Within minutes, he was seated across from her in the living room inhaling the wonderful aroma of grilled salmon Florentine. Kayleigh was equally pleased he seemed to enjoy this one little thing she did for him. "Thank you," he said before taking a taste. "You seem to enjoy cooking. Did your mother teach you?" he asked. Kayleigh knew there'd come a time when they'd talk about themselves, but she wasn't quite sure how she felt. She'd wanted Derek Sloan for so long, and getting to know him was a good thing, but she still found herself shy around him.

"I come from a pretty large family, as you know. I'm the youngest of four, and Mom was always in need of an extra hand in the kitchen. Since that was where everyone usually was, that's where I wanted to be. I've been concocting recipes since I was around six years old. It's really not fun cooking for only one person though, so it has been a treat to have someone else to cook for."

Oh, God! Did that just sound like a desperate attempt at getting him to ask me to cook for him permanently? Stupid, stupid, stupid!

"You're very talented. I can't remember the last time I had real home cooking. Since my grandparents retired, I don't see them much. But then again," he added with a chuckle, "my grandmother wasn't all that much into cooking. She was as invested in the business as my grandfather was."

Kayleigh felt sad for him and even more so for Emery again. The more she learned about the Sloans, the sadder it made her. "My grandmother was always in the kitchen. She was baking pies and cooking huge Sunday dinners up until the day she died," Kayleigh said with a sigh. "I am so thankful for all she taught me. Every little girl should have that kind of influence in her life." As soon as the words were out, she regretted them. Her mind raced as she thought of something intelligent to say to cover up her blunder. "I mean…um…"

"It's okay, Kayleigh," Derek assured her. "You were very fortunate to have those influences in your life. I can only hope someday Emery has a mother figure who'll guide her." Not *the* mother, just a mother figure. *Hmm, interesting.*

They sat in silence while Derek finished his meal. As he sat back to relax, he focused on Kayleigh again, eager to learn more about her even at this late hour. "When you're not saving helpless bachelors and abandoned infants, what do you like to do with your spare time?"

Had he phrased it any other way, she might have stumbled on a reply, but worded so playfully, she couldn't help but chuckle. "Well, when my red cape is safely packed away," she said cheekily, "I enjoy spending time with my family and babysitting my nieces and nephews. They seem to take up most of my spare time, probably because I'm a free babysitter." She smiled. "I don't mind, really."

"What do you do for fun? Do you have friends you go out with or a boyfriend?"

Ah, now we're getting deep. "I go to an occasional movie with friends or shopping at the outlets. As for a boyfriend"—she glanced up at him shyly—"not at the moment."

He made a noncommittal sound, and Kayleigh hoped this part of the conversation was over. Emery was sound asleep in her arms, and Kayleigh was ready to put her back in her bassinet. Standing carefully, she looked down at Derek in the chair. "I hope you enjoyed your dinner. I'm going to put Emery down and head back to sleep myself."

He made that sound again but said no more. As she walked away, Derek noticed tonight's sleeping attire—a faded Whitesnake concert T-shirt and silk pajama pants.

There was nothing sexy about the ensemble, and yet it had his mind racing more than any lingerie ever had.

Upstairs, Kayleigh put Emery down and kissed the top of her head. Little wisps of blond hair were starting to emerge. Soon, she'd be able to put bows in it and cute little headbands… *No*, she thought sadly, *someone else will get to do that.* Kayleigh wouldn't be around much longer. With a sigh, she turned to leave the room and bumped into the very solid frame of Derek Sloan.

He wrapped an arm around her waist to steady her and Kayleigh felt all the breath leave her body.

Oh my.

"Sorry," she whispered, slowly raising her eyes to see his face. He looked very serious, and as their eyes locked, she watched his expression change to one of wonder and desire.

Oh…my.

Kayleigh tried to find something to say, but she was too afraid of breaking the spell. Memories of the kiss they'd shared on that fateful first afternoon together flashed through her mind. She had dreamed about it countless times, never thinking she'd have the opportunity to experience it again. But as Derek's head began its slow descent, she thanked her creator for making it possible.

"Kayleigh," he whispered raggedly before his lips touched hers. They were firm at first, but when Kayleigh sagged against him with a sigh and opened for him, his desire was unleashed.

Derek wasn't sure exactly why he'd followed her up the stairs. It hadn't been his intention to go up there and kiss her, but something happened when her body made contact with his, and it was all he could do to hold back as long as he did. Since the moment he'd first noticed her in his office, he had thought about touching her, kissing her. Even after their brief kiss the day of Emery's arrival, he'd wanted to explore his attraction to her further.

By this point, Kayleigh had wound her arms around his neck. Derek banded his arms around her tiny waist, pulling her tightly against his body. She felt so good against him, he wanted to carry her out of the nursery to the nearest horizontal surface.

Over and over, he nipped at her mouth, his tongue mating with hers—imitating what his body wanted to be doing with hers. She met his every passionate response and clearly wanted him as much as he wanted her. Moving one hand away from her waist, he brought it slowly up her rib cage to gently cup one glorious breast. It felt exquisite in his hand—he had known it would. Kayleigh had a fantastic figure, which he'd have loved to have been touching all over at that very moment.

Just as thought was registering, he felt her begin to pull away. "Derek," she said breathlessly, "I can't."

Her words slowly sank in. *Can't? Can't what?* He pulled back and looked down into her flushed face. Her lips were moist and swollen from his kisses and her breathing was still a little erratic. He liked that.

"I'm sorry," she said softly, "but this shouldn't have happened."

He gently took her hand in his and led her out of the nursery and into the dimly lit hallway. "Why?"

She expected him to be angry, but his softly

spoken question had her asking herself exactly the same question. *Why?* With a fortifying breath, she said, "It's just…you're my boss, and I'm here to take care of Emery. I don't even want to imagine what everyone back at the office must be thinking of this setup, and I certainly don't want to prove them right. I don't *do* casual affairs, Derek. It's just not who I am. I'm sorry."

He had to admire her in the moment. Most women would have jumped at the chance to sleep with the boss in hopes of furthering their own careers. But not Kayleigh. Leave it to him to find himself attracted to the one woman he'd ever met who declared herself off-limits. It was a definite first. He silently observed her and noticed the wide-eyed wonder in her gaze. Was she expecting him to rant and rave? To demand she finish what they started?

As much as he wanted her, he'd never force himself on a woman. He thought about that for a moment. He may not have ever forced himself on her, but he knew without a doubt he wanted her in his bed. He'd give her time—although he was unsure just how much of it they would have before it was time for her to leave. He didn't want to think that far ahead. One way or another, Kayleigh Mitchell would be his *and* on his terms.

Reaching out and caressing her face, he said, "I'm sorry, Kayleigh. I didn't mean to get so carried away. I've thought about kissing you ever since that very first day, and when I saw you in the nursery, with the soft lighting, you just looked so incredibly beautiful, and I had to kiss you." Every word was true, but Derek had never had to use the sweet-talk approach to seduce a woman; he was usually the one being pursued. He kind of liked it this way. No matter how much time they had left together, he was going to enjoy every moment of it.

Chapter 4

SOMETHING CHANGED THAT NIGHT, BUT FOR THE LIFE OF her, Kayleigh couldn't quite figure out what it was. Derek made no attempt to touch her again, but they settled into a simple domestic bliss she had never thought possible.

Derek began to leave for the office a little bit later in the morning—after they shared a cup of coffee—and came home earlier, so they actually ate dinner together. The first time it happened and he came strolling through the door at six thirty, Kayleigh was pleasantly surprised. They were so at ease with one another and the conversation never lulled. He finally began to interact with the baby who could be his, holding her while Kayleigh was busy, and talking and cooing to her while she sat in her infant swing. Kayleigh took it as a good sign that Derek could quite possibly be coming to grips with the situation.

At midnight, when she woke with Emery for one bottle the infant couldn't seem to do without, she found Derek sitting on the sofa with reports spread out in front of him on the coffee table.

"What exactly has you working all hours of the day and night like this?" she asked as she nodded toward the mass of paperwork. She knew Derek normally worked long hours, and even though he was home more, that didn't mean the work had miraculously gone away.

Reclining slightly and running his hands through his hair in frustration, he replied, "We've grown tremendously in the last five years. But our marketing is showing its age. Most of my designers have been with the company for so long that they're out of touch with today's market." With a sigh, he stood and stretched.

Kayleigh's eyes caught a brief glimpse of a well-muscled torso before he turned and walked to the windows to look out at the lake.

"They're all good designers, don't get me wrong, and I don't want to let any of them go, but at the same time, I'm ready to do something big. I want to expand beyond the commercial wall coverings and fabrics we do and move into the residential realm, but I can't seem to get my ideas across to anyone. They're a little set in their ways."

Kayleigh remained silent as she fed the baby. His idea excited her because it was exactly the type of thing she had wanted to do. Finding Emery done with her bottle and back to sleep, Kayleigh quietly excused herself and placed the infant back in the nursery before returning to the living room.

Derek was a little puzzled at Kayleigh's quick and quiet departure and was even more confused by her sudden reappearance. Sitting down on the sofa, she began shuffling through his papers.

"Um, Kayleigh…"

Finding a sketch pad at the bottom of the heap, Kayleigh began sketching like a woman possessed. "Oh, wait," she said before bolting up the stairs and then back down again with a small case in her hands. Derek stood back and watched her work. The case held a mass of colored pencils, and soon the drawing came to life. Colors, patterns, accessories—it was as if she had seen into his mind and was able to put it all down on paper.

Minutes passed before she finally seemed to breathe. Placing the last of the pencils back down on the coffee table, she silently handed the paper to Derek and waited.

"This is good," Derek murmured as he came around to sit beside Kayleigh on the sofa. "This is exactly what I've been talking about." He tossed the pad on the coffee table and stared at her, puzzlement written all over his face. "What are you doing wasting your time answering phones in customer service when you have talent like this?"

Awkward. How could she possibly explain to him that *he* was the reason she was withering away in that cubicle? It would be incredibly embarrassing to admit she'd had an enormous crush on him for years and stayed in a job that was technically beneath her just so she could stare at him in the mornings when he got to the office. Worse yet would be to go on and remind him of how he had never even glanced her way. This would all, inevitably, lead to him assuming she'd taken the job as Emery's caretaker just so she could be close to him and then, knowing Derek as she had come to, he would think she was some crazy stalker chick. There would of course be a lot of apologizing as she would have to pack up her things in the middle of the night, and then she'd be forced to look for another job, which, in the grand scheme of things, might be a good thing. Maybe then she'd finally—

"Kayleigh?"

"Oh, right. Sorry. You asked a question." Nervously,

she fidgeted in her seat and stayed clear of meeting his eyes. "Well, I originally took the job at Sloan's to get my foot in the door with a design firm. I thought eventually I'd move on or up. There just were never any openings."

"So you stayed on even though your talents were being wasted?" His tone revealed how insane he thought this was.

"I guess time just got away from me and I got too comfortable." Rising from the sofa, Kayleigh walked to the kitchen to pour herself some water. Derek followed.

"Okay, so now that the cat's out of the bag, I'm curious about your thoughts."

"On what, exactly?"

"Well, for starters, on my plans for the company. Do you think it's something that can be done, or am I looking to pursue too broad a spectrum?" Derek almost cringed as he heard himself. Never had he asked for advice from anyone where his company was concerned. Not even his grandparents, and it was their damn company to begin with! Now he stood here, at one in the morning, talking to an employee—a lovely employee at that—about the future of his empire.

Not wanting to seem too anxious, she took a sip of water before answering. "Okay, well, I guess I think it's a great idea and you should do it. You've always been successful before in your expansions, and so I see no reason why this one wouldn't succeed."

Annoyance flooded through Derek. "Okay, you can put the pom-poms away. I'm not looking for the yes-man attitude here, Kayleigh. I thought you of all people would be honest with me." Slamming a hand on the counter, he stalked back to the living room and picked up a report to read before sitting down on the sofa again.

Realizing her mistake immediately, she stormed after him. "You want honesty? Okay. Here it comes. Yes, I think it is about time Sloan's broadened its horizons, so to speak. I think while the products you produce now are fine and are selling well, they're boring. They're almost generic. I can picture each and every one of them in a doctor's office. Sometimes when I have to send out a sample to a customer, I think it wouldn't matter if I got the item number wrong because so many of them look the damn same!

"I think it's time to introduce your design team to a little something called *color* and *imagination*." Pacing the room, waving her arms around as she spoke, she went on. "I'm not talking about taking on places like chain restaurants or anything remotely corporate. I'd like to see Sloan's get to the residential, high-end homes, for us to work with architects and decorators so we can do model homes. And not just your average run-of-the-mill homes—luxury homes, villas, exotic locations… I mean, the possibilities are endless."

She was reaching down for the sketch pad again as Derek sat in stunned silence. "Take this living room here for example," she began as she furiously sketched the room they were in. "The colors are great, your decorator did a fine job, but it still lacks warmth. If we went with warm, earthy colors here and used solids on this piece and more textures here…" Kayleigh was so caught up, she had almost forgotten Derek was sitting there. She could see it all in her mind, the room exactly as she wanted it. She wandered around the room, sketching and touching things as she went. "Textured wallpaper for the vaulted ceiling would be amazing. So much better than the popcorn stuff that's up there now. You'd want to be able to offer a complete room; everything a decorator could possibly want to finish a room, they should be able to get from Sloan's." Finally finished, she handed the sketch pad to Derek while she continued to prowl the room.

Looking down at the paper in his hands, Derek was speechless. He had always thought the room was fine, but staring at the picture Kayleigh had presented to him, he saw all it lacked. "Surely this didn't just come to you this minute?"

"What? Oh, no… It's something I've been thinking about since I came here with Emery. I do that sometimes, sit in a room and make it different in my head."

"Do you have other ideas down on paper? Not just about my house, but other ideas in general about fabrics and patterns?"

Oh, this was all getting way too tempting. This could be the exact opportunity she had been looking for. The chance to get into the design department and out of customer service while still working for Sloan's was suddenly looking like a very real possibility.

"I do," she said cautiously. "All of my stuff is back at my place. I didn't think I'd have time for it while I was caring for Emery."

"Maybe tomorrow you can stop by and get it and we can look at it together after dinner. What do you think?"

Her stomach was full of butterflies. "I think I can do that." Taking a deep breath, she turned and caught a glimpse of the time. "I think it's time I headed back up.

Emery is still an early riser and I need to get some sleep. I'll see you in the morning." Afraid to get too close to him, she backed out of the room as she spoke. "Good night, Derek."

He gave her a smile that turned her knees to jelly. "Good night, Kayleigh."

~

Derek couldn't wait to get home the following evening. His mind had been stuck on Kayleigh all day. Who would have thought finding a baby in his office would lead to so many possibilities?

Baby in his office.

Crap. When had he last put any effort into resolving that particular issue? Between work, business trips, and his attraction to Kayleigh, he had put the whole business with Emery out of his mind. He knew she was there, but he tended to block out the reasons why—mainly because her arrival had brought so many bonuses with it.

Focus, dammit! Picking up his phone, he first dialed the number for his lawyer and touched base with him regarding finding Brian. The man had nothing new to report, so Derek hung up and dialed his private investigator, hoping to have more luck with the location of the birth mother.

By the time he arrived home that evening, his head was roaring. Never in his life had he felt so out of control. Everywhere he turned, there were loose ends, and that could not continue. With no real leads to go on, the private investigator promised to keep in touch but hadn't sounded hopeful. With Brian still out of the country, they were at a dead end in just about every way. Derek had no doubt Emery was Brian's daughter. After going through his own social calendar and following up on the women he had been involved with in the last year, nothing had turned up.

The thought of the baby belonging to his brother bothered him more than it should have.

Walking through the door of his home, he was immediately hit with sensory overload. Something wonderful was cooking, there was classical music coming from the house's sound system, and Emery was having the kind of meltdown she'd exhibited that first day in his office. Tossing his briefcase down at the door, Derek rushed into the living room in search of Kayleigh.

"What's going on? Is Emery all right?" His voice was laced with concern and without thinking, he reached out and took the crying child from Kayleigh's arms to comfort her. He was rubbing the baby's back, speaking softly to her as he gently bounced her while walking around when he noticed the stunned look on Kayleigh's face. One dark, arched eyebrow in her direction said more than any question.

"She's been fussy ever since she woke from her nap this afternoon," Kayleigh said, rising from the sofa. She gently placed a cloth on his shoulder to protect his shirt from anything Emery might do as she walked to the kitchen to check on their dinner. "I called my brother, and he said there are a million reasons why a baby could be fussy." She turned and stirred the sauce on the stove before adding, "We have an appointment with him first thing in the morning."

Derek was more than a little relieved Kayleigh was being so thorough in her care of the infant. Carefully, he lifted Emery from his shoulder and cradled her in his arms. His heart ached. He wasn't sure how it had happened, especially since he'd had to remind himself earlier that she was a part of his life, but looking into Emery's tear-streaked face, he realized he had come to love her.

And she was Brian's.

She was still his niece, but that bit of information did nothing to make him feel better. It bothered him that his irresponsible brother was going to come home and find out he had a daughter. There was no way Brian was going to take kindly to the news of being a father. He was selfish and had no desire to settle down. How was he going to take care of Emery? *Who* was going to take care of Emery?

Glancing over at Kayleigh, Derek imagined Brian would try to get Kayleigh to help him. Rage built in him and he started to feel the tension rise. Apparently, so did Emery because her face started to scrunch up as she prepared to cry. Carefully placing her back on his shoulder, Derek continued to rub her back, doing his best to keep her calm. It was a bit awe inspiring to realize this tiny person was so sensitive to his moods. Would his brother appreciate this incredible gift? Would he look down at his daughter in wonder?

"Derek? Are you okay?" He looked up at Kayleigh, who was across the room, concern written all over her face.

"I'm fine." He sighed, realizing he wanted to share what he was thinking with her. "We finished part of the search into who Emery is."

Kayleigh felt all the blood drain from her face as

she dropped the spoon she had been using onto the counter. "And?" She gripped the granite to keep from going across the room to Derek. She had known this day would come, and there was a very real possibility of Emery being his daughter, but that thought just made her ill. The thought of Derek creating a child with another woman was almost more than she could bear.

"She's Brian's."

All the breath Kayleigh had been holding seemed to whoosh out of her in relief. "How can you be so sure? I mean, without Brian being here?"

Noticing Emery had fallen asleep, Derek gently placed her in the cradle Kayleigh had set up in the living room. Once he was sure she wasn't going to stir, he turned to Kayleigh and explained how all the women in his life for the last year had been eliminated. He noticed her shoulders sag. Was she relieved? Had it bothered her that there had been a possibility of Emery being his?

"Well, I guess that's one obstacle cleared," she said carefully, not making eye contact with him. "Any word on Brian's whereabouts?"

"We know he's in Africa. We just can't get in contact with him."

"So what happens now?"

"Unfortunately, until he's back, we're no closer to knowing who Emery's mother is."

Unable to help herself, Kayleigh stepped around the counter separating them and placed a hand on Derek's arm. "Are you okay with all of this?" she asked softly. "With Brian being Emery's father?"

"A week ago I would have said yes, but now…" He

let the statement hang, unsure if he was ready to admit out loud what his heart was telling him.

Kayleigh wanted to push him for more information but could tell Derek was struggling with all of this. Quietly, she turned back to the kitchen and finished the meal preparation. Within minutes, they were seated at the table, making small talk over dinner.

"I went to my apartment today and picked up some of my sketch pads and supplies," she said hesitantly, unsure if she should have waited for him to ask for her drawings.

Derek's head snapped up, and for the first time since he'd walked in the door, he looked happy, hopeful. "Great. I'm anxious to see what you've been working on." For the remainder of the meal, they talked business. Once the dishes were cleared and Kayleigh went to grab her portfolio, Emery started to fuss.

"I'll get her," Derek said. "Go get your stuff."

She wanted to argue; he was paying her a small fortune to be Emery's caretaker. It seemed like, since Derek had found out the baby was his brother's, he was getting more hands-on. Kayleigh didn't know what to think of that, but surely it couldn't be a coincidence.

When she walked back into the room, Derek was seated on one of the sofas with Emery in his arms, speaking softly to her. Taking one of her tiny hands, he examined it as if seeing it for the first time. Then he did the same with her feet. Kayleigh's heart nearly broke as she watched this big, strong man gently caress the infant's cheek in wonder.

Sensing her presence, he looked up. "She's so small," he said, his voice laced with sadness.

Dropping her portfolio next to the sofa, she sat next to him. "She won't stay that way for long. In the last week, I've seen a difference in the way some of her clothes fit. Jared said she's fine. We'll get her weight and measurements tomorrow and you can see for yourself she's growing."

He merely nodded.

Rising, Kayleigh went to the kitchen and prepared a bottle for him to feed to Emery. Within minutes, she was back beside him. There wasn't a need for conversation, so they just sat and enjoyed watching the baby take her evening meal. Soon, it was time to change her and get her ready for bed, which they did together, and Derek was the one who placed her down to sleep for the night. Standing in the doorway, Kayleigh could sense his inner turmoil.

When they were back in the living room, she knew they should go back to talking business, but she was unwilling to do so without addressing the elephant in the room. "What's going to happen to Emery when your brother gets back?"

Derek turned to her, stunned by her question. "What do you mean?"

"Well, I realize I don't know him personally, but I know enough about him to make me wonder what's going to happen when he finally gets back and finds out he has an infant daughter. Aren't you the least bit concerned?"

He wanted to yell and scream, to rail at the unfairness of it, but it wasn't his style. He didn't want anyone to know how much the thought of Brian coming and claiming Emery was bothering him. "I'm sure he's going to be fine, Kayleigh. I mean, I adjusted to having her here.

I'm sure Brian will need a little bit of time and then everything will work out."

"But what if it doesn't?"

Derek didn't even want to think about the possibility. He knew his brother better than anyone, and if he was being honest with himself, he'd admit there was a greater chance of Brian screwing this up than of there being success. "He'll be fine."

With a huff of frustration, Kayleigh turned to grab her portfolio and then stopped. "Look, I know you're his brother and you believe what you're saying, but I have to be honest. I'm concerned for Emery."

He pinched the bridge of his nose and counted to ten before allowing himself to speak. "I appreciate your concern, Kayleigh, I truly do, but as you already stated, you don't know Brian."

"I know enough about him," she mumbled.

"You know gossip; not everything you hear around the watercooler is true." There was condescension in his tone Kayleigh didn't like or appreciate.

"Believe me, I know not everything I hear is gospel truth, Derek, but can you honestly stand here and tell me you think your brother is responsible? I mean, where is he? No one knows! God forbid something happens to you or your grandparents, because no one can reach him! Are you telling me he doesn't date a different woman every week? Do you think once he's back, he's even going to remember half the women he's slept with in the last year?"

"Kayleigh—"

"No, seriously. I've worked for you for five years, and I can count on one hand the number of times I've even seen Brian in the office. Why is it you work fifteen-hour days and he doesn't even show up? Where is he while you're planning this expansion of the business? Where does he stand on that? What exactly does he do? I have to be honest with you, Derek, as far as I can see, he's a spoiled brat living off your hard work!"

Rage was building in Derek at each sentence she spoke, but the more powerful emotion was embarrassment. If Kayleigh had noticed his family dynamics, chances were others in the company had noticed it too, and probably looked at him like he was a fool.

"It's okay to love your brother, Derek," she said with more calmness than she felt. "All I'm saying is maybe it's time for him to grow up and face the consequences of his actions. Maybe it's time for you to stop bailing him out."

"What am I supposed to do?" he asked weakly, his arms dropping to his sides. "Do I really set out to teach him a lesson at Emery's expense?" When Kayleigh didn't immediately answer, he went on. "When Brian gets back, we'll do whatever we have to do to make Emery's transition an easy one. We'll find him a nanny and move furniture and...whatever it takes."

Sadness overwhelmed her. She knew her time here in Derek's home was temporary, but hearing the words out loud made her heart ache. Tears began to well in her eyes and she knew if she tried to speak, the dam would break. Turning away, she once again looked at her portfolio, but realized her heart just wasn't in it tonight.

Taking a deep breath, Kayleigh turned to Derek. "If it's all right with you, we'll look at the drawings tomorrow. I guess I'm a little more tired than I thought."

Derek knew it was a lie, but it was one he understood. He wished her a good night and then turned to look out at the backyard until he heard her bedroom door close. Everything she had said was right. He was concerned Brian was going to screw this up, and deep down, Derek was tired of his brother being so damn irresponsible. At the same time, unfortunately, he knew he would do whatever it took this time to make sure his brother didn't fail.

Teaching Derek nothing.

Chapter 5

After a restless night, Kayleigh was thankful Emery had slept in. By the time they went downstairs, Derek had left for work. A quick glance at the kitchen clock showed she needed to leave soon in order to make their appointment with her brother.

Packing up all of Emery's essentials, she loaded the car and they were on their way. It didn't take long for Jared to diagnose a mild ear infection and prescribe an antibiotic. "You should notice a difference by tomorrow," he said with a smile. "How is she doing otherwise?"

Kayleigh filled him in on a day in the life of Emery and was relieved to hear that other than the ear infection, she was a healthy baby. "Derek will be glad to hear that. He was concerned she is so small."

"Well, she's very young," Jared replied. "If he has any questions, tell him he can call me anytime." He hesitated briefly. "Any word on whether or not he's the father?"

With an odd sense of déjà vu, she gave him the *Reader's Digest* version of where they stood in the paternity department. Trying to mask her disappointment with the current turn of events, Kayleigh gathered up all of their things, so her brother could get to his next patient. "It's such a beautiful day out, Jared. Would it be all right for us to go for a walk in the park or will that upset her ear too much?"

With assurances a walk in the park would indeed be fine, Kayleigh and Emery were on their way. The subdivision Derek lived in boasted a beautiful park with a walking trail, so Kayleigh drove there and parked.

Knowing Derek would want to know how the appointment went, she dialed the office and stiffened at Eileen's tone. "He's in a meeting right now, Miss Mitchell. I'll have to take a message." With no other choice, she relayed the diagnosis and wished the woman a good day.

Refusing to let Derek's assistant alter her mood, Kayleigh pulled the stroller out from the back of her car, got Emery situated, and headed down the trail. The day was crisp and clear; there was a gentle breeze coming off the lake, and it didn't take long for some of the tension she'd been feeling since the previous evening to wear off. Looking around, she wished Emery were older so she could see the ducks in the water or the cardinal on a tree branch nearby. It was a perfectly serene moment.

It changed in an instant.

There was no warning, but suddenly there were heavy footsteps behind her and someone shoved Kayleigh aside. She refused to let go of her grip on the stroller for fear of it tipping over and hurting Emery.

"*What the—*" she began to say.

"What are you doing with my baby?" a woman screeched. It took Kayleigh a minute to focus on where the voice was coming from. She was circling Kayleigh, her eyes wild, her long blond hair a mess. "I didn't give her to you! You have no right! Give her back to me now!"

With a deep breath, Kayleigh cataloged the woman's

features and then tried to reason with her. "Look, Miss…?" She waited, hoping the woman would supply her name. When she didn't, Kayleigh continued to talk to her calmly. "I know we haven't met before, but are you sure—"

"Don't you think I know my own damn daughter, you bitch? Brian is supposed to have her! Why do you have her? Where's Brian?" With every question, the woman's voice grew louder and more irate. "I want my daughter back now!" she screamed as she rushed at Kayleigh, knocking her to the ground.

Kayleigh screamed and Emery began to cry, and soon there were more footsteps rushing toward them. "Help!" Kayleigh screamed. "Somebody, please!" She felt her head bang against the concrete path, and out of the corner of her eye saw the stroller fall on its side. *"Emery!"*

Derek was mentally exhausted. Having slept very little the night before, after his argument with Kayleigh, he'd come in early to the office, only to hit one brick wall after another with his design team. Why couldn't they see what he was seeing? If he was going to move this company forward, he was going to have to seriously reconsider the team of designers he currently had on staff.

Loosening his tie, he stepped from his office and asked Eileen for his messages. "Miss Mitchell called," she said flatly. "That baby has an ear infection."

"Is she okay?" he asked anxiously. "Do I need to do anything? Are they at home or still at the doctor?"

She eyed him over the rim of her glasses. "I have no idea."

Annoyed, Derek went back into his office and dialed Kayleigh's cell phone. He was mildly confused when a male voice answered. "Who is this?" Derek demanded. Panic seized him as he listened. He was out the office door and running for the elevators before the call was over.

Racing into the emergency room, it didn't take Derek long to find her. "Kayleigh?" he cried out as he shoved the examining room door open. She was sitting up on the exam room table, a bandage on her head and a doctor sitting beside her on a stool.

"Derek! You need to go and check on Emery!" Tears streamed down her face as she spoke. "They haven't let me see her yet. I got Jared to come, but I haven't been able to leave this room!"

He went to her and wrapped his arms around her, comforting her. "Shh… It's all right. I'll go find her right now. Are you okay?"

The doctor answered for her. "A couple of scrapes and bruises and five stitches on her head. She's going to be fine."

Thanking the man, Derek gripped Kayleigh's hands tightly in his larger ones. "I'm going to get Emery and then we're all going home."

Feeling as if she could finally breathe, Kayleigh let herself relax. Within minutes, Derek was back, Emery in his arms and Jared behind him. She jumped down from the table and carefully took the baby from Derek. "Is she okay?" she asked nervously, scanning the infant for any signs of harm.

"She's fine, Kayleigh," Jared answered. "She was well protected in her stroller; you had her strapped in perfectly."

"What happened?" Derek asked.

Kayleigh relayed the events to him. "She claimed to be Emery's mother. I've already talked to a policeman and given him a description, but she wouldn't tell me her name."

"Would you recognize her if you saw her again?"

"Derek, I could sketch her for you perfectly right now. I knew it would be important to be able to describe her, especially when Brian gets back."

It took more than an hour to get them both released, and Derek could honestly say he was severely shaken up. When they arrived back at the house and had Emery settled, he sat Kayleigh down and asked, "Can you really draw this woman? It could help the private investigators find her."

Within minutes, Kayleigh had a very detailed sketch of the woman's face. "Do you recognize her?" she asked. A shake of his head told her that he didn't. "I'm so sorry, Derek," she said quietly.

"For what?"

"I should have just come straight home. The day was so beautiful, and Emery had been so fussy, I thought being outside for a bit would be good for her."

Gathering Kayleigh in his arms, he quieted her. "There was no way for you to know this woman was out there, Kayleigh. It's not your fault."

"But if I'd just come home…"

"Who's to say she wouldn't have tried to get in here?" After saying the words out loud, Derek made a mental note to upgrade his home security system first thing in the morning. "You fought her off and you protected Emery. You heard your brother; she's fine." He kissed her forehead and noticed her wince.

"Sorry," she said softly, "it's still a little sore." Without hesitation, Kayleigh allowed herself to relax into Derek's arms and realized it felt good to be there. It wasn't awkward or strange; it actually felt quite natural. This was all really happening to her—she was there, in Derek's home, in his arms, and he seemed to really want her there.

Turning her head slightly, she looked up at him and found him staring intently at her. "Derek…I…"

He placed a finger over her lips to silence her, as if he didn't want the moment lost. His finger stayed in place a moment before gently tracing her lips and moving to her cheek, her jaw, and carefully winding its way around to her nape. Slowly, as if giving her time to stop him, Derek angled her head up as he lowered his mouth to hers.

The kiss was soft, gentle. He waited a heartbeat to see if she was going to pull back and didn't fully relax until Kayleigh wrapped her arms around him as she shifted to get closer. He couldn't say who took control of the kiss first; one minute it was a sweet exploration and the next, they were intent on devouring one another.

His hands carefully explored her, his brain still functioning enough for him to be mindful of her injuries. But he found he was trembling. For all the women he had been with, for all of his skill in the bedroom, this moment had seemed to come out of nowhere and Derek wanted to savor it and make it perfect for Kayleigh.

She had done something to him in these last two weeks; she had not only saved him with Emery, but she had also shown him how much he was missing in his life. Some would say she'd saved him from himself. His mind wanted to linger on that thought for a minute, but she sighed and pressed herself closer, and Derek was lost. The last two weeks suddenly seemed like nothing; it seemed like he had been waiting for her his whole life and he couldn't wait any longer.

Slowly, he broke the kiss and raised his head, his breathing ragged. "Stay with me tonight." He feared she was going to say no; she was suddenly going to remember her reasons for not getting involved with him. Derek silently prayed she had been waiting for him as much as he'd been waiting for her.

Wordlessly, Kayleigh rose to her feet. Standing before him, she held out one shaky hand, never breaking eye contact. "Yes."

Derek wanted to whoop with delight but figured that might break the spell. Silently, he stood up. He leaned in and cupped her face before kissing her again. Hell, he could go on kissing her all night, but if he was going to do that, he wanted to do it in his bed. Scooping her up into his arms, he carried her to his bedroom. He was about to shut the door but stopped.

"What's the matter?" she asked softly, sensing Derek's hesitation.

"I want to be able to hear Emery. The monitor's out there, and I want to make sure we hear her in case she needs us."

If Kayleigh hadn't been sure about wanting Derek before, that statement made her certain. There was so much more to him than she had ever imagined, so much more than what she had thought she knew from their first meeting. Derek's passion for his business was a given; it was his passion for the people he cared about that was quickly becoming his most endearing quality.

Laying her gently on his bed, Derek could only stop and stare. He didn't bring women to his home, and he had certainly never brought one to this bed. Knowing Kayleigh was the first had him suddenly feeling nervous. Would she read too much into this? Was she right a week ago when she'd said this would be a bad idea?

"Derek," she whispered, her eyes showing her own uncertainty. "Please."

Any thoughts of turning back vanished. He was destined for this moment, and rather than focus on the reasons why it may not be a good idea, all he wanted to do was embrace the reasons it was. With one knee on the bed, he pulled his shirt over his head. Earlier, Kayleigh had changed into a pair of flannel pajama pants and another classic rock T-shirt. She shouldn't have looked so damn sexy, but she did.

One large hand trembled slightly as he reached out and skimmed a hand under the T-shirt. "Have I mentioned how much I enjoy your variety of pajamas?"

Unable to help herself, Kayleigh let out a laugh. "Oh, yeah. I'm sure."

He chuckled with her. "What's that supposed to mean?"

"Not too long ago, I had a rather detailed education on the importance of sexy lingerie. Right now I'm feeling a bit sorry I didn't pay more attention. This was certainly not what I had hoped to be wearing the first time you and I…" She stopped herself before she admitted any more.

"So you have thought about you and me making love," he said huskily and watched her nod. "Good. I'm glad I'm not the only one." His hand continued its journey, and Derek found he liked making her squirm. Her body was so beautiful, so perfect, every move was a turn-on. She sighed his name. "It wouldn't matter to me if you were wearing lace or flannel. I want you, Kayleigh."

And then he poured everything he had into proving it to her.

Emery woke up a little after midnight. Kayleigh went to get up but Derek stopped her. "I'll go get her."

She was momentarily stunned. "Do you even know how to change her?" she asked with a chuckle.

He shrugged. "I guess we're going to find out."

That had Kayleigh on the verge of jumping up, but she felt suddenly shy of doing so completely naked. Sensing her unease, Derek pulled out one of his shirts and placed it on the bed. "You get her bottle, and I'll take care of her." Leaning down, he kissed her softly before heading up to get his niece.

They met in the kitchen, but when Kayleigh went to take Emery into the living room, as had been their ritual, Derek took her by the hand and led her back to the bedroom. She looked at him questioningly but followed. Together, the three of them sat in the bed, cuddling together under the blankets while the baby ate. Kayleigh's heart ached. In a perfect world, it wouldn't be a temporary situation; it would be their reality.

Her. Derek. A baby.

This house would be her home, and there would be no threat of it coming to an end at any moment. Tears began to well in her eyes and when Derek saw, his gut clenched. "Kayleigh? Sweetheart? Are you okay? Are you in pain?" He made to take Emery from her, but she held the infant close.

She shook her head and wiped away a stray tear. "I guess it's all just catching up with me. These last two weeks have been a bit of a whirlwind and then with the attack today and being here with you tonight…" She stopped and looked up at him. "I think the lines of fantasy and reality are starting to get blurred."

Derek understood that more than she knew. He was getting too used to having her here and pretending their little family was really his. Kayleigh made him want it to be true. He didn't want to think about what was going to happen when Brian got back, didn't want to imagine what it was going to be like to come home at the end of the day to an empty house. Would he go back to working endless hours? Would he and Kayleigh even continue their relationship, or would everything come to an end once Emery moved out?

He didn't want to think about it. Right then, in that moment, Derek Sloan had it all. He pulled Kayleigh close and kissed her head, and together they sat in silence until Emery fell back asleep. Derek took the baby back up to the nursery, relieved to find Kayleigh still waiting for him in bed. On some level, he had feared that, by the time he got back, she'd have left, wanting to sleep in her own room.

Silently, he stalked across the room and stripped

before climbing back into bed beside her. She instantly moved into his arms, and Derek thought it was as close to heaven as a man could get. He'd take every moment of it while he could, because he had a feeling it wouldn't be long before it was nothing more than a memory.

Chapter 6

FOR THREE DAYS AND THREE NIGHTS, IT WAS BLISS. KAYLEIGH found herself walking around singing for no reason, and sometimes would actually pinch herself to make sure she wasn't dreaming. Life was perfect. Emery was happy and content, Kayleigh had a perpetual smile on her face, and Derek? Well, from the way he greeted her every morning when he woke up and every night when he came home, she felt pretty confident saying he was damn happy too.

It wasn't something they openly discussed, but Kayleigh had moved into Derek's bedroom. Her things still remained upstairs in the bedroom across from the nursery, but she wasn't sleeping there any longer. Every night, after Emery went to sleep, Derek made love to her. It was as if he patiently waited all day, but once the baby was down for the night, he could no longer hold back.

Kayleigh loved that about him.

For hours, they would make love and talk about their lives, the business, and just whatever came to mind. Kayleigh was certain her sleep time had been cut in half if not more, but she had never felt more alive.

On a whim, she took Emery on a little shopping trip to the mall. The baby had had a small growth spurt and needed some new things, but once they got there, Kayleigh decided on a little shopping of her own.

Valentine's Day was only two weeks away, and she was hopeful she'd be spending it with Derek. Although he'd said he didn't mind her funky sleeping attire, she was hoping to do exactly as Carol had said and break out of her comfort zone by buying something racy to wear for him.

After a quick stop in the baby department to get a couple of new outfits for Emery, Kayleigh placed her purchases in the basket under the stroller and walked determinedly to the lingerie department. She felt odd just being there, and kept glancing over her shoulder to make sure no one was watching her or mocking her choices.

Yes, because everyone in the store cares about your underwear. The simple silk nighties drew her in first, but then she remembered how Carol had called them tame. Maybe to her, but for Kayleigh, they were a big step. *Be daring!* her inner voice prodded.

Moving on to the next rack, she found ones that were a little slinkier, a little sexier, and before she could change her mind, she found one in her size and put it on top of the stroller. It was primarily red silk, but the bodice was all sheer lace. There was a slit in the side that, to her, seemed ridiculous since it was already scandalously short.

Walking through the last of the racks, she decided while the nightie was for Valentine's Day, she might try and build up to it by buying some frilly underwear to surprise Derek with that night. While she always wore what she considered to be very feminine undies, she never wore anything overly sexy. Like a thong. Feeling very naughty, she grabbed a black one and then found a sexy matching push-up bra and put them both under the red silk to hide them from people walking by.

The thought of Derek's reaction had her practically racing from the store. He might say it didn't matter what she was wearing, but Kayleigh had a feeling that might change once he saw her in these skimpy little items. As much as she loved them and was proud of herself for buying them, she secretly hoped Derek would take one look at them and rip them from her body.

Her. Little Kayleigh Mitchell. Sex kitten. She smiled at the label. Who knew?

Funny thing about being happy, sometimes it's short-lived.

Kayleigh had Emery bathed and ready for bed a little earlier than usual. Kayleigh herself had taken a shower and moisturized her body in her favorite scented lotion in anticipation of the night to come. Her new underwear felt very decadent, and while she always enjoyed their time eating together, tonight she couldn't wait to be done with it.

A glance at the clock showed it was almost six thirty. Derek would be home any minute. He hadn't called her the way he usually did on his way home, but Kayleigh just figured he had forgotten. Dinner was cooking and the table was set. She had lit a fire in the fireplace, and now all she needed was for Derek to come home.

The sound of a car door slamming had her heart rate kicking up. "Here we go," she said with a hand on her nervous tummy. Would he like the way she set up a romantic evening? Would he be pleased by her new purchases? The sound of a second car door brought her out of her thoughts as she walked toward the front door, coming to a halt as it opened.

Derek walked in, and with one look at his face, Kayleigh knew something was wrong. She was just about to speak when she caught sight of someone behind him.

Brian.

The prodigal son had returned.

Kayleigh felt as if the world beneath her fell away and she almost fainted. Derek sensed it and immediately came to her aid, wrapping an arm around her waist and leading her into the kitchen. Emery was in her infant swing and Derek cursed the fact that all of this was happening now. He took in the fire in the fireplace and the scent of whatever it was Kayleigh had prepared for dinner. He would have given anything for it not to end like this. Now.

Ever.

Her eyes frantically searched his, willing him to say something, anything. "Kayleigh Mitchell, this is my brother, Brian," was all he said as his brother strolled into the kitchen.

"Wow, nice setup," Brian said, but his tone was smarmy and Kayleigh had a feeling he wasn't referring to the decor. "So is this her?" He motioned toward Emery.

"Do you see any other baby here?" Derek snapped impatiently.

"Oh yeah. Right." Brian knelt down in front of the baby and smiled and made some goofy faces before standing up and facing Derek and Kayleigh. "So you're sure she's mine?"

Kayleigh felt ill. This moron didn't deserve Emery. Even the thought of him touching the baby, let alone raising her, made her want to scream.

"Paternity tests prove she's a Sloan, and the woman who attacked Kayleigh said she was yours." Derek walked across the room and found the sketch Kayleigh had done of the woman. He handed it to his brother. "Does she look familiar to you?"

"Yeah, that's Melissa. We dated briefly about a year ago. Great in bed, crazy as hell once she's out of it."

"Charming," Kayleigh muttered, as she went to take dinner off the stove.

"Something smells good," Brian said, coming up to stand behind Kayleigh as he peered over her shoulder. "Looks good too."

Derek wanted to pull his brother away from Kayleigh and tell him he wasn't allowed to go near her. But he couldn't. This whole scene wasn't going to go well, and it was important for him to keep a clear head.

Kayleigh shrugged Brian away from her and began to prepare their plates. Without a word, she made up three plates and placed them on the table. It was awkward to say the least. There were at least a dozen questions racing through her mind. Was Brian really back for good? Was he going to take Emery home? Did he even know how to take care of a baby? Was Derek going to allow this to happen?

They sat down, and it was as if she wasn't even there. The brothers conversed with one another, seemingly unaware of her presence.

"Can you get in touch with this Melissa person?" Derek asked.

"I'm going to have to. The kid is hers."

Derek tensed and had to fight off the urge to scream. "She's your child too, and her name is Emery."

"What kind of name is that?" Brian asked. "Is it even a girl's name? Are you sure she's a girl?"

"Yes, Brian. For the three weeks I've been caring for her, I've made sure to take note of the fact that she's a girl."

Brian shrugged. "Look, all I'm saying is this is not my responsibility. I didn't have any idea Melissa was pregnant—she never contacted me. Now I'm just supposed to…what? Be a dad?"

"Yes," Derek snapped, his patience quickly coming to an end. "That is exactly what you're supposed to do!" Next to him, Kayleigh rose to comfort Emery. Derek's loud tone had startled her and she was starting to fuss. "In case you haven't noticed, that's what I had to do. Emery was dropped off at the damn office and I had to step up and take care of her. She's your daughter. You need to do what's right!"

"Yeah, okay. From where I'm sitting, bro, you didn't do all that much. You hired yourself a hot nanny," he said as he leered at Kayleigh, "and played house. You probably didn't do a whole hell of a lot to take care of the kid. You had your playmate here handle it."

Derek nearly knocked the table over as he rose. "First of all, Kayleigh isn't my playmate; she came here and helped to take care of *your* daughter because you couldn't be found! Instead of making crude comments, maybe you should be thanking her for sacrificing her time to help you out."

Brian looked at Kayleigh, then Derek, and back to

her. "I'm sure it was a real hardship to leave your boring job at Sloan's to come and sit in a mansion and play with a baby. And my brother. Thanks."

Derek saw red. He yanked his brother up out of his seat. "What the hell is wrong with you?" he demanded.

Brian shook him off and took a step back. "What's wrong with me? You're standing here telling me what to do, what to say, how to act, and I'm tired of it! I had to cut my vacation short—"

"You were already gone a week longer than you originally said!" Derek yelled and then cursed when Emery started to cry. Out of the corner of his eye, he saw Kayleigh leave the room with the baby. "Vacation time is over. It's time for you to get your head on straight and take care of your responsibilities."

His brother shook his head. "I didn't ask for this responsibility and I don't want it."

"What are you saying?" Derek asked with a deadly calm he didn't feel.

"I don't want a kid, Derek. I enjoy my freedom. I like to travel. There's no room in my life for a kid, let alone a baby."

"You can't just walk away from her, Brian. She's your daughter."

He shrugged. "Melissa just walked away. Why can't I?"

Derek couldn't believe his ears. Why had he never realized just how selfish his brother was? When had he changed so much? Unfortunately, he knew the answer to that question. While Derek had been raised and groomed to take over the company, Brian had been indulged. And this was the end product: a grown man who didn't have a connection to anything or anyone but himself.

"Don't do this," Derek pleaded. "Don't make a rash decision. Take her home and bond with her. I didn't think I'd be able to handle it and I didn't want to. Hell, if you had seen me the first day, you'd see I reacted exactly like you are. But I changed. You can't just abandon her, Brian. She's family. She's your daughter."

Bryan looked from his brother to the now-empty infant swing. "You and I both know I can't do it alone. And if we're being honest, I don't particularly want to. If I decide to do this, I'm going to need someone to help me. Can Kayleigh come with us to make the transition easier? Clearly she likes the kid and the kid knows her. It would be a great help."

Kayleigh stood at the foot of the stairs in the shadows and held her breath. Surely Derek wouldn't just hand her off to his brother? Even if it was for Emery's sake! The sound of her own breathing was the only thing she heard for several long moments. "That's Kayleigh's decision," Derek said slowly right before Kayleigh burst into the room.

"You can't be serious?" she yelled at Derek. "You cannot stand here and honestly tell me you think he should take Emery out of this house! He doesn't want her! He doesn't even know how to take care of her!"

She was right, but Derek knew he had to be firm. "Emery is Brian's daughter, Kayleigh. He just needs time to get used to her, just like I did. I didn't settle in with her immediately. You know that."

"But you at least wanted to try," she reminded him. "You didn't immediately throw her out or ask someone to take her away. You sacrificed and made sure she was taken care of. He's not going to do that!" she cried.

"Um…I'm right here," Brian said.

"Shut up," Derek snapped and turned his attention back to Kayleigh. "Yes, I did what I had to do, but that's who I am. I'm responsible, and I make sure I do everything I can to keep my life on track. I hired you so I didn't have to do anything. You made sure Emery was safe and taken care of. I just footed the bill."

His words were cold and callous. "Why are you doing this?" she asked sadly. "Where is this coming from?"

Her words and the disappointment in her voice were nearly his undoing. "I'm stating the facts, Kayleigh. I needed to take care of the situation so I could keep doing what I had to do for the business. You made it easy for me to do that." The look of shock on her face was killing him. Didn't she know he had to do this? He had to physically and emotionally detach himself from the situation; otherwise, he would fall apart.

It wasn't fair that his brother constantly got to be carefree and even got rewarded for his bad behavior, while Derek worked night and day to make a success of himself. It killed him that Brian would get to come home, waltz in, and take Emery away. He didn't deserve her. But what choice did Derek have? Biologically, Emery belonged to his brother, and while he would always have a connection with her, he'd have to learn to deal with the role of uncle.

If Brian kept her.

Kayleigh's blue eyes filled with tears. "Don't let him take her, Derek. Please." She clutched his shirt in an attempt to get him to snap out of it, to make him see how desperately wrong he was.

Although it pained him to do it, Derek wrapped his hands around Kayleigh's wrists and pried her hands from his shirt. "You'll need to explain to Brian about Emery's schedule. You can help him find a nanny, or maybe you can help him during the transition," he said coolly.

In that moment, Kayleigh felt all the blood drain from her face. "Go to hell," she said before leaving the room and going up the stairs to her former room. She was packed within minutes, and although part of her was appalled neither Sloan brother came to her aid, she was relieved to make it out the door without having to look at either one of them.

When the front door closed, Brian sat back down at the table and looked at his brother. "Good job, bro. Now what the hell am I supposed to do?"

Chapter 7

It didn't take long for Kayleigh to realize she had made a colossal error in judgment. The man she had fallen in love with didn't exist. She had always known he was ruthless in business; she just hadn't realized he played by the same rules in his personal life.

Lesson learned.

It took a couple of days before she was able to go back to work at the office, and it took her less than a day to realize she couldn't stay. Derek had told her she had talent, and Kayleigh had to believe that if she put an effort into a job search, she'd be able to find something as a designer. Besides, seeing Derek every day, being that close to him and not being able to talk to him or touch him was more torture than she was willing to endure.

To say her supervisor was shocked was an understatement. If she suspected Kayleigh's sudden resignation had anything to do with her time away from the office, she said nothing. "We're going to miss you," she had said, and Kayleigh knew she was going to miss all of her coworkers as well. It was just time to move on.

The original plan had been to give at least a two-week notice, but after the first time she saw Derek from a distance, Kayleigh knew she wouldn't survive long. It might not have been the most professional move on her part, but a one-week notice was all she could do.

The extra money she had made while caring for Emery would go a long way in keeping her covered until she found a new job. She only had herself to take care of, after all.

"I still can't believe you're leaving," Carol said later that day at lunch. "I mean, you were gone for three weeks, living with the boss no less, and then you come back and quit." She gasped. "Oh my gosh! Is that why you're leaving? Is Derek as big a jerk at home as he is at work?"

It would have been easy to lie, but Kayleigh had a feeling she wouldn't sound believable. "He's not a jerk. I just realized this is not my dream job."

"This is nobody's dream job," Carol said dryly. "It's a paycheck."

Kayleigh shrugged. "I'm tired of just getting a paycheck. I need to move on and do something that gives me a sense of accomplishment."

"Do you know what you're going to do?" Kayleigh told her about her designs and her plan to seek out a firm that would be interested in them. "Why not apply here? You and I both know this place could use a bit of new blood and some inspiration in the design department. You've gotten to know the boss pretty well, obviously. Why not ask him for a chance?"

Because it would be emotional suicide. "It's just time to move on," she said instead. They ate their lunch in silence for a few moments. "I'm really going to miss you."

"It's not like we can never hang out together again. I just hope you don't forget me when you're a big, famous designer."

Kayleigh laughed. "Of course I won't."

With the last of her personal items in the box, Kayleigh looked around her cubicle. She had spent five years in the space and it was weird to see it look so bare. She had barely gotten any work done that day; there had been cake and everyone took her to lunch, and most of the time had been spent organizing her files and passing them on to the people who would now be handling her customers.

The department looked a lot like the SuperTarget had several weeks ago. There were flowers and balloons everywhere in celebration of Valentine's Day. While most people were excited that it fell on a Friday this year, Kayleigh would have been perfectly happy not to have to spend the day surrounded by everyone's stories of their big plans for the evening.

Her big plans consisted of ordering Chinese takeout and watching anything that didn't involve love.

Maybe she'd rent a horror movie.

The thought made her chuckle. She could barely stand the sight of the covers for those movies; she'd never get through more than the opening credits of one. Well, there went that plan.

At four o'clock, her supervisor came over. "Eileen said for you to come down for your exit interview as soon as you're ready."

"Exit interview? What's that?"

"Apparently it's something new. When an employee leaves, the brass wants to talk to them, do a survey on work conditions and get a general idea of your thoughts on the company. There's paperwork to be signed for human resources, that sort of thing. Plus, I think because you had shared some designs with Mr. Sloan, there may be some paperwork involved in that as well."

It was the first Kayleigh had ever heard of such a thing, but she shrugged. "Where do I need to go? Human resources?"

"Mr. Sloan's office."

Kayleigh's heart sank. "Wh…why? I thought this was a human resources thing?"

"No idea. Besides, after taking care of his niece for three weeks, I would think this would be easier than going down to human resources." With that, she left Kayleigh alone.

Great. Now she would have to deal with an up close and personal meeting with Derek, rather than having the freedom to run away without notice. "My life sucks," she muttered as she made her way down to Derek's suite. Eileen was at her desk and motioned for Kayleigh to take a seat. At least she knew what to expect from Derek's assistant: cool disdain. What was going to happen once she stepped into his office? Was the human resources director going to be in there? Would there at least be other people, or was she going to be forced to deal with him one-on-one?

"Mr. Sloan will see you now," Eileen said without even glancing in Kayleigh's direction.

"Always a pleasure," she mumbled before standing and thanking her.

Her feet felt like lead and her heart was beating way too rapidly as she walked through the doors to Derek's office. A quick look around showed it was only the two of them. Kayleigh saw Derek sitting behind his desk, sorting through some paperwork. "Please have a seat, Kayleigh," he said, as if he were speaking to a stranger and not someone who had shared his home and his bed just weeks before.

Kayleigh slid into one of the chairs opposite his and waited, secretly hoping someone else was going to join them.

"I have your employee file here," he began, effectively crushing her hopes for company. "It looks like we have some paperwork for you to sign regarding your health insurance," he said as he placed the papers in front of her along with a pen, "and your 401(k)." He shuffled through the papers some more. "You have two weeks of vacation time due to you and payroll has been instructed to send that to you with your final paycheck next week."

Kayleigh nodded, studying the papers in front of her rather than looking at Derek. Once she had signed everything, she slid them back toward him—and then had nothing to do but look at him. "Was there anything else?" she forced herself to ask.

Derek leaned back in his chair and drank in the sight of her. He knew her well enough to know she was nervous and she would rather be anyplace else in the world but there with him. "Did you find the working conditions here favorable?" he asked, searching for something to say to keep her there.

"Yes. Everyone has been great to work with."

"Did you have any trouble assigning your customers to other reps?"

She shook her head. "We are a team out there, so everyone stepped in to help." Silence. She wondered why he was dragging this out, and for that matter, why he felt the need to conduct this meeting himself. It would have made more sense for him to have Eileen handle it.

"What are your plans now?" he asked quietly. "Do you have another job lined up?"

"Not yet."

He nodded. "Well, I realize the designs you shared with me were done off the clock, but I shared them with the designers here and we would like the rights to them. I have some papers here for you to sign if that's all right with you. You'll be compensated for them, of course."

So this was it. Not only had he gotten someone to take care of his niece so he wouldn't have to, he had also gotten some new designs for his company and a couple nights' worth of sex. All in all, Derek Sloan had made out like a bandit. When he slid the contract her way, she practically ripped it from his hands and signed it without even reading it.

He pointed that fact out to her. "You should never sign something without reading it first."

Looking up, she stared at him. "Is there anything else?"

A small smile played at the corner of his mouth. "As a matter of fact, there is. But before I give it to you, I want you to pay close attention to it before signing it."

"Sure. Whatever." She just wanted to be done with all of this and leave. He could have the damn designs for all she cared. She had dozens more and with any luck, some other firm would appreciate her talents and not take advantage of her as Derek had.

Watching her intently, Derek slid a contract across the desk to her. "Make sure you read it, including the fine print."

Sitting back in her seat, Kayleigh took the paper from him and began to read. It didn't take long for her to look up at him, confusion written all over her face. "I…I don't understand."

"Keep reading," he said softly.

She did, and by the time she got to the bottom, she was crying. "When…? How…?"

"Did you read the fine print?" Kayleigh quickly scanned the document down to the fine print and her heart felt full to bursting. "Are those terms agreeable to you?" he asked as he stood and walked around to the front of the desk.

She was shaking. This couldn't be happening. The papers dropped to the floor beside her as she stood. "Why did you do this?" Her voice trembled as she spoke and she had to fight the urge to reach out and touch him.

"Are you going to sign that?" he asked, motioning to the papers.

"Derek, those are adoption papers. I don't understand what's going on."

Taking her by the hand, Derek led her over to the sofa on the side of the room where they both sat. "After you left that night, Brian and I sat down and had a long talk. Not just about Emery, but about everything. This company is my dream, not his. He has no interest in it. I guess I knew that for a long time but didn't want to fully acknowledge it. He likes living abroad, and he's made some business contacts over the years during his travels. Apparently, he has the opportunity to get involved with some resorts. He enjoys numbers and financing, and he seems pretty good at it. Either way, he doesn't want any part of Sloan's."

"What does have to do with—?"

"We came to an agreement, and rather than buy him out, he signed over his share of the company to Emery."

"Is that legal?"

Derek nodded. "He also signed over his parental rights to me."

"But...but what about Melissa? She's Emery's mother!"

Just the thought of the woman made Derek sick. "She never wanted Emery. She was hoping to get money from Brian. She also signed away her parental rights. To me."

"So you're...you're Emery's adoptive father now," she said shakily. "Wow. When did all of this happen?"

"It's been a fairly busy week," he said with a sad smile. "My grandparents came to visit, and they are spending time with Emery and helping take care of her, but she's not doing well."

"Who? Your grandmother?"

He shook his head. "No. Emery."

"Why? Is she ill? Is she cutting a tooth? The books all said teething can be—"

"She's not sick, and it's not a tooth," Derek interrupted. "She misses you." He waited a beat until Kayleigh's eyes met his. "I miss you."

"Oh," she sighed.

"Come home."

"But—"

"Sign the papers and come home with me. Make a family with me. Marry me."

It was all happening so fast, Kayleigh wasn't sure it was real. "I don't know, Derek. That night, you said—"

"I know what I said, and I'm sorry. I was devastated by the thought of Brian being back and taking Emery away. I had to detach myself because I didn't want to feel the pain. I know I was horrible to you and I'm so sorry. Please say you'll forgive me. Tell me I'm not too late. I love you, Kayleigh."

Those three words did it. "I love you too," she finally said, launching herself into his waiting arms. She kissed him with all the pent-up frustration and longing of the last weeks. Never in her wildest fantasies could she have imagined being here like this. Derek's mouth and touch were so familiar and so much a part of her that Kayleigh wondered how she had gotten by for almost two weeks without them.

Raising his head, Derek took her by the hand and led her back over to the desk. "As much as I want to keep kissing you and touching you, I certainly don't want to risk having Eileen or anyone walk in on us, because if we keep it up, I'll end up making love to you right here in this office."

The thought made Kayleigh blush. She reached down for the papers she had dropped earlier and quickly signed them. Looking up with him, she smiled sexily. "Then we'll have to go home and do it in private."

"I like the way you think, but there's just one more thing we need to do."

She was about to growl in frustration when Derek picked up the phone and simply said, "We're ready," before turning back to her. The door opened and in walked an elderly couple who she assumed were Derek's grandparents. His grandmother was carrying the infant car seat, and there she saw Emery, dressed in a beautiful red dress with a matching bow in her hair. In her lap was a heart-shaped box Kayleigh presumed to be chocolates. It was the most precious sight she had ever seen.

Introductions were made and soon she was able to lift the little girl who was now hers out of her seat. "Did you bring me a present?" she cooed to the baby.

"You should open that now," Derek said from beside her, leaning down to place a kiss on the baby's head. "She spent hours shopping for it."

They are both adorable, Kayleigh thought. Humoring him, she shifted Emery in her arms and did her best to open the box of candy. After all, it was Valentine's Day; you had to eat chocolate. It was the law.

Only it wasn't chocolate she found inside but a ring. A beautiful, antique-cut stone set in platinum. She gasped. "Oh my." Derek took the ring from the box and placed it on Kayleigh's finger. She stared at it in wonder. "Mighty confident of yourself, aren't you?"

"I was…hopeful." He reached down to Emery's car seat and pulled out another box. This one was velvet and rectangular. He handed to Kayleigh. "Open it. This one's from Emery."

"I thought the last one was from her," she teased.

"She was simply the messenger. I figured you might be tempted to say no to me, but you wouldn't be able to say no to our daughter."

Our daughter. No words had ever sounded sweeter. Smiling, she took the box from him and opened it. Inside was a platinum chain with a diamond heart pendant surrounded by blue topaz stones. "Emery's birthstone," Derek said as he took the necklace from the box and went to place it on Kayleigh. "She wanted you to have something pretty for Valentine's Day from her."

"She's gotten pretty vocal since I left."

Derek laughed. "You have no idea."

Epilogue

It was after midnight and Kayleigh was exhausted. After they had left the office, Derek's grandparents had offered to babysit so the two of them could go out to dinner. She had wanted to protest; after all, what she really wanted was to get Derek into bed. Unbeknownst to her, Derek had made dinner reservations for them, and after leaving Emery at home, they had gone to Kayleigh's, so she could change her clothes.

She had managed to get him into bed before dinner.

Now, as they lay tangled together in Derek's bed—now their bed—she sighed with contentment. "This has been quite a day. It started with me wondering where to send résumés. I never thought it would end here. I had planned on Chinese and a slasher flick."

"I can only hope this is better."

"Much," she said, placing a kiss on his chest.

"We can still find a slasher flick on cable if you'd like," he teased, knowing full well she never would have watched one.

"Thanks, I'm good."

"Yes, you are." He pulled her in close. "I was afraid I'd lost you, that you would turn me down."

"I was afraid you were going to let me leave again."

"I didn't want to let you leave the first time. I just didn't know how to handle everything. I was so completely overwhelmed and I handled it badly. I promise never to do that to you again. You have it in writing."

She lifted her head from his shoulders. "What are you talking about?"

Derek laughed. "I knew you didn't read the fine print!"

"Fine print? What?"

"The adoption papers," he said as he tucked her head back under his chin. "In the fine print, it said not only are we now officially Emery's parents, but also that we promise to love each other forever, you forgive me for being a grade-A jackass, and I promise never to let you down again."

"Wait a minute. I didn't see that."

"Sweetheart, it's too late. You're stuck with me. The papers are already signed and filed."

Kayleigh smiled against his chest. She didn't need to sign any papers; she knew she was going to love him for the rest of her life, no matter what the fine print said.

Baby, I'm Yours

Prologue

IT WASN'T OFTEN NICOLE TAYLOR LET HER HAIR DOWN OR threw caution to the wind, but if ever there was a time to give it a try, it was now. She'd spotted the perfect guy standing on the opposite side of the bar where she'd gone to grab a drink. Well, she didn't especially know if he was the perfect guy, but for right there and then, he certainly was.

Picking up random guys in bars was so not her thing. She had been raised in a fairly straitlaced, conservative home where she was taught not to chase men. Her focus had been on getting an education and a good job. Well, seeing as she had gone to school for what seemed like forever to get her master's degree in education, and had graduated at the top of her class, she figured now was a good time to relax the remainder of those rules a little bit.

He was tall, easily over six feet, and had jade-green eyes. Even from across the room, Nicole could feel the intensity of his stare. Not used to anyone looking at her with such carnal interest, she glanced over her shoulder just to make sure it was indeed her he was looking at. Lowering her eyes, she blushed and busied herself by playing with her bottle of beer. Normally she never drank the stuff, but it had seemed like the thing to do in a place like this.

On the other side of the room, some of her former

classmates were either playing pool or dancing. She had no interest in either activity. Glancing quickly back to the guy, she risked a smile. He returned it with one of his own, and Nicole actually felt her insides turn to goo. He had a hint of a dimple, and before she knew what she was going to do or say, her mystery man was headed her way.

Uh-oh. It was foolish to put any real effort into meeting anyone, she reminded herself. Tomorrow she had an interview with a school back home, where she wanted to teach, and the day after that, she was moving. The closer he got, the more her mind spun.

People had one-night stands all the time, didn't they? Why couldn't she? In forty-eight hours, she'd be six hundred miles away and beginning her new life. What harm could one little reckless night cause? Of course, with her strict upbringing, Nicole knew she wouldn't be *too* reckless. She was a good girl, after all. Well, for the most part.

Maybe she was overthinking it. Maybe Mr. Hot-and-Sexy was just going to come over and say hello, buy her a drink, and maybe ask her to dance. In the blink of an eye, he was standing right in front of her, and all Nicole could think was, *He smells so good.* Looking up into his lean and ruggedly handsome face, she smiled. "Hi."

He returned the greeting with a sexy grin of his own. "Hi."

Extending his hand to her, he took one of Nicole's small hands in his and simply held it. In that instant, Nicole knew she would be as reckless and wild as he wanted, because someone who looked like that did not come around every day. For this one night, she would gladly walk on the wild side.

As long as the incredible man was right there, leading the way.

Chapter 1

THE CELL PHONE SITTING ON THE KITCHEN COUNTER might as well have been a hand grenade. She certainly didn't want to touch it and was frantically trying to come up with an alternative method for making the call she didn't want to make.

Pacing back and forth next to it, Nikki couldn't help but frown. There was no way what she had to say was going to be well received. Tonight, she was due to go to a prewedding dinner for her best friend, Denise. As maid of honor, she had been wrangled into all sorts of wedding-related festivities, and tonight's dinner was supposed to be an intimate one, with Denise; her fiancé, David; his best man; and Nikki.

Unable to find a replacement babysitter for her daughter, Nikki now had to call Denise and pull out of the evening. Sighing with resignation, she scooped the phone off the counter and scrolled through her favorite contacts until she got to Denise's number. She hit it with all the enthusiasm of hitting a launch button that would start a war.

"Please let it go to voice mail, please let it go to voice mail," she chanted softly.

"Oh my God, Nik, I am so glad you called. You are not going to believe what just happened."

So much for going to voice mail. Denise was rambling on about issues with linen colors for the wedding when Nikki interrupted. "Look, Dee, I know it's last minute, but my sitter canceled, and I can't find anyone to stay with Ellie on such short notice. I'm so sorry, but I can't go tonight."

"But you have to!" Denise pleaded. "You're my maid of honor, and David and I wanted you and Josh to meet before the wedding, and we had a heck of a time organizing this dinner. Josh's schedule is crazy, and it's the only time he was willing to take off to do this. There's got to be somebody else you can call."

"I've been through my entire list, and no one is available. I'm really sorry."

"You could bring Ellie with you!" she suggested, clearly pleased with herself for solving the evening's problems.

"Have you completely lost your mind? I am not bringing a toddler to a fancy French restaurant, Dee." Nikki rolled her eyes in disbelief. "I'll admit my daughter is well behaved, but bringing her into those surroundings past her bedtime is just asking for trouble."

"But, Nik, you've got to be there!"

At this point Nikki was ready to bang her own head against the wall in frustration. "I wish I could, but it's just not possible tonight. Maybe some other time…?"

"Maybe we can bring the dinner to you!" Denise said excitedly.

"What are you talking about? Please tell me you're not going to bring me a doggie bag or something. Because seriously, I'll survive without the French food."

"No, no, nothing like that. I was just thinking maybe we can skip the French thing and grab some Chinese takeout or something and have a casual dinner at your place instead. That way, you won't have to worry about a sitter, and Ellie will be in her own bed. What do you think?"

"I think it's doable, but won't David be disappointed to miss out on going French tonight?" Nikki teased, knowing full well that David was more of a beer-and-potato-chip kind of man than a fancy-French-restaurant one.

"Please, he may very well leave me for you for getting him out of this tonight," Denise said flatly. "Excuse me for trying to introduce a little *culture* into our lives."

"You're lucky David loves you so much, you know." Nikki sighed wistfully. What she wouldn't give to have a man who was as devoted to her as David was to Denise.

"Unfortunately," Denise said, sighing dramatically, "I think he has feelings for another woman. A *younger* woman."

"Oh no! Dee! How do you know? Are you okay? Why haven't you said anything?" Nikki asked.

"Well, I was worried at first, but then I realized it would be a long time before Ellie is old enough to date." Denise chuckled.

"Ellie? *My* sweet baby girl? You nearly gave me a heart attack with that one!"

"What can I say? David is a sucker for those big green eyes of hers and the way she laughs at all his corny jokes."

"She's a flirt, that's for sure. She certainly doesn't take after her mother. Maybe if I knew how to flirt, I would have had a date in the last year or so."

"I have to agree with you there. And it's been more like three years. You really do need to get out there more. It's not good for you to be alone. You're too young to just be sitting at home all by yourself. You should let me fix you up with someone."

And that was when it hit Nikki.

"Oh. My. God. Is that what tonight is about? Are you trying to fix me up with David's best man?"

"Are you kidding me?" Denise choked. "Please, I love you and Ellie way too much to fix you up with Josh."

"Why? What's wrong with Josh?" It was a reasonable question considering Nikki was not only going to have this man in her home for dinner, but that she was obligated to spend some time with him on the day of the wedding as well.

"Don't get me wrong. I love Josh. He's a great guy, and he's David's brother. But Josh is not a family kind of guy, you know? At all. I would never try and fix you up with someone who wouldn't be good for Ellie, and unfortunately, that's Josh."

"He hates kids, huh?"

"It's not so much that he hates them as it is that he has just made it abundantly clear he has no plans to settle down and have a family."

"Oh. So he's what, like a player?"

"No one says *player* anymore, but no, he's not. He was engaged once, and as soon as his fiancée started making plans for their future, he bailed." Denise paused as if trying to remember more. "Actually, Josh had come to visit David up at school right after graduation—he had missed the actual ceremony because of a work commitment—just to get away from all of Erin's wedding plans. After that weekend, they called it quits."

"Wow. What did David say to him made him decide to call off the wedding?"

"Nothing! As a matter of fact, we never even got to see him. He showed up there, but David and I went away for the weekend right before we all moved back here. We went to the Poconos. Remember I told you about the champagne glass bathtub?"

Nikki had hoped to erase that story from her mind because Denise had given such graphic details of all the things she and David had done in said bathtub. "Yes, yes, I remember."

"Well, Josh showed up at the school, we played phone tag with him for the better part of the weekend, and by the time we got back, he had gone home. David felt bad about missing him, especially after Josh admitted he had come up there to get his head together."

"Clearly didn't happen."

"Or maybe it did. If he had really wanted to get married, then he would have. Personally, I think it's great he didn't prolong the inevitable. He didn't really love Erin, so she was better off without him. I'm kind of glad we didn't meet up with him. I would have felt partially responsible for whatever decision he made. I'm glad I have the memories of the weekend in the Poconos instead. Ooh, we have got to go back there and make some new ones!"

While Denise's reminder of the champagne tub story was enough to make Nikki feel extremely uncomfortable, her own memories of that particular weekend made her feel sick. That had been the weekend she had met Tyler. Closing her eyes, she could still see those green eyes and feel the touch of his hands on her skin. Their night together had been every fantasy she'd ever had come to life. Nikki had never told anyone the details of that night; she was ashamed to admit to having a one-nighter with a stranger. Of course, the fact that she had gotten pregnant with Ellie that fateful night meant plenty of people knew what she had done; Nikki just didn't feel the need to share all the details.

After Tyler had walked over and introduced himself, they had talked for hours. The crowd at the bar and the noise level had done nothing to hinder them. By the time midnight had rolled around, Nikki had realized she really should be going, and Tyler had offered to walk her out to her car.

Which was where he kissed her.

Just the memory of that kiss brought a tingle to her body. They had kissed up against her car for long minutes before he'd suggested they go someplace more private. Saying no was never even an option. She had wanted him badly. And then, in an act she regretted to this day, she had woken up while it was still dark out, slipped out of his hotel room, and gone back to her apartment to get ready for her job interview. And then she'd moved away.

They hadn't even exchanged last names. Too ashamed to go back to the hotel and ask for his information, Nikki had figured it was all for the best. Until she found out she was pregnant. Never in her life had she been so scared or felt so alone. There had been no way to find Tyler to let him know he was going to be a father. It was a burden she'd carry for the rest of her life. Someday, Ellie was going to ask about her father, and Nikki had no idea how she was going to answer her questions.

"Anyway," Denise said, interrupting Nikki's wayward

thoughts, "tonight is in no way, shape, or form a setup. That baby girl of yours deserves a man who will love her and want to raise her as his own. You do too, you know, but you'll never find someone if you don't get out there and date!"

"I will eventually." Nikki sighed, anxious to change the subject. "Anyway, back to the dinner plans." In the background, Nikki heard David's voice as well as another man's. *It must be his brother*, she thought. Before she knew it, David was on the phone with her.

"If things don't work out between me and Denise, you are the first woman I am looking up," he teased.

"What are you talking about?" Nikki laughed.

"You and your beautiful daughter have saved me from a night of phony French accents and food I cannot pronounce! Thank you, thank you, thank you!" he praised. "Whatever it is you want, Nikki my love, that's what we'll bring to you."

"Well, you certainly have swept me off my feet! I'll tell you what. You bring me some Chinese from Jade's, and I'll make sure we get to catch at least the third period of the Rangers game. Deal?"

"I love you, Nik," he said with awe. In truth, David loved Nikki like a sister and was very protective of her and Ellie. The fact that she was Denise's best friend and loved hockey was just a bonus.

"I know, I know. Unfortunately, Denise found you first." Nikki had never thought of David in a romantic kind of way, but she still wished she could find someone like him. "So, what time are you guys going to get here?"

"Is seven too early? My girl will still be awake then, won't she?"

"I promise to let Ellie stay up until eight. You know she'd be devastated if she didn't get to spend time with her favorite man."

The fact that this was not a setup made getting ready a breeze. Nikki hated the thought of having to fix herself up and pretend to be something she wasn't. Stepping from the shower, she looked down at the pile of blocks Ellie was happily building with on the white-tiled floor. Her daughter's curly, blond head tipped up and she smiled, saucer-eyed. Every time Nikki looked at her, her heart filled with more love than she'd ever thought it possible to feel for another human being.

"That is a fabulous tower, Ellie." She beamed. "Maybe someday you'll build real towers like that."

"This is weal, Mommy," Ellie said as she began work on a fourth short tower. Nikki smiled as she dried off and got ready for their dinner guests.

Choosing a pair of comfortable blue jeans and a teal-blue shirt, Nikki pulled the towel off her head and began detangling her mass of blond waves. Cursing mentally during the entire process, she reminded herself it was time for a haircut. She could easily chop off a good six inches right now and not even miss it. Tears came to her eyes during one rigorous bout with a knot.

Once the battle with her hair was through and it was drying naturally, Nikki applied a minimal amount of makeup and considered herself done. Had they been going out someplace, she would have put forth more of an effort, but since this was a casual night in with friends, she didn't feel the need to fuss.

She scooped Ellie up, and they headed back downstairs and looked around the main floor of their townhome. It had an open floor plan with hardwood floors and big, comfortable furniture; the space was small, but it was perfect for the two of them. Nikki sang a silly song and made a game out of getting Ellie to put her toys away, and by the time the doorbell rang, the place was clean.

Ellie squealed with delight at the sound of the bell because she knew who was coming over. David and Denise let themselves in and Ellie ran over to greet them but came running straight back to Nikki and hid behind her legs.

"Where'd my favorite girl go?" David called as he walked into the living room. Nikki was sure Ellie was just being shy with David's brother. Picking her daughter up, she headed toward David and nearly dropped the toddler as a man came into view behind him.

It was Tyler.

Nikki felt as if all the air had left the room. She couldn't breathe. She reached out and braced one hand against the wall, doing her best not to let Ellie fall.

David raked a hand through his brown hair and smiled brightly as he took Ellie from Nikki's arms. "How's my sweet girl doing tonight?" he asked in a cheery voice, his brown eyes twinkling. Ellie's only response was to stick her tiny thumb into her mouth and hide her face against David's neck.

"Nikki, this is my brother, Joshua. Josh, this is Nikki."

If Joshua remembered Nikki, he hid it well. After a rather gruff hello in Nikki's direction, Denise led him to the kitchen to help her start unloading and setting up all the food.

"I can't believe Ellie's being so shy," David observed when it was just he and Nikki standing in the entryway, Ellie still in his arms. He placed his index finger under the child's chin to get her to look at him. When he finally succeeded and had Ellie smiling, he let himself relax and took her toward the kitchen to help with dinner. "Don't worry, baby girl. That's just my big brother. He won't hurt you," he cooed to Ellie as they walked away.

Nikki stood rooted to the spot, trembling; all the color had drained from her face. Denise walked over with a concerned look on her face. "Nik? What's the matter? Are you all right?" she asked, placing a hand on Nikki's arm.

"I…I, um." Nikki cleared her throat in an attempt to speak. "I was just a little surprised by David's brother, that's all."

"He's good-looking, isn't he? Too bad he's not into kids or I would have set the two of you up a long time ago." Denise turned and looked into the kitchen at the brothers. David was placing Ellie in her booster seat, chatting with her the whole time. Nikki noticed that, oddly, Joshua had joined in and was playing peekaboo with Ellie as well.

"So, what's got you all freaked out? You look like you've just seen a ghost."

"I can't tell you right now, Dee," Nikki whispered.

"Tell me what?"

Huffing in agitation, Nikki said, "Didn't I *just* say I can't tell you right now?" Without a word, Denise walked across the room, poked her head into the kitchen, and told David to start dishing out the food. "I'm going to go upstairs with Nik and grab a pair of slippers. These new shoes are killing me."

Rolling her eyes at her friend's flimsy excuse, Nikki followed her up the stairs nonetheless. Once inside her bedroom, Denise closed the door and demanded to know what was wrong.

"That's Tyler," she whispered nervously.

"Who?"

"Tyler. Ellie's father."

"Where?"

"Oh, for crying out loud, your future brother-in-law!"

Denise looked at her as if she had grown a second head. "That's impossible, Nik. Obviously he just *looks* like Tyler. You're just being a little paranoid."

"I guess that's possible," Nikki said, but she wasn't one hundred percent convinced. "But if that's not Tyler, then he most certainly could be his twin." It took a moment for her to relax. They said everyone had a twin, and it had been more than three years since she had seen Tyler; it was possible her mind was playing tricks on her. Besides, the man downstairs was named Joshua, not Tyler. Laughing at her own anxiety, she gave Denise a quick hug before throwing a pair of slippers at her and heading down the stairs.

Joining the men at the table, Nikki could feel Joshua watching her but chose to avert her eyes. It was a bit unnerving to look into the eyes that had haunted her dreams for so many years knowing they weren't the eyes she had thought they were. Conversation flowed and Ellie was the center of attention. They all laughed at how she flirted shamelessly with David and shared her food with him, and by the meal's end, she was even offering to share her food with Joshua.

In a perfect world, this would be a typical Friday night—she and Tyler would be together, sharing a meal with their friends and their daughter. While she knew there was nothing wrong with what was going on in front of her, it still brought a pang of regret to her heart. She had cheated her daughter out of the chance to have a father, a real family.

Ellie's squeal of laughter shook Nikki out of her reverie and soon she found herself enjoying the meal and the company. When they all stood to clear the table, Denise shooed her out of the room so Nikki could get Ellie ready for bed. Carrying her daughter up the stairs, the sound of laughter coming from the kitchen made her smile. *Yes, in a perfect world this would be exactly how it would sound*, she thought sadly.

Deciding to give Ellie a quick bath, she had her stripped and in the tub quickly. She was kneeling on the bathroom floor and singing "Itsy Bitsy Spider" when her daughter looked up and waved. Turning her head, Nikki was shocked to find Joshua standing in the doorway.

"Joshwa!" Ellie squealed and waved her arms, causing water to splash all over the front of Nikki's shirt.

Joshua smiled at the toddler but then turned and glared at Nikki. She raised her eyebrows at him in question. "Is there something you need?" she asked pleasantly, confused at his look of irritation at her.

"David sent me to ask you if you wanted dessert. He's going on an ice cream run and wanted to know if you wanted anything before the third period of the game begins." It was a logical reason for him to be up there, she thought to herself, but she wondered why David, or Denise for matter, hadn't come up and asked her themselves. Why send this man, a complete stranger, up to her bathroom?

"Ice cream sounds great," Nikki said as she rinsed Ellie's hair.

"Ice cream!" Ellie shouted and then splashed around some more.

"You can have yours tomorrow," Nikki said mildly. "It's time for bed now." Pulling the plug from the drain, she prompted Ellie to stand and reached for a towel. "David knows what I like. Tell him to surprise me."

"Bye, Joshwa!" Ellie yelled, and Nikki didn't need to turn around to know he was gone. Once she had Ellie dried off and changed into her pajamas, she quickly changed into a dry shirt before leading her daughter down the stairs to say good night to everyone.

David and Joshua were getting ready to head out the door but stopped when they saw Ellie. She jumped into David's arms and planted a very wet, smacking kiss on his cheek, giggling when he did the same to her. He was about to put her down when Joshua took the toddler from his arms and planted a soft kiss on the top of her head. "Thank you for sharing your dinner with me," he said softly as he placed her back on the ground, his eyes unwilling to look away from her.

"Bye, Joshwa." Ellie waved as she walked back over to her mother. Nikki watched as the men left, still a little in awe of what she had just witnessed. It was a very sweet scene. It was Denise, however, who looked as if she was going to need CPR.

"What's the matter, Dee?" Nikki asked. Denise just stared at the now-closed front door, her mouth agape. When she received no answer, Nikki turned and picked up Ellie, taking her upstairs to bed.

While she was reading *The Poky Little Puppy*, she heard the men return. Ellie was nearly asleep when a shadow fell across her bed. Looking up, Nikki found Joshua leaning in a doorway for the second time that evening. Nikki held her fingers across her lips to signal him not to speak, and then she finished the final page of the story.

Confident her daughter was asleep, she placed the book back on the shelf and walked toward the door. She looked up at Joshua questioningly as she turned off Ellie's bedroom light.

"David's got the game on," he said quietly.

"Oh, okay." Nikki realized they were standing close together. Very close together. He smelled really good and his resemblance to Tyler took her breath away.

"Do you read to her every night before she goes to sleep?" he asked.

"Like clockwork."

"Does she have a favorite book?"

"We went through a *Goodnight Moon* phase, but now she only wants stories about farm animals. Her mood changes weekly." They stood there outside Ellie's room for what seemed like an eternity, eyes locked intently, but the sound of David's cheering broke them out of their trance and forced them to head back down the stairs.

Nikki had to remind herself over and over that the man with her was not Ellie's father. *Not* Tyler. How was she supposed to spend time with this man, even if it was only for the day of the wedding, when he reminded her so much of the man she had walked away from?

Sitting on her oversized sofa next to Denise, she picked up the chocolate milk shake David had brought her and focused all her attention on the hockey game playing on the TV and not on the man sitting across the room. As the game progressed, Nikki did her best to shrink from his field of vision, but when Denise stood to get herself a glass of water, there he was.

Still watching.

They cheered when required, cursed the goalie's timing, and, in general, had a great time. When the game ended, Denise stood and stretched, the telltale signal she was ready to leave.

"Thanks so much for bringing dinner to me tonight," Nikki said as she stood and began clearing their ice cream mess away. "It was quite a treat. I know Ellie appreciated having someone other than me to play with."

"Thank you," David gushed, "for saving me from having to wear a suit and tie for dinner." He bowed before Nikki, kissing her hand in a comical manner. "Now, when are you going to let us take the baby girl for the night?"

"When her mommy isn't afraid to be left alone in the house," she said with a laugh as she playfully swatted him away.

Coats were gathered and put on and good-byes were said. Joshua stood on the outskirts of the small group, observing it all. He mumbled a good night to Nikki as he walked out the door. She took no offense at his behavior; after all, he had been very kind to Ellie, and knowing how he felt about kids, she was impressed he had stuck it out with them for the entire evening and with such a pleasant attitude.

At the car, Joshua turned and looked at Nikki one last time before climbing in. He was so ruggedly handsome, Nikki placed a hand over her heart to try and calm its erratic beating in response to his heated gaze. There was a question in his eyes—eyes so green she wanted to lose herself in them—and Nikki had to once again remind herself it wasn't her Tyler looking at her.

Her Tyler. Why hadn't he found her after such a glorious night? As usual, there were no answers. If it weren't for the sleeping child upstairs, Nikki would have questioned if Tyler had ever existed at all or if he had merely been a fantasy.

Chapter 2

A GLANCE AT HER ILLUMINATED BEDSIDE CLOCK TOLD Nikki it was near midnight. The shrill ringing of the phone continued. Who would be calling her at that hour? She had gone upstairs to bed almost immediately after everyone had left over an hour ago.

"H'lo," she said sleepily into the phone.

"Nik, I'm so sorry to wake you, but David and I felt we had to call," Denise said, her voice laced with anxiety.

Nikki instantly sat up and tried to focus. "What's the matter, Dee? Is everything all right?"

"Well…depends."

"On what?"

"On you."

Turning on the bedside lamp, Nikki settled in for whatever dramatics Denise had in store. Propping her pillows up behind her, she got comfortable. "What's going on?"

"I told David about your initial reaction to Josh tonight, you know, how you thought he was Tyler."

"Oh-kay," Nikki said slowly, silently willing her friend to get to the point so she could go back to sleep. Denise had an infuriating habit of taking the long way around.

"Anyway, on the way back to our place tonight, Josh asked a *lot* of questions about you and Ellie, particularly about Ellie. Normally I wouldn't have thought anything of it, but seeing as it was Josh asking, well…it just seemed a bit out of character."

"I'm not following you, Dee," Nikki said with a loud yawn.

"By the time we got home, Josh seemed really agitated, and even though he had originally planned to spend the night here with us rather than driving all the way back to his place in Wilmington, once we turned the car off, he hopped in his truck and took off without a word."

"And this applies to me…why?" she asked in frustration.

Denise paused. "Josh's middle name is Tyler."

That bit of information hit Nikki like a ton of bricks. Suddenly wide-awake, she kicked off the blankets and began to pace the room. "So then I was right?" Her heart began to race like she'd run a marathon, and her throat went dry. "He's Tyler; he's Ellie's father." Her words were barely there, but she wasn't really saying them for anyone's benefit but her own.

"I can't be one hundred percent certain, Nik, but it all makes sense. Joshua was like a different person tonight and now, looking back at him and Ellie, you can see the resemblance. I just wish he had stuck around a bit longer so David could have talked to him." In the background, David was cursing, saying he wished he could get his hands on his brother.

"Yeah, I suppose that would've—" Nikki's words were cut short by a loud knock at her front door. A quick glance out her bedroom window showed a dark-colored pickup truck in her driveway, and although the front door area was not visible from the window, there was no doubt in her mind who was standing down there.

"What kind of car does he drive?" she asked with a sense of impending doom.

"A black pickup. Why?"

Nikki thought she was going to be sick. The room began to spin and her stomach clenched hard. "I think he's here," she whispered.

"What? Oh no. What are you going to do? Do you want us to come over?"

"I don't know," Nikki said honestly as she grabbed a robe to throw on over her nightshirt. "But to prevent him from waking up Ellie as well as the whole neighborhood, I think I'm going to have to let him in." She reached the bottom of the stairs and took a steadying breath. "Stay on the line for a minute, okay?"

"Okay," Denise said and then began relaying to David what was happening.

"I can be there in ten minutes if you need me!" he yelled and Nikki smiled. If she hadn't been so freaked out right then, she'd have thanked him. Unfortunately, all she could focus on was the man she was about to face.

The front door had an old-fashioned chain on it, so it only opened enough for her to peek out and see him standing there. Playing dumb, she whispered, "Joshua? What are you doing here?"

"I want to talk to you, Nicole, and you know why." Tyler had been one of the only people in her life to ever call her by her given name.

"It's after midnight," she hissed. "Can't this wait until morning?"

"No," he said flatly and crossed his arms over his chest. "I'm not going anywhere."

Wearily, Nikki closed the door and unchained it before opening it to let him in. "I'll talk to you in the morning," she said quietly into the phone.

"Call us anytime tonight if you need us," Denise said.

"Thanks." Hanging up, Nikki dropped her arms to her sides. They stood in the entryway, which now seemed very tight and crowded thanks to Josh's presence.

He was bigger than she'd remembered, and for the life of her, Nikki wondered why she hadn't noticed that fact when he had been there in that exact spot earlier. At over six feet tall, he towered over her. His hair was a mess, as if he'd been raking his hands through it all night. But it was those eyes, the ones that mirrored her daughter's, that made her catch her breath.

"Come in," she said hoarsely as she led him into the living room, switching lights on along the way. Tying her robe a little more tightly around her, she motioned for him to have a seat before sitting down on the opposite side of the room. They sat there in silence, assessing one another. Joshua spoke first.

"Ellie's my daughter, isn't she?" *Okay, quick and to the point*. Nikki couldn't seem to force herself to speak; she merely nodded her head, taken aback by his hiss of breath. "Why didn't you tell me?"

In all the times Nikki had dreamed of this moment, it had never gone like this. She had dreamed of it being peaceful and full of declarations of love, not accusations. In her fantasies, he'd see her across a crowded room, rush over to her, and tell her how he'd never stopped searching for her. Unfortunately, life was not like one of those romantic movies she loved to watch. Nope, right now it was more like a bad soap opera.

Her voice returned with a vengeance. "Oh, and how was I supposed to do that, *Tyler*?" she spat. "I can't believe you gave me a fake name! Why would you do that?"

He at least had the good sense to look remorseful. "Hell, I don't know. I just can't believe I have a daughter, and I didn't even know it." He stood and raked a hand through his hair before he came to sit beside her.

"Well, you would have if you'd bothered to give me your real name or maybe even a phone number."

"I'm not the one who took off in the middle of the night," he reminded her.

Now it was her turn to feel remorse. For more than three years, she had agonized over this man. No, she had agonized over Tyler. The man sitting next to her was a stranger.

"I want to get to know her, Nicole. I want to spend time with her and let her know I'm her father. Does she know about me at all?"

"Would I be telling her about Joshua or Tyler?" she asked sarcastically, raising an eyebrow.

Angrily, he stood. "Look, I don't know why I did what I did that night, okay? There's nothing you can say that would make me feel any worse than I already do, but you're not completely blameless here either. You could have left me your number or at least told me your last name, you know." His voice was raised, and then he suddenly remembered the child sleeping upstairs. Taking a deep breath, he willed himself to relax and sat back down. "The fact remains that you had my child, and now I'm here, and I want to get to know her. I don't think that's asking too much."

"She's only two, Ty—I mean, Josh," Nikki corrected herself. "She doesn't understand why she's never had a father here before." Nikki rubbed her temples, willing the whole situation to go away. "You can come by tomorrow afternoon and spend some time with her if you like. She naps from one to three. You can come by after that."

"No."

"What do you mean, no?" she asked incredulously.

"I mean, I will be here in the morning and I am spending the day with her," he said firmly.

"Look, I don't know who you think you are coming in here at this hour and throwing demands at me, but that's not going to fly! This is my home, and Ellie is my daughter and—"

"*Our* daughter," he corrected, and Nikki saw red.

"You have no claim to her! Your name isn't even on her birth certificate. Either you come when I say it's okay, or you won't see her at all." She jumped up from the couch and put some space between them.

Rising from the sofa, Josh walked slowly toward her. When he was scant inches from her, he stopped and looked hard into her wide, blue eyes, searching for something he couldn't quite put his finger on. "She's beautiful, Nicole. Please let me spend the day with her. I've missed so much already." His words were spoken so softly, so sincerely, and his breath on her cheek felt so wonderful, Nikki had no choice but to concede. "I know I don't deserve your kindness after what I put you through, but please…" His words trailed off with a sigh as his eyes continued to soak up the sight of the woman standing in front of him.

"You can come by around ten," she said with resignation. "That will give us time to get up and get dressed before you arrive." She was having a hard time keeping herself from swaying toward his body. She could feel his heat. Smell his cologne. And she just wanted to melt into him. For years she had dreamed about this moment, but nothing could have prepared her for the reality of it. He was here, he was close, and Nikki wanted to touch him so badly her fingers itched.

All of the anger she had felt toward him moments ago vanished, and in its place was remembrance. She remembered how his hands had felt on her body, how his mouth had felt on hers. She longed to feel those things again. Meeting his gaze, she studied his features. The strong line of his jaw, the full, soft lips, and his eyes…

As if battling his own demons, Joshua's eyes softened. His hands reached up and cupped Nikki's face. "Thank you."

Those two simple words reached Nikki's heart like no others had. She merely nodded in response, unable to control her body's reaction to his nearness. Her skin tingled, her nipples hardened beneath her robe, and her tongue darted out to lick her lips.

Joshua's eyes honed in on that action, and he wanted to lean forward and taste her for himself. His thumbs traced the fullness of her lower lip, and he was mesmerized by its softness. Seeing Nicole tonight had been like a hammer to his gut. Finding out about Ellie had turned him inside out. It may have been three years, but he could still vividly remember what Nicole felt like.

If he were a different kind of man, he would take advantage of this situation and claim her as his right now. His body was screaming at him to do so. But he would respect her at all costs. He had already changed the course of her life with his own selfish behavior, and he was going to do all he could to rectify that. He had a lot of time to make up for, and it had to start immediately.

Nikki stood there, silently hoping he would kiss her. It had been so long, and she needed to feel his lips against hers, needed the confirmation that he was real. Sensing his uncertainty, she boldly shifted closer to him, and then they were lost. His mouth came down softly on hers, a gentle brushing. Once, twice. With her face still cradled in his hands, Nikki leaned into Josh and sighed. His kiss was everything she had remembered and yearned for.

Tenderly, he slanted his mouth over hers again and again, reining in his self-control so he didn't scare her off. Truth be known, the intensity of what he was feeling right then scared him. When his tongue teased her full bottom lip, she opened for him, and he groaned. It was sweeter than his dreams, hotter than his fantasies. Forcing his brain to function, Josh reluctantly pulled away. Nikki stared up at him with dazed eyes that were clouded with passion.

"I'll see you in the morning," he whispered before planting a light kiss on her forehead and heading for the front door.

She watched his retreat and stood in the middle of her living room long after the front door had closed. All hope for sleep that night had left with Josh's kiss.

~

The next morning, Nikki was a bundle of nerves as she and Ellie went through their morning routine. After a light breakfast, they went upstairs to get dressed. Because she hadn't slept a wink after Josh left, Nikki had Ellie bring some toys into the bathroom so she could take a hot shower to wake herself up.

The water stung her weary body, and as she lathered up with her favorite lavender body wash, several scenarios played through her mind of how the day was going to go. In the first, Josh would come over, play awkwardly with Ellie for a little while, and be gone by lunch. If Denise's description of Josh was true, this was the most likely scenario. In the next one, he hung around all day, and by the end of it, he would gently inform Nikki that fatherhood just wasn't for him and say good-bye. While not ideal, it would cause the least amount of disruption in her life.

Unfortunately, there was a third scenario that was always a possibility. Josh would arrive looking ruggedly handsome and smelling absolutely delicious. He'd have flowers in one hand for Nikki and a teddy bear in the other for Ellie. He'd be equally attentive to them both, and Ellie would simply fall in love with him, finding it easy to call him "Daddy." They'd spend the day together as a family. And then begin planning the rest of their lives.

"I have got to stop watching so many romantic movies," she muttered softly. Sighing at the ridiculous direction of her thoughts, Nikki finished rinsing her hair and body and then switched to cold water to give herself a final jolt. Letting out a tiny screech, she counted to ten and shut the water off. Ellie's laughter greeted her in the silence of the shower stall.

"You're funny, Mommy." Ellie giggled. Nikki peeked her head out from behind the shower door and smiled at her daughter. "Did the water tickle you?"

"Yes, it did, princess. Mommy needed a good, cold tickle to wake her up." That was an understatement. "We're going to have some company in a little while."

Ellie's eyes lit up. "Uncle David?"

It suddenly occurred to Nikki that David was now truly Ellie's uncle—a fact she knew would thrill him to death. "No, not Uncle David, sweetheart. Remember Joshua who was here last night?" Ellie nodded. "Well, he's coming back over to visit with us."

"Why?" Ellie frowned. The thought of another man being in their house was probably going to take some getting used to.

"Well, he really liked meeting you last night and wanted to come over and spend some time with you today. Won't that be fun?" She knew for this meeting to be successful, she was going to have to be as enthusiastic as she could, since Ellie took most of her cues from her. She forced a cheeriness she didn't quite feel. "We'll play, and you can show Joshua all of your toys, and maybe he'll even read you a story!"

"'Kay," she said with some disinterest.

Nikki dried off and dressed in faded blue jeans and a white T-shirt. She wanted to make sure it didn't look like she was trying to impress him. It was a Saturday morning, and she would have no reason to be all glammed up. Using her usual minimal amount of makeup, she checked her reflection one last time before she picked up her wet towel and hung it over the shower door.

"Come on, baby. Josh will be here soon. Let's get you dressed." Ellie followed. It was more important that Ellie look nice for her first real visit with Josh. After much deliberation—two-year-olds certainly had their opinions—it was decided that Ellie would wear navy-blue leggings with a matching top with pink and white lace flowers on it. Finishing off the ensemble with lace ankle socks, the child declared herself ready.

Nikki's nerves were a wreck, and it was hard to keep her anxiety from her daughter. Walking into the kitchen, she picked up the phone and called Denise.

"Are you okay? How did everything go last night?"

Nikki relayed most of what had gone on, deciding to leave out the kiss she and Josh had shared. "He's coming over this morning to spend time with Ellie." She paused. "Dee, I'm scared. What if he wants to be a part of Ellie's life? How am I going to share my daughter with him after all this time?"

"Okay, let's not get ahead of ourselves just yet. It's only natural for him to be curious about Ellie. He just found out he's a dad. Knowing him like I do, I just don't see him wanting to get all involved. I'm sorry. I know that sounds harsh, and I hate that Ellie even has to go through this, but I want you to be prepared."

"It's all right. She'll get over it. I just don't know if I will."

"I still can't believe Josh is Ellie's father."

"You and me both." Nikki looked at the clock and grimaced. "He's going to be here any minute. I better go."

"David and I can drive over and act as buffers if you'd like."

"No," she said sadly. "But thank you. I think this is something we need to work out ourselves."

"Call me later, okay?"

She agreed and hung up, venturing to see what Ellie was doing. She found the toddler playing with one of her dolls and humming softly to herself. She was so blessed. For all their struggles, she and her daughter had made a nice life for themselves. The thought of it all being turned upside down was eating Nikki up inside.

At exactly ten o'clock, the doorbell rang. Why hadn't she taken Denise up on her offer to come and act as a buffer? Ellie looked up at her mother expectantly, gently dropping her baby doll on the floor. Nikki stood and took her hand, and together they walked to the door. She wasn't sure which of them seemed more apprehensive. Saying a silent prayer that scenario number one would play out and Josh would be out of there quickly, she opened the door.

"Good morning," he said, and Nikki nearly fell back in a dead faint at the sight of him. He was freshly shaven and his hair was still a little damp from a shower, but his arms were bursting at the seams with gifts for his daughter. "May I come in, Nicole? This stuff is kind of heavy."

Waking herself from her trance, Nikki picked up Ellie and stepped back so Josh could come in. He strode to the living room and started setting all the packages down, Nikki and Ellie trailing behind him. He stood straight and looked down at Ellie, smiling. "Good morning, princess," he said softly, crouching down to be eye level with her. "How are you today?"

Ellie looked up at Nikki and smiled. "He called me princess just like you do, Mommy!"

"He sure did! Why don't you go over and say hello? It looks like he's got some things here for you."

"For me?" she asked with wonder. "These are for me, Joshwa?" The way she pronounced his name made him smile, but he found himself longing to hear his daughter call him something else.

"Yes, there are presents in all of these bags for you. Would you like to open one?" Ellie looked hesitantly at her mother for approval. Nikki nodded.

"Yes, sir," the girl said shyly.

The first thing Josh handed her was a giant pink teddy bear, and Nikki felt herself sway slightly before she sat down on the sofa. Ellie hugged the bear to herself and nearly fell over backward because it was as big as she was.

"What do you say, Ellie?" Nikki prompted. The child looked at her quickly before turning her bright eyes toward Joshua.

"Thank you, Joshwa." She smiled and anxiously began scanning the room for her next present. Before things went any further, Nikki knew it was time to say out loud what she was dreading the most.

With her heart in her throat, she said, "Before you open anything else, El, I want you to come and sit with me for a minute, okay?" Ellie nodded and skipped over and hopped into her lap. Nikki looked nervously over at Josh, who had seated himself at the opposite end of the sofa. His eyes met hers, and Nikki forced herself to look away before she got sucked into those green depths again.

"Joshua came here today to give you these presents because he thinks you're a very special little girl," Nikki began. Ellie looked over at Josh and smiled. "Ellie, Joshua is your daddy." She held her breath and waited for her daughter's response. How much of this could a toddler really understand?

"I have a daddy?" Ellie asked in a hushed tone full of awe.

"Yes, princess," Josh said softly. "You have a daddy." He sat back nervously, his hands tightly clasped together in front of him as he wondered if his daughter would accept this situation and accept him into her young life.

Ellie sat there and pondered this news for what seemed like an eternity. She stared hard at Joshua and then at Nikki before speaking. "My friend Sam has a daddy," she stated flatly before climbing off Nikki's lap. She looked undecided about what to do next, and Josh found himself holding his breath. Finally, she walked over to him and took his large hand in her tiny one. "Can I open another present, Daddy?"

In that moment, Joshua lost his heart.

The morning flew by as they opened gifts, read books, and introduced Josh to every toy in Ellie's toy box. Nikki stayed in the background as much as possible because she knew it was important for Ellie to bond with her father and spend time with him without Nikki tagging along. As much as the thought of sharing her daughter pained her, Nikki knew there was nothing she could do about it. It wasn't like they were going to be a real family now that Josh had come back into her life. Ellie was going to have to get used to dividing her time between the two of them. And so was Nikki. For so long it had been just the two of them, and she liked it that way. Having to deal with Josh now was going to take some major adjusting.

Deciding to find something to occupy her time, Nikki went up to her bedroom to work on grading some of her students' papers. *Second graders have wild imaginations*, she thought to herself as she read over some of the short stories she had assigned to them last week. She was chuckling softly when she heard Josh clear his throat from behind her.

Nikki turned and saw him standing in her bedroom doorway and felt her pulse begin to race. *Tyler*. It was so hard to look at this man who had been the object of all her dreams and fantasies and accept that his real name was Joshua. If they made love, would she call him by the right name? *Get a grip, Nicole*, her conscience warned her. *There will no rekindling of this romance. He is here to do right by his daughter. It has nothing to do with you*. Now if only her hormones would get on board with that.

"How was the tea party?" she asked lightly as she put her red pen down and pushed the schoolwork aside. She rose from the chair and casually faced him, hoping he couldn't see the way her pulse was racing. He openly appraised her and Nikki crossed an arm over her chest and placed a hand against her throat in an attempt to protect and cover herself.

"I think next time I'll opt to sit on the floor rather

than attempting to balance myself on one of those tiny chairs." He laughed. It was a deep, rich, masculine laugh and seemed to touch every inch of Nikki's body.

Down, girl.

"It's just about noon, and I was thinking about lunch. What time does Ellie usually eat?"

"She's normally eaten by now. You've kept her so thoroughly entertained, she hasn't asked to eat."

"Where would you like to go?" he asked casually, stepping into her room.

The space seemed to shrink. His casual tan slacks and navy polo shirt fit him to perfection, and yet all Nikki wanted to do was have him take them off. Slowly. For her. For so long she had wanted this man in her bedroom, and now that he was here, it was terrifying. Shaking her head clear of those erotic images, she remembered his question. "Go? What do you mean?"

"I thought I'd take you and Ellie out for lunch."

"Oh, that's not necessary. I have plenty of stuff here to make lunch. You don't need to take us out." Her voice shook slightly and she hoped he didn't notice. She nervously began to rattle off a list of lunch options she had before he interrupted.

"I know I don't *need* to, Nicole. I want to. Come on, what does Ellie like to eat?" He stepped closer, and she took a step back, hitting the back of her legs against her desk.

"She's not really fussy," she said quickly, hoping he wouldn't come any closer. Her senses couldn't take much more. After their kiss last night, she had been edgy. It had been too long since she'd been with a man, and now he had awakened the beast inside her. "Why don't the two of you go out together? You know, take some time to get to know each other without me tagging along." It was a logical suggestion.

Josh frowned but didn't move. "What's the matter, Nicole? Don't want to be seen out in public with me or something?" The statement was meant to be teasing, she was sure, but he sounded deadly serious.

"No. No, it's not that. It's just you and Ellie should take advantage of this time you have together. I mean, I know you don't live nearby and you won't see her very often, so you don't need me hanging around during your time with her. It's okay. Really. I insist." There was more enthusiasm in her words than she actually felt, and she crossed her fingers that he'd accept her offer and run with it.

"I guess that's something else we need to discuss," he said, still frowning, still unmoving.

"What's that?"

"Visitation. I know I live several hours from here, but that doesn't mean I intend to ignore my daughter. I want to see her on the weekends for starters. Maybe you can even bring her to Wilmington to see me too."

Inwardly, Nikki groaned. *No, no, no!* This was *not* the way this was supposed to happen! He was supposed to be bored by now! He was supposed to be looking for ways to leave without being too obvious about it. She had to get control of the situation back.

"Whoa, slow down a minute. I work all week long teaching, and the only time I get to really relax and spend time with Ellie is on the weekends. You can't just swoop in here and take all of my time away!"

"Relax, Nicole. That's why I said we'd have to

discuss it. We're not going to get it all figured out right now, right away. Let's just deal with lunch first, okay?"

Her shoulders sagged dejectedly, and she nodded. "Now, where should we go?"

Chapter 3

MUCH TO HER CHAGRIN, NIKKI HAD A GREAT TIME AT LUNCH. Joshua was charming both her and Ellie. After eating at a local family restaurant, Josh had insisted on taking Ellie to the park, then for ice cream, and even on a trip to the toy store—even though he had purchased half of it that morning.

By the time they arrived back at the town house with more packages, Ellie was near delirious from missing her nap, and Nikki looked exhausted. Josh took his daughter right up to her room and gently placed her in the bed and tucked her in, hating the feeling of loss after moving away from her bedside.

He sat and watched her sleep for a few minutes and found himself completely entranced. Her soft, blond curls framed her little heart-shaped face, and she seemed to have the longest lashes he had ever seen. It was official; he was in love with his daughter.

Josh was perplexed by his feelings. For so long he had been certain he would never have children, he would never *want* to have children. Yet now, as he looked down at Ellie, it felt so right. Like the void that had been in his life was just filled. He sighed and felt complete.

If he was honest with himself, he would acknowledge that he had been against marriage and children until the night he and Nicole had met. That was when he knew his relationship with Erin would never work.

With Erin, they were both about their careers. He cared about her deeply, but he didn't have the kind of feelings you should have for the woman you were going to spend the rest of your life with. There was no heat, no passion. When Erin talked of her plan for the future, it was a series of charts and graphs that laid out their married life with the best time in their careers to have children, move to a bigger house, etc.

On the fateful weekend he had gone to visit David, he had hoped to get his head together. Erin had wanted to start pinning down wedding plans, but Josh had been having doubts about the whole thing. He had hoped his brother would help him find a solution. What he had found was a woman who intrigued and excited him. They had talked for hours on end, and Josh had known, without a doubt, that he had found the woman he could spend his life with.

Nicole was a passionate woman no matter what the topic, and it was as if a light had gone on in his brain. This was what he wanted in a woman. This was what he wanted around him! It had been a long time since Josh had taken a woman to bed on the first date, and although what he and Nicole had wasn't technically a date, it had just seemed like the natural thing to do. Why, then, had he gone and ruined it by lying about his name?

Truthfully, at their first introduction, he had no intention of letting things go beyond a drink or two. It seemed like a harmless little white lie. No big deal. But by the end of the night, when he'd asked her back to his hotel, Josh had known Nicole was special, but he had to end things officially with Erin before moving forward with her.

Things had gotten complicated. When he woke up and found Nicole gone, he had been angry. First at her, then at himself. How had he let her get away so soon? He hadn't been able to find his brother; he'd had no idea how to find Nicole, and by the time he had gotten home and sat Erin down, he'd felt like his life was spinning out of control. Erin handled their breakup with cool detachment, and it simply confirmed what Josh had known all along. She wasn't the woman for him.

For years, Nicole's image had haunted him, and he hoped someday he would find her again—a nearly impossible task considering how little they knew about one another's identity. In all the years David and Denise had talked about their good friend Nikki, Josh never thought to put two and two together.

To have found her, and to have found her with his child, filled him with emotions he'd never felt before. He just had to find a way to make it right, to make it all work out.

For all three of them.

Josh found Nikki in the living room, sorting through the mass of new toys, trying to find a place for everything. He stood back and observed her. She looked exactly the same as he'd remembered. Well, maybe not exactly. Her hair was a little longer; her breasts were a little fuller. Instantly, heat shot to his groin, and he shifted uncomfortably. Now was not the time to be thinking about her breasts. They had some serious issues to discuss about his part in Ellie's life. And hers.

Nikki stood and straightened when she realized she was no longer alone. She smiled at Josh. "Is Ellie asleep?"

"Before her head even hit the pillow." He chuckled as he pushed off the wall and walked into the room. "I'm sorry if I went a little overboard today," he said as he motioned to the mess around them.

"It's a good thing Christmas is so far away," she teased. "You didn't have to do all of this, you know. Ellie would have enjoyed being with you even if you showed up here with nothing."

He frowned. Hell, he knew next to nothing about kids, but he had just wanted to be sure Ellie liked him, so he'd used whatever he could to break through that first awkward barrier. "I promise to tone it down from now on," he said seriously, taking a seat on the sofa. Nikki was sorting books on a small bookshelf. "I think now would be a good time to talk. I mean, with Ellie asleep, we won't be disturbed."

Reluctantly, Nikki agreed. By the tone of his voice, he wasn't about to leave any time soon, and he certainly wasn't bored with the idea of fatherhood. With a sigh, she sat down and faced him. Her spine was stiff, and she braced herself for what was to come.

"First of all," he began, "relax. I can see you're all wound up, and I'm sorry if I've made you feel you have to be that way with me." Nikki shifted in her seat and nodded weakly. "I want to discuss your schedule and try and find a way to fit into it so I can spend time with Ellie. I don't want to miss any more of her life. Are you both free next weekend? Maybe you can come down to Wilmington and see where I live?" His tone was hopeful and Nikki hated to dash it.

"Oh, Josh, I'm sorry, but we have Denise's bridal shower in Charlotte next weekend. David's mom… oh"—she caught herself—"I guess she's your mom too." Nikki blushed and Josh frowned, realizing how ridiculous and confusing this whole situation had become. "Anyway, your mom is hosting a bridal shower for Denise next Saturday, and Ellie and I need to be there." She sat there for a moment, struggling for something else to say, when another dilemma hit her. "Oh my gosh," she whispered. "Your mother is Ellie's…"

"Grandmother," he finished for her. He ran a hand over his tired face. How was he supposed to explain all of this to his parents? *Hi, Mom and Dad. This is my daughter, Ellie. I didn't know about her because I took her mother to bed for a night while I was still engaged to Erin and gave her a fake name, making it impossible for her to find me again.* Yeah, that would go over real well. They were already disappointed in him because he was thirty and nowhere close to wanting to settle down.

At least that's how he'd felt twenty-four hours ago. Now, things were different.

"I'll call them and tell them everything so it won't be weird and uncomfortable for you next weekend." He sighed loudly; it was almost a growl of frustration. "I am so sorry, Nicole. For everything. I didn't want to make things difficult for you. Ever." The pleading in his voice tore at her.

"Well, I'd like to say it hasn't been difficult, but I'd be lying," she said softly. There was no malice in her words, just a simple statement of fact. "It wasn't easy to work once I found out I was pregnant. Especially since I had just started a new job. I was fortunate the teaching staff rallied around me, and if it weren't for David and Denise…"

"David and Denise," he repeated slowly, interrupting Nikki's train of thought. "They know now too. Don't they?"

"I had said something to Denise last night when you first arrived, but she didn't believe me. By the time you left them at their house, she and David had put two and two together."

Josh stood and began to pace. His family was going to think him to be the lowest form of life. He knew how much Nicole meant to his brother and his fiancée, and now they all knew he was the reason her life was such a struggle and why Ellie had been living without a father.

Watching him pace, Nikki knew he was kicking himself to death but didn't know what to say to make it right. She also knew she needed answers of her own before she could even begin to trust him.

"Why did you do it?" she asked quietly, and Josh stopped cold. He stared down at her and noticed she wasn't looking at him but at her own hands clasped tightly in her lap.

Sitting down beside her, he took one of her hands in his. "I honestly don't know. I didn't go up to visit David with the intention of meeting someone. I was there to get my head together because…"

"Because you were engaged to someone else," she said flatly.

There was no point in denying it. Obviously either his brother or Denise had filled her in on some of the details. "Yes." Finally she looked up at him, and Josh saw the hurt in her eyes. "I'm sorry."

She gave a small shrug. "I'm not completely innocent in all of this either. I'm the one who snuck out before you woke up."

"Why?"

How could she possibly explain? "I was ashamed. I'd never done anything like that before. I was never the kind of girl who picked up guys in bars. Or even the kind of girl who slept with someone she just met." She met his gaze. "I thought it was better to leave with a little of my dignity intact."

"When I woke up and found you were gone, I didn't know where to look. We talked about so much that night while we were at the bar, but it wasn't until you were gone and I was trying to find you that I realized we didn't exchange any real personal information." He paused. "I went back to the bar the next night in hopes of finding you there."

She shook her head. "By that time I was in the middle of packing up my dorm room and getting ready to leave the next morning."

"It never occurred to me you could be pregnant," he said sadly.

"Me either. Imagine my surprise six weeks later."

Josh could only imagine. The silence was deafening, and he struggled to get them back on track. "Well, what about the weekend after the bridal shower? Can I come and see Ellie then?"

Nikki was already shaking her head. "We're going to Florida for a quick visit with my parents. I'm sorry." She could see and feel his frustration, but her hands were tied. "The weekend after that, we're helping David and Denise move into their new house, and the one after is the wedding. You'll be in town, and Ellie is going to be the flower girl, so you can see her then." She let out a relieved breath. She had found a solution. But one look at the scowl on his face and she realized her relief was going to be short-lived.

"That's a month away, Nicole!" he snapped. He jumped up and began to pace again. While he knew she wasn't deliberately trying to make this hard for him, he also couldn't help but feel it shouldn't be this difficult to spend time with his daughter. If only he didn't live so far away, he could be there for her more often. The thought began to take hold.

"Obviously it's not ideal, Josh, but maybe you could call her and talk to her during the week, you know? Or you could Skype with her at night after dinner; you could read her a story."

It was better than nothing, but Nikki could tell he wasn't happy. He shrugged and sat back down. Sulking. Nikki found his reaction endearing but didn't want to patronize him. Feeling satisfied they had covered all they could for the moment, she rose to continue her quest for an organized house.

Thursday afternoon, Nikki was enjoying a late lunch, along with the peace and quiet, in the teachers' lounge. Biting into her turkey sandwich, her mind wandered to the previous weekend.

Josh had stayed through Ellie's bedtime on Saturday and left once the child was asleep. Knowing there was going to be a long stretch between their visits, Nikki had graciously invited him to come and spend the day again on Sunday, to which he more than readily agreed.

Sunday was a near duplicate of the day before. He arrived at ten looking incredibly handsome and had given Ellie every ounce of his attention. He had made no attempt to kiss Nikki or to be alone with her, and on some level she was relieved. But when she thought about how he'd looked in those faded blue jeans and black T-shirt, her mouth went dry and her food turned to sand in her mouth.

Frowning, she wondered why he'd pulled a full retreat from her. The kiss they'd shared on Friday night had certainly been hot, and while he'd seemed to enjoy it at the time, he didn't seem inclined to repeat it. Maybe she had been the only one who'd enjoyed it. *Yikes*. Maybe that was the reason for his retreat. She had only slept with one other man beside Josh, so there was a very real possibility that she was awkward and just…not good at sex.

Tossing her sandwich down because she had suddenly lost her appetite, she thought back to their night together. Would he have made love to her two—no, three times in one night if she didn't turn him on? Damned if she knew. She didn't have much to compare it to.

Images of their night together flooded her mind. Their first kiss had been under a large oak tree next to her car. She thought of the way his body had pressed into hers and how right it had felt. *I know this is crazy, Nicole, but I feel like I've known you my whole life.* At those words, she had been lost because she had felt the same way. He had overwhelmed her, and in an instant, she had known she was falling in love with him.

Closing her eyes, she could still hear his words.

You're so beautiful. Touch me, Nicole. Your hands feel so good on me. Heat flushed her cheeks, and Nikki was thankful she was alone.

But what about that last kiss Friday night? He'd seemed reluctant to let it end—or was that just her seeing what she wanted to see? There was no way for her to know for certain, and she wasn't about to humiliate herself by asking.

She'd had plenty of opportunities to talk to him. In keeping with her suggestion, Josh called via Skype every night at seven forty-five to talk to Ellie before her bedtime. He had even purchased several children's books he read to her, which Ellie had loved. "Daddy's on the TV!" she said with delight every time his face appeared on the monitor. Nikki noticed her daughter was getting ready for bed with much more ease since she knew her daddy would be calling.

With the week almost over, she forced her thoughts away from Josh and focused on the coming weekend. The drive to Charlotte Saturday would take at least three hours and Nikki was not looking forward to it. Ellie was a good traveler, but the thought of six hours of driving was completely unappealing, even with Denise in the car for companionship.

The thought of introducing herself to Josh's parents as the mother of their newly found grandchild was also unappealing. Awkward didn't even begin to describe it. Hopefully Josh would have talked to them, and she was grateful Denise would be there with her for moral support. She hated to burden her friend during such an exciting time in her life, but there was no other choice. With any luck, the family would be so consumed with the wedding and getting to know Ellie, so Nikki could just slink into the background completely unnoticed.

At eight forty-five Saturday morning, Nikki opened her front door to find Joshua standing there. "What are you doing here? We're getting ready to go to your parents," she said breathlessly at the sight of him. It didn't seem to matter what the man wore, because apparently, he looked good in everything. Today he was dressed in black dress slacks and a pewter-colored shirt. Her heart was beating rapidly in her chest, and she fought the urge to throw caution to the wind and kiss him senseless.

"Well, I thought it might be easier for all concerned if I was there when my folks meet you and Ellie for the first time." Actually, the thought had not even occurred to him until his mother asked if he would be joining Nikki this weekend. It was her not-so-subtle way of telling him he needed to be there. Not that he minded. It was the perfect opportunity for him to spend time with them both.

"I'm supposed to drive there with Denise. She's going to be here any minute."

"I've already taken care of that. David is going to drive her."

"Oh" was all she could manage to say. It would have been nice if someone had informed *her* of the change in plans.

He followed Nicole into the house and smiled at her appearance. She was clearly in the middle of getting ready. Her hair was still a little damp and she was wearing her blue silk robe. "Make yourself comfortable. I've got to finish getting ready and pack for Ellie."

"Pack? Pack what?"

Nikki chuckled. "I never go anywhere far from home without at least two changes of clothes for her. You never know what kind of mishaps can happen with a toddler." She headed back up the stairs, and Josh admired the soft sway of her hips as she climbed. Before he could let his mind wander in that direction, Ellie came scampering down the stairs.

"Daddy!" she squealed and jumped into his arms. His chest tightened at the sight of her. Only one week away from her and he had missed her terribly. She wrapped her tiny arms around his neck and held on tight. She had missed him too, and it filled him with pride.

Placing her back on her feet, Josh let Ellie lead him to the living room, where she twirled around in her pretty new pink dress and proceeded to tell him about all the times she had played with the new toys he had purchased for her.

Meanwhile, Nikki was upstairs having a nervous fit. She was going to be confined to the car with Josh for a three-hour drive. *No, six hours!* Groaning, she walked to her closet, pulled out the sleeveless purple dress with the long, straight skirt she had chosen for that day, and slipped it over her head. She finger-combed her hair and did a final check of her makeup. She smiled at her appearance; it felt good to look pretty sometimes.

Grabbing a pair of sandals, she placed them on her feet. Out of the corner of her eye, she noticed her own small overnight bag. Deciding being in her dress and sandals all day would most likely annoy her, she threw a change of clothes for herself into the bag for the ride home before heading into Ellie's room to pack her bag.

"Nicole? If we're going to get to my parents' house in time, we're going to need to get on the road," Joshua called to her from the bottom of the stairs. His being there, reminding her it was time to go, seemed like the most natural thing in the world. Like they were a family getting ready for an outing, an everyday occurrence. It felt good. She collected the bags and headed down the stairs.

At the sight of two pieces of luggage, Josh raised an eyebrow at her. "I thought I'd take a change of clothes for myself so I could be comfortable on the ride home," she explained. Nodding, Josh took the bags from her and walked outside to put them in his car.

Nikki grabbed her purse and Ellie's hand and followed him out. She stopped short at the sight in her driveway. "Is this yours?" she asked, confused by the sight of the brand-new silver SUV Josh was placing the luggage in.

"Yeah, I figured it was more practical for when we go out. It was too hard maneuvering the car seat last week. Now there's a full backseat for all of Ellie's things. I even purchased the same car seat you have, so we don't have to keep moving yours back and forth."

She had to admit, she was impressed. In the span of a week, he had given thought to and put into action some of the necessities of being a parent. "I'm sorry you had to get rid of your truck. It really wasn't necessary."

"Sure it was," he said as he closed the tailgate. "I want Ellie to be safe and comfortable when I take her out. Now there's room for all of us to fit comfortably and there's room for us to grow too." The words were spoken lightly, but what they implied gave Nikki butterflies in her belly.

Room to grow? Room for whom? Her mind began to race. Her first reaction to his words was that he wanted their family to grow, but the pessimistic side of her took over. Maybe there was somebody else in his life he was planning on having a family with. After all, he had been engaged once, and no matter what Denise's opinion was, the fact remained that Josh lived several hours away and didn't spend a whole lot of time with his family. Anything was possible.

The thought of there being another woman in his life hadn't even crossed Nikki's mind until right then, and it didn't make her feel good. As a matter of fact, it downright depressed her. Climbing into the passenger seat while Josh got Ellie buckled in, she suddenly felt a great sense of loss. So much for her earlier observation of everything feeling completely natural. Now all she could think about was the family that was going to grow with him and his stupid new car and how it didn't include her. She was frowning by the time Josh joined her in the front seat.

"You okay?" he asked, concern lacing his voice.

"Fine," she lied. Josh didn't give any indication he didn't believe her, and before she knew it, they were on the road.

Interstate 40 was as boring as they came. It was an uneventful drive filled with brief bouts of conversations started by Ellie. Josh marveled at his daughter's chatty nature and wished her mother would feel such ease with him. He remembered a time when they couldn't seem to stop talking. He had hoped their time together today would give them time to relax with one another before being surrounded by his family, but Nikki spent most of the drive staring silently out the window.

He missed the easy camaraderie they had shared on the night they met. Where had that woman gone? That night, they had had endless conversations, and it was only sheer exhaustion that made them stop. He wished she'd share with him what she was feeling, but he was sure she was nervous and didn't want to add to her unease with unnecessary chatter.

They arrived at his parents' home sooner than Nikki was prepared for. As they pulled into the massive circular drive lined with enormous magnolia trees, she sucked in a breath. *This isn't a house; this is a mansion!* Josh looked over at her stunned expression and chuckled. "It's rather large, isn't it?" he said casually.

"I had no idea," she said in awe. "Denise never mentioned her future in-laws lived in such a house." Josh parked the car and moved to get out, but Nikki was frozen to the spot.

The house and the property reminded her of an old plantation home—all white, with large columns along the wide wraparound porch. Wisteria vines climbed the corner columns and she could see a porch swing to one side. Her head began to spin. The whole day was going to be awkward enough with meeting Josh's parents, introducing them to Ellie, and dealing with their opinion of her. But now, Nikki feared she might be viewed as some sort of gold digger trying to trap their son for financial gain.

Nausea rolled in her stomach, and she nearly jumped

out of her own skin when Josh opened the passenger door for her. "Oh!"

"You were planning on getting out of the car at some point today, weren't you?" he teased.

She made a face at him. "I just wish I were a little more prepared for all of this." As she climbed out of the vehicle, Josh was treated to the sight of her shapely calf exposed through the side slit of her dress. She smoothed the skirt and nervously fidgeted with her hair before turning to Ellie to fuss with her appearance as well.

Josh placed his hands on her shoulders and forced her to stand still and look at him. The feel of his warm hands on her skin was like a hot brand. Nikki closed her eyes briefly to the sensation of it before meeting his gaze. His emerald eyes scanned her face, and she knew he completely understood her uneasiness with the whole situation.

"Everything is going to be fine," he whispered. "You are not alone, Nicole; we're in this together." Unable to resist, he pulled her carefully into his embrace and was surprised she went so willingly. Her body molded perfectly to his and felt so incredibly right that all thoughts of his family, this party, and everything else just melted away. His brain was consumed with her and how much he wanted her. Her floral scent intoxicated him, and if he had his way, they'd be as far away from this scene as possible. He wanted Nicole all to himself.

Nikki rested her head on the solid wall of his chest and sighed. Yes, she could get through just about anything if this was the reward for it. Joshua's hands gently stroked her back. She let out a sigh of pure pleasure at the feel of it all. He placed a hand firmly at the small of her back and pulled her just a little closer to him before whispering, “I think we should go inside.”

Reluctantly, she stepped away from his arms and gave him a weak smile. She was thrilled to see the smoky desire in his eyes. It was a heady feeling. Maybe she had been mistaken about there being another woman. It was a subject that was clearly bound to come up soon, especially if they kept responding to one another the way they just had.

“I’ll come back for the bags a little later,” he said as he helped Ellie down from her car seat, and together they walked toward the house, each holding one of Ellie’s hands, looking for the entire world like a solid family unit.

Chapter 4

THEY HAD BARELY REACHED THE FRONT DOOR WHEN JOSH'S parents came racing through it, full of smiles, and immediately embraced the three of them.

"We're so glad you're here! I'm Laura Masterson and this is my husband, Tyler." Nikki blanched a little at the name, but the man embraced her, and her mind instantly cleared. "Is this Ellie?" Laura asked, kneeling in front of the child, heedless of the fact that she was dressed in what Nikki could tell was a designer dress.

"Yes," Nikki replied, coming to kneel next to her daughter as well. "Ellie?" The child turned to her expectantly. "This is your grandma."

Ellie's eyes went wide. "I get a new grandma too?"

Everyone laughed with relief. "Yes, princess, you sure do. And you get a grandpa." In the blink of an eye, Ellie jumped into Laura's arms and hugged her. Tyler promptly joined in, and Nikki felt herself sag with relief. Joshua was standing right behind her to hold her up, his strong hands grasping her shoulders as she leaned into his solid frame.

They entered the grand house and were immediately led toward the back, to a glass-enclosed sunroom filled with too many tropical plants to count, where glasses of sweet tea were waiting for them. The Mastersons kept Ellie with them on a wicker sofa while Nikki sat opposite them in a large wicker chair. Joshua sat on the arm of the chair with his own arm draped around Nikki's shoulder. She couldn't help but sink back into the sense of belonging. His touch on her arm was a gentle caress, and she leaned into it.

"We were thrilled when Joshua called us last Sunday night and told us about the both of you." Laura beamed. "This wedding will be so much more special knowing our granddaughter is part of it."

They sat and talked for at least thirty minutes, discussing Nikki's teaching career and Ellie's young life. Nikki reached into her oversized purse and pulled out a small photo album and handed it to Laura. "It's not much, but I put together a collection of pictures of her for you."

Tears filled the older woman's eyes, and she looked at Nikki with gratitude. "Thank you. This is a beautiful gift." She opened the book, and together they all went through it, Nikki narrating each of the pages.

Looking up, she realized she should have done something like that for Joshua too. Maybe after all the craziness of the wedding was over, they'd have a day where they could go through all the pictures she had and he could pick out the ones he wanted for an album of his own.

There was a flutter of activity in the main hall before David and Denise appeared in the sunroom to greet everyone. When Denise came over to hug Nikki, she whispered in her ear, "Sorry about the ambush. Josh insisted on being the one to bring you here today."

While Nikki appreciated the apology, she still felt a little rankled her best friend had chosen not to call and give her a heads-up. She was pulled from her thoughts at the sound of Ellie laughing with David, who was now thrilled to be a real uncle. He swung her around before carrying her from the room to take her on a tour of the house.

"Our guests should be arriving soon, so why don't we continue this visit later, after the party?" Laura suggested. All were in agreement, but Nikki hung back in the sunroom when the others left. Josh was halfway out of the room before he noticed Nikki's stance.

"You okay?"

"What? Oh…sure. Your folks are really nice, and I'm so glad Ellie's taken to them so quickly." Her arms were crossed against her middle, and Josh could read the uncertainty in her eyes.

"But…"

"Well," she began, trying to organize her thoughts. "It's just I'm in kind of a strange position here today."

"What do you mean?"

"I mean, I'm here as Denise's maid of honor—at least, that was what I was originally here to be. But now," she said as she sighed and turned to look out at the massive gardens beyond the glass, "now I'll be introduced as the mother of your child or as the mother of the new grandchild."

"I'm not sure what the exact problem is here, Nicole," he said honestly. "Are you ashamed I'm Ellie's father?" There was a hint of pain in his voice.

She spun around and faced him. "No! No, that's not it at all! I just really don't want to have to share with a bunch of strangers the fact that you and I had a one-night stand that resulted in a baby. Maybe it's not a big deal to you, but I don't want people looking at me like I'm some sort of gold digger or something, and…" All of her fear and anxiety was coming to the surface. As much as she wanted to, she didn't belong in this house, with this man, with this family, and the day she had been looking forward to a week ago now suddenly felt like torture.

"Why would anyone think you're a gold digger? Where did that even come from?" Josh ran a hand over his face and then forced his hands into his pockets so he wouldn't reach for her again.

"I know nothing about you!" she hissed. "I had no idea your family lived like this!" She waved her arms around, indicating their elaborate surroundings. "But who's going to believe that?"

"I don't care what anyone believes, and if anyone here today has something to say to that effect, then I will set them straight. I'm the bad guy in this scenario, Nicole, not you. I'm the one who lied and made it impossible for you to find me again." There. He had finally admitted his guilt out loud to her, and it felt like a giant weight had been lifted from his shoulders.

"Nikki, do you have any idea how angry my folks were with me when I told them what I'd done?" Nikki shook her head, tears threatening to fall. "They couldn't believe I would do something like that, but they are so grateful you're the kind of person who valued our baby's life and chose to keep her. Right now, I believe they hold you in higher regard than they do me."

"I'm sure that's not true," she said quietly, her attention returning to the gardens outside. The vibrant colors of the flowers were captivating, and it made her smile when she spotted Laura showing them to Ellie and even placing some in the child's curly hair.

"Yes, it's true," Josh said from directly behind her. He too was watching their daughter laughing and smiling as she ran through the garden. "When my mother asked if I was bringing you and Ellie here today, it wasn't a request; it was more like a command. I knew she wanted to talk to you in person and get to know you."

Her heart sank yet again as she lowered her gaze to the floor and furiously blinked away the tears before they fell. She felt Josh move closer behind her.

"What?" he asked. "What did I say?"

She looked over her shoulder at him. "It's nothing," she said quietly. "We'd better go and join your family before the guests arrive." Nikki made to walk around him, but he blocked her and gently grabbed her bare upper arms. The feel of her skin sent waves of arousal though his body. Again.

"I want to know what I said that caused you to look like you were going to cry."

Taking a steadying breath, she looked up at him. "Look, this has been a crazy week, Josh. My whole life is being turned upside down, and when you showed up this morning, I thought you were there because you wanted to be with…" *Me.* "Ellie. But you were there because you had to be."

"That's not true!" His fingers dug into her tender flesh. "It's true it didn't even occur to me to come here today for this bridal thing, but once the idea was planted, I was all for it. I want to be with…" *You.* "Ellie as much as I can. You have to believe that."

His eyes shone with desperation, and Nikki knew he loved their daughter very much. Would he ever care deeply for her?

"I'm sorry for complicating your life so much. I promise to stay by your side the entire time today and answer any awkward questions that get thrown your way. Okay?"

Her eyes grew wide. "You can't do that."

"Why not?"

"It's a bridal shower, Josh. Men normally aren't invited to these things."

"Call me a rebel," he said softly, leaning his head ever so slightly toward hers. "I told you before, Nicole, we're in this together." It was the last thing he said before covering her lips with his own.

Nikki got the impression he had meant to be gentle, but she wanted none of that right now. She ran her tongue along the seam of his lips and was rewarded by a growl low in his throat. Josh's tongue darted out to mate with hers as his arms wrapped around her slender body, molding her to him again.

Nikki threw her arms around his neck and pressed herself shamelessly against him.

It was madness.

It was erotic.

It was…interrupted.

"Ahem." David stood in the archway and cleared his throat, causing Nikki and Joshua to break apart. "Mom wanted us all outside for a family picture," he said with a smirk. Nikki blushed and turned her head to compose herself. "Sorry to interrupt. I'll tell Mom you'll be right out." He walked away with a big smile on his face.

"Are you ready?" Josh asked softly. Nikki nodded and accepted the hand he held out to her. "Oh, and, Nicole?" She met his gaze. "It wasn't just a one-night stand."

True to his word, Josh stayed by Nikki's side throughout the entire party. He had walked around with her and introduced her to all of his relatives, beaming with pride as he introduced Ellie as well. He felt like he was on top of the world.

Much to Nikki's surprise, his family welcomed both her and Ellie with love. There was no condescension or accusing looks; it was a very pleasant day, and she was glad now she had come and that Josh had been there to share it all with her.

To most, they looked like their own little family, and Nikki finally had to admit they were. The situation wasn't ideal, but it was new to them, and they would find a way to make it work. At any point in the day, people could turn and see Josh's arm around her or see him talking softly into her ear. He carried Ellie around with him, and all in all, it was perfect. But what was most unnerving about it all was that, deep down, Nikki knew she was getting very comfortable with the situation very quickly, and she needed to remind herself that come Monday morning, they would go back to living their separate lives.

The shower was a complete success, and Nikki had been more than welcomed into the Masterson family. Denise was giddy with all of her gifts, and Ellie, who was way beyond missing her afternoon nap, was extremely exhausted by the time the party ended.

A cleaning crew had come in to clear away all the

party debris when Laura called everyone back into the sunroom. "I just had a wonderful idea," she said. "It's practically dinnertime, and I know all of you have long drives to get home, but I just thought it would be such a treat if everyone stayed here tonight! It's been so long since I've had both of my sons here for more than a few hours, and with all the chaos with the wedding approaching, I just thought it would be nice to spend some time alone. Just the family," she said with a warm smile. "Besides, we have plenty of space, and we can order dinner in and just take time to visit. What do you think?"

David and Denise readily agreed and immediately headed up to David's room to relax for a little while. Denise kissed everyone and thanked them for a wonderful day while David waved on his way up the stairs, seemingly anxious to be alone with his bride to be. Nikki, however, was unsure of what she should do. It was a very tempting offer, but she hated to impose on these kind people and their hospitality. Even if it was their idea.

"Thank you for the offer, Laura, but Ellie's never really stayed away from home before other than at my parents' house, and I'm not sure she'd do well in a strange bed." It sounded like a reasonable excuse, didn't it?

"Nonsense," Tyler said. "We have a nursery upstairs, which from what I've been told"—he turned and smiled at his wife—"is every little girl's dream."

"What nursery?" Josh asked. "There have never been any girls in the family."

"Your mother went a little crazy this week after your phone call, Son. Now we have a nursery."

Nikki's stomach sank. These dear, sweet people had already made a room in their home for her daughter. How could she possibly refuse them now?

"I even purchased some clothes for her," Laura said with a hopeful smile. "I bought several different sizes, so I'm sure there's something up there that will fit her. Oh, please, Nicole. Please say you'll stay."

Nikki stood and smiled. "Of course."

Laura walked over and hugged her tightly. "Thank you," she said, and when Nikki looked at her quizzically, she added, "For giving us a grandchild and for being so generous in sharing her with us today. I'm sure this was all a bit overwhelming for you, and I just want you to know how much we appreciate your willingness to be here."

"It was my pleasure, Laura. Really. I'm thrilled Ellie has bonded with all of you so quickly." Though every word was truth, it didn't change the fact that she was still very uneasy with the thought of spending the night.

"Mommy! I have a room here! Did you see it? Did you see it?" Ellie danced around excitedly. Nikki let her daughter lead her up the stairs to her new room and gasped in surprise at the sight of it.

The room was enormous, more than twice the size of her room at home. It was princess themed, with a fairytale castle bed, pink walls, and lacy curtains. There was an obscene number of toys and a closet full of clothes.

Nikki turned to the Mastersons. "You really shouldn't have done all of this. It's too much."

"Are you kidding? Ellie is our first grandchild!" Laura said, bending down to pick her granddaughter up in her arms. Ellie gave her a loud smacking kiss on the cheek.

"The pony arrives in a few weeks," Tyler stated with a grin, and both Nikki and Josh stared at him in shock. "Just kidding," he added as he walked over to talk with Ellie.

Laura showed Nikki to the guest bedroom, which was right across the hall from Ellie's. She found out Josh's room was the one next to Ellie's, so should there be a problem in the night, they would both be close by. What did surprise her was the fact that these three bedrooms were the only ones in this wing. David and Denise, as well as the Mastersons, were on the other side of the massive house.

"You have your own bathroom and there's a spare robe in the closet for you. Denise keeps several changes of clothes here, so I'll have her bring you something to sleep in if you'd like." She smiled but must have noticed Nikki still looked a little uneasy. "Don't worry, dear; you'll have plenty of privacy." She left Nikki standing in the guest room as she carried Ellie down the hall and down the stairs.

Taking in her surroundings, Nikki looked around in awe. The room was bright and airy with floor-to-ceiling, arched windows and hardwood floors. The mahogany four-poster bed was covered in a thick, white duvet, and with mental exhaustion plaguing her, Nikki couldn't resist kicking off her sandals and lying down for a moment. It was her first opportunity to be alone all day, and she welcomed it. Closing her eyes briefly, she felt her entire body begin to relax. She assumed everyone had gone back downstairs and she'd have a few minutes to herself.

That wasn't the case.

"We're taking requests for dinner," Josh said as he entered the open door and found her nearly asleep on the bed. He quietly closed the door behind him as he stepped farther into the room. She looked like an angel lying there, and he couldn't resist coming closer.

Nikki blinked her eyes open when his shadow came across her. "Sorry," she whispered. "What did you say?" She pushed herself to a sitting position and found her limbs almost too weak to hold herself up. Joshua sat facing her on the mattress and placed an arm around her to support her.

"Dinner," he said huskily, staring intently down into her sleepy face. Her blue eyes were like saucers looking up at him. "We're taking requests for dinner, and Mom sent me up here to see what you…want."

Oh, there was a loaded statement. What Nikki wanted right now had nothing to do with food and everything to do with the man sitting next to her. Nervously, she licked her lips, and Josh bent forward. "Let me," he whispered before brushing his own tongue lightly over her lips and settling his mouth over hers.

Nikki's hand wrapped around the back of his neck, and she pulled him down onto the mattress with her. Josh stretched out beside her without ever breaking their kiss. *Her kisses are addictive*, he thought to himself as his tongue teased and tangled with hers. He could live a thousand lifetimes and never get enough of kissing her. Nikki strained against him, tangling her fingers into his hair, her nails gently scraping his scalp.

Josh's hand skimmed down one side of Nikki's slim body from shoulder to thigh. The thin linen of her dress left little to his imagination, and he found himself reaching for the hem of her long skirt. The need to feel her bare skin was nearly overwhelming.

Nikki hitched her leg up slightly over his to run her foot up the back of his muscled calf. It also allowed Josh easier access to the elusive hem and soon he found himself touching the exquisite softness of bare skin.

Sighing, she threw her head back as Josh's hand slowly worked its way up her leg and his mouth trailed hot kisses over her cheek and down the slender column of her throat. "Ah, Nicole," he sighed as his hand climbed farther and cupped her bottom. He held his hand firmly there and pressed her into the steely proof of his arousal. "I want you," he growled low against her ear.

Those were the words she had been dying to hear, but the rational part of her brain finally woke up. "Josh, wait," she said breathlessly, placing a hand on his chest to put some distance between them. He removed his hand from beneath her skirt, and Nikki scooted away. "Um…I don't think this is such a good idea," she said as calmly as she could. The reality was she thought this was a very good idea. Her body had been screaming for his touch, his intimate touch, all day long, and now that she'd had a taste of it, her body screamed for release.

"You're probably right," he said, standing and walking toward the window, carefully keeping his back to her so as to not alarm her with the sight of his still-aroused state. He took several deep breaths to calm himself before speaking again. "I'm sure someone will come looking for us soon to find out about dinner and all," he added lightly. He heard Nikki come off the bed and smiled when she came to stand beside him.

"What are the dinner options?"

Dinner was a casual and boisterous affair. Nikki was delighted when it turned out to be catered by the local Chinese restaurant—her favorite form of takeout.

Over the course of the meal, Denise detailed all the final preparations for the wedding, and Nikki was thrilled there was finally something other than her and Ellie and their newfound presence in Josh's life to talk about.

Once the wedding topic was exhausted, Tyler asked Josh how his business was going. "This is my favorite part of the year," Josh admitted. "We've got buildings going up all over the state and a full schedule for the next eight months or so. With the summer coming, we'll get a lot done." Josh was a very talented businessman—Nikki had learned he owned his own construction company where he was the general contractor as well as the master architect.

"Have you ever thought of moving your base of operations away from Wilmington?" David asked, risking a look in Nikki's direction.

"It's crossed my mind a time or two. There just hasn't been a break in the action long enough for me to find a location and take enough time off to make the transition. You have someplace in mind?" Josh knew where his brother's questions were leading, and though he wouldn't admit it to anyone quite yet, the thought of moving closer to Nikki and Ellie consumed him. As much as he knew that most unmarried couples who had children dealt with weekend visitations, it didn't sit well with Josh. He wanted to be free to see Ellie and Nikki whenever he wanted to.

That wasn't the total truth. He didn't want just visitations. He wanted them to live together as a family.

"I just thought with all the growth going on in the Research Triangle Park area, you might want to get in on the action there."

Nikki watched Josh out of the corner of her eye for his reaction, certain he'd shoot David's suggestion down. "I'll look into it," he said lightly.

Typical man, never quick with a straight answer. She hated being in limbo. Once the wedding was over, they would have to deal with setting up a visitation schedule that worked for all of them, and as much as it pained her to lose time with her daughter, the summer vacation coming up would allow her extra time without feeling like Josh was cutting in too much.

The family worked together to clear up the dinner mess, and once it was completed, Nikki said good night to them all so she could bathe Ellie and get her settled into her room.

"Do you need any help?" Josh asked after Ellie had kissed him good night.

"No, we'll be fine," she said, but noticed the look of disappointment on his face. "Well, maybe you could pick out a book to read to her while she takes her bath." Josh smiled warmly at her and the three of them turned to leave the room.

"Hey, Nik," Denise called over her shoulder as she placed the last of the dishes away. "I've got some extra pajamas here. I can bring a pair up for you if you'd like."

"That would be great. Thanks."

Within minutes, Ellie was up to her chin in bubbles and giggling with glee. The bathtub was large and round and could have doubled as a swimming pool for a child her age. She wiggled and squirmed and splashed her mother with pure joy, and Nikki couldn't help but laugh.

Josh picked out a story for Ellie before joining them in the bathroom. The sight of mother and daughter playing together made him smile. "Hey, who's getting the bath here?" he teased.

"I am! I am!" Ellie laughed. "Look, Daddy, I can blow bubbles at Mommy!" Before Nikki knew what hit her, she was covered in frothy bubbles. Father and daughter now laughed together while Nikki stood to get a towel.

"Thanks, princess," she gently chided. "I'm going to see about those pajamas Aunt Denise mentioned, and we'll let your daddy enjoy the wonders of bath time." Her tone was light and it felt nice to be free to leave the bathroom and dry off.

Denise had already dropped the change of clothes in Nikki's room, and when she got a look at what her friend had left, she wanted to throttle her. Lying on her bed was a short ivory-colored silk nightie with very thin straps. This was Denise's idea of pajamas? How in the world was she supposed to change into this and walk around in front of Josh and Ellie? Heck, she didn't know if it was big enough to cover what she needed it to cover.

Remembering the robe Laura had mentioned earlier, she walked over to the closet and grabbed at it like a lifeline. Sighing with relief, she closed the bedroom door before stripping out of her wet dress and sliding into the silk nightie. Looking at her reflection in the mirror, she was impressed. If she had seduction on her mind, this was the number to do it in. The neckline dipped low and showed off plenty of cleavage while hugging her breasts. The hemline came to midthigh with tiny slits on both sides. It was loose enough in the middle to have freedom of movement without being too clingy.

No matter how sexy she felt, unfortunately, that night was not the time for any kind of seduction. She was in Josh's family home, and her main concern was letting Ellie get to know his family.

Slipping on the big, fluffy robe, she tied the sash tightly around her waist. The robe was way too big for someone her size and completely covered her body. Only her red-tipped toes peeked out from beneath it. Laughing to herself, she decided to help Josh out of his misery and get Ellie out of the tub.

Surprisingly, Josh was already helping Ellie into a new pair of Winnie-the-Pooh pajamas. "Well, isn't this a treat?" she said brightly as she entered the nursery. "I can't remember the last time someone else got you ready for bed!" That was probably because no one had ever helped her with Ellie. Well, David and Denise were around all the time to help out with some things, but their nighttime ritual had always been just the two of them. She had to resist the urge to jump in and take over.

Ellie modeled her new pajamas by walking around the room and twirling before climbing into the large castle bed. Josh had picked out a story about a sleeping princess. Nikki noticed her daughter's fidgeting and had a sinking feeling the night was going to be a long one.

Ellie conned Josh into reading a second and a third story before Nikki put an end to it. "Okay, El," she began firmly, "that's enough stories for one night. You've had an exciting day, but it's time to go to sleep." Her voice was soft but firm, and Ellie frowned. "I will be right across the hall, and Daddy has the room right next door. See?" she said, showing Ellie the door that joined her room to Josh's. "If you need anything, we'll be close by, but you need to go to sleep."

The child gave in, but Nikki was certain she'd be hearing from her again before too long. They both bent and kissed her good night and exited the room. "Do you think she'll sleep?" Josh asked, facing her in the large, dim hallway.

"Eventually." Nikki chuckled. "It's a big change for her. That room alone is pretty overwhelming; it's like sensory overload for her." She paused and searched for something to say so she could escape and go to her room. "Why don't you go back downstairs and visit with your family? I'm pretty beat. I'll be here if she needs anything."

Josh frowned at her suggestion. He had hoped to stay up here with her and continue what they had started earlier. He was dying to know what she was wearing under her robe, but he wouldn't push her. Nikki needed to learn to trust him, and no matter how badly he wanted her, he would wait until she was ready. "I've never had the opportunity to help with her during the night. Promise me you'll let me go to her if she gets up?"

Nikki chewed on her bottom lip. "I don't know if I'm ready for that," she said honestly. "She's been my sole responsibility for so long, I'm not sure I could just sit in here while she was upset."

"Fair enough," he said softly. "Then promise you'll let me help."

"Okay." With a nod of his head, Josh turned and walked toward the staircase without another word. Nikki knew she should have been relieved, but a part of her felt a stab of disappointment that he hadn't put up more of a fight about walking away from her.

A soft voice whispered in her ear. It was deep and masculine, and all Nikki wanted to do was curl into it. There was a gentle nudge, and she shifted slightly under the sheets and turned toward it.

"Nikki?"

Wait, was that Josh's voice? Was he in bed with her?

"Nikki, honey, wake up. It's Ellie." Nikki sat bolt upright in the bed and missed knocking heads with Josh by a mere inch.

"What? What is it? What's wrong?" She frantically looked around the room hoping to see for herself what the problem was.

Josh looked a little harried standing beside the bed shirtless, his hair all tousled. "I've tried everything, Nicole, but she only wants you."

Kicking off the blankets, Nikki jumped up from the bed, heedless of her skimpy attire, and walked quickly across the hall. Josh stood back for a moment as a jolt of arousal hit him hard. Her long, shapely legs were in full view and the silky garment she wore concealed little.

"Daddy?" He heard Ellie's pitiful wail coming from across the hall and snapped out of his stupor. He entered her room to find Nikki holding her and rocking her. Kneeling down beside them, he stroked his daughter's cheek. "What is it, princess?"

"I don't like this bed." She pouted. "I wanna go home."

Josh looked to Nikki for some sign of what he should

do. She gave him a shrug, indicating that she was at a loss as well. "Do you want to sleep with me in my room?" Nikki asked her daughter. Ellie shook her head.

"What about me, El? Do you want to try and sleep in my bed?" he asked. Ellie looked at him for a moment and then nodded.

"Can I?"

"Absolutely," he said with a smile. Problem solved! "Come on, princess. Let's let Mommy get some sleep, and you and I will camp out in my room." He lifted her from Nikki's arms and felt the heat from Nikki's body and the silk of the garment she was wearing. Forcing himself to look away, he stood and started toward his room.

"Can Mommy camp wif us too?" Ellie asked, her eyes wide with excitement.

"Oh, no, baby," Nikki said instantly as she stood, shifting slightly to try and cover her next-to-nothing attire. "Mommy can't camp with you tonight. You go with your daddy and get some sleep, okay?"

Ellie's bottom lip began to quiver and Nikki knew the issue was far from over. It had all gone too smoothly and now they were going to have to deal with the consequences of an overindulged child. "Pwease, Mommy." Ellie sniffled. "Pwease camp wif us."

Nikki looked at Josh, who looked just as pitiful as Ellie. It was almost comical. She wasn't sure who was pouting more. She supposed she could stay in there until Ellie fell asleep and then return to her own room. No harm done. Nothing could happen between her and Josh if Ellie was in the bed between them, right? "Okay," she said begrudgingly. "But just until you fall asleep, okay?"

Ellie nodded and Nikki followed them into Josh's room. It was a very masculine environment, she noted to herself—taupe walls crisply trimmed in white, solid navy bedding trimmed in tan on the king-size bed, and all dark wood furniture. Josh's room. This was where he slept. It was both terrifying and exciting to be standing there.

Standing in the doorway, she watched as he got Ellie settled in the center of the bed. He had on a pair of black silk pajama pants, but his chest was bare. She swallowed hard and forced herself to fully enter the room. "Um… which side is mine?" she asked shyly. Josh's expression was closed and his eyes barely met hers as he pointed to the side opposite of where he was standing. Self-consciously, Nikki slid between the sheets and faced Ellie. Josh did the same.

"No more messing around, young lady," Nikki said to her daughter. "It is time to go to sleep." As if on cue, Ellie yawned widely and closed her eyes, sleep claiming her almost immediately, leaving her completely unaware of the tension simmering between her parents.

They lay there silently for several long minutes, staring intently at one another over their child, making sure Ellie was asleep. Nikki made an attempt to get out of the bed, but Ellie noticed and began to whimper. Furious at being at her daughter's mercy, Nikki couldn't remember Ellie being quite so manipulative. Knowing she was stuck in the situation for the remainder of the night, she rolled over, gave both father and daughter her back, and attempted to go back to sleep.

Chapter 5

THE WARMTH WAS BLISSFUL; THE BED WAS THE MOST comfortable she had ever slept in. The hand stroking her back was comforting. *Wait. The hand stroking her back?* Nikki raised her head and realized she was curled up against Joshua and in his arms. With his eyes still closed, Josh asked if she was all right. "Where's Ellie?" she asked quietly but frantically.

"She's back in her bed. You didn't mention her kicking habit," he said sleepily.

"When did that happen?"

"About fifteen minutes after I put her in this bed. She sure is a fickle little thing." He yawned and used his free hand to gently nudge Nikki's head back down to the crook of his neck and shoulder. She fought against it slightly in her attempt to stay upright.

"Why didn't you wake me so I could go back to my room?"

"There was enough noise going on here to wake the dead. I couldn't believe you didn't even budge," he said, now fully awake and more than a little annoyed she wanted to argue with him. "I figured you were exhausted and needed to sleep, so I let you." They sat facing each other in the darkness. Nikki turned and looked at the clock on his nightstand. Two o'clock.

"I should go back to my room," she said as she began to move from beneath the blankets.

"Don't go." His words were quiet but had an edge to them. Nikki sat deadly still. "Please."

She didn't really want to go back to her room because it felt too good being there with Josh. Her only dilemma was figuring out how to agree without losing her dignity. The decision was made for her when Josh lay back down and reached out, gently guiding her back to their previous sleeping position.

"Go to sleep, Nicole," he whispered and kissed the top of her head. Without a word, Nikki snuggled closer to him, their legs tangling comfortably together, her hand held securely against his bare chest.

She wanted to savor the moment, to simply lie there and enjoy the feel of him, of them, so intimately entwined, but she was so tired. It had been a long day, and with all the broken sleep she'd had so far, it wasn't long before exhaustion claimed her. With a sigh of contentment, she closed her eyes and let herself fall back to sleep.

The first rays of sun were beginning to streak through the blinds on Josh's windows. He was slowly waking up, basking in the feel of the woman pressed against him. Looking down at her face, so relaxed and still bathed in sleep, he studied her features. Her skin was so soft and her lips were slightly parted, and Josh could feel her breath on his chest. He gently touched her cheek, reveling in the softness of it. He then let his fingers trail down to her nearly bare shoulder. The thin strap of her nightgown had slid off and was hanging down her arm.

Feeling daring, he allowed his hand to slide beneath the blankets to where she was securely snuggled against him. His hand felt its way down her rib cage and lingered on her bare hip. *Bare?* Thank goodness he'd had no idea about that when she'd first gotten into the bed with him or he never would have slept.

Nikki snuggled closer to him and purred in her sleep at the feel of his strong hand caressing her. When his hand drifted around to cup her bottom, her eyes flashed open and Josh instantly felt her stiffen in his arms.

"Shh... Don't think," he whispered as he gently rolled her onto her back and stretched out beside her. "Just let me touch you."

With a brain too fogged with sleep, she was putty in his hands. His lips found hers and he softly kissed her as his hand continued to stroke up and down her thigh. Nikki wrapped her arms around him and pulled him close, a small, needy sound emanating from her throat. She arched her body into his, reveling in his touch. This is what she'd wanted last night, last week... Hell, she had wanted this since she'd met him three years earlier.

"Nicole," he sighed as his mouth left hers and trailed down her throat in hot pursuit of her breasts. "I've dreamed of waking up with you in my arms. Of feeling your body close to mine." His breath was ragged as he carefully moved the ivory silk aside to get to where he wanted.

Her back bowed off the bed at the contact. "Josh, please..." She needed him desperately and was tired of pretending she didn't.

Hooking a hand under her thigh, he lifted her leg

slightly and positioned himself against her. She cried out at the feel of his arousal covered in silk. "Nikki, I…I…"

"Mommy, can we have breakfast now?"

Talk about a bucket of ice water being dumped on them. Frantically, both of them turned at the sound of their daughter's voice.

"I'm hungry, Mommy. Do you think Grandma will make pancakes?"

Josh rolled off Nikki and shielded her near nakedness so she could fix herself before facing Ellie. "I bet if you told Grandma you wanted pancakes," Josh said lightly, "then she would make them for you." Ellie beamed at his words. "Tell you what, princess," he added, "why don't you go back into your room and let me get dressed and we'll find Grandma together. Okay?"

"Okay, Daddy," she said as she walked toward the bed and kissed him. "Be fast!" she called over her shoulder as she skipped out of the room and closed the door.

Josh fell back down onto the pillows and turned to look at Nicole, who had remained painfully quiet. He rolled onto his side and faced her completely. "You okay?"

It took her a full minute for her voice to work. "I cannot believe that just happened," she said shakily.

He chuckled softly and planted a feather light kiss on her forehead. "It's not a big deal, Nicole. All kids walk in on their parents at some point. She didn't see anything."

She sprang into an upright position. "Excuse me if I don't take it as lightly as you do." Kicking off the blankets, she came to stand next to the bed, her entire body trembling with anger. "In most cases, the parents are at least married and at home in their own bed!" Furiously, she looked around for her robe and then remembered she hadn't been wearing it when she'd joined him in his room last night. With a growl low in her throat, she stalked toward the door.

Josh jumped up from the bed and threw his body against the bedroom door to block her from leaving. "Wait a minute," he said calmly. "Just what is it exactly you're so upset about here?" Nikki arched a brow at him in disbelief over his question. "Well, it seems to me you have quite a few issues." Slyly, he maneuvered her until it was her back against the door and he had her bracketed in his arms. "Are you upset because our daughter saw us kissing?" Before she could answer, he went on with other theories. "Or are you upset we were interrupted when we were about to make love?" His words were a mere whisper against her ear and his hot breath made her shiver.

"Josh," she said weakly.

"Or is there a possibility you're upset because we're not—"

"I have to get dressed," she said quickly as she pulled out of his embrace. "I don't want to talk about this. Ellie's waiting to eat, and it's already past her breakfast time." This time he didn't stop her when she reached around and opened the door. "I'll meet you downstairs," she mumbled without looking him in the face.

Once she was safely ensconced in her room with the door closed, Nikki sagged to the floor. What had she done? She had almost given in and made love to him right there in his parents' home! Was she so depraved she couldn't wait until they were someplace more appropriate and with a little more privacy?

Slowly rising to her feet, she walked into the en

suite and flipped on the shower. Stripping off that damn piece of silk she had slept in and tossing it out into the bedroom as if it burned her, Nikki stepped under the steaming spray. She didn't take the time to luxuriate in the posh surroundings; the sole purpose was to get clean in both body and mind so she could join everyone downstairs as quickly as possible and do her best to act as if nothing had just happened between her and Josh.

Once dressed in the change of clothes she had thankfully brought, she checked her reflection in the mirror and cursed the fact that she didn't have any of her makeup with her. Doing her best to make the bed and straighten up the room, she took a steadying breath and exited the room.

She could hear the voices coming from the kitchen—it sounded like everyone was already up. She walked into the room almost undetected until Ellie called out to her. Then the other five sets of eyes turned to face her with a rush of "good mornings" and offers of coffee. Smiling politely, she accepted a mug from David and made to step around Josh in an attempt to get to the dining room table.

In the blink of an eye, he was seated close beside her. "Did you have a nice shower?" he asked softly, leaning in so only she could hear him. She nodded in response, unable to meet his gaze. "Ellie chose her own clothes. I hope that's okay." He motioned to where Ellie was standing and Nikki couldn't help but smile. Her daughter was perched on a step stool watching intently as her grandmother poured pancake batter onto the griddle.

"That's fine." She slowly sipped her coffee and focused her attention on the floral arrangement in the center of the table. They looked too perfect to be real; maybe they were silk. Or maybe…

"Look, Nicole," he began, taking one of her hands in his, "I'm sorry if I upset you this morning. That wasn't my intention." Brushing a kiss on her knuckles, he continued. "I got carried away, and I'm sorry. We shouldn't have let that happen here. I promise it won't happen again."

Nikki finally looked up at him, her eyes full of dismay. Not happen again? Wait. That wasn't what she wanted to hear! And it certainly wasn't what she had tried to explain to him earlier. She was just about to clarify when he spoke again.

"I don't know what it is about you that makes me lose control." His voice was husky right next to her ear. "Ever since the first time I laid eyes on you." He paused. "But I swear to you, I can control myself."

She turned her head slightly and their lips almost touched. Nikki was ready to lean in when the entire family started walking into the room from the kitchen with platters of food and drinks. They broke apart quickly and Josh rose to help with the setup. Before Nikki could join in, Denise sat down on the other side of her, a knowing smile on her face.

"So," she said coyly, "did you sleep well last night?" She combed a hand through her short, blond hair and smiled, shifting in her seat to face Nikki.

"You are the devil, you know that, right?"

Denise's smile only grew.

"Oh, and by the way"—Nikki leaned in so only the

two of them could hear—"thanks for lending me something to sleep in. What was that thing? A hankie?"

Denise burst out laughing and everyone turned to look at the two of them. Nikki couldn't help it—she was laughing just as hard. Activity resumed around them and once they had regained a little self-control, Denise quietly replied, "I was just trying to give you a little nudge."

"What's that supposed to mean?"

Sighing dramatically, she said, "Look, it's obvious to everyone around you and Josh that you are crazy about one another. I know things are a little awkward right now, but I was just trying to get the ball in motion, that's all. I had a feeling that, if left to your own devices, Ellie would be in high school before you'd make a move." She poured herself a glass of orange juice and leaned in close. "So? Did it work?"

Nikki was just about to answer when someone's cell phone rang. "It's mine," Josh announced as he answered the phone and walked out of the room.

The rest of the family sat down around the table, and Ellie talked nonstop about how she had helped make the food and how Grandma was going to teach her how to bake cookies on her next visit. It made Nikki happy to know Ellie was going to have another set of grandparents who loved her and wanted to be a part of her life.

Conversation flowed and she soon found herself wondering what was taking Josh so long to return to the table. Halfway through the meal, he was finally seated beside her. "Everything okay?" his father asked.

"There's a problem on a job site I have to tend to." Without looking at Nikki, he turned to David. "Would you be able to drive Nicole and Ellie home?"

"Sure," David replied.

Cutting into his stack of pancakes, Josh laughed when Ellie went on to fill him in on the part of the conversation he had missed. He complimented her cooking skills, and she smiled brightly for him. He hated to have to cut his time with her short. The whole day had been ahead of them, and Josh had really been looking forward to it—even though a large portion of it would have been spent on the road. Unfortunately, logistically it was impossible to be the one to take them home. It was a three-hour drive east back to Nicole's, and from there it was another two hours south to get to the job site. By having David take them home, he could make the drive in a little under three and a half hours and be where he needed to be.

Scratch that, he *needed* to be with Nicole and Ellie. He *wanted* to be with them. He *had* to be back in Wilmington, dammit. Out of the corner of his eye, he could see Nicole was just pushing her food around on her plate and not really eating. Placing his fork down on the table, he wiped his mouth with a cloth napkin and turned to her.

"I'm really sorry, Nicole. I tried to find a way out of having to go, but I need to be the one there to oversee the situation."

Her wide, blue eyes stared back at him, and he could see the walls he had been trying to pull down slowly building right back up.

"It's not a big deal. Really. Don't give it another thought." Her words were very clear and concise but were spoken very softly. "If you could, before you go, please move Ellie's car seat from your car to David's for me."

He wasn't sure what he expected her to say, but her quiet acceptance of the situation hurt more than if she'd yelled at him. "No problem." Neither noticed the conversation around them had stopped. Even Ellie was quiet, as if sensing the conversation going on between her parents was important.

After a brief spell of silence, Laura cleared her throat and tried to change the subject. "So, Nikki, I hear your parents are in Florida and you're going to visit them next weekend. Do you see them often?"

Josh excused himself from the table. Nikki imagined he was going to go and pack. "I've only been out there once since Ellie was born. Traveling with a baby was quite an experience." She took a sip of her orange juice before going on. It was good to be reminded of all the things she had to look forward to this week and not what she was losing out on. "My folks have come to visit several times, however, so Ellie could get to know them. I'm really looking forward to this trip. Ellie's very excited about going on a plane, right?" she asked her daughter.

"I'm going to fly in the sky!" Ellie exclaimed, and everyone laughed at her excitement. "Grandma and Grandpa are going to take me to see the fishies!"

"That's right, El. We're going to go to SeaWorld."

Ellie talked about how excited she was to see all the fish while everyone finished their breakfast. And once breakfast was over and cleaned up, preparations for their departure began. Josh never returned to the breakfast table, and Nikki tried not to dwell on it. She let Ellie go and play outside with Laura and Tyler while she packed. The look on the older couple's faces showed their appreciation for the extra time with their grandchild.

Upstairs, Nikki threw her few personal belongings into her bag and then went to retrieve Ellie's things. The door to Josh's room was closed, and for that she was grateful. She'd hate for him to see the longing and disappointment in her eyes.

It wasn't fair! Why did he have to show up again in her life and be wonderful and attentive and have to live so far away? She couldn't blame him for having to leave; after all, he ran a huge business and it would be incredibly selfish of her to make demands on his time. They didn't have that kind of relationship. It wasn't as if he were leaving her and Ellie stranded someplace. David and Denise were right here, as they always were, and more than willing to help out.

Quietly, Nikki made up Ellie's princess bed and straightened the room up. "You don't need to do that." *Josh.* "My mother has a housekeeper who does this sort of thing."

"I don't mind. I'm used to doing it myself." She kept her back to him and continued putting books on shelves and toys in the toy box. On the plush carpeting, she didn't hear him walk toward her. It wasn't until she straightened and they nearly collided that she saw how close he was.

"I really am sorry about having to leave, Nicole," he said solemnly.

"I've already told you it's not a big deal," she lied. "David and Denise live close by, and it just makes sense for them to be the ones to drive us anyhow. I hate being an inconvenience."

Josh's patience snapped. "Dammit, Nicole! You are not an inconvenience! I wanted to be here with you this weekend. I wanted to be the one to drive you here, and I wanted to be the one to bring you home. I hate that I have to head back to Wilmington, but it can't be helped. Can't you understand that?"

Nikki's eyes went wide. She tried to blink back the tears she felt forming. "I do understand. I know you wanted this time with Ellie, and with my taking her out of town next weekend, you're missing out. I get it. I don't want you to worry about us. Ellie will be fine with riding home with her uncle David." She was trying to put an emphasis on Josh's relationship with Ellie and not make this about herself. She wasn't prepared to deal with the fact that, after all these years, she was still hopelessly in love with him and felt as if she was being deserted all over again.

Knowing full well what she was trying to do, Josh reached up and cupped her face in his hands. It was time to put it all out there. "Yes, I'm disappointed about missing out on time with Ellie, but I am equally disappointed about missing time with you too." His mouth slowly descended on hers, giving her ample time to move away. She didn't.

As his lips touched hers, Nikki reached out and clutched at the front of his black polo shirt, pulling him closer to her. Mouths opened, tongues mated, and Josh backed her up against the nearest flat surface. Nikki needed to breathe but was desperate to not break contact with him. She was going to have to go for far too long without feeling him like this, and now she was greedy—greedy for his kiss, his touch, any scrap of attention he would throw her way. She wasn't disillusioned enough to think he felt the same for her as she did for him; that would have been asking far too much, too soon. But she was sure there was still an undeniable physical attraction to one another. There had been no discussion of a future together except for visitation with Ellie. He never even hinted about being with her and making a family together.

Josh pressed closer and the proof of his arousal only confirmed the physical attraction. His mouth left hers and hungrily worked down the slim column of her throat. She arched her head back, grinding it against the wall to give him better access. His mouth felt glorious on her. His hands roamed up and down her sides, gently teasing the undersides of her breasts with a fleeting touch. Releasing his shirt, she raked her fingers up through his hair before sinking them in to hold him to her.

"Nikki? Are you almost ready? David's loading up the car!" Denise called from the end of the hall.

Slowly breaking their contact, Josh moved away. "So much for self-control," he said thickly as he openly appraised her swollen lips and passion-filled eyes. Without another word, he turned and picked up all their bags and left the room, giving her time to compose herself before facing everyone. Luckily for him, the bags could camouflage the arousal straining against his khakis.

Tuesday night, Denise arrived at Nikki's with a bag of takeout and a bottle of wine. Before Nikki could even say hello, Denise was talking. "Okay, I have been going out of my mind with worry for you, and I left explicit instructions with David not to call or bother me unless he is dead or dying." Placing the bag of food on the kitchen counter, she turned and faced Nikki. "Well?"

"Worried about what, exactly?"

"Don't give me any of that!" Denise snapped as she began setting the table. She had been at Nikki's so many times it was practically her home away from home. "I'm talking about you and Josh. What's going on?" As if on cue, the phone rang. "Don't you dare answer that!"

"I have to. It's Josh's nightly phone call to Ellie. Normally he Skypes, but he had to work late tonight and this was the only way to talk with her." Ellie came running into the room at the sound of the phone and was already dancing around Nikki's leg, begging to talk. Handing the phone directly to her daughter, she turned her attention back to Denise.

"Can we wait to discuss this until after Ellie's asleep? It's a little bit complicated."

"Fine, but I'm telling you now, I am not leaving here until I am one hundred percent certain you're okay with all of this."

"All of what?" Nikki asked with frustration. "You know what? Never mind. After Ellie's asleep, we'll talk."

"I brought an overnight bag," Denise said as she finished setting the table. Nikki gave her a bland look. "Just saying."

Moments later, Nikki heard Ellie say good night to Josh. "Thank you, baby," she said, taking the phone from Ellie's hand, anxious to hear Josh's voice. "Hi," she said a little breathlessly.

"Hi." She could hear the smile in his voice. "I hear

Denise is there for dinner so I won't keep you." His tone was as soft as a caress.

Nikki turned and saw Denise leading Ellie up the stairs as the child called out a sweet little good night. Nikki smiled and turned her attention back to the man on the phone. "Actually, Denise is taking Ellie up and putting her to bed. I fed her earlier so we could have a girls' night."

"A girls' night, huh? On a Tuesday?"

"Is there a wrong night to have a girls' night?"

Josh chuckled. "Honestly, I wouldn't know. Any particular reason for said girls' night?"

"None I can think of," she lied. "I'm just glad to not have to cook. Denise brought dinner with her."

"Chinese?"

"What do you think?" she said with a smile in her voice.

"Listen, Nicole, I was wondering," he began nervously, "I have a meeting in Raleigh on Thursday, and I thought maybe I could come and take you and Ellie to dinner. Would that be all right?"

Her heart raced. She hadn't planned on seeing him before the wedding, so this was an unexpected surprise. "That sounds nice. I know Ellie will be thrilled."

"And what about Ellie's mother? Will she be thrilled?" he asked, his tone deep and mesmerizing.

"I think she most definitely will be." She barely recognized her own voice; it was sexy and teasing.

"Will be?" he teased right back.

"Am," she corrected.

"Good," he said, and Nikki could almost hear the tension leaving his body. "I was thinking maybe I could drive you to the airport Friday morning. What time is your flight?"

"We have a ten o'clock flight out of Raleigh, so we'll need to be there around eight."

Josh liked that she hadn't even questioned the fact that he was essentially inviting himself to spend the night. "That sounds good. Are you sure you don't mind? I mean, I don't know who was planning on taking you."

"Your brother was, actually. He was going to go into work late, so I'm sure he won't mind not having to do that."

"I can call him if you'd like."

"Not necessary. Denise is here, so I'll just let her know to tell him." They were silent for a moment. "How about instead of going out for dinner, we stay in? I'll cook, and that way we can get Ellie to bed on time, and it won't be such a chore to get her up before dawn Friday morning."

"That sounds good." His deep voice gave her chills and she could almost feel his breath on her skin. "I'll see you Thursday."

Nikki hung up the phone on a dreamy sigh.

"This is what I was afraid of," Denise said as she breezed past Nikki and began doling out food.

"What is supposed to mean?"

"The hushed tones, the longing sigh as you hung up the phone... Admit it, Nik—you're still in love with Josh."

"Were you spying on me? How long were you standing there?" Nikki asked with a touch of annoyance at her friend's observation.

"No, I wasn't spying. I happened to come down the stairs as you were hanging up the phone. To tell the truth," she said lightly as she sat herself down at Nikki's kitchen table, "I didn't hear what you said, just the way you said it."

Nikki grabbed her plate and sank down into a chair. "Can we even say I'm still in love with him? I mean…I barely know him. We had one night together. Who falls in love after one night?" She was speaking way too fast and could feel Denise's eyes boring into her. She sighed. "Would it be so horrible if I was?" It seemed to take forever for her to get the words out—she was terrified of the answer she would get.

"I don't know," Denise said honestly. "David thinks…" She stopped short, unwilling to finish her statement.

"David thinks what?" Nikki demanded. Denise put a forkful of Hunan beef in her mouth and refused to answer. "David thinks what, Denise?" Still no response. "You'll have to come up for air sometime."

Swallowing, Denise placed her fork down and took a deep breath. Her hazel eyes were full of compassion. "Saturday night, after you and Ellie went to bed, Joshua came back downstairs to hang out with everyone." Nikki nodded in remembrance. "Well, first his parents started talking about how wonderful you are and how much they already adore Ellie." She paused and took a sip of her wine. "We talked about Ellie for a while. Since David and I have known her since she was born, it was easy to fill in a lot of the gaps for them."

Nikki was sure it was all leading somewhere, she just wished it would get there soon. "And?"

"Then they asked him what his plans were where the two of you were concerned." She took another forkful of food. "We could tell he wasn't ready to talk about it, but

David asked him to go outside with him, so they could talk without an audience."

"Oh for crying out loud, Dee, get to the point!"

Huffing spitefully, Denise shoved another forkful of food into her mouth and chewed it slowly. Sometime later, she continued. "David asked Josh about his intentions."

"His intentions?" Nikki parroted. "When did David become my father?"

Annoyance covered Denise's face. "David is concerned for both you and Ellie, and knowing his brother like he does, he wanted to make sure Josh wasn't just killing time here, that he was honestly interested in being a father and playing an active part in Ellie's life."

Nikki's heart was racing and she felt the sickening sheen of perspiration begin to cover her skin. She desperately wanted to know the answer but, at the same time, dreaded it. What if it wasn't what she wanted to hear? What if Josh didn't see himself in the role of father for the long haul? Nervously, she pulled at the collar of her shirt to get some cool air on her clammy skin. Swallowing hard, she looked at Denise expectantly.

"Nik, he's crazy about Ellie," Denise said calmly. "It kills him he lives so far away from her. He questioned David about every minute of Ellie's life until he found out about her. It was very sweet."

Letting out a long sigh of relief, Nikki took a sip of her wine and relaxed a little in her seat. "So he's going to be involved in her life. That's a good thing. Right?"

"It seems that way. How do you feel about it?"

She pushed her moo shu pork around on the plate while she contemplated her answer. Forcing herself to look up, she said, "I'm relieved, actually. I would have hated it for him to start this relationship with Ellie and then disappear. It would crush her."

"Yes, yes, I'm sure it's all good for Ellie. But what about you?"

"Me? I think it's only fair he be a part of his daughter's life. If I had been able to track him down sooner, I would have, so he wouldn't have missed any part of her life."

"Okay, thank you for the politically correct answer. The Miss America judges have marked down your score." Denise rolled her eyes in exasperation. "How do you feel about Josh? About you and Josh specifically? I know what we all saw this weekend, and let me tell you, I hope David and I have that much heat between us on our honeymoon!"

"Oh, stop it! Don't be ridiculous. I haven't seen him in three years. For heaven's sake, I haven't even been with *any* man in three years." She took another sip of wine. "So maybe there's still a little…lust there. It's no big deal. I can handle it."

"Oh, come on, Nikki. I know you better than that. Are you trying to tell me nothing happened that night, even with the slinky nightie I left for you?"

"Did I forget to thank you for that?" Nikki asked sarcastically. They broke into a fit of giggles and then Nikki went on to tell Denise all about their night—from being woken up with Ellie to finding herself asleep in Josh's arms and nearly making love with him before being interrupted by their daughter.

"Wow," Denise hissed. "No wonder you were both out of sorts at breakfast."

"Oh my gosh. Was it obvious?"

"Probably only to me and David because we know you both so well. The Mastersons were so over the moon with Ellie, they probably wouldn't have noticed if you and Josh were consuming each other under the dining room table."

Nikki let out a laugh at the image. "They really were excited about her, weren't they?"

"Absolutely. And if you weren't my best friend, I'd be jealous you gave my future in-laws their first grandchild. I was hoping for that honor."

"Dee, I am so sorry all of this happened right before your wedding. The last thing I wanted was to take any of the focus off you. This whole situation has taken on a life of its own, and I don't know how to tone it down or rein it back in."

"There's nothing to apologize for. I love you, and I love Ellie. If I have to share the spotlight with anyone, I'm glad it's you." She reached across the table and squeezed Nikki's hand. "I'm just glad it's going as well as it is."

"What do you mean?"

"Well, this all could have gone in a completely different direction. Josh could have been furious about having a child and refused to have anything to do with you or Ellie. That would have made for a terribly awkward time for us all at the wedding."

"You don't think he's just—"

"Why are you looking for trouble? Josh isn't that good an actor. He is truly thrilled about Ellie, and if he were honest, he'd come out and admit he's crazy about you too."

Lowering her lashes, Nikki quietly asked, "Did David ask him about how he felt about me?"

"Hey," Denise said just as softly, waiting for Nikki to look at her. "David did ask him how he felt about you, but Josh refused to give him an answer."

"Oh."

"Then David proceeded to tell him if he hurt you again, he'd hunt him down like a dog and kick his ass!" Another round of laughter filled the air. "I'm telling you, Nik, if anything ever happened between David and me, he'd be the first one banging down your door."

"I love David like a brother, and I'm glad he's looking out for me." She smiled. "And Ellie." It was the truth. In all the years they'd all been friends, Nikki had known she could always count on David being there to back her up. Whenever a boyfriend had gotten out of line or did something to offend her, David was right there to straighten it all out. She had no doubt in her mind that where Josh was concerned, David would be just as diligent.

Chapter 6

THURSDAY AFTERNOON, NIKKI AND ELLIE ARRIVED HOME with a handful of grocery bags filled with food to prepare for their dinner with Josh. Nikki had bought enough food for three dinners because she couldn't decide what she wanted to make.

"I help too, Mommy?" Ellie asked as the groceries were put away.

"Yes, sweetheart, you can help Mommy when it's time. But first, we need to get this place cleaned up and all of your toys put away so your daddy can walk in here." It had been a hellish morning. Nikki had been on edge about their upcoming trip, the evening ahead, and Ellie had been slightly out of control. Toys had been strewn about for no reason at all, and now they had their work cut out for them.

Singing the cleanup song, they got the living room put back together. The next item on the list was to get the both of them put back together. "Come on, El. Mommy's going to take a quick shower. Grab some toys and meet me in the bathroom." Within minutes, Ellie was there, building happily with her multicolored blocks while Nikki soaped up in the shower.

Once that task was completed, Nikki reconsidered her plan to bathe Ellie, deciding to let that wait until after dinner, so Josh could have time with Ellie. Dressing in a pair of silky lounging pants and a simple T-shirt, Nikki detangled her hair and quickly blew it dry before reapplying some makeup—with a little more care than she normally did.

Though it was left unspoken, both she and Josh knew what tonight was about. Yes, they were going to have dinner and he was going to have some time with Ellie, but she also knew that tonight they would continue what had been interrupted Sunday morning. A thrill of delight coursed through her body. She felt nervous and jittery and hoped she would be able to calm her wayward emotions enough to actually get through dinner. The thought of making love with Josh again was overwhelming.

Over the years, she had possibly built up their night together in her mind. Was it actually as good as she remembered? Nikki couldn't remember being this nervous their first time. Well, maybe that was because it had all happened so naturally and so quickly, there hadn't been time to be nervous. She knew what was going to happen this time, and now she had to wait.

Sitting down on the edge of her newly changed sheets, her mind wandered back three years.

There are so many stars in the sky, she observed as they walked out to her car. When they reached her vehicle, Tyler placed his hands on her shoulders and turned her to face him. "You are so beautiful, Nicole," he said and lifted one hand up to gently caress her cheek. "It's true," he whispered. "I can't believe someone as beautiful as you walked into my life today. It doesn't seem real."

Nikki reached out and boldly placed a hand on his chest. All night long, she had wanted to touch him. They had held hands as they'd sat in the corner booth and talked, but this was a deliberate touch, an invitation. A serious invitation. With her hand splayed across his chest, she raised her eyes to meet his. "This has been a perfect night."

"It doesn't have to end, you know," he said carefully. Slowly, so slowly, he leaned in and rested his forehead against hers. His body soon followed and they were touching practically from head to toe. "Can I kiss you?"

"Oh, yes," she sighed as she reached up and cupped her hand around his neck to finish closing the gap between them. "Please." Nikki had been expecting the kind of wild, untamed kisses she had gotten from other men, but this was almost chaste. Featherlight. She almost thought she'd imagined his touch.

"God, you're sweet," he whispered against her lips. Nikki leaned farther into him. His green eyes scanned her face before he tasted her again.

"Tyler?"

"Hmm?" He reluctantly raised his head and looked at her.

"Let's go someplace where we can be alone." Nikki couldn't believe she had been the one to say those words. Something about Tyler made her bold. And impatient.

"I'd go anywhere with you, Nicole. Anywhere." Taking a step back from her, Tyler reached out and took one of her hands in his. "I…I'm staying at a hotel not far from here. We can go there if you'd like." His words were hesitant, as if he was afraid to scare her off.

"I'd like that very much," she said breathlessly.

The hotel was within walking distance, and yet it seemed like it took forever to get there. Once the door to the room was closed and locked behind them, Tyler reached for her and she went willingly into his arms. It felt so right—his tall, hard, lean body pressed against her—and it gave her a thrill like she had never known. Heat flowed through her veins and pooled in her middle. His mouth was on her, possessive and gentle at the same time. He kissed her mouth tenderly, adoringly.

"Nicole," he said finally when his mouth left hers; it was a near moan, pleading with her. "I want to make love to you."

"Can we make dinner now, Mommy?" Nikki's thoughts snapped to attention, and she quickly turned and looked at the clock. It was four thirty. Josh would be there soon, and she had been so wrapped up in her daydream, she had lost track of time.

"Oh my goodness!" She rose from the bed and scooped Ellie up in her arms. "We need to get started right away. Your daddy will be here soon."

"Yay!" Ellie squealed as they ran down the stairs.

At five thirty sharp, there was a knock at the front door. Ellie ran to open it with Nikki's permission. Josh stood there and smiled with surprise at the sight of his daughter. "Hi, Daddy," she said as he lifted her up to kiss her.

"Look at you, answering the door like a big girl. Where's your mom?"

"In the kitchen. She said I could." He carried her there, so they were all in the kitchen, and Josh drank in the sight of Nicole. The silky pants, the clingy T-shirt—his mouth went dry. He hoped dinner was going to be quick and time would fly so he could be alone with her.

Ever since she'd left his bed Sunday morning, he had been in a semi-aroused state. Well, that wasn't the total truth; he'd been that way ever since he'd first shown up on her doorstep with David and Denise and seen her again for the first time. No, even that was wrong. Hell, every time he'd thought about her in the last three years, he'd become hard. No woman had ever turned him inside out the way Nicole had, and just knowing they were going to be alone tonight had him on edge.

He was thrilled to have found an opportunity to have dinner with both her and Ellie, and as thankful as he was to have this extra time with his daughter, tonight was truly about having time with Nicole. After all this time, the fire hadn't died. If anything, he felt a stronger pull for her now than he had when he'd first met her. The years hadn't dimmed what he felt for her; it had strengthened it. He hoped and prayed she felt the same.

If he hadn't screwed up that night so long ago, none of this would be an issue. Josh knew for sure that if he had been completely honest with her and had told her his real name—and his last name—they would be married by now and living together, maybe with another child. Could they possibly make that happen after all this time? He didn't want to rush her, and he certainly didn't blame Nicole for being wary and not trusting him outright, but it still stung.

His plan had been to take things slow and let them evolve naturally, but after having her in his arms, in his bed, and feeling her response to him, all hopes of slow went flying right out the window.

Josh didn't want to scare her off, but he had a sneaking suspicion she was burning for him just as hotly as he was for her. So he'd sit and eat dinner, bide his time. He'd play with Ellie and help get her ready for bed, all the while showing Nicole how right this all was. They could be a family together.

Then he'd take her to bed and show her how right they were as lovers.

With the tightening of his groin, he said a quick hello to Nikki and let Ellie lead him out of the room to go and play while Nikki finished cooking dinner. He was relieved for the chance to cool down.

It was going to be a long night.

Nikki was a bundle of nerves. The chicken Marsala was simmering, the potatoes were mashed, and the broccoli was steamed. The sight of Josh when he had entered the kitchen had left her feeling frazzled. It was all a bit too domesticated to comprehend. There was a *Hi, honey, how was your day?* quality to it that felt surreal.

Peeking her head into the living room, she saw Josh had removed his coat and loosened his tie. His shirtsleeves were rolled up to expose the corded muscles of his tanned forearms. Nikki's mouth went dry. He was doing nothing more than sitting on the sofa reading to Ellie, and yet she had never seen anything sexier in her life. As if reading her mind, Josh chose that moment to look up at her. "Dinner ready?" he asked casually.

Nikki cleared her throat. "Actually, I'm just getting ready to serve. Why don't you get Ellie settled into her seat?" His only response was to smile as he rose. Nikki disappeared into the kitchen before she actually started to drool. "Get a grip," she whispered to herself. "He's only a man." *Yeah, right. And Michelangelo was only an artist.*

Placing the dishes on the table, she was a bit shocked when Josh stood and held out a chair for her. "Thank you," she whispered shyly. Once they were all seated and eating, she finally let herself relax.

"Everything is wonderful, Nicole. Thank you for being willing to cook tonight. Although it wouldn't have been a big deal to go out."

"Well, with the flight so early tomorrow and all the chaos that's bound to go with it, I thought a quiet night in would be best for Ellie." She knew sooner or later she wouldn't be able to use her daughter as a shield or an excuse for her every move, but for right now, the means supported the ends. Without meeting his eyes, she quietly added, "She'll probably go to bed earlier than usual."

Had she been brave enough to look up, she would have seen the heat banked in Josh's eyes. He gruffly cleared his throat and turned his attention to asking his daughter how she felt about her upcoming trip, and the remainder of the meal passed quickly.

Standing to clear the dishes, she asked Josh if he would mind bathing Ellie, who, in turn, shouted with glee at the thought of her father playing with her until it was bedtime. If only she had known that her parents needed the time apart to mentally prepare for the remainder of their evening.

~

It was a tense and awkward moment when they finally shut off Ellie's bedroom light. Did they go downstairs? Did they go straight to the bedroom? Nikki watched as indecision marked Josh's face, and she was sure she looked the same way. When he turned to go toward the stairs, she decided to be bold. Hadn't they waited long enough? Why go all the way downstairs only to have to climb all the way back up a short time later? She was all for being efficient.

Taking his hand in hers, she tugged slightly and led the way to her bedroom. Once inside, she shut the door and leaned against it. Without a word, Josh leaned in and claimed her mouth in a desperately hungry kiss. Her lips were parted and waiting for him. He pressed his entire body against hers and growled deeply at the feel of her so close. He could feel her heart beating. He could feel every lush curve, and he was anxious to feel them all skin to skin.

Tearing his mouth away from hers, he trailed kisses across her jaw and down her throat as his hand skimmed up her side and found one full breast aching for his touch. Her nipples had pebbled beneath the flimsy fabric of her shirt, and the brassiere underneath was nothing more than a whisper of lace, barely there. Nikki moaned his name and arched her back, securely pressing herself into his large hand.

"I thought I'd never find you again," he said gruffly before kissing the hardened peak through her shirt. "I've dreamed of being with you again." His words sent a thrill of pleasure coursing through Nikki's entire body, and she twisted and squirmed until he had no choice but to pull her toward the bed. He kissed her again possessively before leaning over and helping her lie down. She looked like an angel, blond hair spread out against the white comforter. Her breathing was ragged and the rise and fall of her breasts kept him mesmerized.

Without breaking eye contact, he began to unbutton his shirt. He reveled in the fact that Nicole seemed unable to look away. When the last button was undone, he toed off his shoes and tossed his shirt onto the desk chair which stood not two feet from him. When he reached for his belt, Nikki raised herself onto her elbows and licked her lips. He paused briefly, surprised she had come to sit fully up. Reaching forward, she placed her hands on his hips and guided him to stand between her spread legs. Without a word, she began to kiss his flat stomach. Josh's head fell back in abandon. Her hot breath on his skin felt incredible.

As she kissed and licked his skin, her hands went to work on his belt. Once it was opened, Nikki focused her attention on getting his pants off. It didn't take long to accomplish. Standing before her in nothing more than a pair of dark-colored briefs, Josh pulled her to her feet. "Your turn."

Without waiting for instruction, Nikki pulled her T-shirt up and over her head. She was beautiful. Her breasts were full and flushed with her desire, and as much as Josh ached to reach out and touch them, taste them, watching her strip was far too erotic to stop at that moment.

Nikki liked the flash of heat in Josh's eyes as she stood before him in her bra. Empowered, she bent and shimmied out of her pants. In nothing more than skimpy red lace, she moved forward until they were touching from head to toe.

"God, you feel so good," he hissed.

"You too."

"Want to feel even better?" he asked thickly, his hands going to her shoulders and slowly pulling the bra straps down her arms.

"Oh, absolutely." In a flash, she found herself down on the bed, her bra gone, and all she could think was that she had finally come home.

~

Much later, they were facing one another by moonlight in Nikki's bed. Josh couldn't stop touching her, still in awe she was really there in his life, in his arms, after all that time. He let out a contented sigh. Three years ago, he knew he had fallen in love with her but thought it would have faded after so many years apart. Looking at her now, however, he knew what he felt for her was real; it would never fade no matter how long they were apart. Nicole was unique. She was wholesome and caring and everything he wanted in his life. That thought brought a smile to his face.

As Nikki watched the smile spread across his face, she couldn't help but match it. She didn't try to speak yet. She didn't want to ruin the moment. She felt a peace and contentment she hadn't felt in a long time. Reaching out slowly, she placed a hand on his chest, over his heart. Moving closer, they shifted until Josh was lying on his back, her head on his shoulder. His arm wrapped around her and held her close, and now it was her turn to sigh.

"You're so beautiful," he murmured after several

long moments. "So absolutely breathtaking." He stroked a hand up and down her arm and placed a kiss on the top of her head. "I missed you."

Slowly, Nikki raised her head. "I missed you too." Leaning in, she kissed him softly on the lips and lingered there.

Josh settled her back against his side. "I just can't believe I'm here with you, we have a daughter, and you've let me be a part of her life. I mean, you could've denied me the chance to see Ellie, and you would have been completely within your rights. I behaved so horribly back then, and you had no reason to trust me." He placed another kiss on her head. "I'm just so grateful to you. I want you to know that."

It wasn't the kind of pillow talk she had been expecting and she didn't particularly want to discuss it. Right then, Nikki was thinking about their future and didn't want to rehash their past. Deciding to just keep quiet, she waited to see if Josh had anything else to say.

"I wish you weren't going out of town this weekend," he finally said.

"It's my dad's birthday. We've had it planned for a while now. Besides, it's only a weekend." She could almost feel him pouting in the dark. "We knew we were going to have to try and work this out. I just don't know how, living so far away from one another."

Josh was silent. In his mind, he knew how much he wanted Nicole and Ellie to come to Wilmington and live with him. He had a large house, and it would be perfect for the three of them. Unfortunately, he couldn't be selfish. Nicole had a job here she loved, and he was already the cause of her having struggled for so many years. How could he possibly ask her to uproot her life for his convenience?

There were no easy solutions; for the time being, they were going to be stuck in this holding pattern. He had hammered out a tentative schedule for the next couple of weeks that allowed him to travel more and, therefore, find time to be in this part of the state, making it easier to try and spend time with Nicole and Ellie.

"What are you going to do this weekend?" Nikki asked sleepily, snuggling up closer to Josh's side.

"After taking you and Ellie to the airport tomorrow, I'm going to head home and do some paperwork. If it would be okay with you, I'd like to be the one to pick you up Sunday night." He held his breath.

Nikki smiled against his chest before placing a kiss there. "It would definitely be okay with me. But isn't that a lot of driving for you? Will you have to be back home Monday morning for work?"

"Actually, I've arranged my schedule so I'll be on the road quite a bit over the next couple of weeks. Most of the time, I'm going to be around the state, primarily west of here. But then I've got a two-day trip up to Virginia and another one down to South Carolina. I haven't done anything like that in a while. I tend to look at jobs close to home, but there are some opportunities for expansion coming up that I'd like to get in on."

"That sounds exciting," she said around a yawn. "How long has it been since you've traveled out of state for a job?"

"Six months, easily."

"How come?"

He shrugged. "I'm not comfortable doing it, the schmoozing and all of that. It's like I can't be myself."

Nikki couldn't quite say why, but that statement bothered her. Something about it just seemed to rub her the wrong way. Before she could examine it any further, Josh shifted and gently rolled her beneath him. "I know you need to get up early," he said softly, leaning forward and kissing her. "And I know I should probably let you get some sleep." Another kiss. "But…I…I…"

"What?" she whispered. "Tell me."

"I need you."

His honest admission put those niggling doubts from just a minute ago on hold. Right then, she needed him too.

"I'm yours," she said as she wound her arms around his shoulders and pulled him closer. Sleep was the last thing she needed.

Chapter 7

"OH MY GOSH! LOOK AT HOW MY BABY GIRL HAS GROWN!" Madeline Taylor exclaimed as she ran through the throngs of people in the baggage claim area and scooped her granddaughter up into her arms. "Nikki, she's so beautiful!" Her stylishly cropped gray hair meshed with Ellie's curly blond locks as she held the toddler close.

Nikki smiled at the sight of her mother and her daughter. It was the first time she had felt like smiling all day. Leaving Josh at the airport had been harder than she had expected, and she found herself second-guessing the trip. But as she looked over at Ellie hugging her grandmother, squealing with delight when her grandfather came up behind her and pretended to scare her, she knew she made the right choice. They made quite a picture, the three of them, and the sight made her smile.

As much as Nikki was used to taking care of herself and Ellie, having Josh there this morning while she was trying to get ready had been a godsend. Ellie had been thrilled to wake up and have her father there, and it made getting up so early a more pleasant experience because they all got to have breakfast together.

He had helped her load their luggage in the car, and at the airport, he had walked them as far as airport security would allow. Watching him say good-bye to Ellie had torn at her heart. It may have only been a couple of weeks, but it was already feeling wrong when they had to separate.

Walking behind her parents, she did her best to stifle a yawn. She and Josh had made love throughout the night, and although she knew she was probably going to need a nap at the same time her daughter did, she wasn't the least bit sorry. Being with Josh again, making love with him again, was everything she had remembered and more. It wasn't that she had a whole lot to compare it to, but Nikki was sure you didn't find that kind of chemistry between two people every day.

"How was your flight?" her dad asked as he picked up her luggage and loaded it onto a cart.

"Uneventful," Nikki sighed thankfully. "It is much easier traveling with her now than it was when she was a baby."

Huddled together in the pure happiness of being reunited, they walked out to the Taylors' car and loaded all the luggage. Nikki remained peacefully quiet and let Ellie chatter to her grandparents about her trip. At the mention of her daddy, Nikki felt her parents' eyes home in on her.

"We'll talk" was all she said in response to their silent query. Why hadn't she thought about this before coming here?

Once back at the house, Madeline made lunch while Nikki settled herself and Ellie into the guest room. Ellie scampered off at some point to play with her grandfather and Nikki relished the brief bout of silence.

"So, Ellie's father finally put in an appearance." She looked up to see her mom frowning in the doorway.

There was no condescending tone, no question; it was just a simple statement.

"Yes."

Sitting next to her daughter on the bed, she reached over and took Nikki's hand. "How do you feel about that?"

That was the million-dollar question, wasn't it? How did she feel? This was so not a talk she wanted to have with her mother. When Nikki had originally found out she was pregnant, her parents had respected her privacy and not pushed for information regarding the father of her child. Now, however, there was no way to avoid the topic. With a sigh of resignation, she turned to her mother.

"I want to thank you, Mom, for being patient with me and never making me feel irresponsible about the choices I've made." Her mother smiled warmly at her and let Nikki continue. "I met Josh up at school right after graduation and fell in love with him at first sight." Meeting the older woman's eyes, she saw they were so similar to her own, she added, "Corny, right?"

Madeline chuckled softly. "That's how I felt about your father the first time I met him, so I don't think it's corny at all."

Nikki relaxed a little and shifted so she was facing her mother. "He wasn't a student there. He was just visiting someone for the weekend. One thing led to another, and we spent the night together." Bracing for some sort of backlash, she was surprised to see nothing but love and understanding in her mother's eyes. "When I woke up, I was embarrassed and ashamed I had actually gone to bed with someone I barely knew, and I sort of…I left while he was still sleeping."

"Understandable," her mother said.

"I was so confused because we had such an incredible connection. We talked for hours and had so much in common, and it was quite honestly a perfect night."

"Did you get in touch with him when you found out you were pregnant?"

Nikki shook her head. "I didn't even know his last name," she said with a hint of disgust. "I spent an incredible night with a wonderful man I thought I was in love with, and I didn't even know his last name! What kind of person does that make me?" She placed her hands over her face and began to sob. Admitting all of this to her mother was mortifying. She so desperately didn't want to lose her respect but hearing her own words out loud, describing what she had done, filled her with despair.

"Nicole, honey," her mother said as she pulled her daughter in for a hug. "Don't cry. You were swept away in the moment. Your father and I are not going to think any different of you because of this. We love you. We love Ellie. We're proud of the choices you've made, and the way you've made a wonderful life for the two of you. I know it hasn't been easy for you, but always know we love you."

Nikki looked up through tear-filled eyes and hugged her mom back. "Thank you," she whispered. "Thank you so much." She clutched her mom like a lifeline. It felt like a great weight had been lifted from her shoulders.

"So how did you find him after all this time?"

"You want to hear about a small world?" Her mom nodded. "He's actually David's brother. I met him when we all got together for dinner two weeks ago."

"No!" Madeline said with disbelief.

"I know. He walked into my house and I thought I had been struck by lightning. The weekend I met him, David and Denise were away. He never saw them, they never saw him, and none of us ever put two and two together."

"But they knew he had been there, didn't they?"

"Yes, but—"

"When you told them his name, didn't they make the connection?"

Oh, this was awkward. "Well, he wasn't honest with me about his name either."

Madeline frowned. "You mean besides not giving you his last name, he gave you a fake first name?" Silently, Nikki nodded. "Oh, dear. I don't think I like this man at all." She stood and looked down at her daughter. "What kind of man does that?"

"He doesn't know why he did it; he's apologized for it over and over. The thing is, he's great with Ellie. He's crazy about her, and she's crazy about him. How could I possibly deny them the opportunity to have a relationship?"

"I think you're being more than generous, all things considered." Her lips pursed with indignation. "Just how involved does he want to be?"

"After the wedding, we're going to work on a visitation schedule. As of now, he's been around on the weekends, and he calls her every night via Skype and reads her a story before bed."

"How touching," she replied, oozing sarcasm.

"Mom," Nikki began warningly. "I am trying to do the right thing here."

"I know you are, sweetheart. I just don't want

to see you get hurt. You've been through so much already, and it's not fair this...this man just swoops in and gets to be a dad after all you've sacrificed to take care of Ellie."

"I'm sure if he'd known..."

"Well, the fact is he didn't, Nicole, because he chose to be deceitful." Nikki couldn't even argue that fact with her. "Who's to say he hasn't done this sort of thing before? Or he won't do it again?"

"What are you talking about?"

"Going out of town, meeting women in bars or clubs, giving them a fake name, seducing them, and walking away? Does he travel a lot for his job?"

The conversation from the previous night jumped to her mind. "No," she lied. "Not really."

"Well, you need to be careful. Who knows how many other children he has out there he doesn't know about?"

That thought did not sit well with Nikki at all. She didn't think Josh would do such a thing again. After getting to know him, she didn't want to believe he'd be capable of it. The truth was, however, for as much as she knew about him, there was so much more she didn't know. Josh wasn't overly close with his family, and she even doubted David would be able to say with any certainty what Josh was and wasn't capable of.

"How do you feel about this man?" her mother asked quietly, interrupting her thoughts.

She couldn't meet her mother's eyes. Instead, Nikki fidgeted on the bed and plucked at an imaginary thread on the comforter.

"I see." Sighing loudly, she sat back down and reached for Nikki's hand. "Come on, let's eat some lunch and let me spend some time with Ellie. I don't get to see either of you often enough."

"Mom, what about—"

"I'll talk to your father about everything, so don't worry. And whatever you decide to do, Nicole, we are behind you one hundred percent. Don't ever doubt that."

Standing, they hugged again, and Madeline wiped a stray tear from her daughter's cheek and smiled. "Don't fret about all of this. Let's enjoy the weekend. Are you hungry?"

"Famished," Nikki admitted, walking hand in hand with her mother to the kitchen, feeling both elated and confused at the same time.

Although the weekend seemed to fly by, once Nikki caught sight of Josh waiting for her and Ellie in baggage claim, she felt like she had been away forever. Ellie was so excited to see her father, she jumped from Nikki's arms to get to him, talking nonstop all the way to his car.

They were on the road for less than five minutes when the child fell asleep. "Wow," Josh said with a chuckle. "That was something."

"She has two speeds: talking nonstop and sleeping."

"How was your visit with your parents? Did you have a good time?"

Nikki told him all about the weekend—opting to leave out the details about her conversation with her mother about him. "It was so rushed and I wish Ellie and I had more time with them, but they're planning to visit over the summer while I'm on break."

"That will be nice for all of you, I'm sure." He drove

along silently for a few minutes. “Did you, um…did you tell them, you know, about me?”

Ugh. So not the topic she wanted to talk about. “Ellie talked about you a lot, so she sort of paved the way to let them know you’re…here.” That didn’t sound good at all, did it? “My mom and I talked, and she’s happy for Ellie and the fact that you’re going to be involved in her life.” *Good, Nikki. Very politically correct answer.*

He nodded and decided not to probe any further. “I know it’s late, but did you have a chance to eat dinner yet?”

“We ate at the airport while we were waiting for our flight and then we snacked on the plane, so we’re good. How about you? Have you eaten?”

He shook his head. “I wasn’t sure what you were doing and thought we’d get to have dinner together.”

“Oh, Josh—”

“No big deal,” he said to reassure her. “If it’s okay with you, I’ll grab something from a drive-thru on the way and eat it at your place.”

“That’s fine,” she said, relaxing. “Actually, I probably wouldn’t mind a snack.”

Josh detoured slightly and picked up their food, and they were back at Nikki’s in no time. With Ellie still asleep, Nikki carried her in and changed her for bed while Josh took care of the food and luggage. They met up in the living room fifteen minutes later, where he’d set up their dinner on the coffee table.

“It is so exhausting to travel with a child,” Nikki said as she collapsed on the sofa. “It’s hard to believe someone so small creates so much chaos.”

“Wasn’t she good for you?”

Nikki reached for a french fry. "Ellie's always good. It's just she has a lot of energy and is exceptionally curious. There is no sitting and waiting quietly for the flight, it's walking around and talking to people, and getting snacks and drinks, and bathroom breaks…it's exhausting."

He laughed. "I know you'll think I'm crazy, but I hope to experience all of that for myself sometime."

"You're right. I do think you're crazy." Her tone was light, and she smiled at him. They ate for several minutes in companionable silence.

"You mentioned you're going to be traveling a bit over the next couple of weeks. Where do you have to be tomorrow?"

"Actually, I'm going to be heading out toward my parents in Charlotte. I'll probably spend the night there and then I have another meeting over in the RTP area. That one should take a couple of days."

"That's not too far from here," she said.

Taking a sip of soda, he paused. "Actually, I was wondering if you'd mind if I stayed here while those meetings are going on. I promise not to disrupt your lives too much. I know you've got school all week, but we'll probably be leaving at the same time in the morning, and I should be back here by six each night. We could have dinner together, and I'd get to spend some extra time with Ellie before I head out on the other trips."

It would have been so easy to just say yes, but unfortunately Nikki feared that letting him stay for more than a night would only confuse Ellie. She shared her concerns with him and was surprised when he seemed to agree. "I'm sorry. I didn't even think about it like that."

"She's too young to understand our…situation,"

Nikki said carefully. "I don't want her getting used to having you here and then being upset when you're not. Does that make sense?"

He nodded. "In my head it does, but my heart is saying I want to spend time with the two of you. I know we still have a lot to discuss with our schedules, but this is all so new, and I've missed so much. What if I explained to her how I live someplace else and I'm just here visiting like her grandmother and grandfather? What do you think?"

It sounded logical, and she really did want him to stay for her own selfish reasons. If he stayed over, they'd get to be together. Spend time together. Sleep together. She sighed. "I guess we'll never know how she'll react unless we try."

Josh frowned. "I was kind of hoping for a little more enthusiasm on your part than that," he grumbled.

Looking at the empty Styrofoam food containers around them, she stood. Without a word, she began cleaning everything up. On her way back to the living room, she began turning off the lights. By the time she was standing beside Josh, he looked confused. Holding out a hand to him, she gave him a sexy grin.

"I was saving the enthusiasm for behind closed doors." Coming to his feet, Josh took her hand and smiled as she led the way up the stairs to her room. True to her word, once the door was closed, she spent hours showing her enthusiasm.

For four days, Nikki caught a glimpse of what it would be like for them to live together as a family. Although

Josh was away Monday night, the rest of the time he stayed with them. Ellie was thrilled, and if Nikki allowed herself to be honest, she was too.

She and Ellie normally arrived at home a little before five and had time together before Josh arrived at six. They ate dinners together, played games, read books, and shared in Ellie's bedtime routine. It was perfect.

It was a little too perfect.

Hating that she had such a pessimistic side, Nikki kept waiting for something to happen, for some bad side to come through, for him to lose his patience with Ellie, but he never did. He helped her around the house, contributed to the groceries, and all in all, was the perfect houseguest.

And the nights?

She almost had to turn a hose on herself when she thought about how the nights were. The man was certainly thorough in everything he did, and by the time Nikki fell asleep at night, she felt completely sated and cherished. It was like living in a dream world.

On Friday morning, Josh packed up as she and Ellie were getting ready. "I'll be in Virginia until Monday," he was saying. "My schedule is pretty tight so I may not Skype, but I promise to call."

"If you're busy, Josh, Ellie will understand," Nikki said as she put breakfast on the table.

"I don't want her to have to understand, Nicole. I want her to know I'm always going to be there for her, even if I'm not right here with her."

His words were sweet, and Nikki knew he was being sincere. "All I'm saying is if you really can't make the call at your usual time, don't freak out."

Easy for her to say, Josh thought; he doubted Nicole ever let their daughter down. Trying to find the balance between work and his personal life was a juggling act he was having a hard time adapting to. For years, he'd had no one to answer to but himself, and now that he had Ellie and Nicole to think about, he didn't want to disappoint anyone.

"I'm going to do all I can to make sure it doesn't come to that, but you have my cell phone number. If she wants to talk to me and I haven't called, promise me you'll call."

"Josh—"

"Nicole," he interrupted. "Promise me."

She rolled her eyes and laughed. "Fine, fine, I promise."

They enjoyed a hurried breakfast together, and as they filed out the door and said their good-byes, Josh felt as though he was leaving a little piece of his heart behind.

~

Sunday night was a nightmare. Nikki couldn't remember the last time her daughter had had such a meltdown, but this one was like nothing she had ever seen.

"I want to see Daddy now!" the child wailed as she kicked a pile of toys around the room, screaming at the top of her lungs.

Nikki had no idea what had prompted the meltdown—the rest of the weekend had gone fine. Josh had called the previous two nights, just like he always did, and although he was late with that night's call, Ellie's reaction was just over the top. "Daddy is away right now, El, remember?"

"I want to see Daddy!" she chanted as she now started to stomp around the room.

Looking at the clock, Nikki saw it was a little past Ellie's bedtime. Maybe it wouldn't be such a bad thing to call Josh and let him at least say good night to her. She knew he was going straight back to Wilmington tomorrow, but he had mentioned being back with them by Thursday for the rehearsal dinner Friday night and for David and Denise's wedding on Saturday.

Hating that she was caving in to her daughter's demands, she reached for the phone and dialed Josh's number. By the fourth ring, she was beginning to think he wasn't going to answer; maybe he was with a potential client or something. She was just about to tell Ellie they would try again in a few minutes when a voice came on the line.

A female voice.

"Hello? Is someone there?"

Nikki was too stunned to speak. In the background, she heard music and laughter, and in that instant, she felt sick. She turned her head toward Ellie and knew no matter what, she wouldn't let her daughter down. Clearing her throat, she finally forced herself to speak. "Yes, I'm looking for Josh Masterson."

"Oh, hang on one minute," the woman said. "He's a little busy."

Yeah, I'll bet, Nikki thought. Less than a minute later, Josh came on the line. "Nicole?"

"Sorry to interrupt," she said curtly, "but Ellie wanted to talk to you and it was getting late."

"Crap," he hissed. "Is it that late already?" He paused. "Sorry about that. How is she?"

Rather than answer, she handed the phone to Ellie and let her talk. What the hell had she been thinking? How was it she had gotten swept up in the fantasy of them having a life together when all she really knew of him was he was someone who lied? Her mother had been right; for all she knew, the woman who answered the phone could be just as stupid as Nikki had been.

Well, she wasn't going to be anymore.

With a bright smile on her face, Ellie twirled over to her and handed her the phone before scampering up the steps to her room. Although she didn't want to talk to Josh, she couldn't simply hang up. She must have been taking too long to speak because she heard Josh say her name. "Thank you for talking with her. She calmed down and is getting ready for bed."

"I'm sorry I didn't call earlier. I hate that she got upset."

"Well, better she learn now that things won't always go her way."

"What is that supposed to mean?" he asked, suddenly noticing her tone of voice.

"Nothing. Never mind. Look, it's late and I've got to get her to bed, and I've got papers to grade."

"Nicole? What's going on? Are you mad at me?"

Ding, ding, ding! Someone should give the man a prize! "Why? Should I be?" she asked innocently.

"I don't know," he said slowly. "You just seem like you're upset."

"You try dealing with a two-year-old having a meltdown and then we'll see how you sound." He made to speak again, but she cut him off. "I really need to go. We'll talk to you tomorrow night." She hung up the phone and shut it off just in case he wanted to call back.

She knew she'd have to deal with him eventually, but for tonight, she just wanted to be angry.

And hurt.

Walking up the stairs, she got Ellie ready for bed before going to her room and sitting down at her desk to grade the last of her papers and prepare her lessons for the final week of school. She had been looking forward to the upcoming summer vacation, looking forward to taking the time to go to Wilmington and see where Josh lived. Now, all that lay ahead of her was dread. How was she supposed to deal with him at the wedding? Hell, how was she supposed to deal with him, period? They had yet to talk about a visitation plan, and Nikki had thought… Well, she had thought it wasn't going to be necessary because they were wordlessly working toward blending their lives a little more.

Hating that it wasn't actually going to happen, she did her best just to remember to breathe and focus on all the good in her life. She and Ellie had managed just fine before Josh came into their lives, and Nikki had no doubt they'd be fine again with a lot less of him there.

If only her heart didn't ache so much at the thought of it.

Chapter 8

SHE HAD PURPOSELY UNPLUGGED THE COMPUTER, AND IF she'd had her way, Nikki would have unplugged the house phone and turned off her cell phone too, but she wasn't ready to risk another meltdown from her daughter like the one the night before.

Right on schedule, the house phone rang and she let Ellie answer it herself. Doing her best to keep busy and not listen to their conversation, she nearly jumped out of her skin when Ellie came up behind her. "Daddy wants you!" she said and handed the phone to Nikki before walking away.

What was she supposed to say? How was she supposed to let him know she thought he was the lowest form of life and she wished he'd never come back into their lives? She looked over at where Ellie was playing and knew that wasn't the complete truth. If nothing else, her daughter deserved a father.

She just wished it were a father who knew how to keep it in his pants.

"Nicole? Are you there?"

"What? Oh, sorry. I was distracted."

"How are you?" he asked in a way that used to make her smile. "How was school today?"

"The last week is always chaotic. The kids know summer vacation is right around the corner, so their attention span is even shorter."

He chuckled. "I remember those days well. So listen, I was thinking maybe after the wedding, you and Ellie could come and spend the week here with me. I think it would be a nice break after all the wedding stuff, and you can relax after a full school year and all. What do you think?"

She sighed and walked to where she was out of Ellie's hearing but could still keep an eye on her. "I appreciate the invitation, Josh, but I don't think it's a good idea."

He was stunned. "May I ask why?"

"I've been doing some thinking and lines are getting blurred here. Neither of us is looking to really get involved beyond being co-parents, and after Ellie's temper tantrum last night, well…it just confirmed what I had thought last week. She's confused. She doesn't understand why you're here one day and gone the next. It's too disruptive to the way things have been. I've made up a calendar of what I think would be the best way for us to handle visitations. You'll see her two weekends a month and we'll divide holidays. I think that's fair."

"*Fair?* Dammit, Nicole, what's going on? You're talking like I'm a stranger. I don't want visitation only with my daughter. I want to share custody of her. I want us all to be together! I thought you understood that!" His voice rose with each word, and he felt like he had been sucker punched. Where had all of this come from?

"I'm sorry if I led you to believe it was going to go that way. After having a couple of days to think about it, I realized we don't really know each other, and it's crazy to try and force the whole family thing." She swallowed the lump in her throat. "It's not what I want."

Josh was silent for so long, Nikki had to wonder if

he was even still there. "I don't believe that," he finally said. "We were fine on Friday, Nicole. What changed? Tell me what I did, for crying out loud!"

"Let me ask you something," she said, her patience at an end. "Three years ago when we met, if your cell phone had rung, would it have been okay for me to answer it? I mean, what if it were Erin on the line?"

"What? What are you talking about?"

"Whoever it was who answered your phone last night when I called made me realize I don't really know you, and what I do know, I can't trust."

"Who? Oh, no, Nicole. It's not what you think. I was out to dinner with the head of another construction company. It was him and his wife. Jack and I were talking to the owner of the restaurant because Jack had been the builder and he wanted to introduce us. That's all."

"Right. And that woman, Jack's wife, just thought it was completely appropriate for her to answer your phone?" God, she hated sounding like a jealous idiot.

"I don't know why she answered the damn phone, but I'm telling you that's who she was. I don't understand what the big deal is."

"The big deal is I don't trust you," she said quickly before she could talk herself out of it. "You lied to me when we met, not only about your name but about the fact that you were engaged to somebody else. For all I know, this is a game you play. You travel on business and sleep with random women. For all I know, Ellie isn't even your only child." Her tone was calm, but her heart was racing.

"*What?*" he roared. "Why would you even think that? Ever since I saw you again, I have been nothing but honest with you! I know the way we started out wasn't ideal, but…I have no excuse for it. It was the only time in my life I've ever done anything like that. You have to believe me."

She wanted to—she really, really wanted to. But she couldn't. "I'm sorry," she said sadly. "But I can't. Every time you go away, travel for business, I'm going to wonder. I don't want to live like that, and I certainly don't want my daughter influenced by that."

"What are you saying?" he asked gruffly.

"I'm saying I respect your position as Ellie's father. I won't stand in the way of the two of you having a relationship, but you and I…" She stopped and took a deep breath. "There is no more you and I. I never should have started anything with you, and I'm sorry I did."

"You're sure about this?"

She nodded because she couldn't make herself speak. He prompted her again. "I am."

He let out a breath. "Email me the calendar, and I'll get back to you," was all he said before hanging up the phone.

There. She'd done it. It was the right thing to do—wasn't it?

By Thursday, Nikki felt even more miserable than she'd thought possible. Josh called faithfully every night, but kept his conversations purely with Ellie. On the night of the first call, she'd taken the phone from Ellie and, as was the ritual, she came on the line to say hello and was greeted with dead air. When the same pattern followed night after night, she just hung up the phone when Ellie was through talking.

There was a part of her that wanted to dwell on the whole thing, but there was so much going on with the last day of school and the rehearsal dinner and the wedding on Saturday. There were so many things she was expected to put a cheery smile on for that Nikki knew she had to do everything in her power to force that final conversation with Josh from her mind and move on. She'd have to see him soon enough.

Soon enough turned out to be Friday night at the wedding rehearsal. Everyone went through the motions of their roles at church—you stand there, you hold this, blah, blah, blah. And the sight of Josh at the end of the aisle standing next to David sent her heart rate soaring. If anything, he looked even more handsome than she'd remembered, and she had to remind herself he wasn't the man for her.

Ellie was the flower girl, and she walked ahead of Nikki down the long aisle. Josh looked full of fatherly pride as he watched his daughter walk toward him. He never looked at Nikki. Of course, she couldn't be completely certain, because she was doing her best not to look at him either.

Standing up by the altar, the pastor explained how the ceremony would go. Ellie went to sit next to the Mastersons during the explanation, which left just Nikki, Josh, David, and Denise standing there.

"Okay, then you'll turn and face your guests"—the pastor indicated to the bride and groom with a wave of his arms—"and walk up the aisle followed by your attendants. Will the flower girl be walking with you,

Miss Taylor, or her grandparents?" All eyes turned to Nikki as if she had this all worked out in her head already. Biting her bottom lip, she paused.

"The flower girl will walk with her mother and me," Josh said instead of waiting for Nikki's answer. He had not once even looked in her direction. Soon, they had Ellie join them and Josh picked her up before taking Nikki's arm and placing it through his so they could follow the bride and groom.

He seemed to take his time walking up the aisle, and several times Nikki had to slow her steps. Her knees felt weak and she was having a hard time with his closeness. The dress she had chosen to wear that night was in no way meant to entice Josh, but when his body brushed against hers, the fabric irritated her skin and made her achingly aware of him. With a groan, she continued to walk.

"Everything all right?" he asked indifferently out of the corner of his mouth.

"Just peachy," she replied, plastering a fake smile on her face as they walked by his parents.

Josh didn't speak another word to her until they were seated beside each other at the rehearsal dinner, which was held at a quaint little Italian restaurant not far from the church. For a Friday night, it was amazingly empty, Nikki thought, and then found out the Mastersons had reserved the entire place for dinner. Had there been an enormous bridal party, Nikki could have been on board with their way of thinking, but with just the parents, her and Ellie, Josh, David, and Denise, it seemed a bit extravagant.

Josh's leg brushed against hers under the table,

and she thought about shifting her position but didn't want to give him the satisfaction of knowing his touch affected her at all. All eyes turned to David as he stood to propose a toast to his bride-to-be.

For all Nikki knew, it was a very romantic speech filled with promises of eternal love. All her mind could register, however, was the citrusy cologne wafting her way from the man beside her. Shaking her head and focusing her attention back on David, she almost didn't realize Josh's hand had come to rest on the back of her chair. If she leaned back ever so slightly, she could make "accidental" contact. Closing her eyes and taking a deep breath, she willed herself to stay in control.

Apparently David's speech ended—Nikki noticed he was no longer standing—and then it was Tyler Masterson's turn to get up and wax poetic about the soon-to-be newlyweds. Try as she might, Nikki just couldn't force herself to hear a word. If anyone looked at her, they probably thought she was soaking up every syllable, but the only thing she was soaking up was a fantasy about her and Josh sneaking off to an isolated corner of the restaurant and letting their hands and mouths run free.

Where the heck had that even come from? What was it about this man she couldn't shake? He made her weak and needy, and ever since she had pushed him away, nothing had felt right. Even more than she had been three years ago. Ellie had picked up on her mood, and the two of them had been wandering around in a funk all week.

"To the bride and groom!" Tyler beamed, raising his glass in a toast. Everyone echoed the sentiment, and while Nikki raised her glass with the rest of them, she took only a token sip of her champagne. She didn't particularly care for the stuff, and she was driving after the dinner.

"Something wrong with your drink?" Josh asked casually.

"I'm not much of a drinker," she admitted quietly, feeling suddenly shy talking with him.

"Oh." He turned his attention back to the crowd around the table before rising to make his own speech. Suddenly, Nikki was all ears. She didn't look up as he stood, instead keeping her focus on her hands, twisting an innocent cloth napkin in her lap.

Clearing his throat, Josh began. "I knew the moment David brought Denise home she was the woman he was going to marry. It was written all over his face whenever he looked at her or even talked about her." The happy couple exchanged goofy smiles and then turned their attention back to Josh. "I envy you, little brother, for finding the woman you love and having her love you back." Without conscious thought, Josh's hand had settled on Nikki's shoulder, his fingers tracing lazy circles on the silky skin exposed from her sleeveless dress.

"I want to thank you for being there and taking such good care of Ellie for me." His eyes began to well up. "It makes me feel so much better knowing even though I wasn't there for her, her Uncle David and Aunt Denise were." He gently squeezed Nikki's shoulder and she closed her eyes painfully. "I wish you two all the happiness in the world." He raised his glass to them and once again everyone toasted with him.

It occurred to him where his hand was, and he

quickly removed it as if he'd been burned. Placing his glass down on the table with disregard, he stalked out of the room. Nikki stared after him and wondered if she should follow. The arrival of their food stopped her, and she helped Ellie with her plate before trying to eat her own dinner.

There was so much noise and commotion around the table that Nikki didn't notice Josh's return some minutes later. The heat of his body so close to hers told her he was there. She turned to look at him, her eyes full of questions he refused to answer. It didn't take long for her to lower her eyes and turn away. The rest of her meal lost its appeal, and she sat silently waiting for the time when she could leave.

After the dessert dishes were cleared away, Denise thanked everyone for coming and shrieked with delight that tomorrow was almost here and she'd finally get to be Mrs. David Masterson. Nikki couldn't help but smile at her friend's happiness. What must it feel like to be in love and secure?

Looking around the restaurant, she noticed that Laura now held Ellie. Collecting their few belongings, Nikki crossed the room to claim her sleepy child. "She's so well behaved in all this chaos," Laura said as she hugged Ellie gently to her. "Grandma was very impressed."

"Thank you, Laura," Nikki said as she took her daughter into her arms. "But if I don't get her home and in bed soon, I'm not so sure she'll be cooperative tomorrow. We'll see you at the church." Turning to walk away, she was surprised to feel a hand on her arm.

Laura looked at her with sympathetic eyes. "I know it's none of my business, but..." She bit her lip and contemplated her next question. "Is everything all right with you and Josh? You both seemed rather distracted this evening."

Sighing, Nikki said, "It's just complicated right now. We haven't settled on a visitation schedule, and between his job and the fact that Ellie and I were already committed to certain things, well…this is just going to take some time and getting used to, that's all."

Laura's eyes softened and she accepted Nikki's words. "Take that sweet girl home and put her to bed. We'll see you tomorrow, Nicole. Have a good night." She leaned in and gave Nikki a kiss on the cheek.

Tears burned in Nikki's throat and she called out a blanket good-bye to everyone as she rushed for the door, hoping no one would notice her emotional state. She had Ellie buckled into her car seat and was walking around to the driver's side when she heard footsteps approaching. She turned to see David walking toward her, his expression painfully serious.

He pulled her into his embrace without a word and Nikki's resolve crumbled. He rubbed his hand up and down her back until her sobs quieted. When she was able to compose herself, she looked up at him and smiled weakly.

"Sometimes it helps to have a shoulder to cry on," he said softly.

"How did you know that's what I needed?"

"I know you better than you think, Nikki. Denise and I both noticed something seemed off, and she asked me to make sure you were all right." Raking a hand through his hair, he looked around. "If that brother of mine had any sense, he'd be out here with you right now."

"David," Nikki warned, "I don't want this situation with me and Josh to come between the two of you. Please. Especially not the night before your wedding. Go back inside and celebrate some more. Normally I'd love to stay, but Ellie's exhausted and I want her at her best for you tomorrow."

David pulled her into his embrace again. "Is there anything I can do, Nik?"

She pulled back and shook her head. "I wish there were. I really do. This is something I have to work out on my own." She stood on tiptoes and kissed him soundly on the cheek. "I'll see you tomorrow, okay?"

He nodded and held the door for her as she climbed into the car. "We worry about you. Don't hesitate to call if you need anything."

"Thank you, but right now all I need is to get home." David closed the door and watched her drive away. Standing in the middle of the parking lot, he turned and faced the restaurant and saw Josh standing in the entryway, his expression pained.

In three long strides, David stood nose to nose with him. "If you ever do anything to make her look the way she did tonight ever again, you'll have me to deal with," David said menacingly. "And believe me, big brother, I'd enjoy taking you down." Without waiting for a reply, David stormed back into the restaurant and swiftly sought out his fiancée, pulling her into his embrace.

The air outside was so still it was stifling. Josh contemplated getting in his car and going to Nikki's. Loosening his tie, he lifted his eyes heavenward as if looking for a sign. How could he possibly make this situation any worse than it already was? He thought about how he'd felt when Nicole had started walking down the aisle toward him earlier today. In a flash, he had imagined it was their wedding day, and he could see her walking toward him in a white silk gown that flowed all around her as she walked. He could even picture his daughter walking with her in a miniature version of the dress.

Emotions welled up in his throat and nearly choked him. Josh had felt so smug and confident he could just charm his way back into her bed, her life, her future, he hadn't counted on one thing—his own feelings for her. It had been painful to stand with her and not touch her. *Be honest with yourself: you found every excuse to touch her. It just wasn't enough.* Taking her arm and walking up the aisle had merely stoked the fantasy in his head. Sitting next to her at dinner had him itch to reach under the table and hold her hand, caress her thigh as it pressed against his.

He deserved to rot in hell for all the ways he had behaved poorly since meeting Nicole. But someday very soon, he would repent and ask—no, beg—for her forgiveness. It was more than he really deserved, just as it was more than he deserved to have her love him. He wanted both. He craved it like he craved his next breath.

When she had told him she didn't want a future with him, it had hit him hard; his reaction to her words had been a knee-jerk one. He never should have just given up, never should have just walked away. It may have only been five days, but it felt like so much more, and instead of doing everything in his power to prove her wrong, to show her he wasn't the man she thought him to be, he'd pouted. True, he'd put the last several days to good use—not that anyone would know it.

And it pretty much confirmed what a grade-A jerk he was. No wonder she didn't trust him.

He needed to show her who he really was; he was a man who was honest and faithful. A man who was in love with one woman and one woman only, and had been for more than three years. Soon there would be no leaving parties separately, no going to separate houses in different cities. They'd go home together.

Josh clung to that thought as he hung his head and turned to go back into the party to say good night to his family. He was staying at David's but had his own key, so he didn't have to wait for his brother. There was no need for him to hang around and drag everyone down with his foul mood.

An hour later, he was lying alone in David's guest bedroom, completely restless. A month ago, he had been fine with the direction of his life. His business was more successful than he could have ever imagined, he traveled, had good friends, and was content. But now, as he lay there in the solitude of the double bed, he came to the grim realization that his life wasn't as great as he'd led himself to believe.

All these years, Josh had convinced himself he had all he needed to be happy. After having Nicole and Ellie in his life, he knew what he'd felt before was all a lie. He had merely been going through the motions. With Nicole and Ellie, Josh could see the fulfillment that was elusive at the moment.

Having the freedom to come and go as he pleased as he had for years now gave him no pleasure. Those few short days he had stayed at Nicole's house had showed him what real pleasure could be. He wanted someone to come home to, someone to go places with him.

Not just someone. He wanted Nicole.

Frowning, he remembered how she'd looked as she left the restaurant tonight—the sadness filling her blue eyes. He had watched her leave and tried to remain detached, but after spotting his brother going after her, he had to see for himself what was going on. Watching her cry on David's shoulder had made his gut clench. David's reaction to Nikki's feelings wasn't surprising—a man would have to have ice running through his veins not to want to protect her from all the sadness in the world. What irritated him more than anything was that it was David who thought to go and comfort her.

Because Josh had been the one to cause her so much pain.

How could a man who was responsible for a multimillion-dollar company be so completely ignorant about how to handle a relationship with the woman he loved? Rolling to his side, he punched the pillow and tried to clear his mind of the image of Nicole crying. His entire body ached with the need to go to her. A glance at the clock showed it was after midnight. There was no way he could just go over there now; it was too late.

The thought of spending the entire day with her tomorrow made him smile sadly. Maybe, somehow, he'd be able to show her how sorry he was, prove to her he loved her and was the only man for her.

He could only hope he wasn't too late.

Chapter 9

NIKKI KNEW SHE WAS IN SERIOUS TROUBLE BY THE time the bridal party exited the church. From the moment of their arrival, Josh had watched her like a hawk. It was a complete 180-degree turn from the cold indifference he had been treating her to for the last week. True, it was at her own request, but she hadn't thought he'd go to such extremes.

At any given point in the ceremony, she could look up and find his smoldering gaze on her. Several times, that look had almost made her knees buckle with its intensity. When David and Denise faced their guests for the first time as husband and wife and headed up the aisle, Josh didn't even wait for Nikki to move before walking over to her and Ellie and claiming them both for the walk to the receiving line. He never said a word to her, but his eyes and his body language were speaking to her in ways that made her want to run for cover.

His fingers gently skimmed the sensitive skin of her upper arm and just as the first of the guests was about to greet them, Josh leaned in close to Nikki's ear and whispered, "You look absolutely beautiful today, Nicole. Denise doesn't hold a candle to you." His mouth lingered just a wee bit longer and his hot breath sent a shiver down her spine. She felt color creep into her cheeks as she averted her eyes.

Before she could even take a breath, wedding guests

were upon them. Out of the corner of her eye, she saw Josh smirk at her flustered state. What was he up to? Why the sudden turnaround? And today of all days!

Plastering her most dazzling smile on her face, Nikki went about greeting everyone who came her way. Josh made sure he introduced her to each and every one of them while placing his hand on the small of her back. If she had been able to see back there, she knew she'd have found his handprint permanently embedded in her skin.

It wasn't much better on the limo ride to take pictures. The driver had installed Ellie's car seat, and luckily only left room for Nikki to be on one side of her while Josh was on the other. Relieved to be free of his touch for at least a brief time, she very nearly jumped out of her skin when Josh placed his arm across the back of the leather seat and began to caress her shoulder while he spoke to Ellie. If it weren't completely inappropriate, she would have screamed in frustration. Unfortunately, the bride and groom only had eyes for each other, which meant Nikki was on her own.

"Ellie looks ready to drop," Josh said quietly as he looked down at his daughter, who was trying valiantly to keep her eyes open. "Will she be all right if we let her take a short nap?"

"Yes," she said casually, keeping her eyes trained out the window, knowing full well Ellie just naturally dozed in the car no matter where they went. Josh's long fingers found their way to the nape of her neck and began tracing tantalizing circles until she had no choice but to look at him. The pent-up frustration was just about to fly when Denise spoke to them.

"We're heading over toward the seminary to take some pictures in their gardens and then we'll go and hang out at the hotel before the reception, okay?"

Sure, like we have a choice, Nikki thought to herself. "That sounds fine," she finally answered.

"Our parents are meeting us for pictures as well. We thought it would be nice to have some family pictures taken in the garden. Don't you think it'll be lovely, Nik?"

"Absolutely." She smiled for her friends, but her heart and mind were elsewhere, focused on the hand that was quietly awakening every cell in her body.

Soon, the large luxury car was parked and the driver was helping Denise out. David emerged next and Nikki handed Ellie to him. Josh climbed out and offered his hand to assist Nikki. Groaning with frustration, she graciously accepted his help and emerged from the car. The champagne-colored silk of her dress shone brightly in the sunlight. The straight, full-length skirt would have been awkward to move in had it not been for the long slit along the side. Almost the entire length of her leg was exposed as she exited the limo, and she watched as Josh swallowed hard at the sight of her.

Within minutes, the photographer was posing everyone and snapping away. For the bridal party shots, Josh continuously had his hands on her, gently, lovingly. Nikki fought hard against the urge to lean back into him when standing in the blazing sun started to feel overwhelming.

When both sets of parents arrived for the family shots, Nikki discreetly stepped aside while the photographer situated everyone.

"Wait!" Josh said impatiently. "Nicole, come stand with me."

Nervously, Nikki stared at him, unsure of what to do. When she didn't move, he walked over to her.

"What's the problem?" he asked casually.

"These are family shots."

"And?"

She rolled her eyes with annoyance. Why was he making her spell everything out? "Ellie is in the pictures. I don't need to be."

"I want you to be in the pictures, Nicole. You're family." His words were so soft; they warmed her already-heated skin.

Staring at him with sympathetic eyes, she said, "No, I'm not. Please go and stand with your folks so we can get out of the oppressive sun." It pained her to say it, but it was the truth. She would forever be bonded to this group through Ellie, but that did not make her family.

"Sir?" the photography inquired, anxious to finish up the group photos while the sun was at its peak.

"Please…" Josh began as he reached a hand out to hers.

"Oh, for heaven's sake, Nik, get your butt in the picture so we can be done with it!" David shouted. "This tie is about to choke me, and as much as I love you, I will hurt you if you continue to prolong my misery!" His face was full of mischief and Nikki took Josh's hand and let herself be positioned into the family portrait.

It was a nice feeling.

The hotel was beautiful.

The reception was magnificent.

The food was absolutely decadent.

The migraine jackhammering in her head was going to be the death of her.

All afternoon, Nikki had made her rounds throughout the room with Josh plastered to her side while he carried Ellie to meet even more members of his family. They had danced together, posed for even more pictures, and now sat shoulder to shoulder at the head table. But now, tears were beginning to form from the pain, and if she didn't get a few minutes of peace and quiet away from Josh, she knew she'd surely die.

Grateful for a brief interruption from one of Josh's cousins, Nikki escaped from the table and walked along the outskirts of the room to get to the ladies' room. There was a small sitting area in there, and once inside, she wet a cloth and molded it to her head as she collapsed in one of the plush chairs.

Josh's father had been toting Ellie around, so Nikki knew she had a few minutes to relax. Josh was just adding to her pain. Her skin tingled all over from his constant touching, and he never let on there was anything inappropriate about it. To the 150 people in the other room, they were a couple crazy about one another. While he had made no attempt to kiss her or have any kind of private conversations with her, his mere presence was driving her crazy!

The cool cloth felt wonderful, and she fished into the bottom of her tiny purse for a couple of ibuprofen to bring the pain down to a dull roar. Just a few more minutes and…

"Excuse me, Nicole?" Nikki looked up from under the cloth to see an elderly woman whom she had been introduced to earlier, Josh's Aunt Marie, standing over her.

"Yes?" Nikki replied weakly.

"I'm so sorry to bother you, dear, but Josh is a nervous wreck out there looking for you. He sent me in here to make sure you were okay. Can I get you anything?"

Josh was a nervous wreck? He was concerned about her? Or was he just at a loss at how to perform without her by his side? Better to keep that comment to herself. "Tell him I'll be out in a minute, please," she said with a brief smile, and the woman reached out and cupped Nicole's cheek.

"He loves you so much, you know." It was a statement of fact, not a question or even an observation. At Nikki's stunned expression, the redheaded woman went on. "It's written all over his face. He's been pacing that hallway like a madman. I thought he was going to barge in here on his own, but I scolded him and told him he'd better behave himself." She chuckled and so did Nikki. Even though it hurt. "I'll see you back inside, dear."

"Thanks," Nikki managed to say as she slowly rose from the chair. A glance in the mirror showed her complexion was pale and her eyes looked bloodshot—all the usual reactions to a migraine. Walking gingerly, she made her way to the door and pulled it open carefully. Josh took one look at her and scooped her up in his arms, carrying her over to a small alcove where there was soft lighting and a sofa.

"Are you all right?" he asked nervously, scanning her face.

If her head hadn't hurt so much, she'd have actually laughed. "I've got a bit of a migraine. As soon as David and Dee leave, I'm out the door." Her voice was small and shallow, and unable to help herself, she completely relaxed into his embrace.

"We'll leave right now. I'll take you and Ellie home and—"

"Shh… Not so loud. I want to stay and see them off, Josh. I'll be fine in a little while. That's why I went to the ladies' room, to have some quiet and try to relax. I don't have my prescription with me because I don't get these very often. All I had was some ibuprofen."

"Did it help?"

"Not really."

"Is there anything I can do? Anything I can get for you?"

She shook her head. "I just need to relax. Most of the time, these headaches are brought on by tension."

"What caused you to be tense today?" His words were spoken softly, but they allowed the irritation she had felt toward him all day to unleash.

"What caused my tension?" she asked incredulously. "Where do I even begin?" He cocked an eyebrow at her. "You haven't left me alone all day!" She climbed off his lap and carefully stood up. "Everywhere I go, there you are, introducing me to someone, putting your hands on me somewhere. I mean, for crying out loud, I was beginning to feel claustrophobic!"

Josh stared at her. "Excuse me?"

"You didn't acknowledge me all week and then—"

"I was doing what you asked!" he shouted as he stood to face her.

Nikki winced with pain at the sound of his voice

and immediately began to rub her temples. Heedless of whether she wanted him there or not, Josh stepped forward, moved her hands, and took over. "Shh… Just relax," he whispered.

She placed her hands over his as her eyes closed. "I can't do this with you anymore. It's all just…too much." Ignoring her, he continued to massage her temples with great care. Nikki felt the tension ebb from her weary body. "I need to go back inside. Ellie—"

"Is being taken care of," he interrupted. "My parents are watching her and loving every minute of it." He led her back over to the sofa and sat them both down. He positioned them so her back was to his chest as he continued his massage. "I agree with you. I can't do this anymore either."

She stiffened against him and made to turn around, but he stopped her.

"I owe you an apology," he began quietly. "I'm sorry I made you feel like you couldn't trust me. I know you have no reason to, not with my track record, but I want you to know you can. When I met you, my whole life changed. If I could, I would go back and tell you the truth about everything—my name, Erin, all of it. I had no idea you were going to be…the one."

This time when she tried to sit up, Josh didn't stop her. "What?" she asked with trembling lips.

"You're the one, Nicole," he said softly, his eyes meeting hers. "When I woke up the next morning and you were gone, I went crazy trying to find you. I didn't even know where to begin to look. And then, last month, when I came to your house? I couldn't believe my good fortune. I was getting a second chance. I should have been honest with you that first night when I came back and told you I loved you. I had been looking for you. Waiting for you. There is no other woman for me, Nicole. Not now. Not ever. It's you."

Her eyes welled with tears. "I don't know how to believe you." The honest admission hurt for her to even say, and when she saw understanding in his eyes, she felt her first glimmer of hope.

Taking her hands in his, he pulled her close. "Let me tell you what I've been up to," he began. "First, those meetings in RTP? Those were with real estate agents. I'm moving my business here."

"But what about—?"

"Shh," he interrupted. "After we spoke Monday night, I sort of went a little crazy. I knew I had already gotten the ball rolling with moving the business, but I knew it wasn't enough. So I did a little restructuring and promoted two of my guys. They'll be handling most of the traveling from now on. I may still have to go to a job site from time to time, but if I do, then I want you and Ellie with me."

"Josh, that wasn't—"

"Hear me out." He placed one finger on her lips. "I'd like to keep the house in Wilmington because it's right on the beach and I'd love for us to have a place to go just to get away, but if you'd like to pick one of your own, I can sell it."

"What are you saying?"

He smiled as he leaned forward and placed a gentle kiss on her forehead. "What I'm saying is I love you. I want a life with you. I want to be there every day for you and Ellie. I want us to have more babies, and I want to be there to see them grow. I love you, Nicole."

"Oh my…"

"I didn't plan on doing this today," he said as he shifted and dropped to one knee on the floor in front of her. "And I don't have your ring with me; it's back at David's." He winked. "But, Nicole Taylor, I want you to be my wife. I love you, and I want to spend every day of my life with you. Will you marry me?"

"Josh, this is crazy," she said as tears freely began to fall. "We barely know each other."

"I knew everything I needed to know about you three years ago. Coming here and finding you again and seeing the way you have loved and cared for our daughter? That just confirmed it all. You are everything I've ever wanted, all I ever needed."

"Me?" she mouthed, unable to speak.

He nodded. "Always."

She took a moment to let it sink in. He loved her. He'd always loved her. How could she have doubted that? Since coming back into her life, hadn't he done everything possible to prove to her how much he cared? Wasn't her self-doubt her own worst enemy? For so many years, she'd been strong, doing all she could to get over the one man who never left her heart. And now here he was, on bended knee in front of her, telling her he loved her.

"I'm scared, Josh."

He reached up and cupped her face. "I know, sweetheart. I'm sorry for making you have doubts. I promise I will make it up to you for the rest of our lives." He stroked a finger down her cheek. "Do you love me, Nicole?"

She nodded. "I do. I have since that first night."

Everything inside Josh relaxed. Standing, he gently pulled her to her feet and kissed her. They had a lot of time to make up for, but for now he would settle for just the sweet feel of her lips beneath his. When they broke apart, he leaned his forehead against hers. "Say it."

Shyly, Nikki looked up at him. "I love you, Josh. I love you so much."

Pulling her into his embrace, he held her tight. "Thank God," he said. He didn't want to let her go, but there was a reception going on down the hall they needed to get back to. He took a step back. "How's your head?"

"Much better."

He held out his arm for her to loop hers through. "Ready to head back to the party?"

Nikki smiled. "I think I'm ready to go wherever you're going." Together, they walked arm in arm back to the celebration.

Epilogue

THE SUN WAS RISING OVER THE OCEAN, AND THE SIGHT OF IT simply took her breath away. Sighing with contentment, Nikki leaned back and rested against her husband's chest. "You were right. This was definitely worth getting up for."

He smiled and placed a kiss on her temple. "You can understand now why I wanted to keep this house, right? The views are incredible."

"Mmm," she purred. It was an incredible sight, but so were the backs of her eyelids after a night of so little sleep. "Can we go back to bed now?"

Josh chuckled. "I would have thought you'd be too tired for that right now."

Nikki jabbed him in the ribs with her elbow. "I meant to go back to sleep."

"Oh," he said slowly. "I think that can be arranged." He stood, swiftly scooped her up into his arms, and walked back into their bedroom, placing Nikki on the bed. "How's that for service?"

She smiled. "Careful, I spoil easily."

Leaning down, he placed another kiss on her temple. "You deserve to be spoiled." He was going to let her get some more sleep, alone, but instead he walked around to his side of the bed, slid under the blankets beside her, and pulled her in close.

"I was hoping you'd stay."

"I guess a couple more hours of sleep couldn't hurt me either. Besides, in another couple of days, we'll be back to early mornings and the real world."

"Shh… Don't remind me." Three months to the day after David and Denise's wedding, Nicole and Josh had said their vows and were now taking a short honeymoon on the coast. "I hope Ellie's behaving for your parents."

"I hope my parents aren't spoiling her rotten. We could have a monster on our hands when we get back."

"Not our sweet little angel. You must have her confused with somebody else." They both laughed. "Seriously, I hope she's okay. This is the longest we've ever been apart and—"

"We'll call her when we get up later, okay? We've only been gone for two days."

"Today's the third one, and it's still long."

"It should have been longer," he murmured and felt that elbow to the ribs again.

"A girl needs time to plan her dream wedding," she reminded him. It wasn't the first time they'd had this discussion. "By the time the wedding plans were all figured out and our date was set, we were hitting back-to-school time. We could have waited until winter break."

"Hell no," he growled and rolled her beneath him. "I waited over three years to make you my wife. I wasn't going to wait any longer." He kissed her hungrily and felt her melt in his arms.

When they broke apart, Nikki smiled up at him sleepily. "Then don't complain."

He knew she was right, but he was disappointed they hadn't gotten to take the kind of honeymoon she deserved. If his plans worked out right, they would get away during her winter break from school and go someplace tropical. He thought about making it a family trip, but he was going to be greedy; he wanted them to have some time to themselves. They had no shortage of babysitters between his parents, Nicole's parents, and David and Denise. He had already spoken to all of them about his plans. All he had to do was say the word and Ellie would be well taken care of.

Nikki yawned. "Sleep," she said as she squirmed out from beneath him.

Looking down at her, he smiled, moving so they were spooned together with him pressed firmly against her back. Over her shoulder, he could still see the beach and the sun rising higher and higher in the sky.

They were blessed with another beautiful day. *A beautiful day, a beautiful wife, and the promise of a beautiful future.*

Baby, Be Mine

Prologue

KISSING THE MAN OF YOUR DREAMS FOR THE FIRST TIME IS an event a girl always wants to remember.

Not this time.

Olivia did her best to hide out in the far corner of her backyard—it was dark back there, and the group of people around her seemed oblivious to her turmoil. Everyone was there to celebrate her eighteenth birthday with her, and all she wanted was for everyone to leave so she could crawl into a hole and lick her wounds. And maybe die.

Maybe that should be her wish when she blew out the candles.

What had she been thinking? How could she have misjudged the situation so badly? Thirty minutes ago, she had thought this was going to be the best night of her life, and now? Well, now it would forever be known as the worst.

Convincing Jake Knight to follow her into the garage under the pretense of collecting more chairs had been inspired. Cornering him and wrapping herself around him had been exciting. Having him shove her away as if she has some sort of disease?

Mortifying.

Jake had been in her life since she was a preteen. Olivia had the opportunity to really get to know him because he was her brother Mike's best friend, and even though he was six years older, she had felt certain that now that she was eighteen, he'd see her as a woman. Not his best friend's little sister.

Clearly she was wrong.

Touching Jake's lips with hers had been like being struck by lightning; a jolt of excitement so powerful it had been hard not to jump from it had shot through her system. For a brief second, his arms had banded around her waist, and then just as quickly, those same arms had pushed her away.

Luckily, the garage was almost completely dark—the only light coming from the full moon outside—and she hadn't been able to see what she was certain was a horrified look on his face. As it was, she could still picture it all too clearly.

The reality had probably been so much worse.

This was so not the eighteenth birthday party Olivia had planned.

It wasn't the beginning of her happily ever after.

If anything, this event would go down as the defining moment of her life.

From now on, Olivia knew she would have to stay away from Jake, no matter how hard it would be. She was done pining after a man she clearly couldn't have. And for that matter, she was done pining and chasing after men, period. From here on out, she would sit back and wait until the perfect guy pined and chased after her. There was no way she could deal with this kind of rejection ever again. College was right around the corner, and she would put all of her time and energy into that.

And her photography.

There weren't many things that gave Olivia pleasure except her love of photography.

And watching Jake Knight.

Oh, if only she could combine the two of them. *So not going to happen.* At least she knew now and could move on.

If only it didn't hurt so damn much.

Chapter 1

"BUT IT'S AN *EMERGENCY*."

Olivia sighed. "Seriously, Mike, to you, everything's an emergency."

"This time I'm serious."

"Look, I really wish I could help you—"

"You can. You're here in town, and you said you need a distraction, something to take your mind off work for a while. I'm just saying this is a pretty desperate situation, and I really think you could help."

A migraine was beginning to throb behind her right eye. "I'm taking the month off so I can relax, and even though you won't tell me exactly what this dire situation is, I can tell it is not something that is going to help me in that department."

"Liv," Mike said with exasperation, "why can't you just trust me? Five minutes of your time, that's all I'm asking."

"I was willing to give you some of my time when we were supposed to meet for lunch this afternoon. You stood me up, remember?"

"Because of this situation!" he fairly growled. "Seriously, haven't you been listening to anything I've been saying?"

"I have, Mike. You're just not saying anything that interests me." Olivia was growing bored with the conversation and yawned loudly to get her point across.

"Okay, I shouldn't have called you."

"You think?" she said sarcastically.

"I'm sorry. There was an—"

"Emergency?"

"Yes, this situation came up, and I had to take care of it. Now I need your help. Please, Liv. You're the only one who can help."

"How is that even possible?"

"If you'd just meet with me, you'll understand."

Olivia knew she was fighting a losing battle. There was no way in the world she was going to get Mike to let this go, and the sooner she went and met with him, the sooner she could say no with a clear conscience. "Fine," she said dramatically. "Where are you?"

"I'm over at Jake's place. Well, his parents' place. You remember where it is, right?"

Everything in Olivia went numb. Jake? Jake Knight? There was no way in hell she was going to do anything that involved him, and there was nothing her brother could say, no amount of guilt he could lay on her, to make her change her mind.

"Liv? Are you there?"

"Huh? What?"

"You remember where Jake's parents lived, right?"

"Lived?"

"Oh, right. You probably didn't know. His parents were killed in a car accident about a year ago. Getting their estate in order has been a bit of a nightmare, but for now, Jake's living in the old house until he has it ready to sell."

What was she supposed to say to that? Why hadn't anyone told her about it? She'd never told anyone about the humiliation at her eighteenth birthday, so that couldn't have been the reason.

"Liv?" Mike said with more than a hint of frustration.

"I…I can't, Mike. I'm sorry. I'm sure whatever the problem is, you and Jake can work it out." No sooner had the words come out of her mouth than she heard a strange sound in the background. "What was that?"

Mike sighed wearily. "A baby crying."

Olivia's heart sank. Why was there a baby crying? Did Jake have kids? Seriously, was her brother looking at her to come over and babysit for Jake and his probably Barbie-perfect wife? Was he out of his mind? She was just about to ask him that exact question when he spoke again.

"It's a long story, Liv, and it's a bit crazy here right now. Can you please just come over?"

She took a steadying breath and counted to ten. "I'm not interested in being a babysitter so you guys can go out or something. You'll have to find somebody else."

"It's not like that!" Mike snapped. Then, a bit calmer, he said, "Look, I didn't want to have to do this, but you leave me no choice. Remember your senior year of college when you needed me to buy you a ticket home from Vegas, and I did it—no questions asked?"

Dammit. "Yes."

"Well, I'm asking for the same courtesy. I need you to come here, no questions asked."

"Mike, you have no idea what you're asking."

"I know, Liv, and I'm sorry, but we really need your help."

It would have been so much easier if she had just decided to have her mental sabbatical back in L.A., where she belonged. But no, Olivia had felt the need to come home and be near her family. She'd know better for the next time.

"Fine," she said once more, only this time with an overwhelming sense of defeat. "I remember the house. I'll be there in a little while."

"Thanks, Liv," Mike said with relief. "You're a lifesaver."

"Don't get ahead of yourself," she said with a sense of bravado. "I only agreed to come over. I didn't say I'd be able to help."

He didn't argue. "I'll see you soon."

Hanging up her phone, Olivia threw it on her bed as she flopped back against the pillows. How was she supposed to survive facing Jake after almost eight years? And how was she supposed to do it without turning into a babbling idiot?

With a sigh of resignation, she stood and grabbed her purse. *Guess it's time to find out.*

The drive over was way too short, and Olivia had hoped to have a minute or two to sit in the driveway and work up the courage to get out. Unfortunately, her brother and Jake were sitting on the front steps of the house, both looking miserable. As soon as she stepped out of the car, she was hit with an overwhelming sense of dread. "What's going on?" She focused her attention and her question at her brother. Her eyes actually hurt from not looking at Jake.

Mike rose and walked over to hug her. "Thank you," he whispered.

That was all fine and well, but Olivia was still clueless as to why her attendance here was of any relevance. Pulling back, she looked her brother in the eye. "Okay, I'm here. What is going on?" she repeated.

In the background, an infant's cry was coming from the house. The kid certainly had a set of lungs.

"Earlier today, Marilyn, Jake's ex-fiancée, stopped by."

Ex-fiancée? Jake had been engaged? That was another bit of news no one had bothered to share with her. "And this pertains to me…how?"

He swiped a hand over his face, and Olivia forced herself to stay focused on him even as Jake came to stand beside him. "He hadn't seen her in months, and she showed up here and dropped them off." He motioned to the house behind him. "And then she left."

"Wait…*them?*" Mike nodded. "As in more than one baby?" He nodded again, and Olivia felt a little faint. The sound of the crying, however, kept her in the moment. "So let me ask you this—if they're in there, why are you out here?"

"They won't stop," Jake said, and Olivia heard the tremble in his voice. At any other time, she might have taken a minute to let the sound of that masculine voice wash over her, but now was obviously not the time. Plus, he sounded like he was near hysterical.

"Have you fed them?" she asked, and both men nodded. "Changed them?" This time two blank faces stared back at her. "Oh, for crying out loud…" she huffed before walking around them and into the house.

It didn't take long to find the babies—they were right in the family room in their car seats, and even louder now that she was standing before them. "Hey, guys," she whispered as she crouched down between them. They were so tiny, Olivia was almost afraid to touch them. "Okay, let's see what we've got here," she said and reached for the large canvas bag sitting between them. Rifling through it, she found diapers and wipes, then lifted baby number one from its seat.

Laying the child down on the carpet, she carefully undressed her. Of course Olivia didn't realize the baby was a her until she pulled the diaper off—her clothes were fairly gender neutral. "Okay, sweet girl," she cooed. "Let's get some dry clothes on you." It didn't take long to get the baby cleaned up and changed into clean, dry clothes. Olivia was hesitant to put her back in the infant seat, but there simply wasn't anyplace else she could currently go.

Once the baby was quieted and back in her seat, Olivia gave her a pacifier, then turned her attention to her twin. "Now it's your turn, sweet pea," she said softly as she laid the baby down. "How about we..." She stopped when she took the diaper off. "Okay, wasn't expecting that." With a smile, she cleaned the baby up. "Well now, young man, now you have some clean pants too." The baby's eyes watched her intently as she worked, and when she settled him back into his seat, Olivia swore he understood her.

She wanted to pick them both up and hug them and snuggle with them and just breathe in their sweet baby smell, but she knew she couldn't. These were Jake's babies. Well, Jake and Marilyn's, and it was too much to wrap her brain around right then. Satisfied they were both all right and about to fall asleep, Olivia backed out of the room and went in search of the two who were responsible for this situation.

Walking out the front door, she found her brother and Jake exactly where she had left them—standing in the middle of the driveway. "What is wrong with the two of you?" she demanded as she stomped down the steps toward them. "Both of those babies were soaked to the skin! How could you have left them like that?"

Jake didn't look at her, and Mike stammered, "How…I…how am I supposed to know how to change a diaper?"

"It's not brain surgery, you moron! Those poor babies cannot take care of themselves. They need the adults around them to do it."

"That's why I called you, Liv! We have no idea what to do!"

She pinched the bridge of her nose and did her best not to wind up and punch her brother in the face. "Where is their mother?" she asked. "When is she coming back?"

"She's not," Jake said quietly.

Olivia looked at him in shock, but Jake still wouldn't meet her gaze. "Excuse me?"

"I never even knew she was pregnant. She said she found out after we broke up and figured I'd be willing to pay child support." He sighed and looked at the ground. "She wasn't planning on twins. When she showed up here this morning, she told me she had met someone, and twins—or any kids for that matter—don't fit into her plans."

Olivia felt sick. "So she just dropped them off and walked away?"

Jake was silent for a long time until Mike spoke up. "Not exactly…"

"Mike," Jake warned.

"She deserves to know. Especially if she's going to help."

"Know what?" Olivia asked even though she knew she wasn't going to like the answer.

Mike waited for Jake to speak, but when he remained silent, he turned to his sister. "She asked for money. Said she'd sign over custody for a lump sum." He said the words with disgust. "So Jake wrote her a check and sent her on her way."

"So basically she used her womb as her own personal ATM?" Olivia asked no one in particular. "Charming." She'd always known Jake picked the wrong kind of women. That was why all those years ago, she had been so sure he would see she was the right one for him.

Pushing those thoughts aside, she straightened and faced Mike. "I still don't see what this has to do with me. I'm not a nanny nor do I want to be."

"It's after five in the evening, Liv," Mike said. "Jake has no idea how to handle a baby, let alone two! He just needs a hand until he can hire someone."

Olivia let those words sink in for a minute. She glanced at Jake, who was still staring at the ground, and then back to her brother. "Sorry," she said and watched as both men paled. "Like I said, I'm not a nanny. I'm sure between the two of you, you can get through the night and begin making calls in the morning. You're both successful businessmen. You'll figure it out." Turning, she walked over to her car.

"You can't be serious," Mike called out to her. "You said you would help!"

Facing them as she threw her purse in the car, she said, "No, I said I would come over. I never said I'd help or I'd stay. That was your assumption and your mistake." She hated how heartless she sounded and yet couldn't stop herself. "Make sure you change them, and you're going to need to get some real baby furniture soon—particularly some cribs."

"But…Liv—" She had to give her brother credit; he wasn't willing to take no for an answer.

"I'm sure you each know some other females willing to come over and help out." Without looking at either of them, Olivia finished climbing into her car and had the key in the ignition before her brother crouched down beside the open car door.

"Why are you being this way?" he hissed. A million plausible reasons played through her mind, yet she couldn't voice any of them. "I get that you're on some sort of mental break, but that doesn't mean you can't help out a friend."

She didn't mean to snap. She'd had every intention of just driving away and forgetting about everything she had seen there. But Mike just wouldn't let her be. Turning toward him, she gave him a blank look. "Jake is your friend, not mine. And if one of my friends called with a real emergency, I'd be there."

"This is a real emergency!"

Olivia shook her head. "No, Mike, it's not. There are two babies in there and two of you. It looks like their mother left plenty of supplies for them. Surely the two of you can fumble through one night with them before Jake hires a nanny?"

His eyes narrowed at his sister before he stood. "I don't know what's happened to you. You never used to be like this."

"Mike—"

"No," he interrupted. "Maybe this is the way you people treat one another in Hollywood, but around here we look out for one another."

She almost wanted to point out that his drama skills were perfect for the Hollywood lifestyle but decided to keep it to herself. Rather than argue, she simply agreed. "I guess you're right. Maybe that's why I left here and moved there. Obviously I don't fit in here anymore. My mistake for wanting to come home for a while." With that, she reached for the door handle, waiting for him to step aside so she could pull it closed.

Without a wave or a smile, Olivia pulled out of the driveway and vowed not to look back.

Jake wasn't sure which was more of a shock right now—finding out he was the father of twins or seeing Olivia again. It had been eight years since her birthday party, and he hadn't seen more than a glimpse of her from a distance since.

Not that he blamed her. He could have reacted with a little more finesse back then, but she had shocked the hell out of him. For years, she had simply been Mike's sister, then she had blossomed into an incredibly attractive young woman and she was off-limits. There was no way he was going to risk his friendship with Mike—they were like brothers. He shuddered as he realized that would make Olivia technically like a sister to him. That was certainly never the image he'd had of her.

As her taillights disappeared down the driveway, he felt completely defeated. She had barely looked at him, and when she had, it had been with disgust. Not that he didn't deserve it. It was just not what he had expected or needed right now. With his head thrown back, Jake closed his eyes and took a deep breath. What the hell was he supposed to do now? When Mike had suggested calling Olivia, he had known it was a mistake. But there hadn't seemed to be any alternative.

"I could call my parents," Mike said as he came to stand beside Jake.

"They're in Arizona while your mom's recovering from her surgery," Jake stated miserably. "They're two thousand miles away. I don't think they'll be able to help us tonight."

Mike raked a hand through his hair. "No, not tonight, but I'm sure if I called them, they'd get a flight out tomorrow."

Jake shook his head. "No. This is my problem, not theirs."

"That's a load of bull, and you know it! You're family, Jake. You always have been. You know good and well if you ever needed anything, they'd be there for you." Mike stopped and paused. "And obviously, you need help."

His head still shaking, Jake turned and looked at his friend. "You have no idea how much I appreciate how hard you're trying to help me out here. I don't know what I would've done today without you here to keep me sane."

"I honestly thought you were joking when you called."

"Lucky for me you're the best lawyer I know, as well as my best friend, and you were able to draw up those papers so quickly."

Mike looked at the ground as he thought about the events of the day. "I still can't believe Marilyn did this. You never suspected she was pregnant?"

"No." Jake's voice was both weary and sad. "She knew how much I wanted kids, wanted a family. It was one of the reasons we broke up—I wanted kids, and she didn't. We were always so careful, so cautious; she was near fanatical about birth control."

"Accidents happen."

Jake glared at him. "Obviously."

"So what do we do now?"

Looking over his shoulder, Jake glanced at the still-open front door. "You don't have to stay. They're my responsibility, and I'm sure you have a life of your own to get back to."

"Don't give me that," Mike snapped. "It's pretty damn clear you're not prepared for this, and maybe between the two of us, we won't traumatize them too much."

Jake couldn't help but chuckle. "I'm not so sure about that. For all we know, we've already scarred them for life."

"Nah, they're too young for that." Placing a reassuring hand on his friend's shoulder, he inclined his head toward the house. "Come on. We'll order in pizza and do a little online research on how to take care of babies. How hard could it be?"

Chapter 2

THE RINGING OF THE PHONE WAS ENOUGH TO MAKE Olivia want to scream. It was barely nine in the morning, and she hadn't gone to sleep until four. Part of the reason for her sabbatical was to get some rest, but it eluded her here. With a growl of frustration, she reached over and slid her finger across the screen without looking to see who it was.

"Honestly, Olivia, it's about time you answered the phone." Her mother. This was so not a good sign.

"Hey, Mom. You're up early."

"One of the hazards of your father's retirement. He still gets up with the birds, but he has no place to go, so he putters around the house, making all kinds of noise until I get up and make him breakfast. Honestly, the man is driving me crazy."

Clearly her mother felt the need to pass it on. "You've spoiled him. He knows exactly what to do to get what he wants."

"I don't think loving and spoiling are the same thing, sweetheart. Your father isn't devious or manipulative."

Wanna bet? "So how are you doing, Mom? How are you feeling?"

"Oh, you know… The doctor told me it would take some time for me to get back to normal. I go to physical therapy—and honestly, that therapist is some sort of sadist! I go and do all the exercises I'm supposed to, but I still don't feel quite like myself."

"You had a hip replaced, Mom. It wasn't like it was some minor procedure."

"Still, you know me. I hate to be idle."

So did Olivia. For three days she'd been home—well, at Mike's guesthouse—and she had yet to be able to fully relax. She was restless, couldn't sleep, and couldn't quite shake the image of Jake Knight from her mind. "You could take up a hobby," she suggested.

"Oh, I have plenty of those. There's my book club and my knitting, and you know how much I love my garden."

"All of those things are good, Mom. So what's going on?"

"Actually, I was calling to ask if you could pick me up at the airport tomorrow."

"What?" This was so not what Olivia had expected. "Why? I mean, why are you flying in? You're still recovering. I didn't think travel was good for you right now."

Her mother made a tsk-ing sound. "Well, normally I wouldn't, but Mike called and told us all about Jake's situation. Poor boy. I can't even imagine what he must be feeling."

"Wait a minute, they called you? They asked you to come and help them?"

"What's wrong with that?"

"You're recovering from surgery! What on earth is Mike thinking?"

"For starters, he's thinking he and Jake can't possibly take care of two infants. Secondly, Mike has that trip overseas he needs to leave for tomorrow. You know how long and hard he's been working on that deal with the Chinese company, Olivia. He has to be there."

Actually, she had forgotten about that, which was odd, considering the reason she had chosen to come home now was so she could have a couple of days with her brother and then the better part of a month to herself to get her head back together without any distractions.

"How would it look if he didn't show up?" her mother continued. "For six months he's been planning this, and apparently it was hard to coordinate schedules, and well…I just couldn't let him miss out on that."

"Why hasn't Jake hired a nanny? What is he waiting for?"

"He doesn't want to hire one."

"What? Why? That's completely ridiculous!"

"One of the things I always had a hard time with was that the Knights left Jake alone so much. I realize we didn't really get to know them until Jake was older, but from what I've been told, they left him alone a lot."

"Completely alone?"

"No, no, of course not. There were nannies and neighbors and the like. Jake doesn't want that for his kids, so he's determined to figure out how to take care of them on his own."

"But he has a business to run!" Olivia said with exasperation. "How does he expect to run his construction company from home? Or is he planning on putting them in little baby slings with hard hats and taking them on the job?"

"Don't be ridiculous, Olivia. Sheesh. Like I said, he is trying to figure it out. Obviously he doesn't have all the answers yet. He's only had the babies for two days."

"Mom, you can't fly in here and take care of them."

"Sweetheart, Jake is like one of my own. He has no

one, Liv. No siblings, no parents… I'm not heartless, you know."

But clearly she was. "Did you already book your flight?" she asked with a familiar sense of dread.

"No, I wanted to talk to you first and find out what your schedule was like."

"I have no schedule, Mom. I'm on sabbatical, remember?"

"Yes, yes, yes, I remember. What is that, anyway?"

"An extended mental-health vacation." So much for that plan. "Look, I'll go over there and help Jake out so Mike can leave. You stay where you are and finish recuperating. You know it's the right thing to do."

"Are you sure, sweetheart? I don't want to ruin your mental-health thing."

Too late. "You're not ruining it." *Jake Knight is*. "It's not a big deal. The important thing is you get better."

"You were always so good with children, Olivia. You were the most sought-after babysitter in town, remember?"

Not really. "Well, it's been a long time since I babysat anyone, and hopefully I'll be able to make Jake see some reason—he needs to hire a nanny. He's not doing himself or those babies any favors by struggling so much."

"Don't go in there with a superior attitude, Olivia! Jake is in a tough place right now, and he needs to be surrounded by people who love him. Now, I'm trusting you to go there in my place and help out, not harp on him."

Olivia rolled her eyes. "I don't harp, Mom." *Much*. "All I'm saying is it would be better for all of them if he didn't try to take it all on himself."

"Please just go and be an extra set of hands. That's

all. Don't try to fix anything, don't lecture, and for the love of all that is holy, don't be so bossy."

There was no point in arguing with her mother, so Olivia simply agreed to behave herself before hanging up. She'd do what she could to help, but if Jake asked her opinion on something, there was no way she was going to be able to keep her mouth shut.

Kicking the blankets off, Olivia rose and looked around the room. Luckily she hadn't unpacked her suitcases, because it looked like she was going to be packing them back up and heading off to play nanny.

She only hoped she wouldn't walk away needing more of a break than she did already.

"Olivia?" Mike said with surprise as he opened the door. "What are you doing here?"

Before she answered, she stepped around him and into Jake's house. "Don't go acting all surprised. You played dirty, and you know it."

"Me?" he asked, all innocence. "What did I do?"

"You called Mom, who in turn called me and laid on the guilt trip."

He couldn't help but smile. "Really? That's so unlike her."

"Oh, knock it off. You knew exactly what you were doing and got your way," she said sarcastically. "Now I'm here, and you can go and play overseas lawyer while I babysit."

It would have been easy to rile her up some more, but instead Mike just pulled her into his embrace. "I knew you still had a heart in there," he said softly. "I really appreciate this, Liv."

Pulling back, she gave him a crooked smile. "Yeah, yeah, yeah, sure you do." Ruffling his hair as she walked by, she added, "Now go get my luggage."

Walking into the family room, Olivia saw what looked like two makeshift bassinets. Essentially, they were dresser drawers now containing sleeping infants. Unable to resist, she ran a hand gently over each of their backs and sighed.

That's how Jake found her. Stepping from the main floor master bedroom after his shower, he was shocked to find Olivia standing in the room. He was shirtless, drying his hair with a towel, and he simply froze at the sight of her. She hadn't noticed his presence yet, so he took a moment just to look at her. Long, chestnut hair pulled back into a ponytail, her curvy body encased in snug, faded denim and a T-shirt had her looking better than he had ever imagined.

And he'd imagined her.

A lot.

All those years ago, he had pushed Olivia away, not because he wasn't attracted to her, but because he was *too* attracted to her. He was older, and there was his friendship with her brother to consider. He had always known she'd grow up to be beautiful, but the woman standing before him was more than that. She didn't even have to try; dressed as casually as she was, she made more of an impact than any of those celebrities she photographed. Was she even aware of that?

He took a step into the room and a floorboard creaked. The silence broken, Olivia looked up and spotted him, a wary expression on her face. She looked down at the infants one more time before walking toward Jake. He motioned for her to follow him to the kitchen and once they were there, he felt like he had a little more control over his emotions.

"Mike didn't mention you were coming over."

Olivia's mouth had gone dry. There were still some drops of water lingering from his shower, and Jake's bare chest was practically glistening. How was she supposed to concentrate on having any kind of normal conversation with that sort of distraction? She may have hated him, but she was still human. Hell, she was a woman who appreciated the sight of a well-sculpted male.

And Jake certainly fit the bill perfectly.

They stood there face-to-face, and she cringed at the possibility of him remembering what a fool she'd made of herself all those years ago. "Mike didn't know," she forced herself to say, barely recognizing her own voice. Jake nodded and waited for her to continue. "My mother called. She's recovering from a hip replacement, and even though she was determined to come and help, I thought it would be better if I…" She cleared her throat. "If I came and helped instead."

Jake studied her. "I thought you weren't interested in helping."

He had her there. Right now, she wanted nothing more than simply to agree with him and leave. Unfortunately, she had gotten a look at those two helpless babies, and everything inside her had turned to mush. "I've had time to think about it." If you could call two hours time to think. "Mike has the China trip, and Mom is still recovering."

He nodded but remained silent. Olivia wished he'd just say something—anything—so she could tell how he felt about her being here. For all she knew, he didn't want her there any more than she wanted to be there. She crossed her arms across her chest and narrowed her eyes at him. "It looks like you're stuck with me." It came out as a challenge, a dare, and she couldn't help but hold her breath as she waited for his response.

With a small shrug, Jake turned and walked over to the refrigerator. "You want something to drink?"

That was it? That was all he had to say? Olivia wanted to stamp her foot and demand he be as outraged by all of this as she was, but as she watched him, Jake simply poured them each a glass of iced tea and placed them on the kitchen table. He sat down and waited for her to join him. Where the heck was Mike? It would have been easier if he were there as a buffer.

No sooner had she finished that thought than her brother walked into the kitchen carrying her luggage. "Thanks for doing this, Liv," he said as he leaned down and kissed her on the cheek. "I have just enough time to stop at home and pack some more stuff and get to the airport."

"You're leaving?" she squeaked. "Now?"

He nodded. "I never canceled my original flight. Jake was aware he'd have to manage for a day by himself if Mom was coming in. Now you're here, there's nothing to worry about." Turning from Olivia, he walked over to Jake. "You're in good hands," he said as he and Jake shook hands. "I hate to take off so quickly, but I have a ton of stuff to do before my flight."

"I can't thank you enough," Jake said before pulling Mike in for a brotherly embrace. "You saved my life."

Mike smiled as he pulled back. "You would do the same for me." It wasn't a question; it was a statement of fact. With a wave and a smile, he was gone.

The silence left in his wake was deafening.

Jake sat back down opposite her, and they simply stared at one another for far longer than was comfortable. Olivia decided to leave her comfort zone and speak up first. "Okay, so I'm guessing you've gotten the basics down—feeding and changing them. But the drawers they're sleeping in have to go. Have you done any shopping at all yet?"

He shook his head. "Neither of us wanted to be left alone with them. They can be quite a handful when they wake up."

Olivia couldn't help but chuckle. "I'm sure. Well, the carriers I saw them in the other day had bases on them, so means they can be used as car seats. How about we go and do some shopping once they wake up? It will be good for them to get used to being in the car and going from place to place." Now was as good of time as any to see what he was planning for the future. "Especially since you plan on being a stay-at-home dad."

"How did you know about that?"

This time it was more of a laugh escaping from her lips. "Please, you think my mother didn't give me the entire lowdown on what you've got planned?" There was a hint of disapproval in her tone, and she watched Jake's expression turn serious.

"You don't think I can do it?"

"You are in construction, Jake. You do massive renovations. How do you plan to do that from home?"

"I have a crew."

She nodded and took another sip of her beverage. "Right. And you're fine with never going on a job site ever again?"

He paled. "Well, I wouldn't say never. I'd just have to find a way to—"

"To what?" she interrupted. "You're clearly against hiring a nanny, even though it's the best thing for all of you, and you think you can still do your job. Babies can't be on construction sites, Jake. You have to admit you'll need help."

He stood abruptly and began to pace in the kitchen. "I'll figure it out, Olivia. I don't have to have all the answers right now. For the time being, I can work from home. I've been on the phone for days with my foremen, and they are all okay with taking the reins for a while."

His tone was defensive, and she was smart enough to let the topic drop for now. "Well then, that's a good thing, right?" He nodded and Olivia stood. "What time do you think they'll be up?"

Looking over at the clock on the wall, Jake tried to remember when they had finally fallen back to sleep that morning. "Sometime after lunch" was all he said.

"Okay, then. How about you show me to my room, and I'll get settled in and start making a list of what we'll need?" Wordlessly, Jake led her from the room and toward the master bedroom on the main floor. The one he'd come out of earlier. "Um…" she began when she crossed the threshold.

"Before they arrived, I was renovating the second floor. This is the only functioning bedroom."

Her mind swirled as she looked at the rumpled sheets on the bed—it wasn't difficult to imagine Jake sleeping there. Shaking that thought aside, she chewed nervously on her bottom lip. "Oh…I guess I'll take the couch. That's where Mike was sleeping, right?"

Jake nodded even as he disagreed with her. "You're the one doing me a favor, Olivia. You take the bed, and I'll take the couch."

Could there be any more torture for her? Not only was she resigned to staying with him for several weeks, but now she had to sleep in his bed. True, she'd be sleeping there alone, but it was still his, and the sheets probably smelled like him. She almost groaned out loud. "If you're sure…"

"Absolutely."

She looked around the room. It was spacious and had a king-size bed, and there was an entire wall of windows as well as French doors leading out to a private patio. She could see the en suite and figured she'd have enough privacy. "What about the babies?"

Jake frowned. "What about them?"

"Well, if the entire second floor is being worked on, where are you thinking of putting the cribs?"

"Cribs?"

"Yes, you know, the beds babies sleep in." She almost smiled at his panicked expression. "You were planning on buying them, weren't you?"

"They're so small, Olivia. Do they really need cribs right now?"

"I suppose you could get by with a couple of bassinets. They're smaller, and they'll easily fit in here, but you are going to have to buy the cribs eventually. I was just trying to get all the basics out of the way for you."

He nodded. "I appreciate that, but until the upstairs is done, let's just get what is absolutely necessary."

"You're the boss," she said lightly and made a quick inventory of the room. It wouldn't be a big deal to have the babies in there with her for now, but the sooner they had their own space and started getting used to it, the better. "How long until the upstairs is done?"

"I had another week or so to go if I kept at it like I had been, but I haven't been able to do anything since they arrived. I'm afraid to hammer anything or to make too much noise." He raked a hand through his hair in frustration. "Now I don't know when it's going to get done."

She wished she had an answer. "Let's deal with one thing at a time. We'll shop today and get what we need, and then we can think about you having time to go upstairs and work."

"Olivia, you can't take care of two babies by yourself."

Well, that sounded like a dare, she thought. "I'm not saying it's going to be easy," she said smoothly, "but you're going to be nearby. If things get hairy, I'll call out for you. We'll see how they do with the noise level and take it from there."

Jake considered her words. "Most of the loud stuff is over," he said as he ran through a mental checklist. "I may have a few pieces of trim to hang, maybe some pictures. It's mostly paint and carpeting."

"I don't think that will be a problem. If the weather cooperates, I'll take them out for a walk while you're doing the loud stuff. How does that sound?"

Unable to do anything but stare at her, Jake couldn't believe his luck. When Marilyn had shown up here and dropped her bombshell on him, he had been certain he wouldn't survive it. He had fumbled through for two days with Mike, but now standing here and talking to Olivia, he finally felt a sense of hope.

It was too much. His emotions were running high and he had to do something to show her how grateful he was. Without thinking, Jake stepped forward and wrapped Olivia in his arms, lifting her off her feet as he hugged her. "Thank you," he whispered. "Thank you for being willing to help me and for giving me the first glimmer of hope I've had in days."

Olivia was too stunned to speak. Jake's large frame completely enveloped her, and her immediate reaction was to stiffen in his arms. When he whispered his soft words against her ear, she felt her body begin to relax.

When she was back on her feet, Jake took a step back. "I'm serious, Olivia. I wasn't sure I could do this, but listening to you talk about how we can get things done is exactly what I needed. I'm so glad you're here."

That made one of them.

"I don't claim to have all the answers, but I'm good at task management. I used to babysit a lot when I was a teenager, and all I can say with any certainty is babies are unpredictable. We can plot and plan all day long, but it won't mean a thing if they don't cooperate."

"Don't I know it," he said with a chuckle. "Who knew such tiny people could turn lives upside down so fast?"

"I'm sure you'll get used to it." They stood in companionable silence for several moments until Olivia heard the first stirrings coming from the next room. She smiled at the sound. "There's just one last thing I need before I go out there and get started."

"What's that?" he asked.

"Their names. In all the craziness, you never told me their names."

"Madison and Ben."

Olivia thought of the two babies in the next room and sighed. The names were perfect for them, and she couldn't wait to go out there and start talking with them. She said it out loud and Jake laughed. "You know they can't understand you, right? I mean, I don't know a lot about babies, but even I know they're too small to really understand what you're saying, let alone their names."

"That may be so, but there's no time like the present to get them used to hearing their names." She stopped and thought for a moment. "Madison is an awfully long name. Would you be opposed to my calling her Maddie?"

Jake smiled at the thought. "Liv, as long as you're here, you can call them whatever variation of their names you'd like."

Olivia couldn't help the wayward thoughts suddenly filled her mind—like staying forever. She knew this was a temporary situation—at least on her part—and she shouldn't let herself get too attached to any of this. Not the babies, and certainly not Jake.

Chapter 3

OLIVIA EXCELLED AT ORGANIZATION, AND AFTER HER FIRST experience feeding and changing the twins with Jake, she was able to figure out what they were going to need to make their lives easier.

She had just placed Ben back in his carrier when she turned to face Jake. "Okay, that was a little bit wild." She said it with a light laugh, but the look on Jake's face made her realize he was clearly overwhelmed. In a flash, she was seated beside him on the sofa, placing a hand over his. "Jake?"

He turned to her, his expression a bit wild-eyed. "What am I doing here, Liv? I mean, I know nothing about kids—zero, zilch, nada. How am I supposed to take care of two infants?"

She wanted to say, "Hire someone," but she knew now wasn't the time to bring that up. Instead, she tightened her hand over his and gave him a serene smile. "No one is good with newborns. It's always chaotic and wild and scary. The good thing is they aren't going to remember this. As long as you love them and feed them and change them, you're doing all right."

He jumped up and began to pace. "But I'm not," he said with a hint of panic in his voice. "When I hear one of them start to cry, I get a little freaked out. When I have to pick one of them up? I'm scared I'm going to hurt them or drop them. And changing them?" He held up his hands in surrender. "I didn't think something so small could smell quite like that."

She walked over to where he had finally stopped pacing. "I think you just described every new dad I've ever met. There is nothing wrong with you or what you're feeling. This is all brand-new, and once we get them on a schedule and you get the house all set up, it's going to get easier. I promise."

"How can you promise that?" he demanded with a little more force than either of them expected.

Olivia simply arched a brow at his tone. "Because you want to give them a good life. And because I know you, I know you are going to do everything humanly possible to make that happen."

He seemed to consider her words and relaxed a little. Jake hated to look weak to anyone—he was always the leader, the one in charge—and now to stand here and practically have a panic attack in front of someone was humbling to say the least. Forcing himself to smile, he looked first at where his children were sitting, and then to Olivia. "Okay, what's next?"

She knew this wasn't the last time she was going to have to reassure Jake things were going to be okay. "Well, if you're up to it, let's load them up in the car and hit the baby superstore."

He paled. "Superstore? There's a baby superstore?" He swallowed the panic that went with the question.

Olivia nodded. "Brace yourself, big guy. It's going to be an adventure." She walked over and grabbed her purse. "Oh, and be prepared to possibly max out a card or two." Walking over, she picked up Maddie's carrier. She didn't look back, but she was certain Jake had turned even paler.

Back in the day, Olivia could shop with the best of them. The weekends of her teenage years were primarily spent at the mall. But this kind of shopping? This had been an entirely new kind of experience, and when they finally pulled up in front of Jake's home again, she could say with great certainty she had shopped till she dropped.

Thank God for the superstore. Olivia wasn't sure how they would have fared without it. While she was certain there were dozens of other places they could have stopped and comparison shopped, for someone in Jake's situation, this had clearly been the way to go. It had taken four hours, three salespeople, and a lot of finagling to convince them to deliver most of the stuff to the house on such short notice. Jake's full-size pickup truck carried a good number of their purchases, but the larger pieces were being delivered the next day.

They sat in silence in the driveway, and Olivia saw Jake's hands clenched on the steering wheel. "Are you okay?" she finally asked.

"I think my head is still spinning."

She nodded in agreement. "Mine too."

He turned and looked at her. "Really? Because you seemed to be completely calm and in control. You knew exactly how to handle those people. I don't know what I would have done if I had to go in there by myself."

She chuckled. "You probably would have spent twice what we did and only gotten half the number of items."

He frowned. "I don't think that's possible."

"Sure it is. They would have fed on your panic and

convinced you to buy the most expensive stuff they had in stock, and you would have believed them."

Sad but true. "Well then, I'm glad you were with me, but I'm still in shock over the amount of stuff you think they need."

Her eyes rolled as she leaned her head back on the headrest. "Seriously? Again?"

"What?"

"Every item we purchased, I gave you a reason for why you needed it. There was not one frivolous item in the lot. What is it you think they don't need?"

"There were an awful lot of clothes," he began.

"This morning alone, I had to change Ben's clothes twice."

He hadn't thought of that. "Okay, then blankets. There were a lot of blankets."

Her head lolled to the side as she gave him a bland expression. "How many blankets were on Ben when I had to change him?"

Jake's mouth flattened into a grim line. "Pacifiers!"

"Oh, for crying out loud," she huffed as she opened the car door. "I am not going to discuss this with you again. You made me justify everything that went into the damn carts, and I'm not doing it again." She pulled open the back door to the truck and reached in for a car seat. With a quick look, she saw Maddie was still asleep, so she carefully pulled the car seat out and walked up to the front door, waiting for Jake to get Ben and follow.

At the front door, he fumbled for the key and then stared down at Olivia. He hadn't realized how different they were in size until that moment. At six feet, he tended to be taller than most women, and the top of

Olivia's head barely came to his chin. Her big blue eyes looked up at him as if she were daring him to question her again.

He knew when to admit defeat. "Fine, they weren't frivolous, but don't get mad at me when I need you to remind me why something is here." He placed Ben's carrier down in the living room and looked around. "Where are we going to fit everything?"

Olivia followed and placed Maddie down beside her brother, both blissfully asleep. "Well, I think until the second floor is done, it's going to be a little cramped down here, but we can make it work. Once you have a room ready to convert into the nursery, it will be easier."

Jake ran a hand through his hair. "I hadn't planned on converting anything. This was supposed to be temporary. I was getting this place ready to sell." He didn't really need to expand on that—Olivia was well aware Jake hadn't planned on staying here.

"Maybe convert was the wrong word," she said quietly. "You can use one of the upstairs rooms as a nursery—for now."

Jake looked over at her with a sad smile. "Who am I kidding? It would be easier to stay here until they're bigger. I can barely get through a day with them without feeling overwhelmed. I can't even imagine how hard it would be to try to pack up and move with them."

"One thing at a time, Jake, let's just take care of one thing at a time." Olivia tossed her purse on the sofa and went out to the truck to begin bringing in their purchases. After her first trip, Jake stopped her.

"Tell you what. I'll carry it all in if you find a place to put it."

"Deal." For the next hour, that was exactly what they did. When all the packages were in the house, Jake began the job of assembling the bassinets. When they were done, he moved the furniture Olivia asked him to move, and when that was done, he collapsed on the sofa. "Please tell me we're done."

Olivia was coming out of the laundry room. "There's actually one thing we forgot."

Jake's eyes were closed, his head tilted back against the sofa. "Only one?"

"Lunch."

He opened his eyes and looked at her. "No, we fed them in the store, remember?"

She rolled her eyes. "Not the babies. Our lunch. We never ate."

"Oh, sh—" He cut himself off. "Jeez, Liv, I'm sorry. I completely forgot. Here you are helping me out, and then I don't even have the decency to let you eat." He jumped up and walked into the kitchen. "I don't know if there's anything here you want, but—"

"Jake?" she interrupted.

"Hmm?" he asked distractedly as he scanned the contents of his refrigerator.

"It's actually dinnertime."

His head dropped in defeat. "See?" he asked quietly. "How can I possibly take care of two kids? I can barely take care of myself."

Slowly, Olivia walked over to him. She pushed the refrigerator door closed and placed her hands on Jake's shoulders until he looked at her. "It's not your job to take care of me. I could have stopped at any time and mentioned lunch." She shrugged. "We were busy, and that's okay. I was just making an observation because, well, I'm hungry." She could feel the tension radiating through him, and her hands gently squeezed his shoulders. "Why don't you go and grab us a pizza? Get out of here for a little while by yourself and just breathe."

Jake looked at his watch. "They'll be up soon, and it takes two of us to get them changed and fed."

Olivia turned him and pushed him toward the front door. "Let me worry about that. You go and grab the food. I think we both really need it." She continued to push him toward the door, and once they were almost there, Jake stopped and spun around.

"Maybe you should go. I'm sure we've made you crazy today and—"

"Jake?" she interrupted.

"Hmm?"

"Shut up."

He frowned at her. "I'm just saying if you want to leave—"

"I don't want to leave!" she shouted with exasperation. "I want you to leave. I want you to get out of the house for thirty minutes and relax. We're going to be fine. Trust me."

"Olivia, you have not been here alone with them. It's not easy."

"I have more experience with kids than you do. Trust me, I was a champion babysitter. I can handle thirty minutes here without you. Especially when the reward is pizza."

"Pepperoni?" She nodded. "Extra cheese?"

"Is there any other kind?"

He still didn't feel good about it, but Jake knew better

than to argue with her. "Okay, I'm going. But if you need anything, call me."

Olivia pulled open the front door and gave Jake a final shove. "Go! In case you haven't noticed, I get cranky when I'm hungry."

"I'm going, I'm going," he said as he walked toward the truck. He turned around and looked at her as she stood framed in the doorway. Something inside him shifted. In a perfect world, this would be his night—getting dinner for his family and coming home to his wife and kids. Things didn't always go as planned though, and for right now, he was grateful for what he did have.

He just needed to learn how to survive it.

Jake wasn't the only one who needed to learn about survival. He had been gone almost forty minutes—she'd kill him!—and the babies were in near-meltdown mode. Things had been pretty peaceful for the first twenty minutes, and then Maddie had woken up. Olivia had been thankful they hadn't woken up together, and she went about getting the baby girl changed and started heating up her bottle. Knowing Ben wouldn't be far behind, she'd started his too.

Midway through Maddie's bottle, Ben had woken up. He was not happy to have to wait, and when Olivia had placed Maddie down so she could get Ben changed, Maddie had started to cry. A pacifier had helped Maddie quiet down for all of three minutes before she spit it out and went back to crying. Once Ben was changed, she'd placed him back in his carrier and ran for his bottle.

"This should be an Olympic sport," she mumbled as she raced around finding burp cloths and getting situated back in the living room. With no other option, she placed both carriers on the floor at her feet and simply held both bottles for the babies and let them drink. Maddie was almost done and needed to be burped, and when she took Ben's bottle from his mouth so she could lift his sister, he wailed in protest.

Scooting down onto the floor, she placed Maddie on her shoulder and awkwardly patted her back with one hand while carefully holding Ben's bottle to keep him happy. "Thank God for Pilates," she said as she twisted and turned in ways that were beginning to make her feel like a human pretzel.

And that's how Jake found her. Her long hair had come out of its ponytail, and she was on the floor seemingly surrounded by his babies. His gut clenched. Having Olivia in his home and around his kids was doing all sorts of crazy things to him, and if she didn't look like she so desperately needed a hand, he would have enjoyed watching her for a little while longer.

Placing the pizza down on the nearest surface, he simply sat down beside her and reached for his son. "Thanks," she said softly as she relaxed against the sofa and continued to pat Maddie's back. Long minutes passed until both babies were back in their carriers, content for the moment. Jake positioned himself next to Olivia and mimicked her pose. "Not as easy as you thought, huh?"

She turned her head and looked at him with a weary smile. "I felt like they were ganging up on me."

"They tend to do that."

"I'll remember that for next time." While she didn't want to move, the smell of pizza was too strong for Olivia to ignore. "Would it be completely inappropriate for us to just eat the pizza here on the floor? Would that be completely uncivilized?"

Jake chuckled as he stood. "Are you kidding me? This is the kind of stuff I live for."

Olivia joined in on the laughter. "A man of simple tastes. Awesome."

He was seated back on the floor beside her and opening the box before she knew it. "It's not a matter of simple, more like a matter of lazy."

As much as Olivia wanted to comment, her hunger won out. Reaching for a slice, she took her first bite and moaned in delight. The pie was halfway gone before either spoke again. "If this is how it feels to be lazy, then I'm all for it," she said.

"Good thing you feel that way, because I'm telling you, with these two here, you'll be eating like this a lot more than you ever thought you would."

Olivia shook her head and finished another bite of her dinner. "It may seem that way now, but I think in a couple of days, a week tops, things will settle down. Before you know it, you'll be eating at the kitchen table again like a grown-up."

"Being a grown-up is highly overrated," he commented and reached for another slice.

"Agreed."

They finished their dinner in silence and when Jake rose to take the pizza box to the trash, he noticed the babies were still awake, watching them. "I can't believe they haven't fallen back asleep."

Olivia stood and stretched. "Get used to it. They're going to start being awake for longer periods of time, and then your hands are really going to be full."

He paled again.

"You're going to have to stop reacting like that," Olivia said as she picked up the rest of their dinner mess and followed him into the kitchen.

"Like what?"

"Like you're going to be sick. You do that every time I mention something new about the babies."

"I'll try to remember that," he said wearily, "along with the ten thousand other things you've told me today."

She was all set with a snarky comeback when she thought better of it. Olivia didn't doubt for a minute she would be feeling exactly as he was if the situation were reversed. Then she realized how ridiculous that thought was and began to laugh out loud.

"What's so funny?" Jake demanded, certain she was laughing at him.

Olivia wiped away the tears streaming down her face. "I was just imagining how I would probably be feeling overwhelmed too if it were me in your situation, and then I realized there was no way I wouldn't be aware of having twins!" She burst out laughing again. "I mean, there is no way someone can just show up and say, 'Surprise, you're a mom!' because I'd have been the one to give birth to them!" She bent over and continued to laugh.

"Yeah, that's great. Lucky you," he murmured, storming from the room to check on the kids. They were just sitting quietly, pacifiers in their mouths, looking around at nothing in particular, and for that Jake was relieved. He wasn't sure he'd be able to handle another crying meltdown.

In the background, he could still hear Olivia chuckling, and it irritated the hell out of him. He wasn't sure why, but it did nonetheless. She might be able to find humor in this situation, but Jake couldn't. His entire life had been thrown upside down and on top of it, he realized just how badly he had misjudged Marilyn. What kind of woman simply walked away from her babies?

The kind who sells them for a lump sum.

While Jake had known for quite some time that Marilyn wasn't the woman for him, he just couldn't believe *how* wrong he'd been to consider marrying her. What had even attracted him to her in the first place? Sure she was beautiful, but didn't he look for more than that in a woman? Or *shouldn't* he look for more than that in a woman? With a sigh, he ran a weary hand over his face. There were no real answers. The only thing Jake knew for sure was it was going to be a hell of a long time before he'd be able to date again. Not just because he'd been burned by Marilyn, but because his focus had to be fully on his kids. He was struggling enough right now, and he had a feeling it was only going to get more challenging.

Olivia came and sat beside him. "I'm sorry."

He turned his head and looked at her. "For what?"

"I shouldn't have laughed," she said solemnly. "I'm not trying to make light of what you're going through. I guess it was just a tension releaser or something. Either way, I'm sorry."

He reached out and took one of her hands in his, almost jumping at the shock he felt at the contact.

Willing it away, he gave a small smile. "You don't need to apologize, Liv."

"Clearly I upset you," she said. "You have enough on your plate without me being a smart-ass."

She had that right. "Like I said, no apology necessary. I need to stop being so sensitive to everything. You're here, helping me out, and for that I'm grateful."

Something warm washed over Olivia. This was all a bit surreal to her, and while her brain wanted to keep her firmly in the present, her heart kept flashing back to the past. Why couldn't she have been the one to attract Jake? Why couldn't he have fallen in love with her? Then these would have been their babies.

Quietly, she pulled her hand from his and put some distance between them. "They look like they're starting to fade," she said as she motioned toward the twins. "Why don't we move them to their new bassinets and get them settled?"

Earlier, Jake had set the two little beds up in the master bedroom, and when Olivia lifted Ben, he followed suit and picked up Maddie. He still didn't feel comfortable holding either of his babies; they were so tiny and fragile, and he felt big and clumsy with them. When he stood in front of Maddie's bassinet, he looked at Olivia. "Now what?"

"Now you swaddle her up in one of the blankets and lay her down on her back."

"Swaddle? What the hell is a swaddle?"

Olivia had already gotten Ben settled, so she motioned for Jake to bring Maddie over to the bed and lay her down. She grabbed one of the receiving blankets and demonstrated how it was done. When Maddie was all snug and secure, she handed her back to Jake. "See? Swaddled."

"She looks like a mummy."

"Babies like to feel snug and secure. Trust me, she's enjoying it."

"But she can't move."

"She doesn't need to move. She's going to sleep."

"What if it's too tight?"

Olivia lifted the infant from his arms and placed her gently down in her bassinet. She left one small lamp on in the room and motioned for Jake to follow her out. They left the bedroom door partially open so they could hear the babies if they cried. "Sit down," she said to Jake.

He complied and looked up at her as she began to pace the room. "You have got to stop arguing about everything," she began. "I'm here to help you, and yet every time I say or do something, you want to argue."

"I'm not arguing. I'm trying to understand."

She nodded. "And I get that, but you are wording everything like an argument."

He stood and stalked over to her. "Look, in the last couple of days, I have been thrown more than my fair share of curveballs, and I'm dealing the best I can! I don't need you telling me how I need to speak in my own damn house!" He knew he was being loud and unreasonable, but he'd hit his limit.

Rather than shrinking back and apologizing, Olivia got right back in his face. "I'm not trying to tell you how to speak!" she snapped back. "I just know what I'm doing, and I would appreciate it if you wouldn't question my every damn move!"

"Oh, that's right. I forgot. You *babysat* like ten years ago, so that makes you the expert!"

Now she saw red. "I never said I was an expert, but at least I have some experience with babies and children, whereas your only experience consists of creating them without knowing it!" The look of pure shock on his face made Olivia realize she had seriously crossed a line. "Oh, God… Jake, I'm sorry. That was…"

He held up a hand and stopped her. "Just…don't, okay? Don't say a thing." Without another word, Jake turned on his heel and walked out of the room. He didn't stop until he made it out the back door and stood in the middle of the detached two-car garage he had converted into a workshop for the renovation.

His hands were shaking, and his breathing was ragged. He supposed he was due for a good breakdown and here it was. Grabbing the first thing he saw, he took the two-by-four and threw it against the wall, gratified by the sound of it smashing and cracking.

Why him? Why now? Why had fate treated him this way? He was a decent person. He was a good friend and a good boss, and his life had been fairly uncomplicated until now. Things may not have worked out with Marilyn, but he had been certain there was a woman out there for him.

Or standing inside his home, probably calling him every name in the book.

That was another thing he'd have to deal with—his feelings for Olivia. If it hadn't been for their age difference all those years ago, he probably wouldn't have been in his current predicament. He had always been attracted to her, always wanted her. If she had been a couple of years older, he would have taken her up on whatever she was offering the night of her eighteenth birthday. For years he had tried to forget her, but he never could. She was always there in the back of his mind.

Of course, that could be because her brother was his best friend, and there was always a reminder of her right in front of him. But having her here with him now and having spent the day with her, he knew he was lying to himself. He'd always wanted her, and he was always going to want her.

And he still couldn't have her.

Why? Age wasn't a factor right now, but everything else was. His life was currently a mess, and Olivia deserved someone who could give her everything she wanted. Jake had a feeling it would be years before he'd be able to give anyone other than Maddie and Ben any of his attention.

And then there was her career. Olivia's photography career had her traveling all over the world, taking pictures of the rich and famous, and her home base was in L.A. How could he compete with that? He wasn't going to be traveling anytime in the foreseeable future, and he couldn't ask her to give it all up so she could play house with him. No matter how much he wanted to do just that.

So he'd have to keep his feelings for her to himself. Again. Forever. He couldn't act on them, and he certainly couldn't go around yelling at her simply because he was frustrated. Jake wasn't sure what he'd do if Olivia chose to pack up and leave right now. He had no one to help him, and there was no way in hell he'd let his kids be raised by strangers. It was something maybe no one else was able to understand, but it was his decision to make.

Unable to help himself, he chose another piece of wood and slammed it against the wall.

It wasn't nearly as satisfying the second time around.

Chapter 4

NOT SURE WHAT ELSE SHE WAS SUPPOSED TO DO, OLIVIA went about organizing the rest of the purchases. She had no idea where Jake went or for how long he'd be gone, but she couldn't just sit still and wait, and there was no way she was going to chase after him. The man was entitled to a few minutes to himself, especially after the week he'd had so far.

Placing the new baby clothes in the dryer—Olivia firmly believed in washing all of them first—she went into the bedroom to check on the babies. Sound asleep. She let out a sigh of relief and took a moment simply to savor the silence. Looking over at the bedside clock, she saw it was barely seven o'clock. Was that all? It felt like much later.

Tiptoeing from the room, she partially closed the door and then made her way to the kitchen to wash all the new bottles they'd bought and get them ready for the night and the next morning. Better to have them prepared now, so no time would be wasted when the babies woke up hungry.

There was something soothing about the task. Olivia's normal day consisted of running around barking orders at people and having to deal with sometimes-difficult clients. The actresses were the worst; they were all spoiled brats, in her opinion, and didn't take too kindly to the fact that Olivia didn't ooh and aah over them.

Olivia had yet to meet anyone who made her want to ooh or aah—she saw them all without makeup, so she knew it took a lot of work to make many of them look so beautiful. Without their makeup artists, they were no different than anyone else.

Carefully, she maneuvered an armful of bottles to the refrigerator and placed them on the shelf. Doing some quick math, she figured they'd have enough to get them through the night and the first bottles of the day tomorrow. By that point, Olivia knew she'd be more than ready to take on the task again.

With still no sign of Jake, she decided to clean the kitchen. It was obvious between the renovations and the arrival of the babies that everyday housework had been put on the back burner. Her brother and Jake must have eaten a lot of takeout, because the trash was overflowing with paper bags and Styrofoam containers. She took the trash to the outside pail and then came in and washed all the surfaces down before cleaning the sink. When she felt the room looked and smelled presentable, she walked out, turning the light off behind her.

The living room wasn't much better. Sure, she'd been hanging out in there most of the time, but now that the baby paraphernalia was organized and put away, she realized this room could use a good cleaning too.

After another quick check on the babies, she found dusting supplies and the vacuum and went to work. At first she had been afraid of making too much noise, but then figured maybe it was better if Maddie and Ben got used to sleeping while there was noise going on—especially if Jake was going to finish up the renovations on the second floor. Olivia didn't know a whole lot about construction or home renovations, but she knew it probably involved a good bit of noise.

Fifteen minutes later, she was putting the vacuum away, smiling when she peeked in at the babies and saw they were still sound asleep. A scream almost escaped her lips when she turned around after partially closing the door and found Jake right in front of her. “Dammit,” she hissed with a hand over her heart, “you scared the hell out of me.” He made to shush her, but she swatted his hand away from his lips. “Please, I just vacuumed in here. They’re fine.”

“But…the noise,” he began and then snapped his mouth shut.

Olivia’s lips twitched. She knew he was catching himself before arguing with her, and it took all of her will not to laugh at his restraint. Rather than comment on it, she stepped around him and walked out into the living room, sitting down on the couch. “I’m not sure they’ll be as cooperative if you are hammering, but they certainly did okay while I vacuumed.”

He joined her on the sofa, looking uncomfortable. “Oh, well…I guess that’s something.”

“Progress,” Olivia supplied. “It’s called progress. You’ll eventually settle in and be able to do all the things you usually do without them getting upset.”

“Somehow I doubt that,” he said miserably.

“Power of positive thinking, my friend,” she replied before reclining slightly against the cushions.

“Everything looks great in here, Liv. I didn’t expect you to go around cleaning the place.”

She shrugged. “It needed to be done.”

"Yeah, I know, but it wasn't your responsibility. I know I should have done a better job of keeping the place clean—especially now that the babies are here—but there never seemed to be enough time."

"Well, there's that and the fact that neither you nor my brother are known for being overly neat."

"Hey," he said in mock protest. "I take offense to that."

Olivia playfully swatted at his arm. "Whenever Mike comes to stay with me in L.A., I need a hazmat crew to come in once he's gone. He makes me crazy."

"Oh, and so you just assume I'm the same way?"

She turned her head and stared at him. "You're forgetting our families have known each other for a long time. I remember coming over here to get Mike when we were younger, and…"—she held her hand up when he went to interrupt her—"I was here the other day when the kids arrived. They hadn't been here long enough for you to blame them for the state of this room." She continued to stare him down, as if daring him to argue with her.

"Okay, fine, cleaning isn't my thing. Sue me."

"I have a feeling I'm going to have to attack the master bath before I'll feel safe using it."

"It's not bad," he said weakly, but caved when Olivia's eyes narrowed at him. "How about I go in there and clean it while you rest?"

"Uh, no," she replied as she stretched and stood. "I need to know it's clean to my standards."

"Your standards? What the hell does that mean?"

"It means clean," she teased before walking away with a smile and a sassy sway of her hips. The sass died away as soon as she got a good look at the bathroom.

"You have got to be kidding me," she murmured as she looked around the master suite.

"Believe it or not, I do have a cleaning woman come in every other week," Jake said from the doorway. "With the construction going on, there didn't seem to be a point."

Olivia could only nod. Between the babies, the shopping, and the cleaning, she was exhausted and this was not a task she was prepared to take on. The way her shoulders sagged must have given her thoughts away. Jake stepped around her and opened the closet to pull out the cleaning supplies.

"Come on," he said. "Between the two of us, we should be able to bang this out pretty quick."

He had a point, and she was too tired to argue. Together they worked in silence until every surface had been scrubbed clean—twice—and there were clean towels out for her to use. Stepping out of the bathroom, Olivia looked at the clock and saw it was now almost ten. A sigh escaped her lips before she could stop it.

"What's the matter?" Jake asked as he stepped from the bathroom and shut off the light. The babies had slept through all the cleaning, so he couldn't imagine what the problem was.

"I'm guessing they're on a four-hour-or-so schedule, right?" Jake nodded. "Then it's almost time for them to get up again. I guess the good news is now that we have everything organized, we can get them changed and fed and back to sleep with a little more ease and then we can go to bed."

Jake's eyes widened at her words, and it took Olivia a moment to realize exactly what she had said. "I mean…

then we…separately…can, um…you know, go to sleep. Separately. Alone. In different rooms." She cringed at her own yammering, wishing the floor would open up and swallow her whole.

"Oh, um…right," he mumbled before making a hasty retreat from the room.

Olivia followed him out. "Actually, I'm going to grab a quick shower before they get up, if that's okay with you."

Jake nodded but didn't make eye contact. "Sure. That's fine." He waited until he heard the bathroom door close before collapsing on the couch. Between Olivia's fumble about sleeping together and now thinking of her naked in his shower, Jake doubted he was going to be able to relax anytime in the near future.

He heard the water turn on and allowed himself the pleasure of imagining Olivia with suds rolling down her body. His eyes closed as his head lolled back onto the couch. The shower was large, certainly big enough for two people plus plenty of room to move around. If he were to join her in there, he'd have enough space to do what he pleased with her. A groan escaped his lips, and he started to sweat.

Forcing himself to sit up, he raked a hand through his hair. "Get a grip, man. You have enough on your plate without complicating things and making Olivia uncomfortable." While there was the possibility Olivia still harbored a crush on him, Jake still wasn't willing to risk offending her. A shake of his head helped to clear his wayward thoughts, and he rose to get himself something to drink.

By the time he returned to the living room, Olivia was

coming through the bedroom doorway, her hair wrapped turban style in a towel, wearing a pair of flannel boxers and an oversized T-shirt. "They're starting to stir," she said softly as she passed him on the way to the kitchen. "I'm going to get their bottles going if you want to get diapers and pj's out for them."

Without a word, Jake simply nodded and did what he needed to do. When Olivia joined him again, he was picking Ben up and taking him over to the changing table. "Do you need a hand?" Olivia asked as she removed the towel from her head and carefully finger combed her hair.

"No, I think I'm getting the hang of the whole changing thing. You'll probably have to show me the swaddling thing again when it's time to put them back down."

They worked together to get the infants cleaned and changed and met up again in the living room. Jake was already sitting with his son but had his daughter's bottle ready and waiting on the coffee table. Olivia sat on the opposite end of the sofa and curled up with the little girl in her arms. Gently, she ran a finger down Maddie's cheek. "Their skin is so soft," she whispered reverently. Then she touched the baby's hand, smiling when Maddie curled her entire hand around her finger. "And their hands are so tiny."

"I don't think I've ever seen babies this small," Jake said. "Their size scares me."

Olivia looked over at him. "Twins tend to be on the small side and they rarely go to term. Do you know if Marilyn carried them all the way through or if she delivered early?"

He shook his head. "She pretty much gave me their

birth certificates and not much else. I was too stunned to think of any specific questions to ask her."

Olivia wanted to rant and rave and rip the woman to shreds, but that wasn't going to happen, and it wasn't what Jake needed right now. "Either way, they're going to grow, and once we get them in with a pediatrician, you'll probably be able to get more information." She looked over and saw the familiar panic on Jake's face. "What? What did I say?"

"I don't have a pediatrician, Olivia," he said, anxiety back in his voice. He must have startled Ben, because he spat out the bottle and began to cry. "Shh…shh… It's okay, buddy," Jake cooed. "I'm sorry." Gently, he placed the bottle back at the baby's mouth and sighed with relief when he took it.

"Well, of course you don't have a pediatrician, Jake. That's not a problem. We'll make some calls tomorrow and get some referrals and get that taken care of. It's okay."

Jake only wished he could believe her. It seemed as soon as he felt things were getting under control, he was thrown another curveball. Pediatricians, cribs, diapers, nurseries—where was it going to end?

"I'm sure if I called my mom, she'd be able to recommend someone. Even if she doesn't know of one, she'll probably know someone we can call and ask."

"Sure, okay."

Olivia knew by the sound of his voice Jake wasn't feeling as confident about the whole thing as she was. At this time of night, there wasn't anything she could do to reassure him, so she just let the topic drop. "So…um, how did they do with sleeping the last couple of nights?"

Jake shrugged. "I hate to admit it, but I was too tired to pay attention to how long they slept and how long they were awake. All I know is it seemed like as soon as I would fall asleep, they'd be awake again."

"Okay, well, let's try and keep track of it starting tonight so we can work on a schedule. Once we get them down after they're fed, we'll estimate they'll sleep about four hours. It would be best if we tried to get them both up together so at some point they'll be in sync, and you'll be able to get some sleep too."

"Are we sure that's ever going to be possible?"

Olivia chuckled. "You're going to have to toughen up a bit, Jake. It's only been three days. You've got at least eighteen years to look forward to."

His eyes grew wide. "Now I may not know anything about babies, but I know kids sleep through the night long before they're eighteen!" He startled Ben again, and the baby began to cry. "Dammit," he cursed.

"It's okay, Jake," Olivia soothed. "I'm sure it's going to take a while to remember to speak a little softer. You're doing great."

"Sure, if by great you mean screwing up more and more each second."

She rolled her eyes. "Jeez, between you and my brother, I don't know who's more dramatic."

"He is. I'm not the dramatic type." Olivia looked at him with disbelief. "What? I'm not."

"You just go on believing that," she said sweetly. Looking down, she saw Maddie's eyes were starting to droop and the bottle was almost empty. Carefully, she pulled it away, braced the baby on her shoulder, and began to pat her back. She noticed Jake doing the same with Ben and knew it wouldn't be long before they had the babies back in their bassinets.

And she could go to sleep.

Ten minutes later, they were each laying a sleeping baby down and stepping back carefully. When a full minute passed without anyone making a peep, Olivia turned to Jake. "I guess I should probably try to get some sleep too. I'm not used to getting up in the night, so I think it would be best if I grabbed a couple of hours while they're sleeping."

"Oh…okay," Jake said hesitantly.

"Is something wrong?"

"No, no…it's just, I thought now that they're asleep and everything else is done, maybe we could just sort of sit and talk—you know, catch up."

Olivia couldn't help but smile. "As much as I'd like to, I'm beat. Besides, you're stuck with me for the next couple of weeks. I'm sure we'll have plenty of time to get caught up." When he continued to stand there, Olivia gave him a playful nudge toward the door. "Go and get some sleep too. I'll wake you up for the next shift."

Jake left the room and watched as Olivia shut the door. He was exhausted; he definitely needed a couple of hours of sleep. As he lay down on the sofa, however, and shut his eyes, sleep didn't immediately come.

Instead, visions of Olivia's smile and the way she had looked as she fed Maddie were there. It was a good vision, and after several minutes of savoring it, he finally fell asleep.

~

It was 3:00 a.m. when Olivia heard the first cry. She thought she was dreaming, and then she remembered where she was and nearly fell out of the bed. She made shushing sounds as she stumbled over to the bassinets to see which one was awake and gauge how upset he or she was. Ben was fussing, but Olivia knew she had a good five minutes before he got frantic.

Quietly, she crept from the room and went to the kitchen to get the bottles started. Jake was passed out cold on the couch, and she decided to wait it out a little bit longer before waking him. Maddie was still sound asleep when she got back into the bedroom, so Olivia picked up Ben and got him changed, then carried him to the kitchen with her to grab the bottles. Maybe if she fed him in the bedroom and had Maddie's bottle waiting, she could swing this without waking Jake.

With a quick peek at Ben's twin, Olivia confirmed she was still sleeping before settling herself and the baby on the bed. She kept the room fairly dark, with only the light of a small lamp to help her see. She wanted to keep the room peaceful and quiet so as not to stimulate either of the babies, so they'd go back to sleep easier.

Halfway through Ben's bottle, Maddie began to stir. Not quite sure what to do, she placed Ben on her shoulder and went to check on his sister. "Shh, sweet girl," she cooed. "Give me five more minutes with your brother and then I'm all yours." Carefully, she reached out and patted Maddie's tummy before turning back toward the bed and nearly screaming.

"I thought you were going to wake me up?" Jake asked sleepily.

"You have got to stop sneaking up on me," she whispered.

"Sorry. I heard them stirring and was waiting for you to come and get me." He gave her a lopsided grin.

"I hoped not to have to wake you at all, and if Maddie had slept for another five minutes, I could have pulled it off."

"You didn't have to, Liv. We're supposed to be doing this together, remember?"

She did, but she hadn't counted on how sexy Jake was going to look in the middle of the night. She had barely been able to keep from drooling a time or two during the day, but as he stood before her now in a pair of jeans and no shirt, she could feel her insides beginning to melt.

"I know, I know," she said, averting her eyes. "Um…if you want to take over with Ben, he's almost done with his bottle and just needs to be burped. I'll get Maddie changed."

"No, it's okay. You finish up with Ben. He looks pretty comfortable." He felt pretty darn good too, Olivia thought as she massaged the baby's back. Ben was curled up on her shoulder, and she was really starting to enjoy the feel of him there.

"Are you sure?" Jake nodded, and Olivia went back to her position on the bed to finish feeding Ben. Five minutes later, Jake sat down beside her, and she gasped. "What are you doing?"

"Feeding Maddie. Why?"

Good question. "I…um…I just thought you'd be more comfortable out on the couch, that's all."

He nodded, yawning. "This just seemed easier."

Actually, it wasn't easier, Jake came to realize. Sitting on the bed with Olivia in a dimly lit room was not going to help with the erotic dreams he'd been having. He kept his focus on his daughter and was actually disappointed when Olivia rose to put Ben back in his bed.

"I'm going to grab a glass of water," she said quietly. "Do you want one?"

"No thanks." Jake watched Olivia leave the room and let out a breath he hadn't realized he had been holding. Why had he thought this was a good idea? Any of this? He should have let Mike's mother come and help out. Hell, he should probably just give in and hire an agency to find him a full-time nanny. One day with Olivia, and he was already losing his mind. He needed to focus on his children and making a good life for them while finding the balance between home and work. Olivia wasn't a distraction Jake could afford right now.

He could only imagine what he was going to feel like by the time the month was up and she was gone.

Chapter 5

For the next week, Jake was too busy to let his attention linger on Olivia for too long. During the day, there was so much going on, he was having a hard time keeping track of it all.

True to her word, Olivia had found a pediatrician for the babies' first checkup. They were also able to find out—with a little bit of help—that the babies had been delivered at thirty-six weeks. The doctor assured Jake both of his children were fine and in good health, and by the time they left his office, Jake felt marginally better about how he had been caring for them.

He and Olivia had worked out a schedule so he could try and get some work done on the second floor of the house each day. Jake did his best to keep the noise and the dust levels to a minimum, but sometimes it just wasn't possible. The spring weather was cooperating, so when Jake told her there would be a lot of noise going on—or dust flying—Olivia would take the babies out for a walk in their new double stroller.

When Jake wasn't working, Olivia took the time to go and food shop and get any supplies the babies needed. Back in L.A., Olivia rarely went food shopping. She'd run in to one specialty food store or another, depending on her mood. But with the current situation, she realized the practicality of doing one big trip instead of a dozen little ones.

That's not to say everything was running smoothly.

The babies ate every four to five hours, so Jake and Olivia did their best to maximize the time the babies were asleep. Unfortunately, as both of them were used to a more active lifestyle, all the sitting around the house was starting to get tedious.

Olivia had brought her camera and her laptop with her, so she spent some of her spare time going through her portfolio and playing around with different effects on her photos. But she longed to do more. Taking pictures was a large part of who she was, and even though she was supposed to be on a break, her fingers were fairly twitching with the need to touch and hold her camera. Going through her backlog of pictures would only take her so far. She craved a new subject to photograph.

Later that night, while she and Jake were sitting on the sofa for the 3:00 a.m. feeding, inspiration struck.

"You know, I came home to take a break from work." Jake nodded. "Well, I'm finding I'm not really quite ready to do nothing at all."

"Liv, you've been extremely busy since you got here. You can't possibly tell me you're bored."

"Actually," she said nervously, "I am."

"Seriously?" His brows rose along with his voice.

Olivia nodded. "I mean, I know I'm doing a lot helping you out around here, but I really want to take some pictures."

He looked at her as if he couldn't understand the problem. "So…take some pictures."

A slow smile spread across her face. "I'm glad you said that."

Something in her tone and her expression waved a

red flag at him. What was she getting at? "Why?" he asked, caution lacing his tone.

"I know you may not have thought about this, but these are your children, and you should be documenting this time. You missed out on the pregnancy and their birth; you should totally be taking pictures of them now."

Jake's head lolled back as he closed his eyes. It truly was never ending. "Really?" he asked wearily.

Olivia nodded again. "Really. I think now that the house is tidier and they're on more of a schedule, we could totally get some great pictures."

"Aren't they a little young for photo shoots and portraits?" he asked with only a hint of a nervous laugh.

"I'm not talking a professional photo shoot. I'm just talking about some casual pictures of Maddie and Ben… and you."

"Me? Why the hell do I have to be involved?" Nerves were now replaced with irritation.

"Because you're their father," she said evenly. "There's going to come a time when you're going to talk to them about this time in their lives, and they're not going to believe how small they were. Or…you won't remember how small they were. Either way, it's nice to have these memories to look back on. Trust me. Don't you have pictures from when you were a baby around here someplace?"

"I found a whole box of them up in the attic after my parents died." Jake grew silent, then startled when he felt Olivia's hand on his.

"I know I wasn't here, but I really am sorry about your parents, Jake. They were amazing people." A lump formed in his throat, and all Jake could do was nod. Olivia gave him a moment before speaking again. "You know they would be over the top with these two little munchkins, right?" Leaning down, she placed a kiss on Ben's head. "Your parents would have spoiled them rotten, and they would have been proud of you for all you're doing for your children."

"I don't know about that," Jake said quietly, and Olivia waited for an explanation. He lifted Maddie on to his shoulder and gently rubbed her back. "My parents traveled a lot when I was growing up. Most of the time, they didn't take me with them. I spent a lot of time with aunts and uncles or with the occasional babysitter until I met Mike, and then I spent a lot of time at your house." He shifted in his seat and shrugged. "I know they loved me, but they were selfish. I think they just wanted to be together, and I was an inconvenience."

"Don't say that," Olivia said, but Jake quietly cut her off.

"I don't blame them, not anymore. They loved each other so much they only wanted to be together. I didn't have a bad life, Olivia, but looking back at how I was raised and knowing how I felt every time I was left behind is the reason why I won't hire a nanny to stay with Ben and Maddie. I don't ever want them to feel the way I did. I want them to know they are more important to me than anything."

Tears welled in Olivia's eyes, and she couldn't hold them back. Silently, she wiped them away as they fell down her cheek, but not before Jake saw them. "You know, you talk about how you don't feel like you're doing a good job with the babies or how you feel inept, but let me tell you something, Jake Knight. What you just said is the reason why you're going to be the best dad in the world. In a week, you totally grasped what it means to be a parent, and I think Maddie and Ben are the luckiest kids on the planet."

Jake felt his heart swell at her words. No one had ever said anything quite so powerful to him before, and coming from Olivia it meant so much more. "Thank you," he said gruffly before standing to get Maddie back to bed. As soon as his daughter was secured in her swaddling, Olivia came up beside him to place Ben down. He stood back and watched for a moment, and when they were certain both babies were asleep, they turned and looked at one another. "Well," Jake began, "I guess I'll see you in the morning."

Olivia nodded, but she wasn't really tired. She had gone to bed at ten—the same time as the babies—and with five hours of sleep behind her, she didn't feel ready to go back to bed. "Sure. See you in a couple of hours." She looked around the room, thinking about what she could do at this hour that wouldn't disturb anyone.

"Aren't you going back to sleep?"

She shook her head. "I'm not really tired. Maybe I'll read for a bit." Then she realized she didn't have anything to read with her. "Or maybe I'll grab something to drink and check emails."

"I'm not really tired either," Jake said, "and we still haven't had much time to just sit and relax and get caught up."

Oh, he remembered, Olivia thought to herself. "Right," she said, frantically searching her brain for a way to avoid having more up close and personal time with Jake. The truth of it was she'd been having plenty of time to sit and talk with him. She had just used that time to talk about anything but personal stuff. How was she supposed to talk about her life for the last seven or eight years without starting with "So remember how you were completely repulsed by me on my eighteenth birthday when I kissed you?" Yeah, probably not the best way to get the conversation started.

"Liv?" Jake prompted. "What do you say? We're both awake, and we've got hours before the kids will be awake and needing our attention. Come on. I'd really like to hear about your life and what it's like to be a photographer to the rich and famous."

She rolled her eyes at one. "It's not nearly as glamorous as you'd think."

"Well, I guess you'll have to tell me all about it and set me straight," he teased as he reached for her hand and led her from the bedroom.

Oh, help, Olivia thought to herself. *Personal time* and *hand-holding?* Why couldn't she have lied and said she was going to go to sleep? They stopped in front of the sofas and Jake released her hand. "I'm going to get something to drink. Do you want anything?"

Yes, to go back to the bedroom and close the door. Not gonna happen. "Do you have any tea?" He nodded and told her to make herself comfortable. Right. Like that was going to happen. The minutes ticked by, and all Olivia could think was how she was possibly going to talk about all of her reasons for hightailing it out of town all those years ago without bringing up the incident.

The incident.

What in the world had she been thinking?

Oh, right, she was eighteen and thought everything she wanted should be hers. Including Jake.

She tossed her head back on the sofa and groaned. *Holy awkwardness, Batman.* She could always simply get up, go to the bedroom, and lock the door, but she figured it wouldn't take Jake long to come over and knock. And then what would she say? "Oops"?

Her eyes opened just as Jake was setting their mugs down on the coffee table. "Milk, two sugars, right?" Olivia nodded as she watched him take a seat at the other end of the couch. "So you're a world-famous photographer," he said with a smile. "I guess I should be honored you want to take pictures of Maddie and Ben. They'll be worth millions someday." He laughed at the thought, then noticed Olivia didn't join in. "Hey," he said softly, "are you all right?"

She almost laughed. No, she wasn't all right. She was at a crossroads in her life, and in the midst of her much-needed break, she was sitting in Jake Knight's living room at four in the morning in her pajamas having tea, and it was beginning to feel like the most natural thing in the world. "I'm fine," she lied. "I guess I'm still a little out of sorts with things."

"Imagine how I feel," he said, and although he tried to sound fine, Olivia heard the telltale nervousness there.

"I guess I should be asking if you're all right," she said softly.

Leaning forward, Jake rested his elbows on his knees and looked straight ahead. Taking a steadying breath, he spoke. "I appreciate all of your help with Maddie and Ben. I don't know how I would have done this without you. I know they're too little to understand what's going on, but I don't want them to be traumatized. I never want them to feel like they weren't loved or wanted. I can't control what Marilyn did, but I can certainly control what happens from this point on. I knew she really didn't have any maternal instincts. I just never knew the extent of it until she asked for a check and just walked away."

His head hung forward and Olivia waited for him to speak again.

"I'm glad they'll have no memory of that—you're here making them feel loved and cared for."

Olivia couldn't remember ever hearing Jake speak like this. She knew he had issues with his family and his upbringing, but there was a vulnerability to him that now made her heart ache.

"You're doing everything you can, Jake," she began, "and you're doing great. Like you said, they're young, and they're not going to remember this, but they will always remember how you make them feel. You're creating a foundation here, a way of life that will help them grow up and feel secure. You should be very proud."

"I don't know about that," he said, his expression grim.

"It's true. It won't be long before they really start to recognize you, and when they're more alert, I know their faces are simply going to light up when you walk into a room. Why? Because you're their daddy, and they'll know that means love." Unable to help herself, she scooted closer and placed one hand over his. "Trust me."

Jake was silent and there was nothing else she could say to reassure him. He was going to have to figure this out on his own. They sat there for long moments, the only sounds in the room their breathing and the ticking of the clock on the fireplace mantel.

When Jake finally spoke, his voice shook. "I don't know how I'm going to do this, Olivia. A week ago, I was a single guy rehabbing a house so I could sell it and move on to the next thing. I wasn't sure what the next thing was, but I knew it wasn't staying here and living in this house. I have no idea how I'm going to handle being a single father of twins. How am I supposed to work and take care of them at the same time? My business is doing well, but it's not completely self-sufficient. I need to be there. And I know I need to be here for Maddie and Ben. How do I possibly do both?"

She moved a little bit closer to him as her grip tightened on his hand. "You're going to find a way, Jake. Not right now, maybe not tomorrow, but in time, you're going to figure out what works for the three of you. I know you don't want to hire someone, and maybe that's not the way to go. Maybe if you hire someone part-time and make the commitment to keeping it that way, you'll find it's a good thing for all of you. You can't possibly be the parent you want to be if you're burned out or broke." He turned and looked at her. "And you love them. That's the best part. Just love them, and soon everything else will fall into place."

"What if I get selfish? What if I get lazy and start relying too much on the person I hire?"

She shook her head. "That will never happen. Why? Because you know what it's like to be them." Olivia went to move her hand away, but Jake clasped her small hand in his large one. Twice in one night and Olivia was starting to get used to the feel of him. He may have hurt her once upon a time, but she knew that right then, it didn't matter. He needed a friend, and she was it.

"You're not going to find all the answers in a day or a week or maybe even a month," she said. "But eventually, you will. And then you're going to wonder why you were so worried. You'll be giving parenting advice to all your friends, and they'll seek you out because you'll have this so under control. I believe in you."

He was stroking the back of her hand with his thumb as she spoke, and Olivia found his touch hypnotic. Jake looked up and she saw myriad emotions there. "I hate that I took away your vacation time." His words were spoken so softly, Olivia wasn't sure she heard him at first. "I know this wasn't the way you had planned to spend your time, and even though I am sorry, I know I can get through this because of you. You're an amazing woman, Olivia."

Oh, hell. How was she supposed to remain indifferent when he said things like that? She blushed and whispered a thank-you as she ducked her head. With his free hand, Jake tucked a finger under her chin and gently forced her to look at him. The gentle expression on his face was mesmerizing, and Olivia felt as if she were being pulled toward him. She swayed. She sighed.

And then he kissed her.

Maybe it was his way of saying thank you.

Maybe he had fallen asleep and his lips just happened to brush hers.

Either way, Jake was kissing her. Gently at first and then it kicked up a notch into something more.

Jake crowded closer to her, and he released her hands so his could roam up her torso to skim her neck and then anchor in her hair. Part of Olivia questioned if she was actually awake or if this was a dream, while another part of her told her to just shut up and enjoy the kiss. Lord knew they didn't get this far the first time around because Jake had pretty much shoved her away. But he was kissing her now. Really kissing her, and oh, how the man could kiss.

Placing her hands on his shoulders, Olivia moved closer. His hands left her hair and smoothed their way down her back until she was wrapped in his arms. It took very little effort until he had her sprawled across his lap. She was warring with herself internally even as she did her best to move closer.

His mouth was hot and passionate, and even as she pressed against him, he was pulling her in. It was like nothing Olivia had ever experienced before. There was so much emotion being expressed without uttering a word, and she wanted him so much—more than she even dared to admit—and he wasn't shoving her away! Once she let that fact settle in, Olivia relaxed a little and let her hands get in on the action, moving from his hard biceps up to his shoulders, his neck, and then into his thick hair. She held on, silently praying he didn't want to let her go, that he wanted to take this to the next level as much as she did.

As her tongue reached out, dueling and mating with his, Jake groaned as if in pain and then hauled her impossibly closer. His tongue teased her, explored her, set off fireworks inside her. She needed air, needed to breathe, but she needed this more.

Twisting in his arms, Olivia went from lying across him to straddling him, and as she settled snugly against what was becoming an extremely impressive erection, she began to move. It felt so good, so right, she was so close and…

She was suddenly sitting alone on the couch.

What the…?

Jake was across the room before Olivia could even register he'd moved. He stood in the far corner, his back to her, and looked out the window toward the darkened backyard. She didn't have to ask if he was all right; his body language said it all. His head dropped to his chest, and he was just as breathless as she was.

Dammit.

When was she ever going to learn? For all she knew, he never intended to kiss her at all. He was probably just going to give her a peck on the cheek to say thanks, and she had gone and pounced. Again. *Yikes.* There was no way to graciously get out of this one, and there was no way she could simply run away. There were babies to consider, and even though she was completely mortified right then, there was no way she was going to up and leave them. They'd already had that happen to them once. In Olivia's mind, that was one time too many.

Tears began to well in her eyes, and she cursed herself. She didn't cry. As a rule, Olivia always did her best to keep her emotions in check—especially where Jake was concerned. And there was no way in the world she was going to let him see her cry. The door to the bedroom was only about ten feet away. She could stand and be there in less than five seconds. The only thing stopping her was the fact that her entire body was trembling, and she didn't think she'd be capable of walking without falling, making an even bigger fool of herself.

With nothing left to do, she wrapped her arms around her middle and bent over, closing her eyes. She did her best to breathe deeply and try to calm herself. Maybe Jake would take pity on her and just leave, go outside or to the kitchen or…anywhere. Just give her a few minutes to make her escape without having to look at him.

"Olivia, I am so sorry," he said gruffly from across the room. "That never should have happened."

Oh God…

"Here you are helping me with the biggest crisis of my life, and I go and…and…maul you." He groaned and banged his head slightly on the glass. "I wouldn't blame you at all if you wanted to pack up and go. Hell, I'll even load your car if you want."

"Wait…what?" Jake was taking responsibility for the kiss? She raised her head and looked over at him, willing him to turn around. "You don't need to apologize to me. I'm the one who keeps mauling you, apparently." She wanted to chuckle, to make it sound like she realized what an idiot she was, but all that came out was a strangled groan. "I know you're going through a really tough and emotional time." *Now make it seem like it was nothing. Like it was no big deal.* "It's okay, really. I'm not going to read anything into it. It was impulsive. It wasn't like you really wanted to kiss me or anything. I learned my lesson a long time ago where that topic is concerned."

He finally turned around, anger and confusion written on his face. He stepped out of the darkness and sat down on the coffee table in front of her. She was used to his scowling. He had been doing it for days. Except now she was the reason for it, and it made her scoot a little farther back on the couch. "What the hell are you talking about?" he asked lowly.

Olivia rolled her eyes. Jeez, was he really going to make her say it? To relive her most humiliating moment out loud? She looked directly at him and saw he was waiting for an answer. "Oh, please... The last time we kissed like that you practically shoved me halfway across the room before taking off. I may not have known a lot about men, Jake, but I certainly was able to tell when one is pretty much repulsed by me."

Why couldn't the floor just open up and swallow her whole right now? She'd go willingly.

"Wait, are you talking about your birthday party?"

Now she was annoyed. "Do you remember us kissing any other time?"

He shook his head. "Olivia, that was like...eight years ago. You were a kid and I—"

"I get it," she quickly interrupted. "It's not a big deal. We don't have to relive it, okay? You weren't attracted to me. It's fine. I got over it. Eventually. Sort of. Message received. Loud and clear." Oh God, now she was babbling. She cleared her throat. "So really, I understand you were probably just letting off a little steam right now. No big deal. We're good. We're fine." *Just shut up!*

Jake reached out and placed a warm hand on her knee. "Olivia, I think you misunderstood what happened. Yes, you kissed me, and yes, I pushed you away, but not because I wasn't attracted to you. I was! But you took me by surprise, and I saw Mike was coming into the garage, and I knew if he saw us...kissing, he'd kick my ass and then start yelling at you. I didn't want to ruin your party."

"But—"

"I guess I did anyway," he said miserably. "God, Olivia, I am so sorry. I had no idea you took it that way. I tried to find you later that night, but you were always surrounded by people." He ran a weary hand over his face. "I should have made more of an effort."

"Wait," she said cautiously, "are you saying if Mike hadn't been coming, you would have kissed me back?" He nodded. "You wouldn't have pushed me away like I had some sort of contagious disease?"

"Liv," he began softly, "if Mike hadn't come in, I just might have pushed you into the corner and kissed you for the rest of the night."

She fell back against the cushions in awe. "Wow. I had no idea."

"I knew it was wrong," he continued. "I mean, I know you had just turned eighteen so legally you were an adult, but you were still so young. It felt wrong to me, like I was somehow taking advantage of you. Suddenly, you weren't just Mike's little sister. You had blossomed into this beautiful woman I found very desirable—so desirable it was hard to control myself around you sometimes." He shook his head. "That's why tonight never should have happened. There is so much going on here in my life right now that I should have known better than to act impulsively."

"Why? We're both adults, Jake, and clearly we're attracted to one another. What's the big deal?"

"The big deal is my life is a mess right now, Liv. I have no right starting something that isn't going to go anywhere. The babies need to be my first—my *only*—priority. I need to get this house done—for them. I need to figure out my business situation—for them. I can't think about myself. Right now, it has to be all about them."

"I get that, Jake, I really do, but…we're not kids. We're both adults, and it's not like I'm asking you for some kind of long-term commitment here." He looked at her as if she were crazy. And maybe she was.

Shaking his head, Jake stood and began to pace. "No," he said adamantly. "That's not… It's just…" He turned and faced her. "It's not right, Olivia. It wouldn't be fair to you."

Now she stood and stalked across the room toward him. She almost laughed when he began to back away. "Who are you to tell me what's fair to me and what's not? I'm a grown woman, dammit, and if I say I'm okay with it, then I am!"

He held up his hands in surrender. "Look, I'm sure you *think* you're okay with it, Liv. And in the right now, maybe I would be too. But we've known each other too long to just jump in and do something like this. There's too much at stake." He shook his head as if to clear it. "I need to focus on the babies. I can't…I can't let myself be distracted by… Damn it, Olivia, I just can't!"

For a moment, Olivia thought it was adorable he couldn't even form a coherent sentence. But she wasn't going to let it deter her either. For years she had pined for this man, and for years she had convinced herself she was over him. But now? Finding out he really had been attracted to her and experiencing the kiss they'd just had was like waving a red flag in front of a bull. There was no way Olivia was going to be able to just stay here for the next few weeks without experiencing the rest of the possibilities.

Maybe Jake was right; maybe she would regret it, but wouldn't she regret it more if she didn't take the chance at all? For so many years, Jake Knight had taken up residence in her head and her heart, and she wasn't about to let go of the chance for him to be a part of her body without a fight.

"Look, I just don't think it's going to be possible for us to ignore the feelings we have for each other—particularly when we're going to be living together for the next few weeks."

"Then I'll get someone else to come and stay with me," he said quickly, his voice laced with panic.

Olivia laughed. "If it were that easy, I think you would have done that rather than calling me in the first place." She began to slowly walk toward him again. "I'm here now, Jake," she said softly. "And I'm not going anyplace. I promised you a month, and I'm not breaking that promise. If you think you can ignore me and what just happened here for the next three weeks, then be my guest. But I'm telling you I have no intention of ignoring it or forgetting it."

Jake closed his eyes and grimaced as if he were in pain. Not her finest hour, Olivia thought. Why did it have to be this man who made her want to be bold when clearly, every time she was, he reacted so badly? You'd think her ego would have been battered and broken by then. But now she knew better. She knew Jake was as attracted to her as she was to him, and he may have been fighting it now, but Olivia silently vowed she'd change his way of thinking.

Soon.

She let out a loud sigh and walked over to the couch

to pick up her forgotten drink. “You have a right to feel the way you do.”

He nodded his head. “Thank you.”

“But…so do I,” she said sweetly. “You may think you know what’s best—for everyone—but I don’t necessarily agree. You’re overwhelmed right now, and I get that. Things are changing all around you, and I’m sure it’s freaking you out.”

“It is,” he said warily.

“I’m still not going anywhere,” she said firmly, staring him in the eye as she said it.

“Olivia, I’m telling you a relationship of any kind between us would be wrong.” There wasn’t much force behind those words, and it gave Olivia her first glimmer of hope.

“So you’re saying I should just forget that I have feelings for you? That I ever had feelings for you?” Jake nodded, and she shook her head. “It’s not gonna happen.”

“But—”

“Let me worry about what’s right and what’s wrong for me, okay?” Leaning over, she turned off the table lamp and sauntered back over to him. Boldly, she placed a hand on his cheek, stood on tiptoes, and kissed him gently on the other cheek. “Good night, Jake,” she whispered. “I’ll see you in the morning.”

Chapter 6

For the next several days, Jake did his best to stay away from Olivia. When the babies were awake, he didn't have a choice but to be around her, but once they went back to sleep, he disappeared. Quickly.

While it was true he did have a legitimate excuse—the upstairs of the house really did need to get done—the truth was he wasn't accomplishing much in that area either. Every task he had, he dragged out. If he had ever done a job at this pace, his company would never have gotten off the ground. He tried to blame his sluggish progress on having been out of the game for a while—having sat at a desk making the connections and overseeing the jobs rather than being out there working them—but he knew it wasn't the truth. Then he tried telling himself it was the lack of sleep causing it.

The truth was he spent most of his alone time thinking about Olivia and the kiss. What if he hadn't stopped? What if he had been the type of guy who simply took what he wanted and didn't worry about being responsible? He'd never been that type of guy, unfortunately, and he couldn't even fathom how something like that would work. It just wasn't in his DNA.

Olivia was his best friend's sister, and if Mike found out Jake had agreed to a no-strings-attached fling with Mike's sister, Jake was certain he'd be a dead man. Not something he was looking forward to, no matter how tempting Olivia was.

He groaned just thinking of how tempting Olivia was. Hell, she was hazardous to his mental health. During the day wasn't so bad because she walked around in jeans and T-shirts and generally was well covered, but at night? She was clearly trying to torture him. The flannel boxers seemed shorter than short and hugged her bottom in a way made his hands twitch, and the tiny tank tops she wore left little to the imagination.

And Jake had a very vivid imagination.

She hadn't touched him—not physically—but her every word, every movement seemed like a caress to him. Watching her take care of his children and seeing how much of herself she gave to the task was far more attractive than anything any other woman had ever done. Ever.

"Jake?" He looked up and saw Olivia standing in the doorway to what was going to become the nursery. "I was hoping maybe today we could do those pictures." Her eyes were big and bright and full of excitement.

"Uh…today's not good for me," he lied. "I've got a lot going on up here I want to get finished." She leaned against the doorway and crossed her arms, staring him down. "What?"

"You're full of crap," she said bluntly.

"Excuse me?"

"You heard me; you're full of crap." She stepped into the room and looked around. "I don't know what you've been doing up here exactly, but I can tell it isn't much."

"Then you don't know what you're talking about," he

said defensively. "There's a lot to get done up here, and it all has to be done in a certain order. Last I checked, you were a photographer, not a contractor."

"I may very well be, but I know when something's being done and when it isn't," she pushed back. "This room looks exactly like it did two days ago, and so do all the other rooms up here."

"How would you know?" he snapped, feeling caged in because clearly the cat was out of the bag.

"Every night when you go in and take your shower, I come up here and see what's going on and how everything is progressing because I'm curious as to when the babies can move up to their own room."

"Why, what's the matter, princess? Don't like having to share a room?"

She actually laughed. "Jake, you can lash out at me all you want. You're slacking, and you know it. You're still uncomfortable with what happened the other night, and you're hiding out up here to avoid dealing with me." She stepped closer and gave him her cockiest smile. "And I'm still not going anywhere."

She was killing him.

"Why can't you just take it for what it is, Liv? I'm up here trying to work things out. Nothing more, nothing less. Not everything has to do with you."

She nodded. "Oh, I would be fine with that…if it were true. I want you to look me in the eye and tell me you're not hiding up here to stay away from me."

Why had he ever thought having her here was going to be a good idea? Or helpful? Taking a fortifying breath, he stepped in close—until they were almost toe to toe—and stared down into her eyes. It was right there on the tip of his tongue, and yet he couldn't force the words out. Jake knew he was many things, but a liar wasn't one of them.

"I'm trying to do the right thing here, Olivia," he growled as his body began to lean toward hers.

"If you recall, I didn't ask you to. That one's all on you, big guy." She winked and smiled at him.

"I've got a dozen reasons why this is all wrong," he said, slowly losing the battle raging within him.

"And I've got a dozen more that say why it's right," she countered, swaying toward him.

"Your brother will kill me."

"My brother isn't here."

"I don't want to ruin our friendship."

"We haven't even talked in eight years."

He inhaled her fresh, floral scent. "I've got two babies to think about."

"That's what I'm here to help you with."

Jake knew he could go on and on and on, but in the long run, he was going to lose. Or win. Depending on how he decided to look at it. His life was spinning out of control, and he had no doubt that sooner or later, he was going to snap under the pressure. Maybe it was time for him to be a little selfish and take what was willingly being offered to him.

Meeting Olivia's eyes, he saw a triumphant glint in them, but he wasn't ready to concede just yet. "Pictures," he finally said and cleared his throat. "You mentioned wanting to take pictures today."

Taking a step back, Olivia nodded. "It's actually a beautiful day out, and I thought it might be nice to take some out in the yard. You have some amazing landscaping out there and so many flowers in bloom would make for great background scenery."

He considered her words for a moment. "How long until they wake up?"

Olivia checked her watch. "I'd say about an hour. Why?"

"Then I'm going to grab a shower now. By the time I'm done, they should be ready to get up, and we can get them changed and fed and then go outside for your photo shoot."

Olivia wasn't stupid; she knew this was simply a distraction to keep him—yet again—from dealing with the situation at hand. "That works for me," she said. "I'm going to go and scope out the spots I want to use so we can maximize our time once they're awake. I've already got their outfits in mind."

"What about me?" The question came out before he could stop it, and his voice was huskier than it had been a minute ago.

"I think you should wear whatever makes you the most comfortable," she said easily and began to turn to leave the room. "I think you look the best in a pair of faded blue jeans and a dark T-shirt." She smiled over her shoulder. "But that's just me."

With one last wink, she was gone. Jake heard her treading down the stairs and almost sagged to the floor when he was finally alone. He was totally playing with fire here.

And one of them was bound to get burned.

As much as he hated to admit it, he was having a good time. The weather was near perfect, and Maddie and

Ben were totally cooperating with everything Olivia had them doing. If he hadn't known better, he'd have sworn Maddie actually smiled on cue for a few of them. Jake knew it wasn't possible—she was far too young—but it still gave him a bit of a thrill.

Olivia posed them on blankets with flowers blooming in the background; then she covered their car seats with blankets, so they looked like big pillows, and took several shots of them on the grass. Jake watched her while she worked and had to admit he was impressed. Obviously she knew what she was doing—she did this on a daily basis with big Hollywood celebrities—but she seemed equally comfortable in his backyard taking pictures of two infants who had no idea what was going on.

"Now I think you need to be in a few of them," Olivia said as she moved the infants to another spot on the grass and laid out a blanket for Jake to sit on. She talked to herself as she got everything situated exactly where she wanted them, and her movements were swift and efficient. Without looking at him, she said, "I'll want you to sit down on the blankets, and then I'm going to move their seats on either side of you." She walked over to pick up each of the babies and placed them into position. "We'll do a few shots like this, and then we'll take them out of the seats and have you holding them. Some shots, you'll hold the both of them, and then I'll take a couple of one-on-one shots, so they'll each have a daddy-and-me shot for when they get older."

Jake had no idea what to say to all of that. He'd never given much thought to pictures—taking them or taking them out to look at them. He knew there were photo albums in his house from throughout his life that his mother had made, but no one had ever made a big deal about them. Maybe he'd have to give them another look and see the kinds of things he should think about documenting in Ben's and Maddie's lives. What Olivia was doing right now was great, but she wasn't going to be here forever to make sure pictures got taken when they should.

For a moment, he let that thought settle in as he watched her continue to set the scene for this next round of photos. She wasn't going to be here forever. This month—which was starting to move way too quickly for his liking—was going to be all they had. Did he really want to spend it walking around wishing things were different? Lying awake at night, wondering what it would be like to hold her, kiss her, love her? Was that the life he wanted?

"Okay, why don't you put a hand on each of their seats and look at me and smile?" Olivia suggested as she crouched down into position just off the blanket. She turned the camera this way and that, and moved around as she directed him where to look and what to do. Olivia knew she should have been focusing on the picture as a whole, but the image of Jake sitting there looking relaxed and happy surrounded by his kids just twisted her up in knots. How was it possible something as innocent as sitting with his babies made him look so sexy?

Clearing her throat, she instructed him to pick up Ben while she moved Maddie out of view and then removed Ben's seat. "What should I do with him?" Jake asked, holding his son awkwardly for a moment.

"Well, first, you want to hold him as if he doesn't

smell like poop," she laughed. "Then just…do whatever seems natural. You hold him all the time. Talk to him, play with him, you know, try to make him smile." She watched for a few minutes and even managed to take a couple of shots before she had to put a stop to the torture. "For crying out loud, Jake," she said with a huff. "What is the problem?"

"It's weird," he said and sat back with Ben casually resting in his lap.

Not wanting to spook him, Olivia engaged him in conversation and kept him distracted while she took a couple of shots. "How is it weird?"

"I know I interact with them every day, but no one's watching, you know?" He looked down and let Ben wrap one of his tiny hands around his finger. He shook it and smiled at how the baby's grip tightened. "It doesn't feel natural to have someone snapping away while I'm trying to get him to smile."

"But you're doing it," she said lightly, managing to catch the look of surprise on his face when he looked up and realized she had been taking pictures the entire time. "See?"

He couldn't help but chuckle at himself. "Wow… you're good."

Standing, Olivia curtsied and then walked over to take Ben and hand Maddie to Jake. When she had them situated exactly as she wanted them—but different from how she had had Jake and Ben—Olivia began snapping pictures, talking to Jake the entire time. "When they get a little bit older, it will be easier because they'll interact with you. Right now it's a lot of serious faces on their part, so you're the one who has to look animated."

Jake looked up and confusion was written all over his face. "Animated? Like a cartoon?"

Olivia nearly dropped her camera as she laughed. "No, not like a cartoon. I mean you have to be the one showing the emotion and having to be a little more over the top than you're used to in order to get a response from them."

"Ah," he said and then turned to make funny faces at Maddie. "I can't wait until they actually smile for real. Earlier, it looked like Maddie was doing it, but I know she's too young for that. Right?"

"She'll be doing it before you know it, and then she's going to learn how to use that smile to wrap you around her little finger."

"No way," Jake said with fake indignation. "Not my sweet girl. There's no way she'll try and manipulate me."

Olivia could only chuckle. "Remind me to check in with you in a year or two. We'll see who's running the show around here then."

Jake was having a hard enough time wrapping his brain around the here and now. Hearing Olivia talk about two years down the road made him feel a little sick.

"Jake?" Olivia asked, concern marking her face as she lowered the camera. "Are you okay?"

"Huh? What?" He swallowed hard. "Why do you ask?"

"You sort of paled there for a minute. I haven't seen that happen to you in almost a week. What's going on?"

Turning, Jake placed Maddie back in her seat before collapsing back on the blanket. "It's just... when you mentioned life for us two years down the road...it hit me. I'm having trouble just getting through one day at a time. I haven't even thought about the future. But I really need to be doing that, don't I?"

She took pity on him. After a quick check that the kids were still content, she sat down on the blanket beside him and then, just because, she lay down on her side and faced him. "Eventually you will," she said simply. "But for right now, you're doing just fine. Don't go looking for trouble. With babies, especially when they're little like this, all new parents simply do one day at a time. You're not any different from the other millions of parents out there. And believe it or not, you're not the only single dad with twins."

"Are we sure about that?" he asked weakly.

Olivia chuckled and nodded. "Pretty sure." She reached out and placed a hand on his arm. "Soon you'll settle into a routine, they'll sleep longer, and before you know it, you're not going to feel so completely overwhelmed."

"I greatly doubt that. No matter how much time passes, there are still two of them and only one of me."

"You'll just have to learn to be faster and a little more devious."

He didn't like the sound of that. "Why would I have to be devious with my own children?" he asked as he leaned up on one elbow, effectively bringing him a little bit closer to her.

"I can't speak from experience, but I've heard stories of twins who…shall we say…work together to try and outsmart their parents."

"Outsmart…how?"

"You know, taking apart their cribs or baby gates. Being the lookout so they can get into things they know they shouldn't. You'll learn to have eyes in the back of your head."

Jake's eyes closed, and he let out a weary sigh. "I'm never going to remember all of this. How am I supposed to do this all by myself?" Opening his eyes, he gazed into hers, his expression imploring.

Olivia wished there was something she could say that would magically make him relax and feel more confident. It was still unnerving to her to sit back and watch the man who had always been the model of confidence suddenly walking around in a constant state of self-doubt. "I don't know, Jake," she said softly, a sad smile on her face. "I wish there was some magic book that gave you all the answers, but there isn't. Parenthood is one of those things in life that doesn't come with an instruction manual. The important thing is you love them and nurture them. You're doing that now."

"But what if it's not enough? What if they need more than I can give them?"

She shook her head. "Not even possible. I can see the difference in you already after a week. They may not have appeared in your life in the most traditional of ways, but your immediate instinct was to take care of them. You worry about them, and you're trying to learn and be everything they need. That tells me you're going to be an awesome parent."

He wished he had her confidence.

He wished he had her optimism.

He wished… Ah, hell. Leaning forward, he did what he was wishing for the most. He kissed her.

It was light, almost teasing, but the moment Jake let his lips settle against Olivia's, he felt as if everything in his world righted itself. He wasn't going to rush it. There was no reason to. All he knew was for right there, right then, he was going to enjoy the sensation of sipping at Olivia's soft lips and listening to her sigh.

It was pretty damn good.

Carefully, oh so carefully, he eased closer, rolling her onto her back. Olivia's arms wound their way slowly around his shoulders and then relaxed around his neck. It was in no way as frantic and wild as it had been a few nights ago, but in Jake's mind, it was definitely better.

He could now focus on taking his time and learning the feel of her. One hand came up and caressed her cheek, and he marveled at how soft her skin was. He let that same hand skim its way down the slender column of her throat, and he felt the rapid beat of her pulse, humbled he was the one to make it race that way.

Deepening the kiss a little, Jake's tongue slowly traced its way along Olivia's lower lip, and before he knew it, hers was mimicking the action. Refusing to take it any further or deeper just yet, he kissed his way across her cheek to her earlobe as a way of distracting himself. But that didn't mean his hands were going to stay still.

His hand had been teasing at her pulse point and slowly worked its way down her arm and across to her waist, where he forced himself to stop and to simply be content. Maybe he gripped her a little harder; maybe his fingers began to carefully tug and pull to move her shirt up so he could feel bare skin.

Maybe he should quit while he was ahead and go back to exploring her lips.

They were definitely worth exploring.

Reluctantly, Jake lifted his head from Olivia's

neck and reclaimed her mouth. He heard her sigh and simply let himself sink into the kiss. This time he did go further—he needed to. His tongue teased at her lips for the merest of seconds before Olivia opened for him and clutched him closer.

It didn't take much to align their bodies, for Jake to be firmly on top of Olivia, her legs slowly winding their way around his hips. He rocked gently and swallowed her soft gasp of pleasure. It inflamed him, turned him on faster than he'd ever thought possible.

"Olivia," he sighed against her lips, raising up slightly to look at her face. God, she was beautiful. Right then, he wanted nothing more than to make love to her. Everything was perfect—the feel of her beneath him, the soft breeze blowing around them while they lay in the grass under the shade of the large oak tree. "Olivia…I…"

Maddie let out a small cry and it was more effective than a bucket of cold water thrown on them. Jake rested his forehead against Olivia's and panicked when he felt her shake and tremble. Raising his head, he looked down at her, surprised to find her laughing. "Are you all right?" he asked.

She continued to laugh until she playfully pushed him off her and went to see what Maddie needed. "Hey, sweet girl," she cooed, "were we neglecting you for a minute?" She lifted the baby out of her seat and stood up. Turning, Olivia looked down to where Jake was still lying flat on the ground. "Are you all right?" she asked with a big grin as her eyes wandered from his face to the erection that was still very evident.

Jumping to his feet, Jake stood and kissed Maddie

on the head before turning and checking on her brother, who was now asleep. "I guess Ben's lost interest in his photo session."

"Give him time," she said, gently bouncing Maddie against her. "By the time we get all of this stuff together and back in the house, he'll be stirring again. He was just bored."

Jake laughed. "Aren't they usually bored? I mean, they can't do anything."

She gave him a bland look. "They are busy growing and developing. It's exhausting. Don't be so quick to judge."

He held up his hands in surrender and began folding up the blanket and gathering their things. "Hey, I wasn't judging," he said with a laugh. "I'm just thinking they have it pretty good right now."

"It's the calm before the storm."

Jake wasn't sure if there was a double entendre there, but he wouldn't have doubted it. Olivia carefully placed Maddie back in her seat, scooping up her camera equipment in one hand and Maddie's seat in the other. Jake stood back and marveled. She was a natural. Did anything faze her? Trip her up? How could she have gone from being so pliant and soft and sexy in his arms one minute to this efficient woman on the go the next? Did their kiss mean anything to her? Was she affected by it at all?

Scooping up Ben and their blankets, he followed her into the house and chuckled when he looked down and found his son staring back at him. "She thinks she's so smart," he whispered to Ben. "She thinks she knows everything, but I'm thinking I can teach her a thing or two."

Olivia looked over her shoulder and smiled at him. Jake had no idea if she heard what he was saying or not, but the look of pure happiness on her face was enough for him. She may know a lot about babies and photography. But Jake knew he was going to teach her how to forget herself for a little. While he appreciated her dedication to the babies, he wouldn't have minded if she had been just as lost as him—if even for a minute.

It was now his goal.

One way or another, he was going to find what it took to make Olivia forget everything around her—except him.

Chapter 7

THE KIDS WERE CLEAN, BATHED, FED, AND ALL THAT WAS left was to put them to bed. Olivia was both looking forward to it and dreading it. In a perfect world, she and Jake would pick up where they'd left off in the yard earlier, and finally—*finally!*—she'd know what it was like to spend the night with him.

Unfortunately, she had a sinking feeling he was going to pull a full-blown retreat once the babies were asleep. Olivia fidgeted with Ben's pajamas and out of the corner of her eye, she watched Jake rocking Maddie. It was such a simple domestic scene, and yet there was something to be said for it. Doing these everyday, mundane tasks with Jake didn't diminish anything. She still felt the pull of attraction as strongly as ever. If anything, she found watching him take care of his kids to be oddly sexy.

Clearly she needed therapy.

"Okay, big guy," she whispered to Ben with a smile, "time for bed." She lifted him off the changing table and walked across the room toward his crib. The digital clock in the corner showed close to ten o'clock, which was their usual bedtime. They'd have to work on getting it a little earlier eventually and getting them to sleep a little longer. *All in good time*, she mused silently.

Laying Ben down, she made sure he was snug and swaddled to his liking, and when he started to fuss, she quietly hummed to him while stroking his head and patting his belly. He was a pushover for a good belly rub. Olivia almost laughed because it seemed so ridiculous, was normally something reserved for puppies, but it worked well on the sweet little boy in front of her. "Whatever works," she whispered when his eyes started to drift closed.

"Is he okay?" Jake whispered from beside her as he went through the routine of getting Maddie settled. Her wide-open blue eyes told Olivia she wasn't quite ready for bed yet, but they were desperately trying to keep them on a routine of going to sleep and waking up at the same time.

"He's fine," she finally said quietly. "You know he always fights it a little bit. He's a snuggler, and he likes to be in somebody's arms."

Jake knew the feeling. "Nothing wrong with that," he said as he found Maddie's pacifier and did his best to get his daughter to take it.

"No," Olivia agreed, "there's not. But if you don't break the habit, he'll never learn to go to sleep without someone holding him. Then you'll be in trouble when you're here by yourself and they're both fussing and you can't put him down. Trust me." She looked down at the twins and smiled. Maddie's eyes were beginning to droop and Ben's were already closed. "See? He didn't put up too much of a fight."

The lights in the bedroom were already dimmed, and Jake took Olivia by the hand and led her out to the living room, partially closing the door behind them. They walked over to the sofa and Olivia sat first. "I'm going to get something to drink. You want something?"

It was a question he asked her every night, and it was starting to become a habit. Normally she wondered if he was really thirsty or if he was trying to find something to keep him away from her for a little longer.

She was hoping he was thirsty tonight.

"No thanks," she forced herself to say, when really all she wanted to know was if he was going to come back and finish what they'd started earlier. Olivia had never been the aggressor in a relationship—especially where sex was concerned—but she was beginning to think there was no other way to make things happen with Jake. It was beyond frustrating. All she needed to do was come up with something flirty or sexy to say to take them back to the way they had been feeling earlier.

Her mind was completely blank.

"Dammit," she muttered. "It shouldn't be this hard."

"What shouldn't?" Jake asked as he walked up behind her, drink in hand. Still in his faded blue jeans and a navy blue T-shirt he had worn earlier for their photo session, he looked even sexier than he had earlier, and her mouth practically watered.

"Relaxing," she said without looking him in the eye. She hoped he wouldn't know exactly what she was thinking.

"Ain't that the truth," he said as he walked around and sat down beside her, taking a sip of ice water. "I think of all the times I used to just be chilling out in front of the TV at this time of night without a care in the world. But ever since the twins arrived, this is the time of day when my brain won't shut down no matter how exhausted I am."

Olivia nodded in agreement. Okay, clearly they were

going to just shoot the breeze. That was good. That was fine. It wasn't like she wanted Jake to come out of the kitchen and simply pounce on her. Much. "Well, I'm sure you also aren't getting much sleep on this sofa. It's all fine and well for a couple of nights, but by now it's got to be getting old." Wait. Did she just make a reference to a bed? Her mind raced and she cringed inwardly. Would he take that as her inviting him to sleep with her tonight? Not that she'd mind…but…that was so not the way she would have played it.

"It's not so bad actually," he said, interrupting her inner ramblings. "I bought the furniture after my parents passed. I knew I was going to be living here temporarily and their furniture was just awful—very stiff and formal. Very uncomfortable. When I went furniture shopping, I did all the man-cave tests."

"Wait…there are man-cave tests?"

He nodded. "It has to be comfortable."

"That's not a man-cave thing; that's a human thing. Everyone wants furniture that's comfortable!" she said with a laugh.

"No, not just comfortable for sitting, but comfortable enough you can watch TV for twenty-four hours straight and not have to get up. So I sat for a long time; then I laid down on it. It was an all-day experience."

"I'm sure they must have loved you in the store."

"Hey, I bought the furniture," he said with a shrug and a smile. "It was a win-win."

"I'm sure you didn't order pizza to the store and see how it felt to eat on it," she said, cracking herself up, and then noticed he had awkwardly looked away. "You didn't."

He glanced back at her and shrugged again. "I didn't have pizza delivered, but I did ask for a beverage and a snack, so I could see how it would be."

She shook her head in disbelief. "Unbelievable. I would never even think to do something like that."

"What can I say? If I'm going to buy something as expensive and important as a sofa, I want to make sure it's something I can live with."

"Well, to be fair, you had no idea you'd end up sleeping on it for so long, did you?"

"Not initially, no. But I have been known to fall asleep on the couch watching TV and not bother to get up and walk the ten feet to the bed."

"That's just lazy."

Picking up his glass, he turned to her and smiled with a mock solute. "That's me."

They sat in companionable silence, and Olivia figured this was all they were going to have tonight unless she made the first move. Her mind raced for something witty to say or some way for her to slink across the couch and get closer to him. Unfortunately, in every scenario, she ended up either getting rejected, falling off the couch, or looking and feeling like a fool.

Talk about a mood killer.

She was so busy going through all of her imaginary, failed seduction scenes, she didn't notice Jake moving closer. Or the fact that he had shut off one of the sofa lamps. It wasn't until she felt his breath warm against her neck that she snapped out of her stupor. A languid sigh escaped her lips as she tilted her neck to give him better access to the skin there. His lips and tongue alternated between kissing her and nipping and licking her. Chills broke out all over her body, and it made her shiver.

"Too much?" he whispered, working his way up to take a tiny bite of her earlobe.

Shifting a little so she could loop her arms around his shoulders, she whispered back, "Not enough." Her lips sought his and soon he had them both reclined, his body nestled securely on top of hers.

Yes, yes, yes! her body screamed. *Finally!* There was no way for her to act casual or pretend this wasn't a big deal. It totally was, and as she wrapped her legs around his hips and locked him in close, she smiled at the evidence Jake was just as crazed as she was right then.

"I tried to stay away," he said huskily as his lips moved from hers to kiss her cheek and then back down to her neck.

"Nobody asked you to," she reminded, her breath ragged.

"I was trying to do the right thing," he panted between kisses. "You deserve someone who can make you the center of his world."

Well, wasn't that just the sweetest thing ever? And as sweet as it was, she still didn't agree with it. She didn't want to be the center of anyone's world. She wanted this moment, this exact moment with Jake, more than she'd ever wanted anything else in her life. Olivia considered telling Jake that, but she didn't want to pull at that thread. Raking her hands through his hair, she pulled his head back up to hers and kissed him. They had more important things to do.

Like this.

Jake was completely on board with Olivia taking a little of the control, and as he kissed her, he did what he'd wanted to earlier—he let his hands wander until they reached the hem of her shirt. This time, he didn't hesitate, he didn't pause, and he simply let his hands slip under the fabric until they found the fullness of her breasts. They sighed in unison at the contact, and he deepened the kiss as his hands began to knead her aching flesh with a little more urgency.

Suddenly, Olivia pushed him away, and Jake thought he had pushed too far, too fast. But once he moved, Olivia crossed her arms in front of her and pulled her T-shirt up and off, flinging it across the room.

Then she pulled him back down.

"This is way better," she said right before kissing him again.

There had only been a flash of white lace before Olivia had brought Jake's head down to hers, and the need to raise his head and look again was almost overwhelming. Carefully, he disentangled himself from her arms and leaned back to look at her. "Beautiful," he murmured and looked at her reverently. "So damn beautiful."

Olivia had never felt that way, never thought for a minute anyone else would see her way. But now? Watching the expression on Jake's face as his eyes raked over her, she actually felt it. A blush seemed to cover her entire body as his words washed over her, and then his hands began to explore her. She whispered his name to bring his attention back to her face. His eyes met hers and everything inside her melted.

"I just can't believe you're actually here," he said, "and I'm really touching you."

Olivia wanted to beg him to touch her some more—now—but it was very sweet the way he was studying her body with awe and wonder. She reached out and touched his face, smiling. "I feel the exact same way."

He was about to lower himself to her again but then stopped. "There's so much I want to do with you, Olivia, but I don't want to do any of it on the couch. We're not kids." He stood up and held out a hand to her. "Let's take this inside."

As much as Olivia wanted to find out exactly what he wanted to do to her and how good it was going to feel, she was uneasy with his suggestion. Jake saw the indecision on her face and immediately began to panic. "I'm sorry," he said quickly, "am I moving too fast?" He cursed under his breath. "I just thought…with the way things were earlier and then how they were tonight, we would… I mean… We were going to…"

Olivia held up a hand to stop him. "Jake," she said and then placed hand on his chest, "you're not moving too fast for me. I'm just not comfortable going into the bedroom and doing…you know…what we're planning to do with the babies in there." She knew it sounded ridiculous, but she couldn't help it.

"They're not even going to know we're there," he said with a nervous chuckle.

"No, I know. But I'll know they're there. I'll be afraid of making too much noise and waking them up, and… well…I just want us to be able to enjoy being together without any distractions."

That was exactly what Jake wanted too, but now he was torn. The thought of making love to her for the first time on his living room sofa was so not what he had in mind. The dreams that had been keeping him awake at night all involved the two of them sprawled out on the king-size bed, and there was definitely a lot of noise.

Dammit.

"I know you're not thrilled with the idea of being out here in the living room," she said as if reading his mind, "but I don't mind." She stepped in closer to him. "I really, really, *really* don't mind. I just want to be with you."

Well, how was he supposed to say no to that kind of declaration? Anxiously, Jake looked around the room and considered his options. The sofa was big enough, and he had already waxed poetic about how comfortable it was, but should he go and grab a blanket? Pillows? Should they set up some sort of makeshift bed on the floor?

Beside him, Olivia chuckled. Reaching out, she cupped his cheek in her hand again and gently forced him to look at her. "Stop thinking so damn hard," she teased. "I know it's not what you envisioned, but I promise you, I'm okay with it." She leaned up on tiptoes and kissed him. "Besides, maybe this will motivate you to get the nursery done faster. Then we'll have big old bed to ourselves, and be able to shut the door and be as loud and as wild as we want."

Just the image of it was enough to bring Jake to his knees. "Done" was all he said as he scooped Olivia up in his arms and laid her back on the sofa. A sigh escaped her lips, and Jake wasn't sure if it was because what he was doing felt good or because she was relieved they were finally getting back to business.

Either worked for him.

Over and over he kissed her as his hand skimmed her rib cage until it cupped one full breast. The satin and lace of her bra contrasted with his work-roughened hands, and it didn't take long for him to reach around her back to unhook it, peeling it away from her body.

If he'd thought the sight of her wearing the lace was sexy, it was nothing compared to her bare breasts. Leaning back, he cupped both of them in his hands and watched as Olivia's eyes fluttered closed and she smiled. "Yes" was all she said, and it sounded like a whispered plea, so he continued to hold them, squeezed them gently, and then finally lowered his head to take one hardened nipple into this mouth.

Olivia's back arched off the sofa, and Jake continued to softly torment her tender flesh until she was writhing beneath him. He was taking his time, learning what made her whimper, what made her squirm, when she reached down and pulled at the hem of his T-shirt. He lifted his head to help her to remove it and watched it sail across the room to join hers.

Leaning back down, they were skin to skin, and Jake looked into Olivia's eyes and smiled. "You're right, that is much better."

"Told you so," she said as she ran her hands over his pecs, down his flat stomach, and to the button on his jeans. Olivia's eyes were sexy and wicked and wild as they met his. "And it's about to get a whole lot better."

"So let me see if I've got this straight," Jake said much later, as they sat on the bed feeding the twins, "you're not okay with us being here in the bed together to make love, but it's okay for us to be here together to feed the kids. Is that right?"

Olivia yawned widely and nodded. "Exactly. And to sleep. It would be totally fine to sleep in here."

"With no sex."

She nodded again. "No sex."

"You've got an awful lot of rules in my house, you know that?" he teased softly.

"One of us has to set a good example," she teased right back. "I don't want to be the reason either of these sweet, innocent children are traumatized and in need of therapy later in life."

He looked at her blandly. "Liv, they don't have a clue what's going on around them unless they're wet, dirty, or hungry. As long as we meet those needs for them, they don't care what we do."

"We don't know that for sure."

Jake rolled his eyes and knew he was fighting a losing battle. It was actually kind of sweet the way she wanted to protect the twins. He didn't necessarily agree with it, but he thought it was sweet.

Actually, everything about Olivia was sweet, he was beginning to discover—from the way she took care of the kids to the way she went about helping him, and even the way she felt in his arms as she came undone.

Sweet.

Leaning over, he kissed her on the cheek before rising to reswaddle Ben and place him back in the crib. Moments later, Olivia was beside him doing the same with Maddie. They made a good team, the two of them, and Jake couldn't imagine anyone else he'd have rather been going through this with.

"They always look so sweet when they first go down," she said quietly. "It's almost as if they're smiling, relieved to be back in their beds, like they're exhausted from all the feeding and changing and snuggling." Beside her, Jake chuckled. "I can already see they're growing. Some of the clothes we bought just a week ago are starting to get snug, or they're filling them out better. Keeping them in the bassinets has been great, but soon you won't have a choice but to put them in bigger beds."

"Do you think they'll notice?"

She reached down and rubbed Ben's tummy for a minute. "Maybe. We'll have to transition them a bit and make sure they feel snug and secure when they're sleeping in a more open space."

Jake knew the feeling. He had a feeling that if he let himself, he'd get used to sleeping next to Olivia, and then he'd have to transition to having the entire bed to himself again. Not a good feeling.

It was too much to think about. Without a word, he took one of Olivia's hands in his and led her back over to the bed. Then, he turned her around, cupped her face in his hands, and kissed her. Slowly. Softly. Deeply.

She sighed and relaxed against him. She was exhausted—not only from the long day, but because they had made love twice before coming in to feed the twins. And as tired as she was, she wouldn't be opposed to stripping down and making love again.

"Sleep," he said quietly against her lips. "The bed is for sleeping." He teased her with her own words as he reached down and threw the blankets back so they could climb in. When Olivia made to protest, he kissed her one last time. "Your rules, not mine." With a gentle push, she fell back on the mattress. "Scoot over," he said and climbed in beside her.

Not letting her get too far, Jake pulled the blankets up and over them before turning off the small lamp next to the bed, leaving only the glow of the nightlight on the wall. Wrapping an arm around Olivia and tucking her in close beside him, he smiled. This was good. This was right. She kissed his chest and hummed her approval. Obviously she felt it too.

Unable to keep it to himself, he said, "This is good."

"Mmm-hmm," she agreed and snuggled closer to him, one leg draped over his, her hand over his heart.

"And you're firm on the whole no-sex rule?"

She nodded. "Stop being such a baby. Think of it as motivation. I'm really doing it for you."

"For me?" he nearly choked out, and laughed out loud until Olivia pinched him and told him to shush. "For me?" he whispered. "Remind me again…how?"

"I told you. Now you have motivation to finish the upstairs and get Ben and Maddie settled into the nursery. The sooner their room is ready, the sooner we can have this bed—and this room—all to ourselves." She lightly traced a circle around one of his nipples with her tongue. "Wouldn't that be nice?"

"You're not playing fair," he growled lowly. "If you're going to throw down a no-sex rule, then you're not allowed to tease."

She shook her head. "I do not agree to those terms."

He couldn't help but laugh at her serious tone. "Maybe I need to find a way to motivate you to change your mind," he challenged.

Olivia lifted her head from his shoulder and looked at him. "You wouldn't dare."

He smirked. "Wouldn't I?" He saw her frown and

took pity on her. Tucking her head back down on his shoulder, he waited until Olivia relaxed against him again. "Okay, fine. I'll play nice." Then he paused. "I guess one of us has to."

Olivia pinched him lightly, and they hugged each other close before settling down. Her eyes felt heavy, and Jake's strong arms around her felt heavenly. She yawned and snuggled so close she was almost on top of him. Her voice was sleepy and a little bit slurred as she whispered, "Yes, this is good."

Chapter 8

Two days later, Olivia stood back in awe. The nursery was done. And not just done like "It's okay to move the kids in," but done like…it could have been in a parenting magazine article about dream nurseries. The walls were painted a lovely green that gave the room a very calm and relaxed feeling. The bright-white cribs made such a beautiful contrast against the walls, and Olivia smiled at how perfectly the bedding they had picked out on that first day went with the decor.

Plantation shutters on the windows, built-in bookcases already filled with books and toys, and pictures from their day in the yard all came together to make for a beautiful room. She couldn't believe how quickly—or how hard—Jake had worked to pull it all together. Although he did all the labor himself, Olivia congratulated herself on her ability to handle the twins as much as humanly possible on her own without disturbing him.

During the day, Jake worked on the nursery and even squeezed in work on the two guest rooms on either side of it. But at night, he was all hers. Just thinking about the hours they'd spent in each other's arms for the last couple of nights made her blush. And knowing that tonight they would be able to go into the bedroom and actually use the bed instead of the floor or the couch—or the kitchen table—had the anticipation building inside her.

"What do you think?" Jake asked quietly from behind her.

Looking over her shoulder, she smiled as tears filled her eyes. "It's absolutely perfect. I can't believe you did all of this, that you even had the vision for something like this. I'm simply blown away."

He smiled shyly. "So then you like it," he said, just for clarification.

Olivia nodded and wrapped her arms around him. "Like I said, it's perfect. Ben and Maddie are very lucky to have such a talented dad."

Jake held on tight, simply enjoying the feel of her in his arms. "Well, eventually they'll each get a room of their own, but for now I think this is a pretty good start."

"Pretty good?" She pulled back, confusion marking her face. "Jake, I'm telling you, it's amazing. But..."—she stepped out of the circle of his arms—"it's missing something."

Now it was his turn to look confused. "What? What did I miss? This was all the stuff we ordered from superstore place you took me to." Stepping around Olivia, he walked the perimeter of the room, searching for what he could have missed. "I'm stumped, Liv."

She smiled and held up her hand. "I'll be right back." Quickly, she turned and left the room, running downstairs to grab her contribution to the room. She had already bought some small frames and put a couple of pictures from their photo shoot on the shelves, but what she had in her hands now was her big gift.

At the top of the stairs, she stopped and caught her breath, praying Jake was going to like what she'd done. "And if he doesn't," she muttered, "then...he's a jerk."

That made her smile, and she took the rest of the steps to get her back into the nursery. "Here," she said with a smile. "This is in no way as big a contribution as what you've done, but it's my way of welcoming Ben and Maddie to their new room." She held out the large, flat package to him and held her breath.

Jake knew immediately it was some sort of picture strictly by the size and shape of the package. But when he opened it, he was speechless. There, in the most crisp and perfect of color, sat him, Ben, and Maddie on the back lawn. He was smiling and looked relaxed, and both babies were looking almost directly at Olivia with the closest thing to a genuine smile he'd ever seen on them.

Looking at the picture and then to Olivia and back again, he struggled for words. "It's…it's absolutely perfect. I don't remember seeing this one in the proofs you showed me the other night."

Olivia shook her head. "I kept it separate. As soon as I saw it, I knew what I wanted to do with it and I wanted it to truly be a surprise for you. It was as if they knew this was going to be the shot because their expressions are so perfect. The three of you look so happy, and I think I'll have to come back once a year and recapture that pose, so we can see how much they've grown and how you've all grown closer together."

They both grew silent, and it wasn't until Olivia closed her mouth that she realized what she'd said. It was a shot of reality neither of them were willing to acknowledge just yet. Her time there with Jake and the twins was temporary and would be over before she was ready for it, of that Olivia was certain. The look on Jake's face told her he was thinking the same thing. But rather than voice that out loud, he simply said, "That would be nice. We could make it a whole wall display, like branches on a tree."

Olivia smiled. "I like that. Your own family tree."

Jake nodded, leaning the picture against the wall while he went in search of what he needed to hang it with. He returned two minutes later and found a spot on the wall between two windows that was perfect for it. Olivia stood back and watched as he carefully hung it in place, then hooked her arm through his when he stood back to admire it. "It's perfect, Olivia," he said gruffly. "Thank you."

Olivia had been complimented on her work more times than she could remember and by some of the biggest celebrities in the world, but something about Jake's words touched her heart more than any others. The photo was perfect just because it captured this sweet, new little family for exactly who they were.

Resting her head on his shoulder, she sighed, a happy, contented sigh. "You're welcome. I'm just glad you like it."

Wordlessly, he took Olivia by the hand and led her from the room to show her what he had accomplished in the other two. Walls were painted and furniture was back in place. "It's not the greatest renovation job I've ever done, but the rooms are freshened up and I can come back to them at a later date. For now, they've got fresh coats of paint on the walls and the trim, all the furniture has been polished within an inch of its life, and there are clean linens on the beds. All in all, I'm fine with it."

"The rooms all look great," she said. "But admit it,

most of the days you were up here, you weren't really doing anything, were you?"

How could he lie to her? He shrugged and gave her a crooked smile. "It was safer up here."

Olivia threw back her head and laughed. "I knew it! I knew you were just pretending to work so you could stay away from me."

"I didn't want to stay away, per se," he began, "but I needed to do my best to get my head together so I wouldn't pounce on you."

"That's funny considering I was waiting for you to pounce on me," she teased as she turned and wrapped her arms around his waist. "There was no need to hide out."

Jake rested his forehead against hers. "I know now. It's just then…well…I wasn't so sure about what to do."

His honesty touched her. "Well, I'm glad you figured it out."

"Me too." He kissed the tip of her nose, then her cheek and lips. It was his favorite thing to do. Kissing Olivia was some of the best times of his day. Jake felt there wasn't anything he couldn't do if he had the promise of Olivia's kisses at the end of it. "What are the odds of us moving the twins up to their new cribs right now and them sleeping through the night?"

"Since it's only four o'clock in the afternoon, I'd say pretty slim to none."

"Damn, I was afraid you'd say that."

"C'mon," she said with feigned weariness, "let's go downstairs and move away from temptation."

Jake pulled her back into his arms and looked down into her eyes. "Sweetheart, as long as you're near me, so is temptation." He kissed her thoroughly before releasing her and heading down the stairs to check on the twins.

Sometimes no matter how much you want something, it just isn't meant to be. Olivia could tell Jake's patience was nearing an end, and no matter what she did, she couldn't make things better. The twins were being particularly fussy, and no matter how much Jake and Olivia rocked them and soothed them, they were not going into their new room quietly.

"It doesn't make any sense," Jake snapped, then cursed himself when he startled them both and they started to cry all over again. "I don't get it!" he hissed in a lower tone. "They can't possibly notice it's another room."

"Sure they can," Olivia said softly, patting Maddie's back as she gently bounced her. "It still smells a little like paint in here—"

"But I used the one that isn't supposed to have a smell! The one that's safe for nurseries!"

"Shh… I know, I know. I guess they're still just sensitive to it." Looking around the room, Olivia racked her brain for what she could do to comfort the twins. Everything was the same for the most part—the crib, their clothes, their swaddling blankets. And then it hit her. "I'll be right back." With Maddie still sniffling at her shoulder, Olivia walked quickly and quietly down the stairs to the master bedroom and found the tiny bumper pads she had been using in the bassinets. She had pulled them out of the bassinets earlier so she could wash them, but they hadn't ended up in the laundry pile yet.

With the bumpers tucked under her arm, she made her way back up the stairs and stopped just outside the door when she heard Jake talking softly to his son.

"It's okay, buddy. I know it seems scary, but I promise you it's not. I made this room especially for you and your sister. I know it's not perfect, but I did the best I could. And you see this?" he asked as he walked Ben over to the picture of the three of them on the wall. "Olivia did this for us." He looked at the picture and then back at his son. "That was a good day, right? The fresh air and lying on the blankets? We're gonna do a lot more of that, and when you get a little bit bigger, we're going to build a big jungle gym and play set out there for you to climb and play on. It's going to be great."

Olivia dropped the bumpers on the floor and put a hand over her heart. She stepped back and stood in the shadows and listened some more.

"And maybe we can even get a basketball hoop, and I can teach you how to shoot baskets. Would you like that?" He tilted his head and tried to get a reaction from the baby. While Ben wasn't showing much enthusiasm, he had stopped crying, seemingly mesmerized by his father's voice. "Basketball may not be your thing, and that's okay. We can get a soccer net and kick the ball around the yard, and we'll try T-ball too. Whatever you want to try, we'll do."

He looked around the room and smiled at the little pink dresses that were hanging in the closet. "Of course, we can't forget about your sister. She's going to be a little outnumbered here when it's only the three of us.

We're going to have to remember she's going to like things like dolls and tea parties. And it's going to be up to you and me to protect her and make sure nobody treats her badly. Once you're in school, you'll be able to keep an eye on her and make sure she's okay. I know it's a big responsibility, but I think you can handle it. You're my boy, and I have faith in you."

Tears began to well up in Olivia's eyes. Jake may not have realized it yet, but this little man-to-man talk he was having with his son proved he was going to be a great dad.

"I'm sure she's going to give us a run for our money," Jake continued, and Olivia noticed the lights in the room dimmed. "I mean, girls can be a little scary and confusing. They're so sweet and pretty, but there are times when you're just not going to understand them. I don't doubt your sister is going to be any different." Ben yawned and blinked up at Jake sleepily. "But at the end of the day, you can't help but love them. Someday, you'll find the perfect girl to love, and you'll be the luckiest man alive." He touched his son's cheek. "I'm sorry your mom left, and I want you to know I'm going to do everything I can to make sure you have a great life. I'm going to screw up from time to time, and… there are times when I'm not going to know what to do. Moms always seem to know what to do…but I'm going to do my best to be the best dad…and mom…to you and Maddie." He placed a kiss on Ben's head and walked over to the crib.

Olivia took the opportunity to slip into the room. She quietly walked up beside him and held up the bumpers. "I had taken them out of the bassinets to wash them.

They're really too small for the cribs, but maybe we can do something to tie them to the new bumpers. I'm not sure it will solve the problems, but maybe the scent of something familiar will help them relax."

Jake stared at her in awe and disbelief. He would have never thought of something like that. He would have walked the floors and rocked them until they all were exhausted.

"What?" she asked, seeing the look on his face.

"It's just…you're amazing. You see a problem, and…you fix it. I would have stood here and panicked all night, but you just looked around, sized up the situation, and found a solution. How do you do that?"

Olivia chuckled. "It's like my superpower. I've always been able to do that. I'm told I'm great in emergencies, but really, I just see what has to be done and do it." Jake took one of the bumpers from her hands and carefully hugged Ben close as he tried to fit it into the crib. "Here, why don't you let me take Ben while you work with the bumpers?"

"I'm still not sure I know what I'm supposed to do with them," he said with a lopsided grin.

"Then how about you hold the twins, and I'll rig this up."

"Deal." Carefully, Jake adjusted Ben again so he could cradle Maddie in his other arm. Olivia made fast work of tying the tiny bumper against one side of each crib and securing it so it wouldn't come undone. Jake simply watched in amazement at her quick and efficient movements and at how quickly the task was completed. "Wow."

"I don't know about 'wow,' but I hope this helps

them to relax." Taking Maddie from his arms, she snuggled her close for a moment before laying her down in her new bed. She positioned her close enough to the bumper so she would be able to maybe see it and smell it, but far enough away that, should she decide to be an infant overachiever and roll over, she wouldn't smother herself. Taking a step back, she smiled when the baby didn't fuss or cry. She simply yawned and closed her eyes and promptly fell asleep. Looking over at Jake, she said, "Okay, now for the real test."

Imitating Olivia's moves, Jake positioned Ben in the crib the same way Maddie was and patted his belly like he'd seen Olivia do a dozen times before. Remarkably enough, his son didn't make a peep. Like his sister, he gave one final yawn before falling asleep. Jake took several steps back and let out the breath he had been holding. "Holy crap…I didn't think it was going to work."

"Me either. Now we'll have to see if these new beds and new environment affect their sleeping pattern."

"What do you mean?"

"Well, they might sleep longer or they may wake up sooner." She looked around the room, spotted the monitor, and turned it on. "We have the other end of this downstairs, so we'll be able to hear them just fine if they wake up." It all sounded good in theory, but Olivia suddenly felt worried about leaving them up there by themselves. Her worry must have shown on her face because Jake asked her what was wrong.

"I'm aware these baby monitors are made for this exact situation, so you can hear the babies when you're out of the room. I just feel bad leaving them up here while we're downstairs." She worried her bottom lip. "Part of me wishes everything was on one floor."

"That would take a bit more renovation than I was willing to do," Jake teased and was relieved when Olivia smiled at him.

"Very funny. I'm sure it's going to be fine. I've just gotten used to having them so close by that this is going to seem weird."

Something in the region of his heart squeezed at her words. While he was standing here breathing a sigh of relief because he had the nursery finished and his kids were asleep in their beds, Olivia was worried about being farther away from them. She may not have been the one to give them life, but she was certainly nurturing them as if she were their mother. Not sure she'd take that as a compliment, he chose to keep observation to himself, tucking it away in his heart.

Taking Olivia by the hand, he slowly led her out of the room, turning off the last light as they walked out. There were two nightlights in the room just in case they needed them, but he didn't think it was necessary to have the room too illuminated. He didn't say a word until they were down the stairs and walking across the living room. He stopped next to the sofa and turned to face her. "Are you going to be okay?"

She nodded, but her eyes looked a little sad.

"They're going to be fine, Liv," he reassured her. "This is what was supposed to happen, right?"

Again, she nodded.

"Okay, so then, rather than letting ourselves be sad about it, let's look at this as one of their first milestones." Then, inspiration struck. "Why don't you go and grab your camera and take some pictures of them up in their new beds. We can title them 'First Night in Our New Room.' What do you think?"

She loved that he completely understood her and how she coped.

Reaching out, she cupped one side of his face and leaned up to kiss him. "I think you are an amazing man, Jake Knight." And then she fairly skipped across the room to grab her camera before running up the stairs.

Jake watched her go and smiled. Who knew such a simple suggestion could bring her so much joy? Olivia was so different from the other women he had ever been involved with—she was uncomplicated and genuine. She was open and honest and real. He had to sit back and watch as Marilyn had just handed over her children without an ounce of emotion, but he had a feeling that, at the end of the month, it would be far harder for Olivia.

And he didn't know if that made him feel good or bad.

Fifteen minutes later, she was back and visibly more relaxed. Jake had gotten comfortable on the couch while he waited for her. She sat down beside him and put her head on his shoulder. "Thank you."

"For what?"

"For giving me the perfect suggestion so I would feel better. As I stood in the room and snapped pictures and zoomed in on their little faces, I could see they were okay. No one was crying anymore, and they were sleeping peacefully. I still don't know how I'm going to feel at three in the morning, when I have to run up the stairs to get to them, but for now, I can see they're fine."

Jake wished he were. Hearing her words after all he

had just been thinking, he had to wonder what exactly was going to happen when the time came for Olivia to leave. She talked as if she was going to be there forever. Not once had she mentioned when she was going to go or what she was going to do once she was back on the West Coast.

He didn't want her to go. That was a given. And as hard as it was obviously going to be on her, he knew without a doubt it was going to be damn near traumatic for him and his children once she was gone. She was building a relationship with Ben and Maddie. She was teaching them that they could trust her to be there for them.

She was doing the same thing to him.

Maybe it wasn't intentional, and he knew for certain it wasn't malicious. Olivia was just the type of woman who did everything with her entire being—heart and soul. He was the one who would have to remember that when it was time for her to go. She was just being who she was, and for a brief moment in time, she had belonged to him.

She had a life back in L.A. He didn't want to think about life or what—or who—she was going back to. Tilting his head, he kissed her on the top of hers and then simply inhaled the sweet scent of her.

She wasn't leaving yet.

For now, she did belong to him.

And he wasn't going to let a moment of that time go to waste.

Nudging her with his shoulder, Jake waited until she lifted her head, and then he stood and held out a hand. "I've been waiting for the opportunity to do more than just sleep with you in bed."

Olivia looked up at him, her eyes heated. “Really? Because I’ve had a couple of ideas myself.”

He arched a brow at her. “Really?”

She nodded. “Really.”

“Then how about we go inside and compare notes?”

“I’d like that very much.” She waited until he took one of her hands and led her to the bedroom, smiling when she saw him pick up the baby monitor in his other hand. There was nothing sexier than a man who took all of your feelings and worries into consideration before anything else.

In minute, what little he hadn’t already claimed of her heart became his.

They got up together when the twins began to fuss at three o’clock. Jake went to heat up bottles of formula while Olivia went up to the nursery to start getting them changed and calmed down. By the time Jake joined her, Maddie was ready to be fed, so Olivia handed the baby to Jake and then took care of Ben. The nursery had two glider rockers, so they would not have to climb up and down the stairs in the middle of the night when it was time to feed the babies.

They rocked in companionable silence until the twins were asleep again. And, as had happened earlier, Jake led Olivia from the room and back down to the master bedroom. It amazed Jake how in sync they were with one another. He had dated Marilyn for two years and never had been able to communicate with her without actually speaking, but with Olivia, it was like they were of one mind. It was a little unnerving and yet calming at the same time.

Olivia immediately rolled over to snuggle against him as soon as the blankets covered them. Jake wrapped her in his embrace, ready to fall back to sleep when Olivia said his name. He shifted in the darkness and looked down at her face.

"It wasn't so bad, right?" she asked softly.

Because he was coming to know her so well, he already knew what she was referring to. "No," he said, shaking his head slightly. "It wasn't bad at all."

That seemed to satisfy Olivia because she instantly relaxed against him and hugged him. In less than a minute, she said his name again. When he looked down at her, she raised her head a bit to make gaze into this eyes. "Was the volume level okay for you on the monitor?"

He chuckled softly. "Yes."

"Oh, okay. Good." She paused. "Do you think they got too frantic while waiting for me to get up there?" Jake shook his head. "Okay. Good." She chewed at her bottom lip. "Do you think it's too cold?"

"Liv?"

"Hmm?"

"What's going on? Why are you so worried?"

She sagged a little. "I don't know. They're just so small and helpless, and I don't want them to think I kicked them out of their space."

Jake sat up a little farther and looked at her like she was crazy. "What are you talking about?"

Olivia flopped back against the pillows and threw an arm over her eyes. "I made you rush to finish the upstairs," she said miserably. "I was being selfish, and I can't believe I did that. I mean, they're babies! This is their home, not mine, and I just swoop in here and start changing everything and…and it was…"—she began to sob—"all for my own…selfish…pleasure." She was openly crying now and rolled over so her back was to Jake.

"Hey," he said softly and reached out to roll her back toward him. "That's crazy. You didn't swoop in here and do anything like that at all."

She faced him and looked at him with annoyance. "How can you even say that? Did I or did I not…dare you…to get the nursery finished so we could have sex in a bed?"

"Well, when you put it like—"

"Put it like what? The truth?" She covered her face with her hands. "I'm so ashamed of myself. I'm supposed to be here helping you, helping *them*, and what am I doing? Thinking of myself!" Tears were falling in earnest again.

Jake didn't know what to do or say to make her feel better. Her uneasiness with the twins being in their new room made much more sense now. But Jake knew this was all for the better, and not just because of the sex. Ben and Maddie were going to need to be in their own room eventually, and if he hadn't been in the middle of renovating the upstairs, they would have been up there all along.

Carefully, he pulled Olivia's hands from her face and forced her to look at him. "Olivia, you need to stop. There is nothing wrong with getting me to finish the nursery. It needed to be done and while, yes, you…motivated me to get it finished, that wasn't the only reason I did it."

"Really?"

He nodded. "Really. They were going to have their own room eventually, and no matter how little or how big they were when it happened, it was going to be a little traumatic. You need to relax. Everything is good."

She wiped away some of the tears and sat up to face Jake. "Are you sure? Do you think they're going to be traumatized because of me?"

"Liv..."

"No, I'm serious. They've already had their mother abandon them, and then I go and make them feel unwanted and—"

Placing his hands on her shoulders, Jake gave her a gentle shake. "Hey, that's enough," he said firmly but gently. "You have done more for them since you've been here than I can ever imagine Marilyn doing for them in their entire lives. Olivia, you've sacrificed your time, time you had set aside for yourself, to come and help me. Help them. You've made them feel loved and secure. More so than I ever could have done on my own."

Her eyes were huge as she looked up at him. "Really?"

He nodded. "I couldn't have done any of this without you." Wrapping his arms around her, Jake pulled her in close. "You're the reason we're a family right now." As soon as the words were out of his mouth, he realized how much he wanted that to be true. He already knew he and Ben and Maddie were a family, but now he wanted Olivia to be a part of it too.

It was too much to throw at her right then, but he'd have to be brave and broach the subject with her soon—before she packed up and went back to her life in L.A. Maybe she'd think he was crazy, and maybe he was. They'd known each other for almost their entire lives.

Now that they'd finally been able to admit their feelings for one another, shouldn't they be able to talk about a future together?

"What's wrong?" Olivia asked quietly. "You've gotten awfully quiet and you're frowning."

He couldn't tell her what was really on his mind. Not yet. Plus, it was nearing four in the morning. Turning, he looked at her and smiled. "Nothing. Everything's perfect." Her eyebrows arched in surprise, and Jake knew the best way in the world to convince her he was speaking the truth. "I was thinking I'm not ready to go back to sleep yet."

Her expression softened, and he could see all the tension of minutes ago begin to fade. "Me either."

Leaning forward, Jake kept moving slowly until Olivia was flat on her back and he was reclined next to her. "That's good because…I don't think we've finished comparing notes on all the things we wanted to do in this bed."

Olivia wanted to tell him her notes would never be finished, but instead, she snaked an arm around Jake's shoulders and pulled him in close. "You know I'm all for being efficient."

Jake's lips hovered mere inches above hers. "It's one of your best qualities."

And for the remainder of the night, she showed him a few of her other ones.

Chapter 9

For the next week, they settled comfortably into a routine. Jake had even gone to the office several times, and Olivia was perfectly comfortable staying at home alone with the twins. While it was definitely easier when Jake was there to help her, she found she could manage all right.

The babies were growing, and the only problem Olivia seemed to be having was that they were growing on her too. Every day, she saw them do something new, and she found she looked forward to it more than anything else.

Well, almost anything else.

Her time with Jake—whether they were alone and in bed or spending time just hanging out and talking with the twins—was something she was beginning to get used to. Very used to. The days he went to the office, she found herself watching the clock in anticipation of seeing him again—and not just for an extra set of hands to help with Ben and Maddie. When he walked through the door, there was a very domesticated 'Hey, honey, how was your day' vibe they both seemed to fall into with little to no effort.

Olivia was a career girl. Ever since she had been old enough to work, she had. From working in the mall on summer breaks to waitressing through college, Olivia knew the importance of having a job and, eventually, a career. Her photography was everything to her. From her first exhibit in her art class in the ninth grade, she knew this was what she wanted to do.

Lately, however, she had grown a little…disenchanted with it. Maybe it was the daily grind of working with demanding Hollywood starlets, or maybe it was just the endless stream of photo shoots and all the traveling that went with it. Either way, it wasn't quite as magical to her as it had once been.

Taking the photos of Jake and the twins had been the first time in a long time Olivia had found joy behind the camera. Every day, she made sure to snap new pictures of Ben and Maddie, because she knew Jake would forget to do it once she was gone.

The thought of leaving made her stomach clench.

Her life was back in L.A. Her agent had freaked out enough at the news Olivia was taking a monthlong sabbatical. If Olivia tried to extend it, she had no doubt a search-and-rescue squad would be combing the area in order to drag her back to the West Coast and back to work.

Sigh.

That wouldn't be good either.

Long-distance relationships were never a good thing. And with Jake having infants to take care of and his refusal to hire any help, Olivia knew there would be no way for them to make anything like that work. She sighed as she wondered if he even wanted such a thing to work. They lived in the moment. She had told him that was how he needed to handle parenthood, and apparently, they were applying it to their relationship too.

He had so many things on his plate already. How could she possibly add one more thing to it? How would it seem if—knowing all she knew about how he'd been feeling—she went and got clingy and started asking where all of this was going?

Jake didn't even know how to make it work for himself and his career. How could she even consider asking him to figure out how to make hers work too?

The sigh escaped before she could stop it. Right then, Jake was in his makeshift home office getting some work done, the twins were sleeping, and apparently Olivia was stuck trying to figure out how to win in a no-win situation.

Some relaxing vacation this had turned out to be.

She wasn't ready for it to come to an end. At best, she had a week and a half before she needed to get back home. Her ticket was already booked and paid for. In the distance, she heard Jake's voice and her heart skipped a beat. Maybe they needed to talk. If she could only think of a way to broach the subject without making him feel cornered or pressured, she knew they'd figure something out. Anything.

Unfortunately, she had a feeling no matter what solution they came up with, it wouldn't be fair…or enough. For either of them.

Or the twins.

Damn. It had all seemed so simple when Jake had kissed her that first time. They'd have their fling—for lack of a better word—and she'd finally have her time with him; then she'd move on.

But now she didn't want to move on.

But she didn't want to give up her career either.

She'd worked so hard to get to the level she was at—it was an extremely competitive field, and to be as young as she was with the client list that she currently had was nearly unheard of. And she didn't even want to think of the waiting list of the rich and famous who wanted her attention, her talent in taking their pictures.

It was too exhausting even to contemplate.

But she had to.

And soon.

Because all too soon, she'd be faced with a decision to make.

And she wanted to be certain she was making the right one.

Jake paced the confines of his temporary home office and listened as his assistant ran down a list of things that required his attention. The longer she spoke, the more overwhelmed he felt. In his mind, this should have been simple. He was going to pass on the bulk of his responsibilities to his management team, and they would meet maybe once a week via Skype or some other conference call setup.

Apparently, he hadn't trained everyone as well as he'd thought, because all hell was breaking loose on multiple job sites, and he knew the only way to get things under control was to go there in person.

But how?

He already felt guilty about the number of times he'd gone into the office and left Olivia home alone with Ben and Maddie. She'd never complained, but

Jake knew it wasn't an easy task to take on alone. What if they both got cranky at the same time? What if they weren't feeling well? What if Olivia was feeling overwhelmed here all by herself with his kids, and he was putting out fires his management team should have been able to handle?

Should he hire more experienced managers? Was that the answer? He sat down at his desk and made some notes as his assistant continued to talk. God, when was this one-way conversation going to end? Jake looked at the clock and saw it was almost time for the twins to get up from their afternoon nap. "Helen?" he interrupted. "I need to let some of this settle and figure out what I'm going to do."

"I hate to say it, Jake, but the guys just aren't ready to take on this much responsibility. You always did too much, and you handled everything for everybody. Now they don't know how to do it for themselves."

He wanted to argue, but unfortunately she was right. Jake had always found it easier to just do what needed to be done himself, rather than sitting back and watching someone else fumble through it.

Lesson learned there.

Except with his twins. He had sought out help immediately—first, he had Mike, and then, he had Olivia. That thought made him drop his chin to his chest in defeat. He was no better than his team. He had let other people come in and help him out in a difficult situation, and now he had no idea how he was going to handle it on his own when Olivia left.

He felt a migraine coming on. "I'll call you in the morning," he said distractedly, hanging up the phone and slouching in his seat. Dammit. What did it say about him that he had so quickly turned into the type of person who let other people fight his battles and solve his problems for him? What the hell was he doing?

Scrubbing a weary hand over his face, Jake considered his options. He needed to stop putting all the responsibility for the twins on Olivia. She was leaving soon, and he needed to remember that. She hadn't talked about extending her stay there, and Jake—as much as he wanted her to—didn't think asking her to stay was the right thing to do. It pained him to even think it. With the way his life was spinning out of control right then, maybe some time apart would help to put things into perspective.

Jake knew he cared about Olivia. A lot. He might even say he was in love with her. Oddly, that didn't scare him. What did scare him was the possibility that he was using her as a solution to his problems. And that wasn't fair. To either of them. How could he possibly convince Olivia he loved her and not just her babysitting skills? He needed to figure out how to run his own life—the life he was now faced with—without help from Olivia or anyone.

Yeah, that definitely scared him.

It was time to man up and figure out how to get his life back on track. As much as he hated to do it, he was going to have to use the time he had left with Olivia to get his company back in line and find the kind of managers and foremen who could handle the job without hand-holding. Then, once that was done, he could figure out how to work from home and maximize the time he spent working while the twins were napping.

All of this meant less time with Olivia. That made him feel uneasy. It was not at all what he really wanted to do, but he had to make sure he was ready when she went back to L.A. They'd have to take the time now to evaluate what they had and for Jake to learn how to take care of his kids on his own.

None of it sounded appealing.

He wanted to cry out that it wasn't fair. None of this was fair. Just a few weeks ago, he was a single guy with a successful company, good friends, and a fairly carefree life. Now he saw it was all an illusion. His company was successful because he worked his ass off to make it that way, and he was clearly overpaying his staff for work he was doing himself. And as for being carefree, how could he have been so oblivious to the fact that Marilyn was pregnant with his babies? They had been involved with each other for years and had mutual friends! How was it even possible no one had let him know what was going on?

Maybe they had, and he just wasn't interested in listening. No one had come out and said, "Hey, Marilyn's pregnant," but they had suggested he give her a call, and he had simply ignored it. The old ignore-the-problem-and-it-will-go-away approach had clearly not been the way to go on this one.

Dammit.

Sitting up straighter, he looked at the notes he had written. All five pages of them. He was totally screwed. As it stood, he was going to have to get up at the crack of dawn tomorrow to get into the office and begin searching for new employees while fixing the problems his current ones had caused. *Great.*

And if things didn't get worked out quickly, he'd be repeating that same pattern for the rest of the week. *Awesome.*

Cursing under his breath, he stood. In the distance, he heard the first cries coming from the nursery. Looking at the clock, he saw it was going on four o'clock. *Right on schedule*, he thought with a grim smile. Great, he'd be able to set his watch by his children—thanks to Olivia—but he had no idea how he was going to manage his time so he could be everything to everybody all the time.

Like a condemned man walking to his execution, Jake left his office and went to take care of his children.

~

Something was wrong. Olivia knew it the moment she stepped into the nursery to get the twins. Jake's shoulders were slumped, and he wasn't talking with the kids like he normally did. She didn't say anything—she knew he'd been on the phone with his office for well over an hour. Clearly things hadn't gone well. She took care of Ben while he got Maddie changed, and together they walked silently down the stairs to the living room, where she had bottles waiting.

Once they were seated on the couch and the babies each had a bottle in their mouths, she turned to him, unable to stay silent any longer. "Is everything all right?"

Jake couldn't make eye contact with her. He just couldn't. One look into those eyes he loved, and he knew he'd cave and beg her to stay forever. What kind of man would that make him? "I'm going to need to be gone all day tomorrow. I have to hire a couple of new guys and there are some situations demanding my attention, so I'm going to have to travel to a few job sites. I know it's going to put a lot of pressure on you, and I'm sorry for that, but I don't really have a choice."

His words were fairly monotone, and Olivia knew there was more to it than he was letting on. She'd leave it be for now, but sooner or later, they were going to have to discuss it. "It's fine. You need to do what you need to do," she said lightly, so she wouldn't let on she suspected anything.

"I'll probably leave in the morning around six, and I have no idea what time I'll be back." It sounded like he was daring her to demand he not go or that he come back early.

"It's fine. I'm sure we'll survive okay." She looked down at Ben. "Won't we, buddy?" she cooed. "We'll have fun. If the weather cooperates, we'll go shopping or to the park. I'll keep them busy so maybe they'll sleep a little bit longer."

"Yeah, good luck with that," he muttered and fairly yanked the bottle from Maddie's mouth to burp her.

Olivia almost demanded he hand the baby to her, but she stopped herself. She couldn't control everything, and there were going to be times when he didn't want to deal with the mundane chores of dealing with infants. He was in a pissy mood, but she knew Jake would get over it, and Maddie was oblivious to her father's mood. So far.

Since Jake refused to engage in conversation, she took the bottle from Ben's mouth and stood up to burp him, talking to him the entire time. She just couldn't stand this particular brand of silence. For weeks, she and

Jake had talked about everything—all of his hopes and fears about parenthood—and suddenly he was shutting her out. Whatever he was dealing with, it must have been pretty big.

Ben let out a little burp, and Olivia sat down and began to feed him again. She glanced at Jake out of the corner of her eye and decided she wasn't going to let him pout all night. "So what's going on? Where are the job sites you have to go to?"

He glared at her. How dare she act like it wasn't a big deal? Like he wasn't being a bastard who was taking advantage of her! "What difference does it make? I've got to go to them. End of story."

"O-kay," she said, beginning to lose her patience. Normally Olivia was a pretty optimistic, glass-is-half-full type of girl, but right now she sensed something bad was coming, and she didn't know what to do about it. Opting to keep her mouth shut, she got comfortable with Ben and finished feeding him. When he was done, she placed him in his swing and went about getting ready to make dinner.

Jake followed her into the kitchen five minutes later. "Don't bother making anything for me," he said as he placed Maddie's bottle in the dishwasher. "I'm just going to make myself a sandwich and then hole up in the office for a couple of hours."

Yeah, something was definitely wrong. If she didn't know any better, she'd think Jake was purposely trying to push her away. Olivia wanted to lash out and demand to know what she'd done wrong or why he was behaving this way, but there was no way she could do it without breaking down.

And she hated that little admission most of all.

"That's fine," she said as she wiped the countertop down. Turning her back on him, she finished what she was doing and walked back out to the living room to check on the twins. If Jake thought she'd offer to make his sandwich or she'd try to engage in conversation with him again, he was mistaken.

The whole thing made her sad. It didn't seem like long ago that she had been thinking about talking to Jake about a future—about what was going to happen when she had to go back to L.A. But she felt like she had her answer now. Nothing. Olivia hadn't been prepared for such an abrupt ending to their relationship, but maybe it was for the better. She'd finish up her time here—not that she owed it to him—and then go back to her life.

Looking over at Ben and Maddie, she felt her heart kick in her chest. She was going to miss the two of them most of all. They definitely owned a piece of her heart, and she knew if they were old enough to understand, they wouldn't just throw it back in her face. They would appreciate it and cherish it.

Too bad their father wasn't that smart.

Jake was exhausted. He could no longer look at the reports in front of him without his eyes crossing. He'd shut the door to the office and turned the radio on to purposely block out any sounds from around the house. He didn't want to hear Olivia or the twins. While he knew that was the wrong attitude—they were his children after all—he just needed a couple of hours to himself to organize his thoughts.

Looking at the clock across the room, he saw it was after one. He cursed as he rose from the desk and stretched. No doubt Ben and Maddie would get up at three for their usual feeding, which meant he had to squeeze in two hours of sleep.

Sleep. How the hell was he supposed to do that? He looked around his office. There was no way he could sleep in his desk chair. There was no sofa in there and the floors were hardwood, so that wasn't an option. He could go and sleep on the couch like he had before he and Olivia had become intimate. That wasn't appealing either, but it was his only real option. After the way he'd behaved earlier, it would be completely inappropriate for him to crawl into bed beside her as if nothing was wrong.

Another curse escaped as he headed toward the living room and came to grips with the fact that he'd sleep for a couple of hours and then have to face Olivia and try to be at least a little civil. He wanted to tell her what was going on. He desperately needed someone to talk to—to bounce ideas off—but he was already too reliant on her, and she was going to be leaving soon. Jake knew he needed to stand on his own two feet—no matter how much it was currently killing him.

Bypassing the living room, he went to the kitchen and grabbed a glass of water. He was so damn tired. His feet dragged as he walked back out and went to sit on the couch. Looking to the left, he noticed the bedroom door was open and there was a light on inside. That was odd in and of itself; Olivia was never up at this hour. She knew the importance of sleeping when the twins slept, so what was going on?

Standing wearily, Jake walked closer to the door and saw that the bed was made and Olivia was nowhere in sight. *What the hell?* Panic seized him. She wouldn't have just left without telling him, would she? What about the kids? Were they okay? Spinning around, Jake ran from the room and up the stairs to the nursery. There, sleeping peacefully in their cribs, were Ben and Maddie. He placed a hand on them just to assure himself they were fine.

That still left the question about Olivia's whereabouts.

Quietly walking from the room, he stood in the hallway and contemplated the situation. He needed to check the master bedroom and see if her things were still there. If her clothes were still… He stopped. At the end of the hall, the door to the guest bedroom was closed. It was never closed. Could she…? Tiptoeing down there, he slowly turned the knob and almost sagged with relief to see Olivia asleep in the bed.

But why? Why would she sleep up here instead of the room she'd been using all along? It didn't take long for Jake to figure out the answer to that one—she probably didn't want to take a chance on him showing up in the middle of the night and crawling in beside her. Because clearly that was what he'd been reduced to—a jackass of a guy who was pretty much obnoxious all damn day and would still expect sex at night.

He was really beginning to loathe himself.

She never moved—never uttered a sound—and yet she called to him. It was impossible for him to leave. He stood in the doorway and simply watched her sleep. As irrational as it was, he wanted to crawl into the bed beside her and just hold her. It wasn't about sex or anything physical; Olivia had a way making him feel like everything was going to be all right.

"Jake?" she rolled over and whispered. "Is everything all right? Did I miss hearing the twins?" She sat up, rubbing her eyes, and the blankets draped around her waist and revealed one of the tiny tank tops she wore to sleep in that drove him insane. He almost begged her to let him join her.

He had to hold on to the door frame to keep from going to her. "No…no…they're fine. Still sleeping. I just got done working and went downstairs and saw… well…you weren't there. I wanted to make sure you were all right."

For a minute, Olivia thought she was dreaming. This was the Jake she knew and loved. This was the man she wanted to be with, the one who was kind and caring. "I'm fine. I just figured it would be…better…for me to sleep up here. I'll be closer to the twins when they wake up or if they need me."

There was no reason for him to speak or to respond. He felt like crap for even thinking she would leave in the middle of the night without saying anything. All Jake knew was he was seriously losing it.

And he was losing Olivia.

He wasn't ready for that.

"Liv—" he began, his voice pained.

"Don't," she said quietly. "Just…please don't say anything."

More than anything, he wanted to give her what she wanted—what she needed—but not this. He needed to talk to her. To tell her he was sorry. For his behavior. For tonight. Everything.

But words escaped him.

Standing in the doorway, Jake watched her. And waited. He was dying to hear if she was going to say anything else to him, or if he was just supposed to walk away and go downstairs. Alone.

Olivia was at war with herself. It was foolish to want him after the way he'd been behaving, and yet she couldn't help herself. Their time together was growing short, and as she had reminded herself earlier, she wasn't prepared for it to end this way. Maybe she was desperate. Maybe she was so sleep deprived she wasn't thinking clearly. Either way, she knew what she wanted and she wanted it right now.

Rather than saying anything, Olivia scooted over to one side of the bed and folded the blankets back. Jake knew what she was offering, and he didn't hesitate before moving into the room and quietly closing the door behind him.

Neither of them spoke, too afraid of breaking the tenuous hold on the truce they were declaring. But as it had been since she'd arrived on his doorstep, they were too in sync with one another.

Jake approached the side of the bed and stripped down to his boxers before leaning forward to caress one of Olivia's cheeks. He opened his mouth to speak, but she placed a finger over his lips to silence him.

"For tonight," she whispered, "just be with me."

He knew it was selfish, and on some level he knew he should be the strong one and just walk away. But he wasn't strong. At least not where Olivia was concerned. She had always been a weakness to him, and if he was only going to have tonight, then he needed to take it and not have any regrets. He'd let his body tell her everything he couldn't. He'd show her everything he wanted to show her—as long as she'd let him.

He only prayed it would be enough.

Chapter 10

To say the next week was a strain would be an understatement. Olivia felt as if these were her babies and not Jake's, because he was never home. Whatever was going on with his company—which he still hadn't shared with her—had to be major to keep him away from home for so many hours each day.

It was a good thing Olivia was so organized; the twins were settled into a routine where they would wait for longer periods of time between feedings, and they were sleeping a little bit longer each night. The first time they slept until four o'clock, Olivia said a thank-you to her guardian angel. When it continued to happen, and eventually they were almost sleeping until five, she almost wept with joy each morning.

She and Jake hadn't slept together again since the night in the guest room. They didn't discuss it—just like they didn't seem to discuss anything these days—but it seemed to be an unspoken agreement that part of their relationship was over. It broke her heart, but deep down Olivia knew it was for the best. She had spoken to her agent, who was picking her up at the airport Friday night. Once she landed, she was going to hit the ground running.

There was a big museum opening coming up for one of the biggest studios in Hollywood, and they'd commissioned Olivia to do a series of portraits of today's hottest actresses dressed as some of the most iconic roles in the studio's history. It was a definite feather in her cap, but she didn't have much enthusiasm for the project. It was being rushed because the head of the studio had just thought of it. While she was used to fast deadlines and all that went with them, she knew for something of this scale, her head was going to need to be completely in the game.

From what was discussed on the phone, she would have access to actual movie props and sets for the sessions—all of which were already set up in the museum—and the models-slash-actresses were already chosen and being fitted for their wardrobes. All Olivia had to do was show up and take the pictures.

She really had to thank her agent for that one. Normally she was much more involved with every aspect of organizing and setting up these shoots, but considering the time constraints, it was nice to have that burden removed.

Thinking of the photo shoot, she looked over at Ben and Maddie, who were happily swinging, and decided she wanted to get a few more shots of them. When she got back to L.A., she planned on making a scrapbook for Jake and sending it to him—maybe for Christmas, maybe for the babies' first birthday. She hadn't decided yet.

Walking over to pick up her camera, she decided she'd get some shots of them in their swings and then maybe some of them playing on the floor on one of their blankets. She'd done some shots like this before, but the way they were growing, she figured they'd still look different.

"Hey, guys," she cooed as she slowed the swings down. "How about some pictures, huh?" Olivia didn't doubt for a second that, if they could talk, they'd have told her she'd taken enough pictures. The thought of one of them saying that made her laugh. "Then it's a good thing you can't talk yet, isn't it?" Reaching for her camera, she continued to talk nonsense to them while she snapped shot after shot after shot. When she was satisfied with the ones she had taken, she walked over and picked up Ben, placing him on the blanket. "I really wish I were going to be here when you learn to sit up all by yourself. That's a picture I would love to have for the book."

Once he was situated, she went for Maddie. When she lifted the baby, Olivia immediately knew something was wrong. She was warm. Very warm. And now that she looked a little bit closer, she noticed Maddie's skin was a little flushed. "Oh my," she said and walked quickly to the bathroom to find the digital thermometer. Not wanting to leave Ben alone any longer, she carried Maddie back out to the living room and took her temperature.

"Uh-oh." One hundred and one. "That can't be good." Without hesitation, she reached for the phone and called the pediatrician. She explained Maddie's symptoms to the nurse and was told to bring her in as soon as she could.

As soon as Olivia hung up, she called Jake's office. "I'm sorry, Olivia," his assistant Helen said, "he's not here. Have you tried his cell phone?"

"Not yet. I figured I'd try the office first. If you hear from him, can you please tell him I have to take Maddie to the doctor?"

"Is she okay?"

"She's got a pretty high fever, but other than that, she seems okay. I called the pediatrician, and they said to bring her in. I figured Jake would want to know."

"Try his cell, and if I hear from him, I'll pass on the message."

"Thanks, Helen." She hung up and immediately dialed Jake's cell and got his voice mail. "Dammit." With nothing left to do, she left him a message asking him to call her and that it was an emergency, and then she quickly packed the twins up and loaded their car seats into her car. By this point, Maddie was starting to get cranky and Ben—seemingly having sympathy pain—began to cry with her.

It was the longest fifteen-minute drive Olivia had ever taken.

Jake was exhausted. It was the first time in a week he was getting home at a reasonable hour, and he was actually looking forward to possibly having dinner with Olivia. She was leaving in three days, and he didn't want them to part ways like this. Not with him acting like a jerk.

He pulled into the driveway and his dashboard clock read six o'clock. He was going to sleep hard tonight. He had been getting home around midnight every night and then leaving at six in the morning. He missed the twins and hated having to be away this much. But if everything went as planned, today was the last of the long days, and come Monday, he'd be able to work from home with little to no aggravation.

He had hired a new manager and three new foremen. The process had been fast, furious, and damn near painful, but Jake was confident he had found the right team of people to help him manage his company while he spent the next couple of months trying to get things settled with Ben and Maddie. Helen had suggested that, if he came in once a week, she could arrange for someone to take care of the twins in the office. That way, Jake would be close by in case they needed him, but he'd still get to be a little more hands-on in the office like he wanted to be. The idea had merit. It wasn't a complete solution, but it would enable him to feel like he was still contributing to the big picture.

It wasn't until he got out of the car that he noticed Olivia's car wasn't there. That was odd. It was late in the day for her to be out with the twins. They were normally having their dinner around now, or just finishing up and getting their baths. Where the hell was she?

Walking through the front door, he called out to her just in case she was there and maybe something had happened with her car. But there was no answer, and as he walked around the house, he didn't find any kind of note or indication of where she might have gone. While he knew he had been working late for a week, that didn't mean he was okay with her just taking off with his kids. This was his one night home, and he wanted to spend time with them. Now. Reaching for his cell phone, he remembered the battery had gone dead hours ago. He cursed when he realized that it was the only place he had stored Olivia's number.

Running to his office, he dug around on his desk for his charger and plugged the phone in. He knew he wouldn't be able to use it immediately and tossed it aside and searched for Mike's number. Why, oh why, hadn't he memorized people's phone numbers, rather than relying on his damn phone?

He found Mike's number and was about to pick up the house phone when he heard noise coming from the next room. Dropping the phone, he quickly walked out and saw Olivia struggling to get in the door with the two infant seats. "Where the hell have you been?" he yelled as he walked across the room to take one of the seats from her.

Olivia had been shocked to see Jake's truck in the driveway, and this was certainly not the greeting she had been expecting. "Didn't you get my messages?"

"No! I was working, for crying out loud! You know that. If you're going to take off with my kids, then you need to let me know where you're going. You could at least have left a note!"

That was it. Olivia placed Ben's seat down in the middle of the living room, shrugged out of her coat, and waited for Jake to put Maddie down. "For your information, I called you eight times! Eight!" she nearly screamed. "And on top of that, I texted you and called Helen at least four times in hopes of getting a message to you!" She got in his face and poked her finger into his chest. "So don't you dare cop any kind of attitude with me, dammit! I did tell you where I was, and I tried repeatedly to get you to answer me because you needed to know what was going on. Maybe you should pay more attention to keeping your damn phone charged and remember you have two children who may need you!"

Her breathing was ragged, and she took a step back and made sure her voice level hadn't upset the babies. "Although for the life of me I don't know what difference it would make—it's not like you're interested in fatherhood anymore," she muttered as she went and got the diaper bag that held Maddie's prescription in it.

She had almost made it by him when Jake reached out and grabbed her upper arm, spinning her toward him. "What the hell is that supposed to mean?"

Yanking her arm free, she stood her ground. "It means for a week, you haven't even spent five minutes with them. You're out of here at the crack of dawn and you're home at midnight. You've slept through all their feedings, and you know what? That's crap. In case you've forgotten, I leave in three days. You're going to have to get your shit together, Jake, because there's no one else here to help you!"

"Don't you think I know that? Has it once occurred to you I've been working like this because you're leaving, and I have to get my affairs in order at the office so I can be here full-time?" He didn't wait for an answer. "No. Of course not. It was too easy to make assumptions and paint me as the bad guy!"

"Well, what choice did I have? Did it ever occur to you to talk to me? To let me know what was going on? I mean, what the hell, Jake? The first few weeks I was here, we would talk for hours about anything, and now? Now I don't even know what's going on with you!"

"I'm getting things in order so I can devote my time to my children, Olivia. They are all that matters to me. Things with the company got a little crazy, and I had to fix it. I think I've taken care of everything, and come Monday, when you're gone, I'll be able to take over just fine."

Something about the way he threw in "when you're gone" hit Olivia like a knife to the heart. She'd deal with it later. Without looking at him, she went and grabbed the bag with Maddie's prescription. Once she had it, she lashed out at him. "Just so you know, we were at the doctor. Maddie was running a high fever, and I called the pediatrician and he took her in right away. I knew you'd want to know, maybe even be there, but you couldn't be bothered to keep your phone charged." She stormed past him and made her way to the kitchen.

Jake immediately followed.

"A fever? The doctor? What did he say? Is she all right? What's wrong with her?" He was rambling a mile a minute, and Olivia knew that for the first time in a long time, he was scared.

"She has an ear infection. It's fairly common in infants. She's going to be fussy for a few days, but he gave us something for the pain, and that should make it easier for her to sleep."

"What about—?"

"I had him check out Ben too, and his ears are fine. No sign of any problems."

Jake nearly sagged with relief. He started to say he was sorry for overreacting, for not having his phone—everything—but she was clearly pissed off and not ready to hear any of it. He watched as she read the instructions on the medication and went to take care of Maddie.

Without Jake asking, Olivia explained everything she

was doing and why. None of it was difficult, but Maddie was clearly upset, and getting the eyedropper of medicine into her mouth was proving to be a bit of a challenge. Olivia managed to get it done and then handed Maddie to him, so she could wash the dropper off.

They worked together to get the twins fed and bathed and changed into pajamas, and Olivia ended up making some grilled cheese sandwiches for them to eat. It certainly wasn't gourmet, but it was good to finally be eating something.

At nine o'clock, she started walking up the stairs with Maddie, and Jake questioned her. "I've been putting them down at nine the last couple of nights. They don't go to sleep right away, but I think it's important for them to be able to be in their cribs without crying about it. Plus, with you being gone all day, I've been pretty exhausted by this time of night."

He felt like ten kinds of crap at her words. "What time are they waking up for their bottles?"

"I've been fortunate—we've had quite a few nights they've slept all the way through to five and even six o'clock. It's been pretty great."

Jake was shocked at how much he had missed over the course of a week. "Olivia…I…" His words were cut off by the sound of Olivia's cell phone ringing. She turned around on the stairs and carefully ran down—with Maddie in her arms—to answer it. Jake was about to offer to take his daughter, but Ben let out a little cry of annoyance at being ignored.

Olivia saw the name on the screen and cringed a little. She looked at Jake briefly over her shoulder before answering the call. He looked curious as hell, and she figured she might as well get this over with. "This is Olivia," she said, forcing a cheeriness she didn't feel into her tone. "Uh-huh… What? No. That's not… That's not… You're not listening, Margo," she snapped impatiently. "That's not going to work for me. We had an agreement…" Olivia listened for a moment and then said, "Let me call you back in ten minutes, okay?" She didn't wait for an answer. She simply hung up.

Without acknowledging Jake, she took Maddie upstairs and got her settled in her bed. When she turned to leave, Jake came in with Ben. She was going to ask if he wanted her to wait, but she figured it was now or never—he was going to have to learn to take care of his children without her there to guide and help him.

Once down the stairs, she picked up her cell phone and walked into the master bedroom, where she closed the door for privacy and called her agent back. "Margo? It's Olivia. What the hell is going on? We had an agreement. The shoot is scheduled to start on Monday."

"That was the original plan, but Jennifer Davis's agent called and said she was needed over in Morocco on Monday, so we need to get her shots done before she leaves the country."

Olivia pinched the bridge of her nose and fought the urge to punch something. "Then I'll do it on Saturday," she said. "Make the arrangements. I land in L.A. Friday night at seven. I don't care how early we need to do it on Saturday morning to get it done."

"Not going to happen, Liv. Sorry. They want the shots finished no later than Friday because Jennifer and her agent need to approve them before they leave."

This was why she hated working with celebrities. "Margo, you have no idea what you're asking."

"Look, Liv, I have done my best to give you the blessed peace and quiet you ranted and raved about needing, and I still don't know what exactly you've been doing, but whatever it is, it's not as important as this shoot. If you get this done in the period of time they gave you, and you do it up right? Sweetie, you'll be able to quadruple your asking price. You'll be the biggest name in photography."

Olivia sighed heavily. "I can't believe you're making me do this."

"Not me, darling. Jennifer Davis, her agent, and the studio. I'm just the messenger."

And because Olivia knew Margo was beyond efficient, she asked, "What time is my flight tomorrow?"

"You leave out of Raleigh at eight o'clock in the morning, and you land here in L.A. noon our time."

"And the photo shoot?"

"We've arranged to have access to the museum from six until midnight tomorrow. I'll have everything ready and waiting for you. A car will pick you up at the airport and bring you home so you can freshen up or whatever, and then you can meet me either here at my office or at the museum."

"I guess the museum," she said wearily.

"Liv, lighten up. This is huge. You should be on top of the world!"

"Yeah, you're right." But her heart just wasn't feeling it. "I'll call you tomorrow when I land." She hung up and sat down on the bed. This was it. It was time to go. She so wasn't ready for it. Knowing she couldn't put off the inevitable, she walked to the door and opened it to find Jake sitting on the couch looking anxious.

"Everything okay?" he asked.

Oh, God. How was she supposed to do this? How was she supposed to pack up and leave after all they had shared? How was she supposed to pack up and leave Ben and Maddie? They may not be hers, but in her heart, they felt like they were.

"That was my agent on the phone," she said carefully as she walked around to sit at the other end of the sofa.

"And?"

Olivia sighed. "And…I need to leave sooner than expected."

"When?" His throat felt as if he'd swallowed glass.

"Tomorrow morning." She looked up at him and couldn't help the tears that began to well in her eyes. "I'm sorry for the short notice. It couldn't be helped. My flight has been booked, and I'll have to leave here before six tomorrow morning in order to return my rental car and catch the eight o'clock flight."

Jake inhaled slowly, then exhaled. He had known the time was coming, and yet he didn't think it actually would. And the fact that she was leaving earlier than expected did little to ease his worries.

"Will you be all right staying home from the office tomorrow?" she asked.

"I'm going to have to be, aren't I?" he said a little too shortly.

"Look, I didn't plan this, Jake. I just got the call a few minutes ago, and you know it."

"Do I? For all I know you set this whole thing up as a way of getting back at me for working all week."

Olivia's eyes went wide at the accusation. "You have got to be kidding me!" she cried. "You are unbelievable, you know that? And an egomaniac besides! Believe it or not, this has nothing to do with you. I was just handed an incredible opportunity with a big production studio. It's the kind of thing I've been working for my whole career. So yes, I'm leaving early to go and take the job. It's no different than you having to go to the office and take care of business. My photography is my business. And this job I'm going back for is going to make my career soar into a whole other stratosphere. So sue me. I need to take it."

"Fine. I'm not stopping you," he said defensively as he stood up and walked into the kitchen. Olivia followed him.

"I'll make the bottles tonight, and all the laundry is done, so—"

"We'll be fine, Olivia," he said as he opened the refrigerator and got himself a can of soda.

"Okay, well…I'll take the car seat bases out of my car so—"

"I'll take care of that too," he snapped. "Why don't you go and pack?" He walked out of the room before she could respond.

"Tell me what I'm supposed to do!" she called after him, surprised when he strode back into the room. He stopped in front of her.

"Marry me."

"What?"

"You heard me. Marry me."

Olivia was stunned. So many times she had dreamed of this moment, but somehow it was a lot more romantic and a lot less…angry. "Why? Why would you even suggest such a thing?"

"It seems you've grown fond of the twins, and they feel the same about you. They may not be able to verbalize it, but you can tell they do. You're really good with them, and you and I…well…we've proven we're compatible. It's a win-win for everyone."

Her stomach clenched. She crossed her arms across her middle. "Let me ask you something, Jake. Do you love me?"

"What?" he asked, confusion marking his face.

"Do. You. Love. Me?"

"What does that have to do with any of this? You don't seem overly thrilled with going back to L.A. I'm offering you an out."

Wow. Just…wow. "And if I said yes, you'd expect us to have sex, right?"

He shrugged. "I think we've proven we're attracted to one another."

"You know what? I think I'll pass." She released her arms and went to walk around him, but he stopped her.

"Why? What's wrong?"

"What you're offering isn't a marriage, Jake. What you're offering is a way for you to have a live-in babysitter for the kids and a plaything for you." She pulled free of his grasp. "Thanks, but no thanks."

He stared her down for a long minute, then just gave a curt nod and walked away.

When she heard the front door close, she knew it was over. There would be no way to keep in touch with him—not civilly anyway. She'd have to get her news about the twins through her brother or maybe her mother.

Her heart was breaking. If she had her way, she'd turn the damn studio job down. It was a phenomenal opportunity, but somehow, as she looked around Jake's kitchen and then walked out into his living room, Olivia realized for all she'd gain by taking the job, she'd be losing twice as much.

At five thirty the next morning, Jake lifted Olivia's suitcase into the trunk of her rental car and closed it. "That's everything?" he asked, and she nodded. He had woken up at five with the twins, and it worked out well because Olivia got to feed them one last time. She didn't have to say anything, because Jake could tell how much it was tearing her apart to leave them. Not him. But Ben and Maddie.

He had a feeling they were going to feel her departure just as much.

And he couldn't even imagine how he was going to feel when it all finally set in.

"I'm just going to go back in and say good-bye to them," she said and turned on her heel and ran back into the house. When Jake found her, she was crouched in front of the two of them as they sat in their bouncy seats on the floor.

"You know I'm going to miss you guys so much, right?" she asked softly. "I can't believe how, for two little people, you worked your way into my heart so darn fast." She swiped away a stray tear. "I want you to behave yourselves and not give your dad a hard time. It's going to be tough with it only being the three of you, so try and give him a break, okay?" Two pairs of dark blue eyes stared back at her as if they were really listening to what she was saying. "But most of all, I want you both to know I love you. I wish I could stay here with you and play with you and take pictures of you and watch you grow up. I'll try to come and visit though, okay?" She reached out and stroked each of their cheeks. "Just don't grow up too fast, okay?" Before she completely broke down, she kissed them both on the tops of their heads and then stood.

It was hard to compose herself, but Olivia forced herself to pull it together. She never heard Jake's approach and when she turned around, he was right there. She gasped in surprise at his proximity. His eyes were hard on hers and he took one of her hands in his. It was the first time in over a week he'd physically touched her. "You can come back anytime, Liv," he said softly, fiercely. "You know that, right?"

She nodded. "I don't know when—"

"It doesn't matter," he cut her off. "Any. Time."

It was too much. All of it. Olivia knew she had to leave—now; otherwise, she wouldn't leave at all. Unable to speak, she simply nodded and went to pull her hand away, but Jake held on tight. It took her a minute, but she found her voice. "I have to go." Her voice was barely audible.

All the while, Jake's eyes held hers. "I know."

This was it. Time to go back to her life and hope that someday she'd be able to look back on this time and her relationship with Jake fondly. Right now it just hurt too damn much. Before she lost her nerve, she rose up on her tiptoes and kissed him with all she had. Jake instantly took control of the kiss as he banded his arms around her waist and hauled her close.

They could have kissed for minutes, seconds, or hours, but to Olivia it wasn't enough. It nearly killed her to pull back. She placed one hand on the side of his face and looked him right in the eye. "I love you. I just want you to know that. I always have."

And Jake stood there dumbfounded as Olivia escaped from his home and his life.

Chapter 11

TWO WEEKS LATER, OLIVIA WAS SITTING IN HER BED, EATING a pint of chocolate brownie chunk ice cream and watching TV—some depressing doctor drama was making her brain go numb. Or maybe it was the ice cream. She couldn't be sure. In the distance, she heard a noise. At first she ignored it, but then she realized it sounded as if someone was trying to break in through her front door.

Putting the ice cream down, she jumped up from the bed and grabbed the baseball bat she kept next to her bed. If someone was going to get in, they were going to get a bat to the face.

Tiptoeing through the apartment, she was just about to open the door when it opened. She screamed. "Mike? What the hell?"

While Mike hadn't screamed, he had certainly had the crap scared out of him. "Holy shit, Olivia. What in the world?"

She slammed the door shut. "Seriously? You break in here and you're going to give me crap for it?"

"I wasn't breaking in. I have a key." He held it up to prove it to her.

"Yes, that was supposed to be used only in an emergency. Not just for the sake of stopping by and scaring me."

He grinned. "Yeah, sorry about that. I was going to

call, but I figured you'd be working. Mom told me all about the big project. Did you get done early today?"

She shook her head. "Not really. I actually got done early, period."

"Is that a good thing?" he asked as he dropped his luggage to the floor and walked toward her kitchen to help himself to something to drink.

Olivia shrugged. "I sort of pushed things along, worked long days, made people change their schedules, and got done five days ahead of schedule. The studio is thrilled, my agent nearly peed herself, and now I can sit back and relax for a bit."

He chuckled. "Be careful. The last time you tried to take some time to relax you ended up playing nanny."

She glared at him. "And whose fault was that?" Walking around him, she went into the bedroom and grabbed her ice cream. She was wearing sweats and a T-shirt, and since it was only Mike, she really didn't even care. Once back in the kitchen, she sat down at the breakfast bar and took a spoonful of ice cream. "So what brings you to L.A.? I thought you were going to be in China for at least another week."

"Well, like you, I got done early, and I was heading home to meet up with Jake."

Her immediate reaction was to ask how Jake was, but she didn't want to know. Well, she did, but it would kill her to hear he was moving on just fine without her, so she just nodded. "Are you going to stop and see Mom and Dad?"

He shook his head. "Not this time. Actually, they don't even know I'm back, so I would appreciate it if you didn't mention it."

She made a zipping motion across her lips. "They won't hear it from me." She took another spoonful of her ice cream. "And why can't they know?"

"Jake and I are going on a fishing trip. A week up in the mountains, like we used to when we were younger. If I tell Dad I'm going, he'll want to come too. I just can't deal with him right now. He scares the fish away because he can't hear well anymore and makes me yell everything to him. It's annoying."

"Wait…what? How are you and Jake going fishing? What about Ben and Maddie? Who's taking care of them?"

Mike uncomfortably looked away and opened the refrigerator again. "Do you have anything to eat here that isn't yogurt?" He closed the door and walked toward the phone. "Does your pizza place deliver?"

"Mike?" Olivia snapped. "What's going on? Who's going to stay with the twins?"

"Look, um…forget I mentioned it, okay?"

"How can I just forget about it? Why can't you just tell me what's going on?"

He sighed and hung his head low. "Jake," he said and then took a deep breath and collected his thoughts. "Jake realized he couldn't handle raising Ben and Maddie alone. He'd already taken custody and parental rights away from Marilyn—not that that would have made a difference—but he knew he couldn't do it anymore and be the kind of parent they deserved."

"What are you saying?" she asked, her stomach churning. She felt like she was going to be sick.

"He contacted a lawyer and social services and an adoption agency. Someone is coming to pick the kids up on Monday."

"No!" she cried and collapsed to the floor. Mike was immediately beside her and held her until she caught her breath. "How? Why? I…I don't understand. They were fine when I left!"

Mike nodded. "He's muddling through, but he's overwhelmed. Not everyone is cut out to be a single parent, Liv. He wants better for his kids. He wants them to be raised in a home with two parents, and that's not what he has to offer."

Olivia thought of the proposal the night before she left and began to cry. Her brother cradled her beside him. When she began to calm down, he placed a gentle kiss on the top of her head. "Hey, I know you got attached to them while you were there, but…you have to understand, Jake's just not cut out to do this on his own. And when you turned down his proposal, well, he just thought…"

"Wait…what? You know about that?" Olivia lifted her head and looked at her brother in shock.

"Well…yeah. He said he asked you to marry him and you turned him down."

"That's because he wasn't really asking me to marry him. He wanted someone there to take care of the twins. It wasn't as if he was in love with me."

Now it was Mike's turn to look confused. "Are you kidding me? Jake's been in love with you for as long as I can remember."

"What are you talking about?" Olivia demanded as she came to her feet. "Why would you even say that?"

Mike rolled his eyes. "Liv, I've been his best friend for most of our lives. I knew. Just like I knew you had a crush on him, and when I saw you guys kissing on your eighteenth birthday, I thought, *Finally!* But then nothing ever came of it. Then you completely avoided him like the plague for like…ever. I thought when you guys saw each other again, you'd finally get it together." He shrugged. "I guess I was wrong." He studied his sister. "Why'd you turn him down?"

She shook her head to clear it. "I told you, he doesn't love me. He talked about me being fond of the kids, them being fond of me, blah, blah, blah…and when I asked him directly if he loved me, he asked what that had to do with anything. Does that sound like love to you?"

Mike was stumped. "Honestly, I don't know why he would do that—unless he thought you weren't in love with him."

"Oh, for crying out loud," she cried out, stomping away to get her ice cream. She took a heaping spoonful and then almost cried out with the brain freeze. "Dammit!"

"Look, I know it sucks, Liv, but it really is for the best. Jake wasn't happy, and he said the babies were crying all the time, and he just didn't know what else to do. So I'm planning on flying out there and being with him when they come pick the kids up and then taking him out of town immediately."

Olivia looked at the calendar and saw it was Thursday. There was still time. Without a word to Mike, she ran over to her computer and began searching for flights back to North Carolina. "What are you doing?" Mike asked, mildly amused.

"He can't do it, Mike. He just can't. I'll go there and talk to him. I'll stay as long as I can—as long as he needs me to so he doesn't have to give Ben and Maddie away."

"Liv, maybe you should just leave it alone. I mean, it's not like you're in love with him. You going back there is just going to mess with him."

She straightened and looked up at her brother's face. "What are you talking about? Of course I'm in love with him! I even said that to him when I left. I told him—right to his face—that I loved him and I always had! He didn't even try to stop me!"

"He didn't want to stand in your way, Olivia," Mike said soberly. "He knew this job was a big opportunity for you, and he didn't want to be the reason you gave it up."

Olivia laughed. "You want to know something funny?" She didn't wait for an answer. "I wanted him to stop me because I really didn't want to leave. I didn't want to come back here and even do this job."

"What? Are you crazy? I hear you've got royalty from all over the world wanting you to come and take their pictures!"

She nodded, clicking a flight to book it. "I do. And you know what? I don't care. I'd rather spend my days taking pictures of Ben and Maddie than sitting with these obnoxious Oscar winners who think they're better than everyone else. I'd give up taking pictures of the queen herself any day for a chance to get the pictures of Ben and Maddie's first steps." Just the thought of seeing that milestone made her smile. She was not going to let Jake do this. She refused to let him do it.

"So what's your plan?"

Olivia spun around and walked toward her bedroom to begin packing. "I'm going to take the red-eye tonight. That will have me landing in Raleigh tomorrow morning at around seven. I'll rent a car and go and plead with him to change his mind."

"I don't think you're going to be able to do that, Liv. His mind is made up."

Olivia remembered another time Jake's mind had been made up, and she'd managed to change it then too. She had every confidence she could do it again. "No, he just thinks it's made up." Marching to her bedroom, Olivia pulled her suitcase out of her closet and threw it on the bed, randomly throwing clothes in it.

From the doorway, Mike stood in dazed amusement. "Olivia, I know Jake. Don't go there and mess with his head."

She turned and glared at him. "Is that what you think I'm going to do? Do you really think I'm that kind of person?"

He shrugged. "Not intentionally, no. But, Liv, your photography and your career are your life. What are you going to do if you walk away from here and go to North Carolina, huh? How is that going to work?"

Dropping her hands to her side, she smiled up at her brother. "I don't know. If I have to, I'll take pictures at the mall. I just want to be with them, Mike. All of them. I love all three of them."

That was obviously what he wanted to hear. "What time do we need to get you to the airport?"

Olivia was near delirious when she pulled in to Jake's driveway the next morning. Her flight had been slightly delayed, and she hadn't landed until eight o'clock, and by the time she got her luggage and her rental car, it was well after nine. She hadn't slept well on the plane because she was so tense about seeing Jake. She only hoped he would be willing to listen to her.

The car was barely parked when she tumbled out of it. She ran to the door and knocked, then remembered she still had her key. In her hurry to leave two weeks ago, she had forgotten all about it. She waited and waited and waited, and just when she thought she was going to have to resort to using the key, the door opened.

And there was Jake.

Looking weary and tired and sexy and…better than anything she had ever seen in her life. "Olivia?" he asked as if he didn't trust what his eyes were seeing. "What are you doing here?"

She didn't wait for him to invite her in. She simply stepped around him and looked around to see if anything was different. "Look, I know things haven't been easy and you're feeling a little overwhelmed with all the responsibility, but you can't go through with it, Jake."

He shut the door and looked at her with confusion. He had been asleep when he heard the knock at the door. Stumbling out of the bed, he had grabbed a T-shirt and jeans from the floor to throw on. His hair was sticking up, and now as he looked around the house, he saw it kind of was a disaster. "What are you talking about?" he asked around a yawn.

"Mike stopped and saw me last night." She paused. "He told me."

He frowned at her. "Told you what?"

She rolled her eyes as her shoulders sagged. "You know…about…sheesh, I hate even saying it." She huffed. "He told me you're putting the twins up for adoption."

"What?" he said loudly, but Olivia wasn't paying attention.

"Here's the thing, Jake, you can't do that. You just can't. We can totally make this work. Me and you. When you asked me to marry you, I was surprised. That's all. I guess I always thought if you asked me to marry you, it would be a little more romantic, and you'd tell me you love me, but it's okay. Like you said, we're compatible. And we both love Ben and Maddie and want what's best for them." She paused and took a breath. "I never should have left. I know that now, and I'm sorry I did. I was being selfish, and I never should have done it. I love you and those babies more than anything, and I should have made you my first priority. Tell me I'm not too late. Please. I don't think I could live with myself if I was a contributing factor in you letting those precious babies go."

Jake could only stand there and stare at her. Olivia took his silence as a bad sign.

"I'll move my business here," she blurted out. "If anyone wants me to photograph them, they'll have to come to me. We'll hire an assistant you approve of who can help me when I have to bring the twins on photo shoots. Or if you prefer I don't work, I'm okay with that too. I can take a million pictures of Ben and Maddie and never get bored. I was planning on making you a scrapbook of all the pictures I had taken. I know that sounds lame, but…it's what I do." She took a slow step toward him. "It's okay that you don't love me. I can live with that. We're friends though, right? And maybe that's going to be even better for the kids in the long run."

"I don't agree," he finally said.

When he didn't elaborate right away, Olivia felt as if she'd taken the risk for nothing. "Oh."

Stepping closer to her, Jake stopped right in front of her and placed his hands on her shoulders. "You shouldn't have to live with someone who doesn't love you, Olivia," he said softly. "You deserve more than that. Much, much more."

She thought she understood what he was saying and nodded sadly. "Okay." She tried to step away before she started to cry—a habit that was really starting to get on her nerves—but Jake held on. "I probably should have called first before just flying across the country and springing all of this on you. Promise me you'll think twice before sending them away, Jake. Promise me. I think you'll only end up regretting that. Maybe not immediately, but you will."

"Oh, I know that," he said and gently squeezed her shoulders. "I've learned letting someone go is not always the right thing to do, and it's not the answer to everything."

"Okay," she said slowly. "Good. So…um…does that mean you're not going to let the adoption people come on Monday?"

Slowly, so very, very slowly, Jake pulled Olivia close, until they were toe to toe, chest to chest. "There never was an adoption agency, Olivia. I don't know what Mike told you, but whatever it was, it's not true. I'm tired and exhausted and overwhelmed and all that, but that goes with the territory, right?" He leaned his forehead against hers and simply breathed in the scent of her.

"I don't understand. Why…why would Mike lie to me?"

He shrugged. "I don't know, but whatever his reasons, it brought you back to me, so I don't care."

She pulled back and still looked confused. "You… you wanted me to come back?"

"Olivia, sweetheart, I never wanted you to leave."

That did little to clear up her confusion. "But…but you told me—"

"I know what I said, and I'm so sorry for the way I behaved. In my head, it all made sense, but it was killing me. I didn't want you to go, Liv. And now you're here and you love me, I'm not letting you go. Not now, not ever."

Olivia tried to process his words, she really did, but her mind was spinning.

Jake knew there was one last thing he had to say. "I love you, Olivia. I know I should have told you that, that day, when you asked me, but I really thought what I was doing was the right thing. I didn't want to guilt you into staying or force you to give up your career. But now I know I don't want to live without you. I don't want a long-distance relationship. I'm going to be selfish again, but I want you here with me. With us. We're a family." He cupped her face in his hand. "I love you."

He closed what little distance there was between them and kissed her with all the love he felt.

When he finally lifted his head, he looked into her eyes. "Will you, Liv? Will you stay? Marry me? And make our family complete?"

It was everything she had ever wanted. "Under one condition," she said, smiling when Jake quirked a brow at her. "I'm going to want to give Ben and Maddie more brothers and sisters. I hope you're okay with that."

He laughed, lifting her in his arms and spinning her around as he held her tight. “Sweetheart, I am more than up for that task.”

Epilogue

Six months later...

"THIS SEEMS A LITTLE EXTREME, DON'T YOU THINK?"

"No."

"But...how are you supposed to handle it all?"

"It's what I do." Olivia looked at Jake, and his expression showed he did not believe her. She rolled her eyes and put her camera down on the table beside her. "What is it exactly you're worried about? You're not the one doing the work. I am."

"Yeah, but I'm sitting here watching it all and I'm already starting to sweat. I just don't understand how you're going to make it work."

Placing her hands on Jake's shoulders, she maneuvered him until he was standing in front of one of the stools on the set and forced him to sit down.

"I just—"

"Shh," she said firmly. "No more talking. I have twelve models I have to get through today, and as we have learned from our own experience, children do not have a lot of patience for standing around and waiting." Olivia looked over her shoulder and saw her first model coming in. "This was all my idea, and I am confident I can get it done. Our children have trained me well."

Jake chuckled. Olivia had thousands of pictures of

the twins, and now that they were a little bit older, she had gotten into the habit of using props and dressing them up. She claimed they were the inspiration for this project, but he still worried she was taking on too much. "I just don't want you to overdo it. We are getting married next week. I wanted you to have this week to relax. I didn't think you'd take on something quite this…challenging."

Olivia had come up with the idea after dressing the kids for Halloween. Taking a cue from her movie studio project, she had decided to approach some of the actresses she had worked with in the past to see if they would consider doing photo shoots with their children, who would be dressed as their famous parent from one of their most famous movie roles. It wasn't until after she had confirmed the first five that the industry caught wind of it and *Vanity Fair* called, asking if they could feature the spread in the magazine. Olivia was thrilled with the idea, and once word got out that *Vanity Fair* was on board, she had no problem gathering up the rest of her subjects.

"I don't want you to worry, Jake," she said sweetly and kissed him on the cheek. "I've got plenty of help here and we are starting on time, and with a little luck and minimal amount of temper tantrums—and not just from the children—we should get all the shots done today. Why don't you take the kids and go to the park or the zoo? Make a day of it. I'll call you when I'm done."

He shook his head. "They're having fun with Annie and the other kids, so until they get restless, if you don't mind, I'd like to watch you work." Annie was the nanny they had hired. Jake had been mildly against it at first, but Olivia helped him to see that having someone come in to help them didn't mean they were neglecting the twins. Annie was there to help them keep things sane when life got a little crazy. Which was an everyday occurrence with Ben and Maddie.

Picking up her camera, Olivia was about to walk away when she remembered something. "My parents' flight comes in tomorrow at three. I had planned on leaving the kids with Annie and getting them myself, but I was thinking if you could get off work early, then we could all go together and surprise them at the airport. They are so excited to meet their grandchildren, I think it would be torture to make them wait. What do you think?"

Jake stood and wrapped his arms around her and, unable to help himself, kissed her very thoroughly on the lips.

"Wow," she sighed when she pulled back. "What was that for?"

"For making Ben and Maddie part of your family and for wanting them to be your own. I love that about you, Liv. Actually," he said with a sexy grin, "I love everything about you."

She blushed and leaned in for one more kiss. "Well, that's a really good thing, because I love everything about you too."

"Olivia?" someone called from across the room.

"I have to go," she said and sighed. "But let's get together later when the kids are asleep and talk a little bit more about all the ways you love me." She winked and walked away to get started on the shoot.

And all Jake could think of was all the ways he was going to spend the night not only telling her, but showing her as well.

Keep reading for an excerpt from the next in Samantha Chase's Shaughnessy Brothers series

Love Walks In

It was completely unacceptable.

"I don't think I understand."

Hugh Shaughnessy straightened the cell phone that sat on his desk until it was completely in line with the rest of the items there—all while keeping eye contact with his assistant Dorothy. "I said," he began slowly, "it isn't going to work for me. It's unacceptable. Tell her no."

Dorothy shifted nervously. "Um…I don't think that's an option, Hugh. You…you can't exactly…" She hesitated, clearly trying to choose her words. "What I mean is, I don't think you get a say in this."

He arched a brow at her. "Really?"

"I could see if it was a request for time off or for vacation, but…"

"Technically, she is asking for time off," he said reasonably.

"No. What she's doing is quitting," Dorothy stated in the same tone.

A sigh of frustration escaped before Hugh could stop it. He rose and crossed the office to stare out the open window. "Tell her we require a minimum of two weeks' notice or else."

"Or else what?"

Looking over his shoulder, he replied, "Or there'll be

no letter of recommendation. If anything, I'll make sure she never works in the industry again."

"Don't you think it's a little harsh?"

Turning and walking back to his desk, Hugh sat down, clearly restless. "Don't you think it's a little harsh for Heather to quit—with no notice—because she fell in love and wants to run off and get married in Vegas?"

Dorothy chuckled, quickly stopping when she noticed the glare on her boss's face. "Personally, I think it's romantic."

"Vegas? That's romantic for you? We run some of the most beautiful and romantic resorts in the country—hell, the world!—and you're choosing Vegas?" he snapped.

"Now I didn't say that, Hugh." She bristled. "What I said was how I thought the whole *thing* was romantic—meaning the relationship. Heather and Dave have waited so long for this and with his military service coming to an end, they can finally get married. And they're going to have a baby and—"

"She's pregnant?"

"She really hasn't told anyone, but clearly you can see why they're anxious to get married."

Honestly, he didn't. People had babies all the time without rushing out and getting married. He didn't agree with it, but that's the way it was. The fact that his special events coordinator was deserting him on such short notice to do it? Well, it just added fuel to the fire.

Folding his arms on the desk, Hugh looked at his assistant pleadingly. "Dorothy, we are getting ready to start a very busy season at our resorts. We've got full calendars. And on top of that, you know I've been courting a new wine distributor. He's due here tomorrow.

Heather is supposed to sit in on those meetings and come up with a presentation to convince him to do business with us. Can't you convince her to stay through the end of the month?"

"Hugh, you're not listening. Heather's gone. She wasn't giving us a heads-up, she wasn't giving us an option. She stopped by earlier—with her bags packed, loaded, and waiting in a cab—and said good-bye. She's probably at the airport right now waiting to board a flight. Face it, we have to come up with a plan B."

"You'll have to sit in on the meeting and come up with the presentation. You know what we're looking for. You can just…"

"Hold it right there, chief," she said sternly, holding out a hand to stop him. "That is not going to happen."

"Excuse me?"

"There are many things in my job description, but party and event planning isn't one of them. From everything you've told me, this guy is a little high maintenance and demands perfection. My idea of a party consists of inexpensive wine, cheese and crackers, and a deck of cards."

Hugh rolled his eyes. "Dotty…"

"I'm serious, Hugh. I'm from another generation. I don't understand yours. My friends and I enjoy going out for a quiet dinner and then playing mah-jongg. We're not into music or the latest trends. Trust me, having me work on this would not help you in any way, shape, or form."

Unfortunately, Hugh knew she was right. He just hated being in a jam like this, and having Dorothy's help would have simplified everything. Scrubbing a weary hand across his face, he looked back at her. "Any suggestions then?"

"Off the top of my head? No. But give me a few hours to make some calls and I'll see what I can do."

"This is a nightmare," he grumbled.

Reaching across the desk, Dorothy patted his hand. "It's definitely not the greatest thing to have happened, but it's far from the worst. We'll make it work. We always do." With an encouraging smile, she turned and walked out of the room.

With a curse, Hugh reached for the phone and began scrolling through his contacts. Surely he had to know someone who could take over the position on short notice. Hell, right now he'd even consider letting his sister come and do it. Darcy was in her first year of college back in North Carolina and he needed someone right here in California, but maybe she could get school credit for this. While she didn't technically have any experience, she was young and social and in touch with the latest trends. Hell, her vivacious personality alone would be an asset.

"Now I know I'm getting desperate," he muttered. Pulling his eighteen-year-old sister out of school was not the solution to this. Although…

The buzzing of the phone in his hand brought him out of his reverie. His brother Aidan's face showed up on the screen and Hugh almost wept with relief. A distraction was exactly what he needed right now.

"Aidan! What's up, man? You don't normally call midday."

"You know, you use that greeting on me no matter what time I call," he replied with a chuckle. "Is there a time slot when I'm supposed to call that I don't know about? Did I miss the spreadsheet?"

Hugh couldn't help but smile. He knew Aidan was right. He should be thankful for a friendly voice on the phone and not nitpick on when it came. "Sorry, bro. You just always seem to catch me off guard."

"Maybe let your guard down every once in a while. Live a little."

"Ha! This coming from the king of control. Nice!"

"Yeah, yeah, yeah…once upon a time that was me. Clearly I've passed the torch on to you."

"Whatever. So what's going on? Everyone okay?"

"Yeah, everyone's fine. I wanted to talk to you about…um…well, Zoe and I were thinking of having a destination wedding. And the more we talked about it, the more we figured, who better to get advice from than you. So? What do you think?"

"Wow! So you're ready to start making plans? That's great! I didn't realize you were there yet."

"If it was up to me, we'd be married already. Zoe wanted us to settle in and spend time getting to know each other more, and get her business off the ground before we started planning a wedding."

"So she's ready to branch out on her own? What about Martha?"

"She's still going to do stuff with Martha, but it's going to be more like a partnership. Martha deals more with commercial accounts and Zoe really enjoys doing residential. They've been playing around with the idea for a while, and they're going to give it a trial run."

"How do you feel about it?"

Aidan chuckled. "I want Zoe to be happy and she's

much happier being her own boss and choosing her own clients. So we'll see how it all goes. But that's a story for another time. We want to talk to you about options for the wedding. We want to meet with you and your event person and figure out which resort fits our needs and what the availability is. I think it would be great for the family."

"What do you mean?"

"Hugh…when is the last time Dad went anywhere?"

Too long. "Okay, stupid question. Sorry. So this is your way of forcing him to break out of his rut."

"He's been making progress since Darcy left for school but…baby steps. He goes bowling with the guys once a week, he went fishing last weekend with the same group."

"For him, it's huge. At least he's spending time with friends."

"Yeah, but it's still… He's still sticking close to home. You travel. Riley travels. Hell, even Owen travels. But Dad?"

"And you."

"Fine. I don't travel either. So it will be good for a few of us. Happy?"

Hugh laughed. "Extremely."

"Okay, so who do we need to talk to and what's your schedule like? Zoe and I are open to flying to wherever you are so we can talk in person."

"Here's the thing—I'm happy for you guys. I really am. You've just caught me at a bad time."

"Oh, I'm sorry. I didn't realize you were busy. Why didn't you cut me off? You can call me later or—"

"No, no, no. That's not what I mean. I mean it's a bad

time—my events coordinator just quit and I don't have a replacement lined up."

"Is that all?"

"Is that all?" Hugh repeated incredulously. "It's huge! We have a lot of events scheduled and without someone overseeing them, it could be a disaster!"

"She wasn't your only event coordinator, Hugh. I mean that would be…"

"Shut up."

"She was your only events person? You own twelve resorts, Hugh! How is that possible?"

If there was one thing Hugh hated more than chaos, it was being questioned on how he managed his business. "Look, Aidan, you run a construction business. You have no idea how to do things in the hospitality business. I know I have twelve resorts, but they're small. Intimate. We're like a family. Each resort has someone who acts as an assistant to Heather, but she was the go-to on all events."

"That's just weird. And probably not the smartest managerial decision you've ever made."

"And we're done here."

"Okay, okay…I'm sorry. Look, give me a call when the smoke clears so we can set up a meeting. Like I said, Zoe and I aren't in a huge rush and we're willing to meet you wherever you are."

"I appreciate it, I do. But you're going to have to give me something to go on here. Are you thinking beach? Mountains? Do you want to stay stateside? Or were you thinking of Australia?"

"Get things settled where you are, Hugh, then we'll talk. Trust me. Zoe and I can wait until you're ready."

"Thanks, man. I'll give you a call soon."

Hugh placed the phone back down on his desk and sighed. Yeah, maybe it wasn't such a great idea to have one main events coordinator, but Heather had been the best. She oversaw her staff and managed to make every event unique. Now he had to figure out how to move forward and find a replacement.

Fast.

He looked up when Dorothy knocked and poked her head back through the door. He knew immediately the news wasn't good. It was written all over her face. "What? What's happened now?"

"Your wine guy? William Bellows?"

Hugh nodded.

"He's arriving today."

"No. He's arriving tomorrow."

She shook her head. "His assistant just called. He's on his way now. He wrapped up his other business early. She called to make sure we would have a suite ready for him."

Cursing, Hugh stood and kicked his chair out of the way. "This is unbelievable! I can't catch a break today!"

"I did manage to tell her you would be tied up in meetings and would have to stick to your original plans with him. She said it would be fine."

"Lucky me."

"Okay," she began, stepping farther into the room. "Again, it's not an ideal situation but it's not a catastrophe either. We'll make sure his suite is ready, we'll arrange for spa services and dinner and keep him pampered like a VIP. In the meantime, we'll continue to figure out who you're going to use as a replacement for Heather."

"Where's Josie? She's worked as Heather's assistant here. We'll use her as a temp."

Dorothy shook her head.

"What? Why not?"

"She's on vacation. Two weeks."

"So call her in. Tell her it's an emergency."

"Already tried. She's in Europe."

"Has everyone stopped working?" Hugh yelled. "How is it possible all of this fell into place like this?"

"Bad timing?"

He glared at her. "Not the time, Dotty."

"Can I ask you something?"

He nodded even as he rubbed his temple to ward off the headache that was building.

"Why are you freaking out so much about this meeting? I've never seen you like this before and you've done business with people from all over the world. What is it about this guy that has you so overwhelmed?"

Hugh dropped his hands into his lap. "He's a little… eccentric. Unconventional."

Dorothy quirked a brow at him. "Unconventional in what way?"

"He's not the kind of guy who follows any kind of plan. He tends to go with the flow and follow his gut instincts…that sort of thing. One time, he was on vacation in Italy and hired a guy to handle sales of a particular wine here in the U.S. just because he liked his shoes! And the guy didn't even speak English!"

"The guy he hired or Mr. Bellows?"

"I'm glad you're having fun with this," he said in a near growl. "The guy he hired! Then Bellows hired a tutor to teach the guy English!"

"And? How did it turn out?"

Hugh raked a hand through his hair. "He's the top salesman in the company."

"Oh dear," she murmured. "And you want to do business with him? You're his complete opposite! How are you going to handle working without any structure? You know how much you hate that."

"I know, I know." He sighed. "Honestly, I'm hoping if I present a completely well-thought-out plan to him, he'll simply agree to go along with it. There won't need to be any gut instinct or flowing because I'll have it all covered."

She chuckled, and when Hugh glared at her, Dorothy quickly placed a hand over her mouth. Clearing her throat, she continued. "You're not counting on that, are you?"

Hugh straightened in his seat. "As a matter of fact, I am. That's why this presentation has to be flawless!"

"Oh, Hugh…"

"Look, I'm getting it all worked out. It's not the way I envisioned but…"

"You're just going to go with the flow?" she finished and then smirked.

"Cute."

"Let's take a walk. We'll go over to the suite we're preparing for Mr. Bellows, check on the grounds. Sometimes a change of scenery can help us brainstorm. What do you say?"

"I'd say you're talking to me like I'm a moron, and I don't like it."

She smiled at him sweetly. "But are you coming with me?"

Dammit. Without a word, he strode from his office and waited for his assistant to catch up.

About the Author

New York Times and *USA Today* bestseller/contemporary romance writer Samantha Chase released her debut novel, *Jordan's Return*, in November 2011. Although she waited until she was in her forties to publish for the first time, writing has been a lifelong passion. Her motivation to take that step was her students: teaching creative writing to elementary age students all the way up through high school and encouraging those students to follow their writing dreams gave Samantha the confidence to do so as well.

When she's not working on a new story, she spends her time reading contemporary romances, playing way too many games of Scrabble or solitaire on Facebook, and spending time with her husband of twenty-five years and their two sons in North Carolina.

Made for Us

Shaughnessy Brothers #1

by Samantha Chase

New York Times and *USA Today* Bestselling Author

Can't make time for love?

The Shaughnessy brothers have spent the years since their mother's untimely death taking care of one another and trying to make their father proud. Oldest son Aidan is hardworking, handsome, successful—and still single. Sure, he'd like to have his own family someday, but who has the time?

She'll show him how to find it

Zoe Dalton, a stunning designer Aidan meets on one of his construction jobs, has the beauty and heart to make Aidan realize how much he's been missing. But it's not easy to break down walls you've spent years building up. Now there's a major storm bearing down on the North Carolina coast, and it could be catalyst enough to force Aidan and Zoe into some major decisions of the heart.

"Chase grabs readers by the heartstrings and reels them right into the antics of the lively Shaughnessy family." —*Publishers Weekly*

For more Samantha Chase, visit:

Return to You

A Montgomery Brothers Novel

by Samantha Chase

New York Times and *USA Today* Bestselling Author

She will never forget their past...

He can't stop thinking about their future...

James Montgomery has achieved everything he'd hoped for in life...except marrying the girl of his dreams. After a terrible accident, Selena Ainsley left ten years ago. She took his heart with her, and she's never coming back. But it's becoming harder and harder for him to forget their precious time together, and James can't help but wonder what he would do if they could ever meet again.

What readers are saying about Samantha Chase:

"Samantha Chase really knows how to tell a story."

"Perfect romance! Love it, love it, love it!"

For more Samantha Chase, visit:

www.sourcebooks.com

Meant for You

The Montgomery Brothers

by Samantha Chase

New York Times and *USA Today* Bestselling Author

She dares to dream...

Summer Montgomery wants to be taken seriously almost as much as she wants her brother's best friend, Ethan. But with a long résumé of seemingly random career choices and a protective brother on watch, those things are nothing more than pipe dreams...

Does he dare to try?

Ethan Reed would like nothing more than to live by his own rules. Not wanting to disappoint his best friend Zach, or any of the Montgomerys, Ethan's had to push aside his long-denied feelings for Summer. But it only takes one night away from watchful eyes to make impossible dreams come true...

What readers say about the Montgomery Brothers series:

"The Montgomery brothers are perfect romance!"

"Great story line, strong characters—a great read."

For more Samantha Chase, visit:

www.sourcebooks.com

I'll Be There

The Montgomery Brothers

by Samantha Chase

New York Times and *USA Today* Bestselling Author

This Montgomery has a head for business

Working for Zach Montgomery is challenging on many levels—coming from a wealthy and powerful family, he lives by his own rules and doesn't answer to anyone.

And a heart for adventure

Zach's perfect world is turned upside down when a climbing accident leaves him broken, angry, and maddeningly dependent. In his slow quest for recovery, Gabriella Martine is always there to help…but as Zach comes to see his assistant in a new light, he is forced to reevaluate what it really means to be a man worthy of her love.

Praise for Samantha Chase:

"A perfect happily ever after." —Carly Phillips,
New York Times bestselling author

Samantha Chase makes your heart skip a beat
and leaves you smiling." —*Tome Tender*

The Best Laid Wedding Plans

Magnolia Brides

by Lynnette Austin

Some Dreams Are Worth Whatever It Takes

Jenni Beth Beaumont has a dream. She leaves her career as a wedding planner in Savannah for the small Southern hometown whose glory days are long past. She is determined to breathe new life not only into her family's once beautiful antebellum mansion, but also into the town itself. And so she sets out to create a premier wedding destination the likes of which this small town can't even begin to envision, and few want.

But Cole Bryson can…and it's not at all what he had in mind when he set his sights on the crumbling Magnolia House. Cole and Jenni Beth also have a past, one that she does not want to repeat. But she needs Cole's help to make her dream a reality, and Cole can't help himself when it comes to Jenni Beth. Can the guy who thoroughly broke her heart become the man who will help her build her happily ever after?

"All about small towns, community, and sweet and sexy romance." —*Booklist*

"An intriguing premiere…well-developed characters and sensual romantic tension." —*Publishers Weekly*

I'll Stand By You

by Sharon Sala

New York Times and *USA Today* Bestselling Author

When no one ever takes your side...

Dori Grant is no stranger to hardship. As a young single mother in the gossip-fueled town of Blessings, Georgia, she's weathered the storm of small-town disapproval most of her life. But when Dori loses everything within the span of an evening, she realizes she has no choice but to turn to her neighbors.

All you need is one person in your corner

Everyone says the Pine boys are no good, but Johnny Pine has been proving the gossips wrong ever since his mother died and he took over raising his brothers. His heart goes out to the young mother and child abandoned by the good people of Blessings. Maybe he can be the one to change all that...

Praise for *The Curl Up and Dye*:

"A delight...I couldn't put it down." —*Fresh Fiction*

"One of those rare treats." —*RT Book Reviews*

"Engaging, heartwarming, funny, sassy, and just plain good." —*Peeking Between the Pages*

For more Sharon Sala, visit:

www.sourcebooks.com

Not So New In Town

Harmony Homecomings

by Michele Summers

You can't go back, and you can't stand still...

Lucy Doolan is a marketing genius. She can sell rain to a frog and snow to a polar bear. Newly single and unemployed, she's lured back to her hometown of Harmony, North Carolina, to help out her pregnant evil stepsister...only to find her former crush, heartthrob Brogan Reese, has returned too, to open a new business in town. To add insult to injury, he's still hot.

If the thunder don't get you,
then the lightning will...

Brogan never noticed Lucy much when they were young, but seventeen people have recommended her to help him. She's got his attention now. With her sweet personality, brilliant imagination, and penchant for doing the completely unpredictable, Brogan is finding a whole lot of excuses to spend his days—and nights—with Lucy.

Praise for *Find My Way Home*:

"A lot of emotion and off-the-charts sexual tension." —*RT Book Reviews*